THE BISLEY BOY

by the same author

STREET LAVENDER

MIGNON

THORNAPPLE

N FOR NARCISSUS

GAVESTON

CHRIS HUNT

THE BISLEY BOY

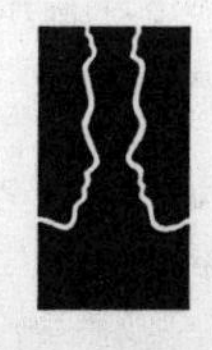

THE GAY MEN'S PRESS

To Ray, Gill and Heather

This book should not be confused with the play of the same name by Shane Scott first performed at the Drum Theatre, Plymouth in June 1995.

The portrait of Queen Elizabeth I on the cover, by an unknown artist, was commissioned for Erik XIV, king of Sweden, and is reproduced by permission of Statens Konstmuseer, Stockholm.

First published in 1995
by GMP Publishers Ltd
PO Box 247, London N6 4BW, England

A CIP catalogue record for this book is available from the British Library.

ISBN 0 85449 211 6

Distributed in North America by Inbook,
140 Commerce St, East Haven, CT 06512, USA.

Distributed in Australia by Bulldog Books,
P O Box 155, Broadway, NSW 2007.

Printed and bound in the EU by Nørhaven A/S, Viborg, Denmark.

ONE

I

We are all deceivers, to a greater or lesser degree.

Some make it their trade to be other than they seem, and we reward them for it – for the danger into which they put themselves for our sake, for their pains and woes in our service, their familiarity with the alleyway by night and the sodden straw of a stableyard in foul weathers, the sudden flight and pursuit, the secret letter concealed beneath the creaking board, the threat of the knife in the dark.

Courtiers deceive, men who have no business to be false, fawning, smiling, simpering; hearts full of lies.

In humankind deception is the way of it; we all are at it, feigning, fooling and dissembling. To achieve our aims we favour those that we despise, we promise that which we shall at the last deny, we tease and we prevaricate. He that has not the skill to do this had best live in the country and tend sheep.

When the Plague takes to the streets of London decked in all its grisly finery, we take to fairer fields. It has always been so. We seek the meadows and the hills where air is sweet and clean. Oxfordshire... Gloucestershire... *As sure as God's in Gloucestershire,* they say. God we may find there, also those selfsame sheep and the windy wold where the winter's rough, with snow whose like has not been seen by those who never crossed the Windrush. And as keen, as excellent a working of deception's craft as ever was discovered in the Cheapside bolthole of a Spanish priest from Douai.

This was the air I breathed. Deception was about me from my birth. Small wonder that I took to it and thrived as at a feast.

It is a tendency with the infant to believe that those whom he calls parents are indeed the very same from whose loins he sprang, the more so if the honest pair encourage this belief; and I was no different from the common in this respect. Father had I none, but such a mother as by warm affection constantly expressed conveyed to me her fondest care and left me no doubt but that I was a most beloved and cherished son, who had been the centre of a circle of devotion which was now unaccountably absent.

Who is there can say where memory begins? I do recall a house of shadows, large rooms, lengthy passageways...the streaming candle flame illuminating a great stairway...bulky linen chests of black wood...the leaded windows and the sound beyond of tall trees soughing, so nearby that the rattling boughs clawed at the panes when the winds came in from the west. More than one face I remember...servants, the patter of their shoes upon the stairs as they brought possets on a tray...and a bed, tall as a ship, it seemed, with heavy curtains that smelt of damp and lavender. And a garden, great in size, high-walled, with roses and long grasses, and beyond the wall the church, and the bell that brought the faithful to their prayers and the dead unto their resting place.

Thus memory. But this house was no forgotten dream distorted through time's vagaries to other than it truly was. I have returned to it and verified it with a clearer eye, a more detached awareness; and this long after we were turned away from it.

This house was to be found at Bisley, Gloucestershire. Its name was Over Court.

My mother – that is, she whom I believed my mother till I knew better – could give no reasonable explanation for our change of fortune. Worse, she implied that we were fortunate to find so good, so kind a protector as dear Master Dutton, cloth merchant, who would now look after us and give us his name. But we had names already. Hers was Catherine Felton, mine John Neville. This availed us nothing; bag and baggage we were taken from the large dark house and brought to Master Dutton's, there in Bisley village, down the hill.

It was a little house, a low one, and it gave upon the springs that gushed out of the wooded crag atop of which stood the church and Over Court. The water made a stream outside our door and flowed thence to the Toadsmoor valley and so to the River Frome. In consequence our house was damp and moist and smelt of mould and fern. Mosses grew in the cracks of its walls, even inside the house. Its inferior position emphasised our shift of fortune. We had been high and now were low.

We are all given, I believe, some prescience, some awareness of our destination in this world. For as long as I can remember I have known that as I lived and breathed it was my ambition to do some act that would make my fame spread abroad in my lifetime, and after occasion memorial for ever.

I also knew that such an aspiration would find no fulfilment in the place where I now found myself. No voice of seer, astrologer or prophet was needed to show me that I would not attain so portentous a goal in Bisley.

Sheep and cloth were Bisley's claim to fame. It lay beyond the wide green Cotswold uplands, scattered up and down a craggy hill, a secret place closed in upon itself. This was a land of beechwoods, combes, and greystone quarries; of ancient ways that crossed the wolds and brought the drovers from the hills of Wales and the packhorses that bore the fleeces. "Bisley's gates are open," they would say when the wind blew from the north. Winter winds and rains lashed the high commons till the trackways oozed with yellow mud, the same that in the summer were floury with grey dust; and still the packhorse trod the steep and winding ways.

I was, under Master Dutton's kindly tutelage, in a fair way of knowing more about sheep than was acceptable to my nature. Even while I watched and listened I knew well enough I never would become the cloth merchant he intended, but I heard all that he had to say respectfully enough, and thus I to this day possess knowledge never put to use at court – that Cotswold sheep are big and sturdy with a thick and curling fleece; that though the Hereford sheep may have longer coats, the which increase their market value, they compare but poorly with the Cotswold, which are by nature hardy.

"These poor sheep have nothing to shelter them but Bisley spire," they said along the windswept wolds.

A small boy with a pony of my own I accompanied this Gloucestershire cloth merchant where he went – to Cirencester's great sheep fair,to the quaysides and warehouses of Bristol, to Mynchen Hampton market, where we rode knee-deep through flocks that shoved and jingled through the streets with bells about their necks, and bleated in their wicker pens.

With the dust of shearing in my nose and ears I watched by waysides in the month of June the men that worked the fleeces. They bellowed for ale in voices rough and harsh, and drank till it flowed in rivulets about the throat, their necks arched and their foreheads glistening with sweat. Their backs were tanned and their faces grimed. The moving blades of their trade flashed in the noonday heat.

I heard the dainty speech of merchants from across the seas who could not pronounce our country names and called the Cotswolds "Choudisgualdo". I knew the watermills that fulled the cloth, the pounding of the wooden hammers as the force of water pushed the shaft to work; I watched the Cotswold broadcloth form, the women with the teasels and the men with shears, the children carding, and I saw the fleeces boiling in raw piss to loose the grease. Familiar to me was the sight of hillsides smudged with scarlet as the Stroud-red cloth lay spread and drying in the sun, while from the mills the streams gushed red as blood among the bulrushes.

He was successful in his calling, Master Dutton, and like to rise. He had a stone house built outside the village, and when it was finished, in we moved – my mother and myself, and the infants younger than I, fruit of the union. It were no shame to live in such a place, a gabled, slated, steeply-roofed domain, with mullioned windows from which could be seen the rolling wolds and those same sheep which ruled our lives and kept the turf so neat and smooth and ourselves in wealth.

Yet having known, as I believed, a finer life, a fairer place, I could not come to regard it as my own. Teased and baffled by dim recollections and half-understood notions of a fall from grace, I saw myself a stranger here, one not in his appropriate sphere; I daily looked for my release.

From my mother I could learn nothing. It was as if she had chosen to deny the past we shared, and that thereby all reference to such on my part was some lapse of common politeness. After a while I understood this and refrained from pestering her, colluding in our peculiar mystery. My mother was a most beautiful creature, with sleek black hair and soft fair skin and gentle hands. She had a clear fine voice, and knew the names of jewels and perfumes. She was very graceful; nothing like the Bisley women, who worked with their hands and had square country faces. Although her hair was black and mine was auburn I believed that I resembled her in mien and manner; certainly we were not like Master Dutton; but we made pretence we were. Our difference lay mostly in our speech – Master Dutton spoke the rich broad language of the wolds; Catherine Felton did not, and I chose to emulate her way of talking rather than his. She could read, and taught the same to me; this was not the way of Bisley huswives. She knew courtly ways and graciousness, and sometimes my stepfather would reprove her.

"Catherine! All that must be forgotten! There is no place for that here. The boy must learn what now befits his station."

But what my origin had been I did not know; and when my mother died in giving birth to one more stepbrother, one sorrow more to me was that I never did pursue my questioning.

Never unkind to me, Master Dutton nonetheless plainly favoured those infants sired by himself, the three small fry romping with their nurse, all of whom resembled him, square sturdy curly-headed stock, and not unlike the Cotswold sheep. Plain enough for all to see in me some changeling.

Slim and pale I was, small for my age, with long white fingers and, strangest of all, hair of a reddish amber, resembling no one in the village. My face was oval, neat, with clear grey eyes. Taught by my mother I walked daintily and ate and drank fastidiously. ("This they do at court," she told me once, and blushed, afraid that she had said too much.) Now she was gone, her secret with her, and I in a fair way to grow up to be a cloth merchant. That such would never be my fate I knew, for I would sooner run away to sea; indeed, such was my intent, the thought sustaining me as I sat long into the nights, my face at my small window, as if I would see into the days to come, looking over greensward flecked with sheep. My future did not lie in this quiet place, I knew it, but the thread that bound me to where I should be was tenuous, and broken now. I stood like one beside a maze, half guessing where the gateway lay, but knowing nothing of the heart of it.

That gateway was the big old house in the village. There, only there lay explanation.

This same house lay beside the church, divided from it only by a wall and wicket gate. It was built of grey stone with a grey slate roof, furry with lichen. It was tall and gabled, dormer-windowed, half hidden by the rooky trees whose branches rustled at the leaded panes, whose soughing I remembered when I slept there as a babe.

Time and again I was drawn back to that house. Empty now, it stood locked and barred. A little solitary stranger, I frequented that deserted garden, moth-like flitting here and there between old roses and the wilderness of woody herbs now untended, a place where foxes slipped by silently at night.

By dint of climbing I could see through the windows. I beheld fine rooms where nets of cobwebs hung, some furniture remaining – heavy oaken chests, a great dark table, carved stools and tall-backed chairs. No one lived there. No one spoke of it in Master Dutton's house.

When Master Dutton learned that it had been my habit to hover about that selfsame house where I believed I had been born he grew as angry as I had ever witnessed, and seized and shook me.

"I forbid it, John," he trembled, quivering with rage – and fear, I thought, though I could not imagine why. "You never must go to that house again. I may not tell you why; 'tis best you know not. Trust me – it is for the best. It would much grieve your mother. If ever I do hear that you go there, much as it pains me, I shall beat you with my belt, and in such wise you never shall disobey me more."

"But why?" I cried, amazed and expecting reasoned explanation.

"Ask me no more," he answered. "And believe me, it is not through malice but through love that I advise you. It is for your safety and your comfort."

"Was I not born there?" I demanded. "Why am I there no longer? Why did my mother leave that place? Is not that house mine?"

He clouted me about the head. "Have you learned no respect?

Have you grown so wild? Will you prove a thorn to me who treat you well for your dear mother's sake?"

"I only wish to know and understand that which I half remember."

"Then memory is false," he snapped. "You never lived there. You were not born there. You were born in the little house in Bisley where we lived before we came to this house."

I knew he lied and I said nothing. But I despised him; for I have always held that if one does embark upon deception, that deception should appear to all observers perfect truth.

"Content you," Master Dutton said, relenting. "Settle yourself to the worthy life of a merchant's child. You will never know how fortunate you are in this, believe me. Learn happiness in small things."

Wretched fellow. How he must have lived in dread that one day I might ask him: "Who was my father?"

But at that early time it was the house that was my lodestone, and of course I went to it again, in secret.

Five or six years old I was, a little shadow, quite unnoticed in the dark untended place with none to see me enter that wild garden or press my cheek against those weather-grimed windows to peer within.

Impelled by curiosity, and by a stronger force – the impression I maintained that this large house belonged in some strange way to me – I found it possible to insert my hand into a broken pane and touch the latch and then by climbing on a water butt to open the window and carefully make my way within. I dropped on to the floor, my thudding heart the only sound in that great emptiness. Here I was in the forbidden place, an explorer in a strange land, my footfalls in the dust the only sign of humankind.

The house smelt cold and was so. All the hearths were empty, tapestried with cobwebs. I went where I would, like an elf that brings good fortune, all unseen. Of myself, my birth, my mystery I learnt nothing. But I saw the house, its rooms, its passageways, its creaking staircases; I trod them all. I saw the furniture, some of it covered by old cloths, some of it bare. I lay upon a bed that smelt of must and matting. I marvelled at the carvings on the bedposts and the size of them. And lifting the heavy lid of an oaken chest I fingered rich embroidered cloths that smelt of lavender.

I was an interloper; this place had no messages for me. I came away. I carried with me more questions and confusions than I had had before.

But there are always folk to gossip, and a child may always find some satisfaction for his thirst for knowledge amongst the common folk; and my informants were then Jenny the huswife spinning in her doorway, and Jem Ickley the slatter with his feet on the ladder, tapping and hammering the Througham slates while he held the knotched whippets steady, leaning on the eaves.

"The big house? Over Court? They hold it for the Crown."

"But why does no one live there?"

"They have their own houses in London town, bigger and better than we have here. What do they want with such as Over Court? Over Court's a cottage to the king when he has all his palaces."

"But whose house is it then? Is it the king's?"

"They hold it for the Princess Elizabeth. It belongs to she."

Let it not be thought that we who lived so far from London were as far removed from knowledge of the great. We knew of Princess Elizabeth. We knew her to be a most unhappy maiden. When she was an infant her mother the queen had suffered execution, and shortly before that time had miscarried of a dead boy. Yes, we knew even that; for the King's Majesty was the father of his people, noble and just in every way, and we cared for him and wished him well and hoped to see him happy in the birth of a son and heir; we knew it was his dearest wish. He had once had a son, a strong and handsome son who grew to manhood, but that son had been a bastard and had wasted and died; and all the King had then were but two daughters, Princess Mary, born of the Spanish Queen Catherine, and Princess Elizabeth, born of Queen Anne Boleyn who was dead. And now those princesses themselves were become bastards, for the king had married Queen Jane Seymour, and had got the son he longed for, Edward, an infant; but the queen had died.

Jem the slatter saw the king in Gloucester when His Majesty came visiting us – for Gloucestershire was in no way a forgotten place. Kings and queens came here, knowing well that Gloucestershire was famous for its good air and its hills of sheep whose presence betokened wealth; and at Sudeley there was a fine castle for the royal folk to use, and hunting lodges in the forests round about. The fame of Gloucestershire had certainly reached London.

"King Henry?" Jem recalled. "Oh aye, a golden man. Gold hair, gold beard. A yellow feather in his hat, and gold about him, at his neck and on his royal chest and sleeves and hands. Aye, even on his horse; aye, even on his horse's rump."

He had made changes, had King Henry. Now we had an English prayer book in the church. And there were foul tales told about the monks.

"Buggery at Bath Priory, regular as eating and drinking," Jem said nodding.

"But what is that, Jem, buggery?" I enquired. Jem said he did not know; but he knew that in order for the king's men not to tell about the buggery the prior offered them his Irish wolfhounds. And the prior at Maiden Bradley only lay with pretty maidens and would send the plain ones back, and all his children ran about the cloisters. And at Winchcombe it was said the monks used alchemy and called the Devil to them in the crypt and got their wealth from necromancy.

This was why the king must make a clean sweep and so rid the land of villainy that passed for holy living.

And with such vigour was the new godliness brought to the people that it was deemed necessary to destroy the tombs of old Saint Cuthbert and the Venerable Bede with sledgehammers, and to bring some of the abbots to the gallows.

Master Dutton wept. He was not of the popish faith, but he was saintly in his way. Once he went on a pilgrimage to Hailes, some miles away across the hills. It was the most memorable moment of his life.

"A lovely holy place," he said. "An abbey sheltered by a hill, all set in meadowland where bees hum in the flowers, the air so mild that vines grow thick and lush. And such a large and beautiful abbey, meet enough to hold the Holy Blood. One day I'll take you there. It is a sight you'll never forget. The Holy Blood was brought to Hailes by Edmund Earl of Cornwall, who was the nephew of the king, three hundred years ago. Christ's blood, John, that dripped from the Cross into a silver salver and was brought here from the Holy Land to be the hope and salvation of us poor folk that live in Christ's love. So thankful were the holy monks that their abbey was to be the place where Christ's blood should repose, that all the eastern end of the church was taken and reformed to make a shrine for it. And thus it is a place of pilgrimage. We make our slow respectful way towards the shrine and when we reach the holy phial we kneel. The phial is made of glass and seems to contain only water; then we pray and call upon Our Maker and He grants us the most blessed sight of a miracle – the cloudless liquid becomes His Holy Blood – we see it flow before our eyes – we see the scarlet of His blood – we weep and pray and we give thanks. It is not given always to behold the holy flow. But I was blessed and I thank Him for it."

"But is Hailes Abbey safe? Safe from the sledgehammers?"

It was not. Poor Master Dutton was to live to hear the last bell rung at Hailes on Christmas Eve.

It was to ring a change for me.

II

Up from the port of Bristol on fast horses one fine April day came Ambrose Neville and Zachary Mountshaft, who by diligent enquiry in the village discovered my present whereabouts and came forthwith to find me. Never in my life had I seen anything like these golden strangers.

Travel-stained and muddy-booted as they were, they were magnificent. Mere description can barely convey the impact of their presences, but to prise away the radiance that surrounded them, in plain truth they were thus:

Ambrose Neville was a man of middle height, a courtier by his graciousness and bearing, a man of quality and elegance; and very beautiful. He had an oval face, beardless, pale, with a fine mouth, fair eyebrows and grey eyes. His hair was tawny gold. His hands were long and slim with very white fingers, such as any woman of our time might envy. He wore a dark flat hat trimmed with a feathery plume; he wore slashed breeches with an embroidered codpiece and silk hose, and a velvet coat lined and edged with fur; all of the very best quality.

His companion Zachary Mountshaft must have been six feet tall, broad in the shoulder and tanned of complexion. His eyes were of the most piercing blue beneath black bushy brows; he had thick curling black hair and a black beard. He wore gold earrings. His laugh filled the whole room. He wore a leather doublet and a crimson swirling cloak, and his boots reached to his thigh.

What splendour! What confusion! And what mystery! Master Dutton would have me hustled from the room, but I lurked in the passageway, wide eyed, at the half-open door; I heard it all.

"But what have you done to the boy, Master Dutton? Dorothy's child to live his time on earth amongst the Cotswold sheep! The prospect makes me shudder! Ugh!" And Ambrose Neville did so, flamboyantly, like a player, looking about our abode, which was considered a very fine place to live, as if it were indeed a sheep pen. I giggled; he was very droll.

"'Tis for the best," Master Dutton declared, defensive, yet plainly sure in his own mind. "No other possibility is safe. And you know it in your heart of hearts, sir. Best he know nothing. Best we take no risk."

Zachary Mountshaft laughed, a risk taker, who believed such talk mere foolery.

"Would you have truly kept his secret to the grave?" said Ambrose Neville. "A bold man, Master Dutton, so to toy with fortune. I daresay you believed I'd never come to claim him. I daresay you believed that I was lost at sea."

"Indeed, I thought about you not at all," said Master Dutton stoutly.

"The more fool you then, sirrah," Ambrose answered piqued. "For I shall have some say in how the boy is to be reared, and you shall like what I propose."

"I'll hear the proposition first. I'll not have aught to do with that which I consider contrary to his best interest."

"Bring the boy in," Zachary suggested lazily. "Let him give his opinion." His boot kicked the door wide open, he not moving from his chair, thereby revealing me where I waited; and he laughed, and beckoned me, and I came in.

Then Ambrose Neville strode across the room and caught me in his arms and held me close. I breathed in heady scents of coriander.

"Young John, sweet John," he said, his smooth cheek to my own. "I am your uncle, come from a ship that docked at Bristol. Shall you like me, do you think?"

"I like you very much, sir."

"Better than Master Dutton?"

"Yes sir, very much so."

He squeezed me in a tight embrace, pleased by my answers. "And now come shake the hand of my friend Zachary Mountshaft. He is a sea captain. And is his not the handsomest face that ever you clapped eyes upon?"

"Indeed it is, sir," I replied, my hand enclosed in the strong and leathery palm that Zachary extended.

Master Dutton interrupted this bonhomie with a noise of irritation. "Master Neville, you surely do not intend to take the boy from here? This is his home. What can you offer him? As I understand it, you are not a man of great fortune and have been at sea for these five years. Have you some property to call your own? The boy is not my own flesh and blood but I feel duty bound to him and want what's best for him in all things. You do not mean to make a sailor of him? He is not strong. He is much like his mother."

"You presume, sir, to remind me of it," Ambrose answered haughtily. "Do you suppose I may not see for myself the sweet face of my sister in his looks? But Master Dutton," he continued in a tone laden with meaning, "he is also the living image of his father."

"Enough!" snapped Master Dutton. "We agreed...we promised..."

"Very well," said Ambrose, tight-lipped. "All I meant thereby was that the boy has every right to education of a gentler sort. He must have a tutor, he must have the education of a nobleman, and he must have less to do with sheep!"

Zachary Mountshaft laughed again, and I with him. Ambrose's voice had grown querulous in his passionate distaste for fleece and mutton.

"If it is commensurate with your own position," Ambrose continued in more placid tones, "let the boy remain here in your care. But let him be at his books. Together let us undertake to find a tutor worthy of him, and let us groom him so that he may take his place...wherever fortune intended him."

"I am content that he should have a tutor," Master Dutton answered warily. "But Master Neville, is it for the boy you do this – or for yourself? If you have plans at some future time to use the boy to advance your own state...I tell you now, it is not wise."

"You wrong me, Master Dutton," Ambrose cried. "Just as yourself, all I want is that which is best for the boy."

I plucked at his gorgeous sleeve. "But uncle – you are not going back to sea and leaving me, now that you are here?"

He hugged me once again, my new discovered kinsman. "My dearest lad, fear not. I shall be with you, and Zachary also, until we are convinced that all is well. And we shall have the best of times; and you shall know us better."

My heart, which had plummeted like a stone when I heard that I was to remain with Master Dutton, even with the tempting promise of learning put before me, now leapt with pleasurable excitement. Nor was I to be disappointed.

"As I recall," said Ambrose, "the best May Day games are to be found at Nailsworth."

It was the first time in my life that I had travelled anywhere merely for enjoyment. No warehouse dealings with merchants, no fleeces to inspect nor cloth to weigh, nothing waited for us at the end of our short ride but what should please us. Down into the valley village we rode, Zachary, Ambrose and I, through springtime woods of blossoming hawthorn and the carolling of birds, and there found Morris dancers and a maypole raised and a Robin Hood, and hobby horse and revellers and music from pipe, shawm and drum, with everybody out for frolic.

We joined in the dancing. Pedlars tried to sell us ribbons and trinkets, from pie makers we bought pasties, and we drank beer at the tavern. We watched mummers playing greenwood tales. Although it was long past dawn, the people came and went into the woods that overhung the village, gathering mayboughs, they said, and some indeed came back with mayboughs.

"Shall we also gather mayboughs?" I requested, and in great good humour Zachary and Ambrose acquiesced, and Ambrose said: "O

Spring! O Love! The fairest time of year, when every man doth find a maid and know the sweetest joy of all."

And off we set amongst the trees, I riding upon Zachary's broad shoulders. And though we picked boughs of blossom, neither of my new friends went in search of maids, for all that Ambrose sang it.

"They told you that Catherine Felton was your mother, did they?" Ambrose said to me, as we sat over our beer at a trestle table outside the inn. "It is not so. Catherine was your mother's maid. Your mother was Dorothy Neville, my sweet sister, whose life was taken in the same way as poor Queen Jane who gave birth to Prince Edward. She was the loveliest of creatures, Dorothy; but ask not of her, for the past is gone, and all we do is done in the moment wherein we draw breath. And this same moment should be passed in mirth and not in sadnesses recalled."

"But – " I protested.

"Not another word more," said Ambrose briskly. "To pleasant pastimes!"

The Nailsworth May Day was but the first of many pleasing expeditions undertaken in the company of these two merry gentlemen, whose intent it seemed was entirely to give me delight. To Bristol went we, but not Bristol as I had been accustomed to be acquainted with it, a place of counting-house and storeroom; no, we strode about the quaysides and drank ale amongst the sailors, and I was brought aboard the *Sainte Marie*, the ship that Zachary took to the Azores and across the seas – a privateer.

As we made our way along the quaysides I saw the building of a ship. I saw the great wooden props against which the curved sides rested; I saw men with saws that split the timbers on the benches, and the frames whereon men worked to seal the joins. From underneath, where we stood, this ship seemed like a mountain.

Not at all alarmed, I climbed the gangplank of the *Sainte Marie*; I went wherever Zachary directed, relishing the stink of rope and pitch, the creak of timber, and the dark beneath the deck. I saw the galley with its fireplace, and the hold, empty now, but later to be stacked with water, food and gunpowder. Rats scuttled into the shadows. We were below the waterline. At sea, the oak was all that lay between men and the ocean. How brave they were, the mariners that ventured life and limb aboard ship! I saw the great guns, and the tiller steering such a vessel. Then Zachary took me into his cabin.

This cabin was a fine place, furnished in red velvet, with a table covered with a mass of charts the which he let me handle and peruse. He poured me wine, which I preferred to beer and ale, and talked to me of many things – of the African gold trade, and the Cape of Good Hope, and the long sea route that led to Calicut; and the islands of Columbus. I saw the astrolabe which showed the altitudes of sun and moon and stars. Zachary spoke names of high romance – Tingitana, Manicongo, Mauritania – and told me of the ships that came from Santa Cruz with sugar, almonds, dates, molasses; and of the men that risked their lives for tropic gold, and died of the Great Sweat. But also in his cabin he had jewels in an old sea chest. He let me run my fingers through them – emeralds he had, and amethysts and rubies, and amongst them Spanish gold coins; and he laughed and said mysteriously: "Flowers of the sea, my boy. These grow in the oceans; and a man may reach his hand out and pluck them if he dare."

I looked up at this mighty man with adoration. He was the tallest man that I had ever seen, and broad and handsome. I could see the muscles of his thighs. "Tell me about the places you have seen," I begged; and he obliged and sat me on his knee and told me tales of marmosets and parrots and steaming swamps with tentacles of roots that pulled men to their deaths, and Indians with poisoned arrows, and fruit made up of both bread and wine that dropped from trees at the touch of a hand, and snakes as big as fallen tree trunks; and I believed it all. Zachary possessed that skill – that if it were a yarn he spun me it had all the ring of truth because of the conviction in his voice, the glowing fervency of his blue eyes. The best deceptions give no cause for doubt. I vowed that when I grew to be a man I also would sail the seas for Spanish gold and see the wonders of strange lands. I would seek out a man like Zachary for my companion.

I clung to my uncle Ambrose in distress; I could not believe that after so short a time he must depart and Zachary with him.

"Trust me," he replied, "We leave you in the hands of Brother

Xavier. With him you shall have the education of the best in the land. When the moment is right we shall return. Your future lies with us and we shall not abandon you. Believe me, we shall meet again."

"And when you return," said I, "shall I then go to sea with you and Zachary? That is my dearest wish."

"If God so wills it," Ambrose answered piously. "But in the meantime set about to study. Make us proud of you. Apply your mind to learning's joys. I know you will do well. And though he is of lowly station Master Dutton is good-hearted. Do not despise him overmuch. All men are equal in the sight of God."

I said nothing, knowing full well that Zachary and Ambrose sniggered at my benefactor and called him Master Mutton when they spoke of him; but the sorrow of parting overrode all other emotion, and when they two went and I turned back to Brother Xavier, I considered him a poor exchange.

III

They found me Brother Xavier from amongst the disaffected monks of Hailes. I thought no ill of him at that time, though the strangeness of his name and its foreign quality perplexed me somewhat. Master Dutton said that we should pity him, for now he had no home but what ourselves could give him.

The abbey had been stripped of its wealth and power. Abbot Segar was paid off with land, and the Holy Blood was sent to London for the wise ones there to test its authenticity. Canterbury had been plundered - Rochester and Waltham likewise, but that anyone should doubt the Blood of Hailes to Master Dutton was as if one doubted that the sun would rise; he shook his head despairingly.

The world was not as once it was. In London the king had taken an ugly wife; and in Bisley they whitewashed a painting of Our Lady from the north wall of the nave of All Saints' Church, and said it was no longer holy. Ten feet square this painting was, and showed Our Lady sheltering the trembling souls of those about to come before their Maker. Facing her Saint Michael stood, with scales to weigh the little quivering hopeful naked souls; a demon hung upon the balance to pull down the soul to Hell; and all was blues and crimsons and flecks of gold, and Our Lady with long flowing tresses and the richness of a queen held wide her arms. I was there with Brother Xavier and we stared in silence at the shadowed place where through the whitewash showed the smudged and indistinct remains of what we once had venerated.

I learned in that instant that truth is the judgement made by those present at the time; that when we say a thing is so, so be it; but if we say that selfsame thing is other than we said before, then so it be: the saying gives the thing its definition, not the thing itself.

Brother Xavier and I came home, returning to our books.

For three years Brother Xavier hid the truth of his character from me, or, my mind as yet unformed, I had not the capacity to perceive him as he was. He was my tutor and I was left much alone with him. Master Dutton, sensing that through Ambrose's fleeting influence I was become more than before a thing apart, now turned his own attention to my stepbrother Will, and on his journeyings about the wolds and to the market towns it now was Will that accompanied him; and I was left to study in the upstairs room allotted to my tutor and myself.

Here, for the next three years, we set about my education. When it is made clear that in that time I acquired some understanding of Latin, French, Italian and Greek, cosmography, astronomy, logic and arithmetic; and of perfecting both the Roman hand and the flourishes of the Engrossing style, it will be seen that there was not a deal of time for much besides. However, Ambrose had stipulated that I was to learn archery and horsemanship; therefore we spent many hours at the butts down in the meadow, and we rode; nor did it occur to me to wonder why a monk should so excel at both these skills; yet it was plain he did so.

Because of what Brother Xavier was to become to me I am aware of an unwillingness to dwell upon the details of his appearance, indeed to speak of him at all. He wore at first a monkish habit, and I believe that when he first came to us the tonsure of his calling also was a feature of his general appearance; this he soon relinquished. His hair was pale and fair, transparent when the light shone through it, wispy round about his face, and never thick, but like a little aureole of feather-down, close to his head; therefore the shape of the skull beneath was well pronounced. His face was gaunt and square-jawed, his eyes hazel, hooded, seeming sleepy, but not so; and he did not smile.

Yet at first I did not fear him, and he gave no cause for disquiet in the daily round of scholarship we shared. He was, it seemed, by nature taciturn, and in the company of others silent and respectful, grave in manner, very like one would suppose a monk, though dispossessed, to be.

That Christmastide some of the village boys, myself included, bonded by our churchgoing, performed a brief enactment of the Holy Nativity under the direction of our vicar Ralph Hauchell; and I, because of my gentleness of bearing, slender build and lack of height, portrayed Our Lady.

Into the dim church we would go, its small interior lit by the glow of candles. Here in the flickering gloom we acted out the sacred story, watched by the ancient stone carvings of those musicians from another time, and the heads in foliage and the dragon belching leaves. We tweaked the ears of the hound on the tomb of the knight in chain mail while we waited for our turn. By lanthorn light we returned home, past the old stone monument where mass candles were lit for the souls of those too poor to buy their own – a spot we dreaded, for it covered a well where once a priest was drowned, and he was said to climb out from beneath it on dark nights, all wet and black with slime, looking for that dead man for whom he had been bringing the Blessed Sacrament.

Brother Xavier who was my constant companion would help me dress, would comb my hair, would instruct me how best to comport myself; but it was plain to me that I had natural gifts enough to represent the Holy Virgin, and looking round about me at the other boys I could not help but see that none but myself could have played the Lady. Even those that played the angelic host were large square boys upon whom the white gowns and the painted aureoles sat a little oddly.

"A godsend to me," Sir Ralph murmured many a time as we rehearsed. "Without a Virgin of some verisimilitude our little play would be a laughing stock. But John, when you come forth and speak, you are the very Maid."

"Do not you perceive," said Brother Xavier afterwards to me, "with what respect he treats you – how he does not pinch your cheek or chuck your chin as he does with the others?"

Such had not occurred to me till Brother Xavier pointed it out. I felt that I was treated courteously, but this had seemed entirely natural to me and not worthy of remark.

The first time I became aware that Brother Xavier's thoughts went deeper than we guessed was when he catechised me on the subject of my name.

"Neville is a name of the nobility," he said.

"It was my mother's name."

"A Plantagenet name," he pursued.

"Oh, not in this instance," I assured him laughing.

"But why not?" said he.

"You have met my uncle, Ambrose Neville. You have seen the manner of man he is, a swaggerer. If we were of Plantagenet stock he would have said so. Would he not?"

"But did he speak at all about your forebears?"

"He did not."

"You did not think to ask him?"

"In the short time that he was with me we did not hold a deal of converse. It was a time of doing, not of talking. Such intercourse as passed between us was mostly on the subject of the sea, of ships, of foreign parts, of – of beasts and monsters, of the Indian in his swamp. As I recall, these at the time seemed of more import."

"But what a wasted opportunity!" he marvelled.

"I was younger then," I said by way of explanation.

"Neville," he said then. "It is an ancient name. A Yorkist name," he added.

"I know that," I replied.

"You know also that these very hills are no strangers to the passing of the Yorkist troops? Before the battle at Tewkesbury King Edward the Fourth sought his enemies here, the two armies narrowly missing each other, up and down these hills and valleys. They made their camps by Birdlip and Leckhampton and crossed the Frome in such great numbers that the river mud was stirred up and the horses could not drink the water. And Edward the king...his mother was a Neville."

"All this was long ago."

"Not so very long at that. And you will find the Rose of York carved within the church, and the shield of the Duke of York. Nevilles owned Bisley. Nevilles owned Over Court House."

I stared. "No, that I did not know."

He was gratified to have at last my interest. He saw that it was with the house that he would draw me.

"Yes," said he. "King Edward the Fourth gave Over Court to his mother, Duchess Cecily Neville, the Rose of Raby. And she was of the house of John of Gaunt."

I paled. "All this has naught to do with me." My heart was beating fast. "You speak of things long past."

But he maintained: "Not so long past."

And at that time he said no more of it; but he had sown the seed.

Possessing from birth a careless assumption of my own importance, I confess that Brother Xavier's hints in no way contributed to humility and self-effacement. Of Plantagenet stock? It seemed entirely likely, eminently reasonable. Yorkist armies had wandered these hills of ours, and that youthful Edward who became king of England was reputed to love women peasant and high-born. What more natural than that he should have passed his mother's name on to a child conceived in secret, and this infant become ancestor of mine? Or if not Edward himself (though fancy preferred the monarch, given choice) then some kin of his, some high-born Neville, scion of a different stem whose flower became my mother? My mother...it was she that bore the Neville name and not my father, it would seem, for Ambrose Neville was her brother. Reluctant as I was to assume my father low-born, I must needs come to this conclusion, and with no sure facts at my disposal, my favoured interpretation was that my mother, a lady of Plantagenet origin, made a love match with a squire of low degree, much as the widow queen of King Henry the Fifth had done. The mystery of my birth now occupied a great deal of my thoughts; and though I gave my mind to study, it was true that fancy also very much possessed me.

It then occurred to me that Master Dutton had spoken of risk and danger in connection with my situation. Could this be so? Was I, if Plantagenet indeed, at risk? Was that why the matter was so cloudy, so enigmatic, so little spoken of? Would it not be better for me to remain here, hidden from the world, to live my life out in obscurity, amongst the sheep? What might befall me if my existence were revealed? I had no way of knowing. King Henry had been monarch now these thirty years, following his father, first of the Tudor line, and though he was secure in power and status it was understood he still feared any man or woman who pretended claim to the throne. But would he fear a boy of seven years old?

My head bowed over Latin prose I pondered this. Astonishingly, considering the very slight evidence for it, I never doubted the possibility of my royal blood. The question that I asked myself was, given that possibility, was it right for me to remain unknown in Bisley, or had I a duty to discover more about my origin and then to take the matter further? My conclusion was always the same: in spite of danger I would wish to take my true place on the world's stage and let come what may.

In London King Henry's marriage was declared null and void; Thomas Cromwell was executed for high treason; and the king then married Katherine Howard. We heard that she was young and beautiful.

In Bisley it occurred to me that now, amongst my Latin and my Greek, my tutor had begun to pay more attention to my stance and manners. Courtliness and deportment figured more largely in our daily conduct. With the Dutton family we had less and less to do. Master Dutton now was frequently from home; his new young wife was simple-natured and, it seemed, content to rear her brood in separateness from Brother Xavier and myself. I had the impression that, without withdrawing general sustenance, the worthy cloth merchant had washed his hands of me; that though he wished me well, he understood that others had the manipulation of me.

Those others now returned, and showed their true intent. My days of ignorance were numbered.

TWO

I

"You have done well," said Ambrose Neville to my tutor Brother Xavier. "He is exactly as I would have wished."

I stood before them in the suit of clothes they gave me, the epitome of a well-dressed boy of eight years old. I wore long hose of wool, soft leather shoes with high tongues, slashed breeches, a green velvet doublet over a shirt with a linen frill. I had a short green cloak, and a neat cap with a feather. I was never dressed so well before.

Ambrose glowed with a peculiar excitement, as if some private knowledge rose and leapt within his breast, the which he would not share and yet whose existence threatened to consume him with its passionate intensity.

"Look at him!" he gloated meaningfully. "But look at him I say..."

They needed no encouragement. Brother Xavier – who had long since cast off monkish robes and wore a suit of sober grey – and Zachary Mountshaft, always too large for the room that contained him, watched me, each with calculating stares, which in no way troubled me, for I believed myself most beautiful and worthy to be the object of such gazes. I am one born under the sign of Leo. We believe ourselves the centre of the stage. And now I understood that I had passed some kind of test.

Ambrose then conversed with me in Latin far more ricketty than my own, and we continued, a little stumblingly, with Italian and French. Zachary had ridden with me at great speed across the common towards Mynchen Hampton, and had taken aim beside me at the archery butts; he pronounced me skilled. They questioned me on the Catechism, the Articles of the Faith, and the Ten Commandments; on aspects of grammar, logic and cosmography, astronomy and arithmetic; and on the *Colloquies* of Erasmus. Brother Xavier told them I had a natural aptitude for learning.

"We rise early," said my tutor. "Whatever I may teach him, he shows an eagerness to learn; he swiftly masters all I set before him and then asks for more. It has been my pleasure to instruct so diligent a pupil."

"Better and better," Ambrose said. "And my felicitations to you, Xavier. It seems that in the wilds of Gloucestershire we have contrived between us to produce the education of a gentleman to the benefit of all. Remain here, if you will, and wait upon events. I will send word to you of all that passes. John!" – he pounced upon me, kestrel-like,and held me by the shoulders – "how would you like to go to London town and meet your grandfather?"

"My grandfather!" I gasped elated. "In London! Oh yes indeed, I would like that very much."

It was now spring, the month of March, and this proposed excursion was the longest journey I had ever made. Familiar places rapidly we left behind – Oakridge Common, Water Lane, the river Frome – the edge of Oakley Wood, and so to Cirencester and across the wolds. We had no servants with us, no one but ourselves – Ambrose, Zachary and myself – and because of the smallness of our party and the speed at which we travelled, somehow I had the impression that there was an illicit aspect to our business.

I asked no questions – partly because I sensed that Ambrose would not answer them, and partly because I had every hope that soon all questions would be answered. I was to meet my grandsire. I pictured an old gentleman living alone in a big house in London – on the outskirts, perhaps, in the green countryside of Islington or Whitechapel or Charing Cross. For some reason he had not wished to see me before now – perhaps my mother had made an elopement and caused him distress – but at last, victim of mortality's privations, he must have sent for me, and, won over by my amiability and elegance of bearing, he would repent of past coldnesses and restore me to my inheritance. Gone would be the world of Master Dutton and the wolds of bleating sheep. Ahead of me would lie the radiance of a gentleman's life, with wealth, acceptance, and the power to purchase ships of my own and to sail beyond the seas. I was content to bide my time, certain that the boundaries of my knowledge were about to be increased.

My knowledge was to grow in other ways also.

When dusk fell we would seek an inn beside the way or in the town through which we passed. Warming ourselves at the good fires that burned in the hearths, we ate either in the smoke-filled tavern or upstairs in the room that was ours for the night. Ambrose and Zachary slept in the bed, and I upon a trundle. As I pulled the rough blanket about my shoulders, Zachary blew out the candle, and we all wished each other goodnight and sweet sleep. Darkness fell around us; sometimes from below came the raucous laughs of those that drank, and always the creak of the beam, the shifting of the thatch, the rustling of mice and bird. I dozed.

When they believed me sleeping, in low voices Zachary and Ambrose talked, not of the venture upon which we were embarked (for in hope to learn more I made every effort to hear what they said), no, but of themselves; that is, endearments, toyings and fond words. I heard them move in an embrace; I heard the panting and the sighs, the muffled kisses and the grunts of satisfaction. Then I slept, the strands of borrowed pleasure woven into my dreams.

I observed them in the morning, my heroes; I watched them as they washed and dressed. Ambrose was so slender, lithe and smooth. Apart from at the crotch where there was a smudge of gold, he had no body hair. His limbs were shapely, pale-skinned, slightly freckled. He moved gracefully, sinuously, lazily. He perfumed his body carefully, amber-tinted in the shaft of sunlight from the window. He laughed apologetically.

"The males of our family, John," he said, "never need to shave. My father was the same. As for the growing of a beard, this bounty is completely denied us. I doubt that I have seen the smallest hair upon my chin in all my twenty-seven years." He pouted petulantly. "Unlike Zachary."

Zachary Mountshaft! The curiously suggestive nature of his very name excited me. Neither Ambrose nor I could take our eyes from him. Naked he was bronzed and hirsute, his muscles rippling as he moved. His arse was big and firm, his cock in its bush of black hair seemed a living creature. He laughed, comfortable in our admiration, his teeth white against the blackness of his beard, his blue eyes full of merriment.

I envied Ambrose. I could think of nothing more wonderful than to be with Zachary aboard ship under a wide sky, sailing for treasure across the wild ocean towards the Islands of the West.

And now we drew near to London. Everyone, it seemed, was going that way. Horsemen like ourselves, pedlars, farmers, carts and wagons, beggars, the cavalcades of the great, all converged upon the rutted roads that led towards the great and famous city.

Passing through the fields of Holborn, with Smithfield to our left, we reached the city wall, and entering the gate, now found ourselves in Cheapside. The sounds and sights of London closed about us. To my wide-eyed wonder and my quivering senses it was a wonderful place. My heart leapt as a lover's might on first glimpsing the beloved. Grandsires, sheep, confusion – everything that previously dominated thought fled from me, dissipated by the marvels that surrounded me. The noise, the crowds, the stink (yes, the eye – or nose – of love must tell it: London has more than its fair share of stenches) enraptured me. I was one on a cloud blown by the breath of Zephyrus. This was my element, this my true sphere. If I were never more to set eyes on Bisley I would weep no tear.

Which of us may say what is that vital spark which causes passion's flame to leap within the docile breast – and what was London but a mass of houses, churches, taverns, alleys, beams and straw? What were its folk but citizens about their daily grind – the huswives, water carriers, apprentices, the gallants and the coney catchers, and the thieves and drabs? What were its noises but cart wheels rumbling and the clamouring of bells, the raucous shouts of street vendors and the yelps of dogs, the snatch of music and the brawls of drunkards? Who dare say what constitutes true love and whether it be possible that one poor town provoke that love? I speak but as I find; and London town was instantly my heart's desire.

But in plain terms we left our horses at some hostelry; we took lodgings at the Goshawk, and we passed a week in London. An odd week, for I found that I was left much to my own devices. Somewhat to my surprise Ambrose took off "to see what he should see". More than that he would not say. In Zachary's company – that is, in Elysium – I saw the wharves, the ships that lay at anchor, and the quayside taverns; here he made enquiries as to voyages and vessels and which nobility were like to lend support to ventures of discovery. Because I had not seen the sights, he showed me London Bridge, Saint Paul's church and the palace of Whitehall; and took me to a bear baiting.

Ambrose returned at night and drank so much he fell asleep and must be put to bed; and this became the pattern of the days. Polite and trusting I said nothing about grandfathers, believing that in their own good time, my benefactors would make all known to me. Besides, I had so much to occupy myself withal I was content to let the matter rest, for either with Zachary or without, I led a wondrous life for seven days, ankle deep in mud and grime, and gawping at the business of the streets, one more speck among the riffraff of the bustling antheap.

Then one day, such excitement! Word went about that King Henry was in procession outside the city gate, and having by then some fair idea of the pattern of the streets I knew my way, and joined the throng that went to see the king. It seemed at first that the intelligence was false, for there was no sight of king or company upon the road that led to Westminster, and sore of foot but hopeful we pursued the rumour as it flew before us in the air; and passing by the houses of the great we came at length to Charing Cross and here good fortune smiled on us. Those citizens who had persevered now savoured their reward.

Towards Whitehall rode a procession: guards to lead the way and guards about the royal personage, the Master of Horse beside, and the nobility behind, and at the centre of it all in splendour rode our monarch.

My first sight of the father of our land! He whose doings Bisley weighed and pondered as if his deeds were personal to themselves. A golden man, had Jem the slatter said. This was not my own impression.

Certainly there was gold enough, and velvet and brocade, the flash of jewel, the glint of silver. But placed as I was, about the level of the royal knee and looking up, my startled eyes could see that the king was very fat and very sad. Each shoulder, beneath its fur and padding, seemed as wide as a sideboard; the bulk before and aft the width of woolsacks heaped for handling; the legs in their white hose all wound about in bandages. There were pearls sewn in his hat, and beneath its brim the face was grave and lined, the mouth's expression obscured by a grey-gold beard. Monstrous and majestic the king rode by; all cheered and one or two amongst the nobles flung some pennies; then it was over.

"How sober his face!" said I to the woman standing by.

"How else should he seem?" said she and shrugged. "'Tis barely a month since he gave orders for his poor young wife to be beheaded, she who went mad with fright and ran about the palace screaming, till they quietened her. How lonely must his bed seem now!"

A man beside us guffawed in contempt. "No king sleeps lonely. All they do is crook a finger...you remember King David and the virgins?"

The wayside crowd dispersed. I ran back towards the city, breathless, joining Zachary at the Goshawk where he drank in preoccupied silence, the which he broke to greet and embrace me.

"I saw the king!"

Ambrose did not return till dusk and then he slumped down at the table and called for wine. Zachary put his hand on Ambrose's wrist.

"No more wine now; and no more sullen nights. This business must be concluded."

But Ambrose pulled away, and filled his throat with wine, and his intent was plainly once more to drink himself senseless.

"The boy has seen the king," said Zachary. "He thought him fat and grave."

Ambrose laughed, but not in mirth, and left us and went out without explanation.

"Won't you follow?" I frowned, puzzled. "Won't you bring him back?"

"No," said Zachary. "But when he returns I'll clout him. He has gone to find a boy."

"What boy?"

"Any boy. When Ambrose is dispirited he gets into a street boy's bed and fucks his way into oblivion."

The complexities of this remedy for ill not entirely clear to me, I yet marvelled.

"But how could he bear to leave one such as yourself? You are in every way superior to all, and certainly to any boy. I don't understand. I would never leave you if I and not Ambrose were your friend."

Zachary hugged me. "You are my friend, indeed you are, lad. You honour me with your companionship."

"Thank you," I said, much gladdened. "Then shall you and I remain together this night and let Ambrose do what he will?"

"We shall, and be the better for it."

I passed the night in Zachary Mountshaft's bed, both of us naked and asleep. I never slept so well as then. In his strong arms I was well secure, his big body my shield and safeguard, his steady breathing the rhythm that rocked me into slumber. And in the morning when I woke, my head upon the dark hairs of his chest, he let me touch him where I would, and lay and smiled indulgently at my delight in his male beauty.

When at about mid morning came Ambrose crawling back I dressed and slunk away. I felt a sense of loss so palpable I knew that I would bear the void of it for ever. I wept against a post in Saint Paul's churchyard; but a stranger said if I would go with him he'd cheer me with a penny and some cakes and a pleasant surprise after, and that so frighted me I stopped my tears and fled.

Back at the Goshawk Ambrose had a blackened eye, and he and Zachary were talking about a journey. As if I were of no importance it had been decided in my absence that, our time in London being at an end, we should return to Gloucestershire. This I could not believe.

"Our business here is not concluded," I declared. "As I recall, our object was to find my grandfather. What of that now?"

"It has not been possible," said Ambrose sourly. "My hopes were misplaced. There has been a change of plan."

"But did you look for him?" I cried. "Did you make attempt to find my grandsire? I believed that in your daily absences this was the matter upon which you were about. Was I mistaken?"

"You were not mistaken," Ambrose answered quietly. "But I did not succeed. And therefore we return."

"To Bisley?" I screeched in an eldritch voice.

"Indeed to Bisley. Where else? That is where you live."

I found Ambrose's manner cold. I felt that he had changed towards me. I did not understand. Too well bred to cause discord where we were now, amongst folk, I pursed my lips and maintained silence. I believed that Zachary would explain all to me later, and that perhaps upon the journey I might persuade them both to reconsider their decision. This hope alone sustained me as we regained our horses and began the journey westward.

Heavy of heart indeed was I with each mile travelled. With London lost to view, now all was field and wood, or villages devoid of bustle. Gone the camaraderie of our previous journey, gone all the excitement and anticipation. We were all gloomy, Zachary perhaps the least, for he had voyages arranged and his thoughts already turned toward Bristol and the sea and Spanish gold.

No such pleasure was on my horizon. Bisley and its sheepwalks, the companionship of Brother Xavier and the loss of Zachary...it was a poor exchange for London.

It was upon a hill in Oxfordshire that I made clear my doubts and my despair. We had dismounted for a piss, knee deep in cowslips, and my outrage overmastering me, I shouted: "Why must we return? I cannot bear the great confusion of it all. You told me I should see my grandfather. What, is he dead? Or living does he refuse to see me? What is my crime? What has befallen us? Are we no longer friends? I need to understand. I will not mount until you tell me the truth. Rather I will lie down in the cowslips till I become a clod of earth!"

Zachary then smiled, but kindly. "There is no need for such extremity," said he. "Sweet Ambrose, pity him and say."

Ambrose sighed. "It would be against my better judgement," he answered. "I believe it best that he be kept in ignorance, for safety's sake. Who knows what follies and calamities might lie in wait for him if he were in possession of the truth?"

I sensed him wavering. I planted myself before him, hands on hips. "Come folly or calamity I'll hear the truth," I said.

"Remember, it was not my choice," said Ambrose.

"The choice is mine," said I. And then, to prompt him, I added:

"So. Why did I after all not see my grandfather?"

"You saw your grandfather," said Ambrose dourly. "That fat grave man you were so glad to gawp at, that was your grandfather. And that you got no closer to him is because I lost my nerve and dared not bring you to him."

II

"I could not do it," Ambrose said to Xavier, as we sat, the four of us, in the upper room of Master Dutton's house at Bisley, in varying postures of disappointment and dismay. "As may be well imagined, I despise myself. I believed myself so bold. I have fought duels. I have fought the storms at sea. I have confronted mutineers with murder in their eyes. But though I came within a yard of him I dared not speak to that great monarch. I dared not tell him who I was or what I had to say."

"It was not as easy as we had supposed," said Zachary in mitigation. "It was not the right time. Oh, we had heard, yes, that the queen had been beheaded, that it was true she had had many lovers. We had not foreseen that, this so fresh in his mind, the king is grown morose and wary as a watchdog, growling in anticipation. And London is a restless place. We in our ship at sea, you in the silence of the wolds, have no conception of the undercurrents in that city. The king is gross and full of flesh. They wonder that he yet moves. He cannot last, they say; and yet he does. He has the carcase of a rotted ox. The prince is four years old. The nobles move about him like chessmen; and the more devious, they say, are secretly in touch with the Lady Mary, hoping that the boy will die. He barely recovered from the quartan fever; he was ill for months. So fragile is the thread of life...The factions are already in position. There is no party for a new contender."

"Do you see?" cried Ambrose desperately. "We were naive. To bring forth a claimant to the throne – and such John would be, however innocently we brought him forward – you would need an army and a man powerful in the kingdom to put his name to it. Those boys that came against King Henry's father had the backing of the old nobility, and Ireland, Scotland and the Low Countries. I knew this. But I believed we would succeed through sentiment. The old king loved his son the Duke of Richmond. He wanted him to succeed him. Illegitimacy would have been no bar. And so with John. Bastardy may be revoked. We've seen it done. I thought that could the king but see his grandson, all paths would be smooth. But when the moment came, fear stayed my hand."

"You should have spoken," Xavier said.

"I know it. But yet I thought the court a strange and dangerous place. I feared the hand of an assassin."

"You should have let me take the boy," said Xavier. "I would not have hesitated. I would have feared nor knife nor poison. Ambrose Neville, you are a fool. I half suspected it. You say the moment was not right – I say it was. When but in the darkness of despair and doubt would the king welcome news of an unknown cousin for the prince, and dear to him for the sake of the father? How long will you leave it now? Who will believe you if you wait? You must return. You must bring John into the presence of the king. For all our sakes."

I listened to these interchanges, weighing each. My mind, now rational and free from confusion's misty clouds, knew at last the truth and could make stance on its firm base, a most pleasing progression, and I welcomed it. That knowledge was to my eager senses much like a jewel which, through pleasure in its novelty, I must take out and polish, time and time again. In exchange for the vague claim of a tenuous connection with the old house of Plantagenet I had been handed on a plate the gratifying information that I was born of royal Tudor blood.

My father was the Duke of Richmond, son of King Henry. Twenty-three years ago King Henry fell in love with a beautiful lady-in-waiting to Queen Catherine. She was eighteen years old; she came from Shropshire. Her name was Elizabeth Blount; they called her Bess. This was my grandmother. In the priory of Saint Laurence in Blackmore, Essex, she gave birth to a son. The infant was named Henry Fitzroy. He grew to be auburn-haired and handsome, with a pale oval face and grey eyes. King Henry loved him with a passionate devotion. Bastard though he was, the boy was groomed to take his father's place. King Henry made no secret of it: this healthy son, so like himself when young, would one day rule England. Young Henry was made Knight of the Garter, Earl of Nottingham, Duke of Richmond and Somerset. He was given a household of his own, and four thousand pounds a year for all that he required.

He was made Warden of the Cinque Ports and Lord of Ireland. He was given the best education. He studied at Cambridge with his tutor, a famous Greek scholar. Everybody knew the king was contemplating the revocation of all the laws concerning bastardy. The Duke of Richmond was to have married Princess Mary; but the duke was wayward and would please himself. At Cambridge he learned more than Greek. Young as he was, he fell in love. The maiden of his choice was Dorothy Neville. When it became known the lady was with child, the Duke of Richmond made arrangements for her accouchement far from court and gossip, for he was by then upon the point of marriage to Mary Howard, daughter of the Duke of Norfolk and sister to the Earl of Surrey.

So Dorothy came to Over Court, in the royal manor of Bisley, with Catherine Felton her maid, and a small household. Here she gave birth to her son, but died so doing. For three years here we lived, Catherine and I, she who said she was my mother, and our income came from London. Thus my memories of the big old house, of servants, of a fall from riches. And then our source of wealth came to an end.

The Duke of Richmond died of a wasting consumption, still young, a mere seventeen. We in our Gloucestershire fastness were forgotten, nay, unknown, left to our own devices. Catherine married Master Dutton, and considered she had done her best by me. Ambrose was at sea and knew nothing of our change of fortune. Had he not returned, I never should have known my forebears. I never would have known that, just as the ladies Mary and Elizabeth, I came of Tudor stock; my place was at the court.

"You will, of course, make a second attempt," said Xavier in a cold hard voice.

Ambrose fidgeted. "I think not..." he began.

"But you must!" cried Xavier, white with rage. "You have here the wherewithal for all our futures. It is a chance that men would give their eyes for."

"A chance," agreed Zachary in a placatory tone. "But this is a child of which we speak, not a principle or a theory. Ambrose believes the boy would be in danger were his existence to be known."

"It was said that the Duke of Richmond was poisoned by Queen Anne Boleyn," Ambrose said.

"What was not said of Queen Anne Boleyn?" shrugged Xavier.

"Indeed," conceded Ambrose. "But what if it were true? You know the way it is at court. The little prince, the two princesses. Behind each lurks the power of those who would benefit by their accession. There is no place for a fourth contender, and a male at that. Spain would not have it. Spain counts upon the Lady Mary to succeed Prince Edward should he die."

"Then let John turn papist," said Xavier with no change of expression.

"And you a holy man!" laughed Zachary reprovingly.

"We speak of policy, which must at times override matters spiritual," said Xavier, eminently reasonable. "And since you profess to show concern for the boy's welfare, why not ask him what he wants? I know him well. I know the mazes of his mind. Ask him – if you dare."

Now all eyes turned to me. Unhesitatingly I said: "I want to go to London."

"John is too young to know what he wants," Ambrose snapped. "He answers like a child – 'I want, I want'. I as his kinsman know what he should want."

"What use are you to him?" said Xavier in contempt. "Either at sea, or if on land, a man that knows not how to act for his own advancement."

"Of what do you accuse me?" Ambrose bristled, reaching for his sword.

"He accuses you of indecision only," Zachary said mildly. "And 'tis true, we are not bound by singlemindedness. Myself I am inclined to agree with Ambrose; and yet, who knows? Mayhap in a year or two...when we return..."

It seemed that Zachary and Ambrose were running true to pattern; with a voyage planned, a ship awaiting, and their scheme a failure, they were off to sea. Nor would they be persuaded otherwise.

I opened my mouth to say: "Let me come with you. Let me be your cabin boy." Then I closed it again. Ambition's hand was on my shoulder. An arras had been lightly drawn aside, a vision glimpsed before it fell back into place. I had the strong impression that Zachary and Ambrose had lost interest in the prospect of a golden future for me and, though they might well return from travelling, it would not be to contrive my accession to the throne of England.

Inimical and unprepossessing as I had so far found Brother Xavier, I knew instinctively that his was the force would promote my change of fortune, his the power would work for my advancement, for he, untroubled by the bonds of friendship and its moral duties, and propelled by self-interest alone, had the incentive to pursue the matter in whose toils we were now entangled.

"Forgive my weakness, John," Ambrose cajoled me. "When you are older...when we return..."

"When we return," said Zachary embracing me, "we'll take you with us and together we shall make for the golden lands of the west. Never forget this, boy. Depend upon it. You shall be with me in my ship. How will that please you?"

"It will please me very well," I answered, and added with a smile: "If I am not to be a prince of England, then I will gladly sail the seas with you."

We parted friends, and I was left with Brother Xavier.

I was nine years old. I disliked Brother Xavier, but I respected his ambition; I sensed that we were bound. With Ambrose and Zachary gone, in the whole of England there were but Xavier and myself possessors of this piquant secret. Inevitably our lives must be intertwined. Indeed, my tutor said as much.

"Why do you remain?" I asked. "By his general comportment Ambrose has well indicated that his plans for me are all too nebulous to succeed. He speaks of armies, patronage at court. What may you do that he did not? Nothing will change. You have no more power than he. What may you hope for?"

"For the present, nothing more than the payment I receive for your education," answered Xavier. "Nevertheless, I live in hope of other, and therefore my intention is to live close to you as any leech."

Our daily round was much the same as it had always been, partly because it was expected of us as tutor and pupil to be seen to study; and partly because I loved to learn and Xavier was content enough to teach. But now there was a difference; it was understood that nicety was at an end, and in our communal deceiving we were more honest than we had been hereto.

I found that Xavier was a man without scruple, a man amoral and entirely lacking in the warmth and sentiment which are the hearth fires for the chills of man's existence.

"The Blood of Hailes?" he laughed in scorn. "'twas I that stood behind it. The legend goes that in the presence of a true believer the cloudy liquid turns to Holy Blood. Behind the shrine I stood, observing through a spy hole all who passed, and if I liked the look of them I pressed the spring; thus flowed the blood. Sometimes I did not even look, but munched my breakfast, leaning my elbow on the spring. The blood was made of honey, wine and piss."

I gasped, awed at the magnitude of his deception. I remembered Master Dutton's shining eyes as he described his journey to the sacred place, his joy at witnessing the sight, the tremulous reverence in his voice as he recounted the enactment of the miracle.

"There are no miracles," said Xavier. "Who tells you otherwise is a fool. You have heard of the Rood of Boxley? That crucified Christ worked miracles, answering prayers by the nodding and shaking of the head, the twitch of lip and eye; but like a puppet master there stood one behind it, working the device, pulling its strings. It is always so. It is so for miracles and it is so for men and women – always one a little further back that pulls the strings."

I shuddered then, for I suspected that he then referred to our two selves.

"The other tales about the monks...?" I asked him cautiously one day, when pen in hand I sat over my Latin.

"Which in particular?"

"The wives... the necromancy..."

"Men call it necromancy when they understand it not. There exists a knowledge which men fear through ignorance, and if such knowledge may, when put in practice, threaten king and state, then laws are passed to prevent its blooming in the light of day. Then it will go underground and men will call it evil. Some monks do possess this knowledge and no doubt some of them will use it for devilish purposes, the more so now they have been driven from their sanctuaries. There is much bitterness let loose in the world, a creeping malevolence that seeks the soil wherein to root itself. And there are always some who know through herbal lore the ways to kill that seem to show that death came in the course of nature."

Was Xavier one such? I did not dare to ask.

"And then...the sodomy?" said I.

"Ha!" laughed Xavier amused. "What would you know of that?"

"I would know all that you may with propriety reveal."

"Have you yet gleaned what such entails?"

"I think it is something to do with what we see with the rams and ewes, and it is spoken of in Holy Writ?"

Then Xavier without preamble told me in detail all that pertained to sodomy; indeed, it was not exactly as I had imagined, and, always eager to learn, I was grateful for the information.

Then Xavier was beside me, and he took me by the hair in a firm hold, and curled his lip and stared into my face. Through a trick of the light how like a death's head seemed his visage, all his bones revealed, the facial hollows emphasised by shadows!

"You are a pretty boy, John, with a dainty arse. Had you been sent into a monastery there would have been no chance whatsoever of your having to learn of sodomy by enquiry; a dozen lusty fellows would by now have beaten a path to your plump white buttocks and those yet waiting would have thrust their bursting pricks into your throat."

I gasped at the coarseness of his words. My tutor smiled. "Afraid, John? What is there to fear? Believe me, sodomy is very pleasant. I could show you here and now precisely how agreeable the deed."

"No!" I said wide-eyed, and closed my mouth because his breath was on my lips, something tangible, something I might almost taste.

"How may you prevent me?" murmured he, teasingly, much as a cat toys with a mouse. "What if I chose to perpetrate that upon you which would please me and which, if not entirely without pain to you, would add to the sum of your education. How might you hinder me?"

"Thus," answered I, giving gaze for gaze. "By reminding you that if ever I came to greatness I would reward all those that played me fair, and punish those that took advantage of me."

"I congratulate you, John," he answered, and he let me go. "You have fixed upon an argument that I may not refute."

"Assassination," said he comfortably, as we rode at an ambling pace across Mynchen Hampton common, "in certain circumstances is permissible, nay, worthy."

"But what of the respect we owe to human life – life given us by God? What of the love for humankind that ought to bind us all?"

"Humankind!" he spat. "We are no more than worms that wriggle in the apple of the earth."

There was a low alehouse on the road from Mynchen Hampton – it was called the Black Sow – where it was understood the innkeeper received and hid those goods which others stole upon the highway. This watering hole we well knew, Xavier and myself, pausing here upon our rides for beer. While I drank I observed the company from my seat in the corner, and Xavier met up with rogues and vagrants. The first time that we visited this place I was surprised to learn that he who was a monk in other times knew men like these; but soon it seemed completely natural that we should pause there and that Xavier should rub shoulders with the footpads and the rufflers, the whipjacks and the thieves. Once when Xavier was gone into another room, a cheery fellow with a warty face taught me the different ways to cheat at dice, and seeing my interest in the same, he sold me a weighted die for my own use, the which I kept and still possess.

"What business can you have with these men?" I once asked Xavier, not in judgement but in curiosity.

"Why? Are you afraid of them?"

"They take no heed of me; no, I don't fear them."

"You should fear them," said Xavier bluntly. "There's not a man there who would not do murder for a groat."

"Then Xavier, look to yourself," I said. "You have other greater dreams, in which the common footpad has no part."

"What, would you advise me, sir?" he laughed maliciously. "Believe me, I know what I am about."

Once, when we were shooting at the butts, a poor old woman slunk across the meadow, Beth Pegler, who lived alone in a shack below the Springs, and her cat with her. Xavier about to release his arrow, turned, and to show his skill at archery and for no other reason, spun round at speed and let fly the shaft. His arrow pierced the cat which squealed and died. I made a noise of protest.

"Squeamish?" sneered Xavier. "Squeamish for a cat?"

"It was her own thing."

"You like not sport?"

"It was not sport; the beast was fat and slow, and now the woman is bereft."

His eyes grew hard and cold. "The action scarcely merits comment. It was a moment's fancy, without meaning. He is a fool that pities those beneath his feet."

I let Xavier into Over Court through the downstairs window. Daylight it was, but no one saw us. Like me, he seemed at first to share the sense of mystery produced by such a vibrant emptiness.

"Here ghosts walk," murmured he. He padded silently across the uneven boards, gazing about him, pausing now and then to touch the dust-grimed furniture, to lift a cloth, to take between finger and thumb the edges of a folded tapestry. We spoke in whispers, warily. In an ancient house, parts of it four storeys high, and gabled, with a maze of rooms and passages empty of humankind yet full of noises of its own, there hung the wherewithal to make one apprehensive. But then habituated to our situation Xavier grew careless, roughly searching chests and cupboards, ransacking drawers, casting aside that which incommoded him.

"What would you find?" I wondered.

"Proof," he answered.

"Proof of what?"

"Of whom you may or may not be, young muttonhead."

"We need no proof; we have the word of Ambrose."

"That painted ninny?"

"Don't speak of him so. He is a man of honour."

"He is a coward. But that is not the point. No doubt he spoke the truth. But who is there that will believe it? If we could find a letter, document – a will – or some memento of the Duke of Richmond...that would much help our cause."

"That is the philosophy of a small-minded man," I cried stung by his impertinence. "I know it in my heart. I know I am descended from a king. My very blood tells me my grandsire is the king of England. I need no document nor letter!"

"Fortunate one to possess such certainty," said Xavier lightly mocking. "Alas, but others, being prone to doubt, may question more than you do. And some, reserving the inalienable right of the free-born man to cry 'It is not so!' may send us roundly on our way. How happy were we then had we some half-torn fragment from a letter found abandoned here, bearing such words as 'infant...my dear son...signed this day at Westminster...Harry Richmond'."

We found none such, and if indeed there were ghosts in that old house, none spoke to give us aid in such a quest. Little did we know that with the turning of the year, there lay in wait for us a drama of such magnitude as would disturb for ever the restless silences of Over Court, and cause them to reform and merge with unquiet spirits yet undead.

THREE

I

The winter snows had barely melted from the lower fields when all that bustle on the rutted highways which betokens the approach of spring began anew. But this year of 1543 there was in Bisley seen amongst the general mess of travellers the glamour and uncertainty of the new – strangers from London.

We in the country, who are aware of every leafburst, every footfall, every shift of earth, could hardly miss the arrival of the party from the east. And that its destination was to be Over Court had been apparent ever since the fires were lit and smoke was seen to curl up from its chimneys. The gawping observer then might clearly see the windows wide flung, and servants shaking bedding in the garden, cloths hanging to dry upon the bushes; while voices from within came wafting on the wind.

"For whom do you make ready?" I asked a manservant.

"For the Lady Elizabeth's Grace," and as if that in itself had not the ring of ultimate splendour, he added: "She that was at birth a princess of the realm."

Natural curiosity would have impelled me to return to Over Court and squint and gaze from wall and tree, but to inquisitiveness was added that possessiveness I felt towards the house – my house – and like a lodestone it drew me now more sharply than before.

I lay along the surface of the wall that bounded the garden, and watched. I saw the comings and goings of the household. I could tell that it was small – only a few servants, a poor stable, sufficiency rather than excess. I made guess as to who slept in which room, by the lighting of the candles. And inevitably then, as the days unfolded, I saw the players in the play. I saw portly Master Thomas Parry, and Mistress Katherine Champernowne with her breezy laugh and her motherly care of her young charge; and I saw the Lady Elizabeth whom I thought cold and haughty. Her quick bright eyes missed nothing. They certainly saw me.

"Mistress Champernowne! There is a boy upon the wall."

I slithered down and waited, lurking outside.

"I see no boy."

"Yet he was there."

"Some village lad."

"Well, indisputably so. I prefer not to be watched without my wishing it."

I did not go away. I leaned against the wall, excited, challenged. I knew well enough her voice was meant to reach me. After a while she called out: "Boy! I know you are still there. Climb up again. I do permit it."

I clambered up and lay once more along the wall. Below me in the garden stood the Lady Elizabeth, hands on hips, surveying me. I still thought her proud.

She was nine years old. She had a small pale elfin face, and auburn hair loose to her shoulders. She wore a green gown over a skirt of amber brocade, muddy at the hem, with little skinny ankles below. Behind her, Mistress Champernowne in a dark dress.

"You see," said Elizabeth turning to her governess. "I said he was of pleasing appearance. It is no mere village lad." She gestured to me kindly. "Tell us who you are."

"My name is John Neville," I replied.

A glance of approval; so, they were not wrong.

"And where is your home? What is your situation?"

A dreadful hotchpotch of half-truths came to my lips. "My mother is dead; my father Ambrose Neville is away at sea. I lodge with Master Dutton the cloth merchant, in a large house on the hill. I study with my tutor, a very learned monk."

"You have a tutor!" Elizabeth cried enviously. "Kat – he has a tutor. Oh, come down from that wall, John Neville – you remind me of a picture of the Serpent lurking in the Garden."

I bounced down into the garden. I landed inelegantly but soon righted myself and bowed before her.

"I am honoured to meet you, my lady Elizabeth."

"Ah, so you know who I am."

"Naturally. Your fame spread before you."

"Amongst those I consider my friends I am called princess." She corrected me lightly. I hesitated.

"I am content for you to be my friend," she prompted.

"Thank you, my lady princess."

"Your manners are excellent. Are not his manners excellent, Mistress Champernowne? It would be permissible, would it not, for him to become my friend while we are at Bisley?"

"Whatever pleases you, my sweet," said Kat warmly. "And lord knows we shall need entertainment in this distant place."

Now those who have accused dear Kat of easiness and folly might stand vindicated here, for thus readily did she give me access to the royal presence, simply for my name and my demeanour. But she was ever thus, tender-hearted, affable.

"We were at Hunsdon," Elizabeth explained to me. "That is the name of a royal manor near London, one of many such. But sweating sickness broke out suddenly. It was feared that, Hunsdon being vulnerable, then Hatfield or Hertford might also be so, and it was suggested we come to our manor of Bisley, where the air is known to be very good."

"We have had no sweating sickness here," I agreed.

"Have you brothers or sisters, John?" enquired Elizabeth.

"None," I answered.

"To be the only one," she said, "induces a certain sense of solitude."

"But you are fortunate, Your Grace," I said. "You have both brother and sister."

Her cheek twitched. "We are not close," was all she said then.

I learned more later. She confided to me as we played. We climbed the trees in the garden. We practised archery together. On wet days she taught me how to dance. It made us laugh. To my surprise a dance was no simple matter, but every part therewith had meaning relevant to the virtues of existence – the placing of a foot or hand conveyed prudence, industry, judgement, modesty and circumspection, enhancing by its wider implications the pleasure of the dance.

Strange indeed it was for me, to be at Over Court and not by stealth...How wondrous then it seemed to walk in rooms cleared of their mustiness, to see the bright spring sunlight stream across floors smelling now of herbs and beeswax.

And now I saw them at close quarters whom I had once watched merely from a wall —

Kat Champernowne was buxom of face and figure, not pretty, but of an engaging sweetness of disposition that gave to her face a pleasant openness of countenance. Her eyes were brown, big and gentle, her lips full. Her hair was dark, and parted at the centre of her brow.

Thomas Parry was plump and portly. His hair was close cropped. His eyes were bright, his nose bulbous and his mouth firm. His dimpled chin was well-rounded – indeed, if truth be told, he had more than one chin. By nature he was choleric and prone to irritability. He was steward to the young princess.

The maidservants also I saw, who paid me small regard, and it was clear to me that Kat alone had close access to the princess and was her especial confidante.

How strange then, I reflected time and again, to be in this company, and to dance here, with the girl in the green gown – a cousin to me, though she knew it not – while Mistress Champernowne did play the flute for us till she grew out of breath, and the maids-in-waiting sewed and smiled.

It pleased those women to watch us dancing. They would smile and clap and cry "Well done!" and then turn to each other laughing.

"As like as two peas in a pod!" they marvelled; but we paid no heed.

"So you have a tutor, John," Elizabeth said wistfully. "I was not permitted to bring one with me. They are all needed for my brother; I share his tutors when I study. I suppose your tutor would not consider joining us here? I long to pursue my studies."

"I think my tutor would be most eager to take up such a kind offer," answered I; and Brother Xavier came to Over Court. As an eyelid closes over an eye, so Xavier's careful grey persona came down over his true character in the presence of the young princess. You would have sworn him God-fearing, austere and good. I marvelled at his capacity to deceive. I could not help a certain admiration. Now, in an upstairs room at Over Court, at a small table, sat Elizabeth and I about our work, with Xavier to teach.

"Why, you know almost all the same books as I myself, John!" cried the princess in delight. For our amusement we conversed in Latin and in French.

"It is vastly more agreeable to study with you than with Edward," she declared. "There is some pleasure in competing with you, being of an age, and it greatly pleases me when I find that I know more than you. To know more than Edward is no achievement, he being four years younger. Although," she added, scrupulously fair, "for one of five years old he has an excellent capacity for learning. But he has a tendency to grow pompous." She laughed. "Once in his French studies he muddled up two words, and speaking of 'the works of the great ones', he wrote 'the eggs of the great ones'! I corrected him before his tutor saw what he had writ. Edward was crimson with mortification. He has a horror of appearing stupid."

I asked her more about her life.

"What would you know?" she shrugged. "It is very humdrum. I live sometimes at Ashridge with my brother, sometimes at Hunsdon or at Hatfield. When I am with Edward we begin the day with Mass; we ride, we study, we shoot or we play bowls up in the gallery. It's very pleasant when we are with Edward's companions. There is Barnaby Fitzpatrick who is dull but steady, and Henry Sidney who is well read; but the best is Robert Dudley, who is my own age, as yourself."

I felt a swift and sudden dislike for the one so singled out by her admiration.

"What is particular to Robert Dudley?" I demanded.

She swished her skirts and smiled. "He is handsome," she admitted. "And," she shrugged, "he can do anything he sets his mind towards. But," she added firmly, "I would never tell him that I liked him best. He is arrogant enough already."

On other subjects she proved more cautious and guarded in her speech. But I learnt thus much: she feared and loved her father, but he had no time for her; she did not like her sister Mary; she cared greatly for her little brother, but she sensed that men worked to keep them apart; she felt that Mistress Champernowne was her only friend.

"I had a friend," she blurted out. "I may tell you this, John, because we shall not meet again when I go from here. One did love me. It was Queen Catherine Howard. She gave me place of honour at her table. She said that we were kinswomen, of the same blood and lineage – my grandmother was a Howard. She would have been a mother to me. I began to confide in her, my thoughts, my fears. At last, I thought, there is one at court who cares for me. And you know what happened to her." Her lips tightened. "I learnt then never to give my heart. She gave her heart too freely. In this world that is a crime and you will die for it. When she died I sorrowed, crying in my bed. But I vow I shall never cry again, nor permit one to be privy to my secret thoughts."

My company proving so pleasing to the Lady Elizabeth, and Xavier's skills deemed necessary for her instruction and entertainment, it was suggested that we two should lodge at Over Court for the duration of the royal visit. We accepted with alacrity, both for the pleasures this entailed and for the undeniable improvement in our situation. Master Dutton put up no objection, but I daresay we would have paid him no attention if he had, so distant were we now grown from him.

I was given a small room in the upper part of the house. A single step led down into it from the passageway, and, the ceiling being low, this little room was always dark, the window letting in small light. A second door led to Xavier's room. We were private here. We could speak as we would, unheard.

"Well, John, we have landed on our feet," murmured Xavier. "I cannot help but feel that we may turn this present situation to our advantage."

I felt uncomfortable. No doubt what he said was true; but yet I wished he had not said it.

The Lady Elizabeth could play the lute and sew. I was required to sit with her while she did these things. I liked to hear the lute, but it would have been tedious to watch her sew if I had not made use of the time to satisfy my curiosity, gleaning all I could of how the great ones lived.

However, it soon became apparent to me that up till now her life had been a simple one. She – and in this respect I noticed a similarity to myself – recalled a fall from grace. She could remember a time when she was called 'princess', and then merely 'my lady'. She remembered the christening of Prince Edward at the palace of Hampton Court. She had been four years old and had been carried in the procession by Edward Seymour, he who was later Duke of Somerset; she carried the baptismal robe, and it was very heavy.

But she lived quietly, she said, with Mistress Champernowne and Master Parry, in one or other of the royal houses within easy access of London. "I have lived with my sister Mary," she conceded. "But her household is no more splendid than my own."

"The similarity of the situation in which you find yourselves, you and your sister, must surely bind you in a mutual support?"

"Yes, one would think so," she mused, "but it does not. It may have done at first, in that I do believe my sister showed me some sympathy when I too was obliged to take a place of some obscurity. She was kind to me, I don't deny it. But it was an odd kindness, one cannot help but sense it. She has few friends, and I believe she chose me as an object of her love, and on to me she poured excess of it, as if to heap me with so much of it that I must of necessity love her in return. She did not love me for myself, as Kat does. And when I was lukewarm in response she grew sullen, as if I were at fault."

"Your father no doubt cares for you?"

She looked me in the face. "I don't believe he does," she said. "He may have loved me when I was an infant. But now he dare not love me, because of who I am. I am become a symbol of something that is past, a horrid reminder of all he would forget. He never asks for me. It's all Edward, Edward. I best please him by keeping quiet, far from him. If he is fortunate he'll marry me to a prince beyond the seas and make a good alliance. Such I believe is his intent. Meanwhile I doubt that I am ever in his thoughts."

"There yet remains Prince Edward, whom you cherish."

"Yes..." She wrinkled up her face. "He loves Jane Dormer better. She is of his age. He calls her my sweet Jane. I am too old to be his confidante".

She shrugged, disdainfully. "It doesn't matter; I don' care". I did not believe her.

I looked at her thoughtfully. She was as solitary as myself, for all she was the daughter of a king.

II

The Lady Elizabeth said to me: "My governess believes that you and I are as alike as two peas. It is my intention to prove her wrong."

"There is no need for proof; we are alike, but not so alike that we cannot be told apart."

"Precisely. And in order to show Kat the folly of her pronouncement I propose that you and I change clothes. In my gown you will look like a gawky little boy with a thin chicken neck, and she will see our likeness superficial."

"My neck is no thinner than your own, Elizabeth!" I cried outraged. "I warn you, I have played ladies before now – the best Lady of all, the Virgin Herself. And all who saw me praised me."

"My Lady Elizabeth!" she snapped back at me. "Never call me by my name again."

I bit my tongue. I almost blurted out what I should not – that I considered us as equals. Instead I made apology. And I vowed I would show my boast to be a true one.

We undressed in a little curtained room, she on one side, I on the other, reaching round the curtain with our hands, giggling at the immodesty of our action, passing breeches, kirtle, stockings, teasing each other: how do you wear this? how do you tie this? how can you bear that? Then we emerged, and in blatant curiosity we stared at one another. I saw her face darken in a frown. I understood. She saw that in her dress I much resembled her, and she was vexed.

"Your hair is too short," she snapped at me.

"That will be remedied when you help me into the head-dress. Do it," I cajoled. "We should disguise ourselves to perfection if we do it at all."

She relented, and, a thin boy in my hose and breeches, she showed me how to bind the hair into the linen and to drape the little veil behind the shoulders. Thus, I wore a brocaded underskirt and her green kirtle. The shoes were uncommon tight; and mine, on her small feet, were loose. We fixed her hair inside my cap.

"We are nothing like," she grumbled. "This was a foolish notion."

But I began to run downstairs.

"No, John – come back – "

When Elizabeth came down I was ensconced in her own chair, seeming to sew, and Mistress Champernowne, also at her sewing, asked me absently if I would like potato soup along with my mutton when we dined.

"John!" I called. "Don't skulk there; come and join us." But Elizabeth would not, and went into the garden.

"John is out of sorts today," I said complacently.

I sat with Kat all afternoon, and answered easily when she spoke. She wondered if I had the starting of a cold; I said that I felt very well; we spoke of John and praised his virtues; and we spoke of Bisley and agreed it was a fresh clean place; we wished, however, that we were back at Hatfield which, we both agreed, was our favourite palace. Catching a glimpse of Elizabeth in the doorway I said: "I have half a mind to go early to bed..."

"To bed!" shrieked Kat, dropping her sewing. "You are not becoming ill, I trust?" She moved towards me and she took the garment from my hand. "Why, not one stitch, my love, not one stitch have you sewn, and you would go to bed? Why so?"

"Why so?" fumed Elizabeth now rushing in and throwing down the sewing to the floor. "Because he knows not how – and you are the more fool, Kat, for sitting and conversing with him and indulging him in his monstrous play-acting! Are you so blind? Can you not see that this is John?"

"Lord save me!" Mistress Champernowne said in a low voice. "I was fooled; I was entirely fooled."

"You did not look at me; you saw what you expected to see," I said tactfully. "If you were to study me closely you would see my eyebrows are a little heavier, my hair a little shorter."

"Kat, how could you!" Elizabeth seethed, and stamped her foot. "How could you sit there and be so deceived!"

I giggled. "Particularly since I have more shapely legs than she has. You see it now, Kat, now that you see my lady in her hose – we are nothing like at all."

Elizabeth now flew at me. She was beside herself with rage. Her eyes burned red. Her fingernails went for my cheeks. She fastened both her hands upon my ears and shook me.

"Give me back my clothes!" she screamed. "Vile impostor! Leave this house! Never see me more!"

We became an undignified scuffle of half-strewn clothes, bare limbs and tousled heads, with Kat between, half laughing, half dismayed. When we were clothed again in rightful guise Kat smacked Elizabeth and made her speak me fair; and though Elizabeth was sullen for a while she did apologise, and I in spite of smarting ears remained.

Elizabeth was henceforth cooler towards me, taking refuge in that original haughtiness which I believed to be a feature of her character when I first saw her. I took pains to remember to call her 'my lady' when I spoke to her, but it did not come easily to me to appease this proud princess whom in my heart I thought a cousin, and in some ways inferior to myself, since I possessed at least by rumour some trace of the Plantagenet.

One day, a dark overcast day with rainclouds heavy in the sky, we found the entrance to what seemed to be a secret passage, hidden in the garden. It was down in a kind of ditch, obscured by foliage, the which we pulled aside, and, finding a low tunnel before us, we took a lanthorn and went carefully within. In trepidation and excitement we continued, moving slowly forward in the dark and eerie gloom, the lanthorn like a quivering will o' the wisp leading the way. Suddenly the candle was extinguished. We were obliged to retrace our steps back to the daylight. We attempted once again to make assay, but at the same point, once again the small flame died, and so a third time. Always at the same place, almost as if snuffed out by a goblin thumb.

We stood there for a moment in the dark, its blackness absolute.

"Perhaps there is a hidden meaning in it," whispered Elizabeth. "Perhaps there exists a point of enquiry beyond which the human spirit must not venture."

"No, that isn't so," I said. "We have enquiring minds and must pursue where thought leads. And to prove it I will go on alone, without the light."

"I forbid it," she said swiftly.

"Why? Do you fear for my safety?" I asked in surprise, but notwithstanding pleased.

"No," she answered. "Naturally I have no wish to see you hurt, but

I would wish to accompany you, and I am too important a person to risk death in such a careless manner. And it would be a risk if we continued, because to lose the light means that the air is bad."

"If I understand you aright," said I in rising anger, "you consider my loss unfortunate, but your own the more so because you are more important than I."

"Well, certainly," she answered, her voice pert and penetrating in the darkness. "I am of royal blood and you are not."

"There you are wrong," I answered, and, I have to say it – albeit with shame – I relished every word I spoke. "I am as noble as yourself. Have you not paused to ask yourself why it may be that we so resemble each other? It is no freak of chance. My father was the Duke of Richmond. King Henry is my grandsire. In truth I have more claim to the throne than any one alive."

This last was spoken in bravado with intent to goad. I did not of course consider what effect my horrid boast might have upon the sensibilities of my companion, and no doubt its enunciation from a disembodied voice in an underworld of threat and shadow must have sounded chilling.

"You speak treason," she whispered, her voice hoarse and trembling.

"That was not my intent," I answered chastened.

"I perceive that you are not as I supposed," Elizabeth's voice came clear and querulous. "I believe that you are now become a danger to me."

I cursed myself for having spoken. What an imbecile! I should have bitten off my tongue.

"Your claim must be investigated," said Elizabeth.

"I was jesting."

"I think not. But the truth shall be discovered and you shall answer before others who will best know what to do. Now let us leave this place."

I was so frightened at the implication of her words I wished the earth would fall upon us and we be buried with our shared secret intact. But I answered merely: "By all means." I vowed that in the night I would sneak out and run away to sea.

Silently we stumbled from the pit. When we emerged the rain was gashing down like knives. We were both drenched to the bone by the time we reached the house. Mistress Champernowne fussed and wept over Elizabeth and took her away upstairs. Xavier took charge of me. Up in my room he stripped my wet clothes from me and rubbed me with a rough towel.

"Xavier!" I shuddered. "I told Elizabeth who I am. I couldn't help myself. Forgive me. But she said that I must be investigated! Xavier! I am afraid! What can they do?"

"Hush now," Xavier murmured. "It will make no difference. They will do nothing, believe me. Sleep now."

Then he brewed me a monkish potion and I wondered whether he were one of those that knew the strange herbs that wrought wonders or disasters; but when I said as much out loud he cuffed my ear and made me go to bed.

In the morning we learned that my Lady Elizabeth was very ill of a fever. Mistress Champernowne remained with her in her room and there were murmurs among the servants about the sweating sickness. Two vile days passed. Voices whispered on the stairs. I heard muffled weeping. A tapestry was laid along the passage so that the servants' shoes would make no noise. Outside the princess's door platters of food, goblets of wine waited untouched. The door remained shut.

Mistress Champernowne, white-faced and swollen-eyed, came looking for Xavier. She plucked at his arm, half incoherent in her distress.

"You must know some remedy...our potions have no effect...in the abbey – was there not some herbal brew known only to yourselves? Believe me, I am desperate..."

Xavier went into the sick-room and the door closed after him.

On the evening of the third day I went to bed as usual. I was awoken by a scream. I sat up, my heart pounding. I jumped out of bed, and opened the door. The sound of sobbing, fierce and uncontrolled, came up from below. Lights wavered on the wall, as candles were borne to and fro. It was very cold.

Xavier came quietly up the little winding stair.

"She's dead, John. The maid is dead. Come down."

"Must I? I am afraid."

"You must." He held out his hand to me. Reluctantly I took it and accompanied him downstairs.

I was taken to the princess's bedside. I could not bring myself to look, but fell into a swoon and must be carried from the room.

"I fear that it was I that killed her," I confided to Xavier from my bed. "I told her who I was. And she was shocked. She may have died of rage or fright. It is myself must bear the blame."

"Peace, John," said Xavier holding me against his breast. "You did not kill her; such is not possible. Rest now...drink this...sleep...trust me."

"I swear that I will never blab again," I whispered. "Never, not about anything."

"Just for this day," said Xavier in the morning, "we want you, John, to perform a kindness for us. For fear of spreading alarm among the servants we have decided to keep the sad news quiet. None of them need know, not yet. And therefore, will you wear the Lady Elizabeth's gown, as you have done before, and walk about a little, to be seen, to show them that the maiden is recovered. It would be a great kindness to us, John, and it would make it easier for Mistress Champernowne to go about her business."

"Does Kat wish it?" I asked dubiously.

"She does."

"Bring her to me and let her say as much."

Kat Champernowne knelt down by my bed. Her pleasant face was streaked with tears.

"For my sake, John," she whispered. "Until I think what would be for the best."

"But why, Kat, truly?"

"Because I am afraid," she answered simply.

"What do you fear?" I asked. "It was no fault of yours. It seems plain enough that the Lady Elizabeth, whom God keep in His mercy, caught a chill and died of a fever. It happens. In Bisley one year half a dozen children died that way, in the houses down by the Springs where there is excessive damp."

"I fear His Majesty," said Kat. "And that's the truth. Since the young queen died he has been fierce and strange. I doubt it not but that I shall be held to blame. I would have died for her, my sweet young mistress, and you know it, John. But who knows it at court?

I shall be thought a light and careless woman and I shall be put in prison for it. And Master Parry with me. Yet we did all we could. I'll swear it before all the world. But who will believe it, who I say? And who will take the news unto the king and face his wrath? Who dares? But if we wait awhile, perhaps...with time...and if you help me,John, no one need know, not yet..."

Her eyes beseeched me. Entirely to cause Kat to lose her fear I let her clothe me in the gown she chose. It was a dainty thing, brown velvet over an underskirt of honey-coloured lawn, with white woollen stockings and a cap of tawny velvet.

"Leave it to me," said Xavier to Kat. "I will provide the shoes. She had such little feet, it seems. As for the rest the match is perfect. And Kat..."

"Master Xavier?"

"Weep not, especially when you are in the company of folk. Your little treasure lives, see – there she stands before your eyes."

But in her room, Kat wept in secret.

For myself the matter was an easy one. I had seen enough of the Lady Elizabeth's comportment within the walls of Over Court to know well enough how she would speak, act, walk; and this I did. Once, as I sat with a book in my hand, a maidservant rushed up to me and curtseyed and thrust a bunch of primroses into my hand.

"God be thanked, my Lady Elizabeth," she said to me. "I prayed for your recovery."

"Thank you, Ann," I answered, self-composed.

The first night that I slept in that great bed I hesitated.

"Send for Xavier," I said suddenly.

"My Lady would not send for him by night," Kat murmured dubiously.

"I have a query regarding a Latin translation and I need to know the answer," I replied, haughty and serene.

Xavier came to me. We closed the door.

"Xavier – is there sickness in this bed?" I quivered. "Tell me the truth."

"All the sheets are changed and the mattress turned," said Kat. "The windows are opened also. John, you must sleep here – it is where she slept."

"Xavier," I whispered trembling. "Where is she now?"

Kat covered her face in her hands and rushed from the room.

Xavier said to me in low tones: "She is buried in a coffin in the garden. Master Parry and myself, by night...no one saw us. There was no moon."

"A coffin, Xavier? How did you come by it?"

"Do you recall how in the garden there is a small stone wall some eighteen inches high, close by the enclosing wall? Half covered over by a bush of hawthorn? One would say it was a water trough. Indeed we did suppose it so. When I shifted the foliage, thinking that this trough would well do for a hiding place, I found it was an ancient coffin. I could scarce believe my good fortune. It seemed to have been sent in answer to prayer."

"Lord save us," murmured I. "A coffin sent, like the ram in the thicket."

"Seven foot long and tapering to the foot. It must have been the coffin of a giant."

"Oh Xavier, but were prayers said over her?"

"What do you take me for? All was done with due reverence. Later, when the house is empty once again I will oversee her burial in a more apt place. Think not of it, John, think only of how best to play your part."

"But in her bed..." I hesitated.

"Would I permit you, John, to lie therein if I feared for your safety? Believe me, John, you court no danger, sleeping there, I promise you. Trust me...trust me."

Trust him! I never would – and yet I must.

I slept that night in the great dark bed, and as the trees beyond the window soughed and clawed the panes in the workings of the wind I knew this was the very bed in which I slept when I lived here as an infant, this room the source of my half remembered dreams, this place my home when first my mother came from London. By strange ways had I come to claim my inheritance.

April passed, with Xavier, Kat, myself and Thomas Parry in possession of our guilty secret.

The servants were informed that young John Neville had been sent home for fear of the princess's sickness recurring. The little princess, however, seemed fully recovered now, and all continued much as usual. For me this new life was no hardship. I lived as I had done before but for the fact that I was dressed in girl's clothes and must remember always to sit upon the close stool instead of standing, in case I was observed. It was amusing and curiously pleasing to find all the world respectful to me. It was like a living play, unreal, yet by the participation and collusion of the players, real enough. How long we would have continued so, staving off the wrath of our great monarch, sparing Kat and Master Parry from the pains they dreaded when the truth be known I cannot say. But one day came a messenger from London and his news threw Over Court into a turmoil.

It was His Majesty's pleasure that the Lady Elizabeth and her household should return to Hatfield and without delay.

I see them, ranged about my bed, disputing in hissed whispers. Master Thomas Parry who had shared that deed of darkness when there was no moon, Kat so tearful that she scarce could stand – and Xavier like Chorus in a play, all knowing and all seeing, never faltering, willing us all by the power of his belief to carry our deception to the portals of the great.

"What do we risk?" he said. "You have seen how competently John is able to perform the part. He so resembles the Lady Elizabeth, God rest her soul, that no one will suppose him other than he is. Yourselves will never leave his side, always at hand to prompt him should he hesitate, and he shall be primed before he goes as to the shapes of rooms and palaces and what he must expect to find there. You have said how rarely did the maiden meet her father, nor has she seen her elder sister latterly. The boy prince is too young to prove a hindrance. Any discrepancies in John's behaviour may be put down to the illness she has recently endured. A quartan fever which has left her a little disordered in the head. And in John we have a willing player. I would not suggest the notion if the boy were frightened or incapable of undertaking what we propose."

"He is so young...does he understand the nature of the situation?"

"He does. And what is more, he longs for it, for your sakes and his own. It would be so easy. So little would be demanded of him – the exchange of a simple life in Bisley for a simple life at Hatfield. No one is asking him to live at court."

"But what if his appearance should change?" suggested Master Parry. "At nine years old his features may be girlish. But suppose he were to grow a square jaw and thick neck, the muscles of a youth, or – Lord save us – an early beard?"

I tittered stupidly; they ignored me.

"Here we are fortunate," said Xavier smoothly. "He comes of a family whose males are pale, slender, effeminate. Through some natural lack they grow no beard, nor hair upon the chest. They are a little below the common stature for a man. But this is idle speculation. We are not suggesting that John grows old in petticoats. We speak of a matter of a few weeks, do we not, while the king is in a torment of distress. Either His Majesty will soften and the news be broken then, or he will in the course of time expire. The boy prince will be very much easier to deal with. Meanwhile we all gain time, a breathing space. Your good selves keep your reputation and your safety and John enjoys a strange adventure."

When he and I were alone Xavier murmured: "Chance has played into our hands. This falls beyond my wildest hopes. We would never have got to London playing by Ambrose's rules. But this...who would have thought it possible? And yet it is so! We may feather our nests with riches that shall last our lives long."

"I would have preferred to go in my true character," I temporised.

"But so you do!" he said. "Your own true character but bound about with petticoats! And John," he smiled, chucking me under the chin, "they do become you well. Maybe I shall come to Hatfield and see you in your fine surroundings and pay court to you. And then it may be I shall prove to you the secret joys of sodomy, and you shall not refuse me, for fear I tell the world what you hide beneath your skirts!"

He made me write letters saying I had run away to sea in search of my uncle Ambrose and Captain Mountshaft – one to himself and one to Master Dutton. I wrote that since the princess was leaving Bisley I had no wish to remain here, having tasted the delights of pleasant company after whose passing all would be dross. He said he would remain behind and do all that was required to cover up what had befallen and give credence to my story of a flight to Bristol.

The coffin must be properly interred and all traces of the deed obscured.

We were all, I think, a little startled to learn that he would not be coming with us, he who was the master mind behind it all; but he assured us he would join us later when the business at Bisley had been concluded. He said that to build an edifice the base must be secure.

In early May, with baggage packed and every preparation made for the journey across country, we left Over Court behind; we said farewell to Bisley, and we set our faces eastward – our servants, Mistress Champernowne, Master Parry, and I, Elizabeth.

FOUR

I

At once we were plunged into deep waters.

We arrived at Hatfield in the dusk. The weariness induced by the journey, and the gathering excitement and anticipation rising in my breast, combined to make the homecoming memorable. A manor house of a hundred years ago, the palace rose, red-roofed and turreted, above the blossom of the pear and apple orchards, at the heart of its wooded parkland. As our procession wound its way along beside the wall I remembered what Mistress Champernowne had urged upon me: "Embrace Blanche. She has known you since birth. She rocked you in your cradle."

Blanche ap Harry. She had a face like a weasel. She hung over me, gaunt and thin in grey. There was no warmth in her welcome.

"That is her way," Kat told me afterwards. "It means nothing. She seems cold natured, but her heart is kind."

"You look peaky," Blanche commented, perusing me.

"She has been ill – oh so ill!" cried Kat. "Kiss Blanche, child, and let me put you to bed."

It was done, the gladness and confusion of arrival, the shepherding by Kat through meal time and to bed – only to learn that Prince Edward's household was expected here next day and that we were to go on together to Greenwich. Safe behind the closed door of my room, night descending to obscure the gardens below, Kat and I gaped at one another in a desperation that bordered on hysteria.

"Oh! If only Xavier were here!" said Kat. "A quiet life in Bisley for a quiet life at Hatfield! If he but knew! We barely are landed, and tomorrow we have Edward to face – and no sooner that than pitched into a crowd of beholders and no breathing space! And all without his guidance and advice. O wretched man! That which seemed so simple far away at Over Court seems other now we are in truth arrived amongst those whom we must deceive!" She wrung her hands. "We shall send word that she is ill, that the Lady Elizabeth has a recurrence of her fever. We can take no other course. We were mad ever to suppose we could succeed with this deception. Dear Lord, whatever will become of us? We'll answer with our lives for this day's work..."

I padded over to her in my nightgown and took her hand.

"We have not Xavier," I said in a low voice. "And thus we must do all that must be done alone, that is, we two, Kat! There must not be in all the land two souls more close than you and I – our lives depend upon it!"

Kat's fit had passed. She sat in silence, biting at her lips. Then she said, calm enough: "Bless you, John. You teach me forbearance."

"Kat," I answered ruefully. "You never must call me by that name again, not even when we are alone, as we are now."

Tears came to her soft eyes; I knew that she recalled the dead princess. She blew her nose upon a handkerchief.

"What must we do?" she said. "We have one night before we are called upon to play before the crowd."

"I must know Hatfield Palace. I must be as familiar with it as once I was with Cotswold sheep."

By candlelight in whispered silence, Kat and I traversed the rooms and passageways of Hatfield. We crossed the great hall, peered through the oriel, stood in the embrasure at the dais end. The moonlight shone through the many windows, for the palace was illumined from both north and south, lively with our shadows as we passed. We climbed the turret stairs, the necessity of that which we were about vanquishing all weariness, all fear of night's alarms. As I fell asleep beneath the covers of the bed in which I lay, my mind retraced in fancy where my steps had been, and consequently in the morning I was able to go where I would and know what I should see. With daylight I made swift acquaintance with the courtyard and the knot garden, the orchard and the green, the archway that led to the park; the stables and the rabbit warren. When in the afternoon my brother's entourage was sighted and we went to greet him I could in general have accompanied Edward anywhere he wished. I prayed that Hatfield held no secret known only to his sister and himself.

Here I was fortunate. Prince Edward, not yet six years old, was taken up with one matter above all other, and therein his interest lay.

"We are to have a mother!"

The prince was plump and rosy cheeked; there was no sign of what was yet to come. No, he had been thoroughly fattened up since his illness and recovery. He had red-gold hair and sober grey eyes beneath finely shaped eyebrows. His great delight was his small dog.

"What we supposed is true!" he told me, breathless with excitement. "Our father is to marry Lady Latimer."

"Lady Latimer?" I said stupidly.

"Who else? She that was Katherine Parr. Don't look so strange, Elizabeth. We have spoken of it often."

"It's that – I never truly thought that it would come to pass."

"And we are sent for! I mean, all three of us, that is, also Mary. We will all be together. How will that seem, I wonder?"

"Monstrous odd," said I with feeling.

"O Elizabeth! I shall be very glad to know a mother's love!" said Edward, shining-eyed. "Will not you?"

"I hardly know," I murmured cautiously.

"We heard that you were ill in Gloucestershire," said Edward.

"I had a fever; it has left me somewhat weak."

"It was the same with me," said Edward sagely. "Therefore I understand."

Sweet child that he was, he made allowance for those small discrepancies of which he must have been aware and to which I may have been oblivious. In superficialities our time was passed; next day we went to Greenwich.

The palace of Greenwich should by rights have daunted me. One would have supposed it a young town, so vast it first appeared – its crenellated walls and towers, its many windows glittering in the sunlight, its curls of smoke from countless chimneys; and beyond, a prospect of trees and meadows; a town that clung to the river's edge, where the tall ships rode at anchor on the shimmering water.

But my first memories of Greenwich, though of splendour and

magnificence, were all diffused with the soft and overwhelming presence of she whom Edward called our mother; therefore I was daunted not at all and knew there only warmth and unexpected love.

Lady Latimer...She was to become important to me. Ah, how could I then have foreseen the turbulent events that were to bind us, when upon that day in June she clasped me to her bosom and said lovingly: "Elizabeth! My dear! I think we shall be friends!"

Lady Latimer of Snape was at that time some nine and twenty years of age. She was tall with pleasant features, though her eyes slanted upward somewhat and her mouth was small. She had – it almost seemed obligatory here – auburn hair, and her dress was of crimson and gold. As a young girl she had studied at court with Princess Mary under the great Spanish teacher and nobleman Juan Luys Vives, who had taught her that learning was the answer to the ills of the world and that women must beware the silver tongues of the predatory male whose words of love hid the tricks of the sorcerer. In practical terms it meant that the young Katherine Parr could read the Holy Writ in Latin, knew the works of Plutarch, admired Thomas More and followed the humanist doctrines of Erasmus, believing that knowledge was the right of the people and the only means whereby we might raise ourselves up from amongst the beasts.

At twelve years old she had been married to an old husband who died two years after. She returned to court where she became close to Princess Mary and Lady Jane Seymour, and to Kat's beautiful sister Joan who later married Anthony Denny of the Privy Chamber. But Queen Anne Boleyn would have no thriving educated ladies about her person and it was with some relief that Katherine left the court to become Lady Latimer and live in the north. Somewhat against her will she and her husband had become involved in the Pilgrimage of Grace and had to justify their position to the king, but Katherine so successfully convinced our sovereign of their loyalty that they suffered no reprisal, and indeed, her passionate sincerity and warmth of character made a sharp impression on him; he would not forget her. Lord Latimer had died only last year, and it was understood that His Majesty had paid court to the fair widow while she was visiting Princess Mary. And now she was to be his bride.

"We shall be friends," she said and held me close. "And if you will permit me I shall be a mother to you."

It was not the false image of Elizabeth that answered – it was I. Not until then had it occurred to me how desolate was my childhood, how bereft of that particular solicitude which maternal succour might provide, that tenderness offered by one who truly cared for the infant at her knee. Then of a sudden I understood my loss – my mother gone and I never to have known her, never to have heard her voice or felt the soft touch of her hand. When Lady Latimer embraced me I began to weep, and though I knew that Kat nearby grew fearful, knowing that Elizabeth would not have wept, I could not help myself, and Katherine loved me for it.

"You shall be safe," she told me fiercely in my ear. "Your days of sadnesses are gone."

"Sadnesses!" said Kat afterwards, affronted. "My lady knew no sadnesses with me. She was a happy girl; I saw that it was so."

"But she had no mother," I said. "Lady Latimer has understood that loss, and to the best of her ability she will redress the balance."

To Princess Mary, Lady Latimer could scarcely be a mother of the kind she wished to be for Edward and myself, for she was but two years senior to the elder daughter of the king, and a companion of long standing. Indeed, she had been named after Princess Mary's mother, whom she admired for her patronage of learning. Mary was a citadel protected by a hedge of ladies. Her nature was such that she seemed taciturn and severe. Kat had warned me about this. It was ascribed to the tribulations of her early years. Brought up to be the king's heir she had been obliged to give precedence to the six-year-old Duke of Richmond, that is, my father, whom the king hoped would succeed him. She was affianced many times but never married. She witnessed the degradation of her mother, from whom she then was torn apart. With a profound sense of her own importance – it was innate in those of us of royal blood – she was made bastard by the king's new marriage and the birth of the Princess Elizabeth.

"She must ride behind the infant's litter," Kat had whispered, "and she made herself ridiculous by silly devices to cheat this rule, by sneaking into first place when she could, and sitting down with a great show in the place of honour, as if daring anyone to remove her thence. Her life has been one of petty humiliations and small victories at great cost. They say she is grown cunning with long practice."

Even I at nine years old knew well enough that there was some ambivalence in the position of a lady yet unwed at twenty-seven years. Mary seemed an old maid, unwanted, like to lead apes in Hell, as the saying goes. Had she been beautiful, her situation might have held a certain poignancy; but she was plain. She was of medium stature, squat of build, and she walked as a hen does. Her waist was thick. There were many jewels about her person, and her gown was of amber-tawny brocade. What I particularly remarked about her face as she bent over me to bestow a brief kiss was that she had no eyebrows whatsoever and had rectified the omission with a fine line so plainly drawn that it merely served to emphasise the lack. She laughed like one that looked over her shoulder expecting to be chastised for it; and in repose her mouth was tight and grim, her face an aged face.

"Lord, Lord, Elizabeth, are you grown stupid?" she declared; she had no patience with me. She turned to her ladies. "Every card game I have been at pains to teach her she has all forgot; and either I must teach her again or she must sit by while we others play."

"I am content to do so," murmured I.

At another time she would perhaps have pursued the matter further, this so strange aberration on my part, but she was nervous and preoccupied because the king was soon to join us, and his presence caused her visible distress. She plainly longed for his approbation, and her longing made her graceless and clumsy. While constantly preparing herself to make a good impression, her mind was ill at ease and absent, and her sister's unaccountable lapse of memory the least of her worries. She supposed Elizabeth's forgetfulness an act of mischief.

"Your heart was never in the cards," said Mary with a brittle laugh. Cards were her passion. When she and her ladies played, they strove to win, and teased and praised each other in the playing.

Mary's voice was low and gruff. Katherine spoke of poultices for the throat, and possets of alehoof and honey, but Mary said impatiently: "My voice was ever thus and well you know it."

I put my book up to my face to hide my foolish grinning. Mary's voice was like a man's voice, and I had the notion of a sudden that she had died at ten years old, that she, like me, had secrets, and beneath her petticoats a prick.

That June was wet and stormy; we were much indoors. One day Edward pausing from his Cato looked up at me across the table and said in a whisper: "I know a foul lewd rhyme. Robert Dudley taught it to me."

"How does it go?" I whispered back.

He told it me with surreptitious giggling:

"Gay go up and gay go down
The sun the wind the rain
I am a jolly tinker
And I go up Cherry Lane.

And gay go up and gay go down
The sun the wind the rain
I am a saucy sailor
And I go up Cherry Lane.

And what of you, kind mistress fair?
Your answer give it plain
Do you go up that cherry lane?
No – I am Cherry Lane."

Edward looked at me anxiously. I gave no response.

"Is it not foul?" he whispered eagerly.

"I know not," answered I in disappointment. "I cannot tell its meaning."

"No more can I," said Edward. "I hoped you might explain. I did not wish to seem a fool and so I laughed when Robert told me. You are supposed to laugh when the lady answers," he added helpfully.

The Lady Mary had heard our whispering and giggling and half the verse besides. She made us repeat it.

"Where did you learn that?" she frowned.

"I have forgotten," Edward answered stoutly.

"Whoever it was, he should be whipped," said Mary, tight lipped.

"Why?"

"Because it is a song of fornication," Mary answered, cool now, with her self-control returned. "And fornication is a sin and very filthy. It brings man down to the level of the beasts – the rutting pig, the lecherous goat and the promiscuous she-cat. Is this the company you wish to keep?"

"No, no!" we answered, firm and sure.

"Then sing no more beastly rhymes."

"And do not think that I don't understand your game, Elizabeth," she added venomously. "You have not forgotten how to play at cards. You simply do not want to be in my company when you may have Edward's, who will be king. Don't think I don't know how your devious mind works. You were ever thus, a seeming innocent, at heart a schemer."

Katherine had us work to please our father, whose arrival we expected shortly. Mary learned new music for the spinet, and Edward and I composed a poem in our father's praise, with a refrain in Latin, this to be learned by rote and spoken. Carefully we persevered, all under Katherine's direction.

"And thus shall you best please your father," promised she.

"Truly?" I said wistfully.

"I know it," she replied.

Lord save us, but he was enormous.

I had not at that stage seen the ropes and pulleys necessary to get him upstairs. Suffice to say that to my astonished eyes he seemed big as a house. He came in upon a scene of unrivalled domesticity, superbly contrived by Katherine Parr. Mary at the spinet, Edward and I at a table over our books, and Katherine over her sewing – from these positions we arose to make obeisance. However, since His Majesty could barely stand, he settled himself into a vast chair brought for the purpose, and indicated that we should be grouped about him to be seen; and we in our turn gazed at our great progenitor.

His face was red and glowing like a fire. His hair was short, the neck above his collar piled in ridges. His mouth was little, like Mary's, and his eyes were sunk into his flesh, but bright. His beard was ginger streaked with grey, and his brow furrowed. This head, topped with a cap of velvet flecked with pearls, rose up from the vast bulk of his body like a cherry on a loaf. His gross shape was much magnified by crimson padded sleeves and the silken layers of his jewel-encrusted shirt and doublet, a shifting breathing wheezing mass of shimmering cloth.

And now his narrow topaz eyes were turned on us.

Edward, of course, received complete approbation, this most of all because he was in radiant health, rosy and plump; moreover, he was fair of face and beautiful to see. Who could not be proud of such a son? Respectful and good-natured, dutiful, intelligent, Edward was a model prince, and, it was plain to see, the apple of his father's eye.

For Mary the reception was a little tempered with caution. So much hostility, such pain, such conflict of wills had passed between them. I sensed a powerful mutual desire for harmony, a deep and binding love, all overlaid with the briars of distrust and wariness and the recollection of ancient hurts.

"Dear daughter," wheezed the king, extending both his arms. "From this day let us vow to start anew...Your kind mother...here beside me will bind up all the wounds. Her touch is sure."

A momentary stumble – he had been about to say 'your kind mother, Katherine', which of course could not be said without recalling she who had been her true mother; this small lapse had, I guessed, been understood by Mary also, and, slight as it had been, was an outward symbol of their greater rift, the reason why their differences could never heal, though Katherine Parr apply every poultice known to medicine. Mary withdrew politely from the formal embrace, and curtseyed once again.

"And now Elizabeth..."

I looked him in the eye, my grandsire, face to face at last. He held my gaze and though my heart was pounding fast I stood my ground and I saw tenderness in his expression. I smiled. I saw then pass across his face the spasm of a strong emotion. He bent towards me, then he half turned to the woman at his side.

"Katherine," he said, half in a laugh, half mystified. "My Harry! I swear it is my Harry come again...Lord save me, but I never saw the likeness clear as I do now. I'd swear it was my boy..."

Now this did monstrously alarm me. I grew cold and pale. His words had stripped me; I believed I stood there naked, everybody seeing that which must have been clear as daylight all along. I clasped my hands together, as in a plea for mercy. My eyes were full of fear. I had to speak.

"Your Majesty," I stammered stupidly. "I am Elizabeth!"

His vast belly quivered before me, and a chuckle rose up from his chest and he began to laugh. It was a kindly laugh.

"Poor wench," he gasped in throaty mirth. "Be still. You are Elizabeth. And the more cherished in my bosom for that you call to mind my dear dead son. Take it not amiss, my dear." Then he added to Katherine: "Put her in breeches and hose and she would be my Harry as a lad – but fear not, poppet, none shall take your petticoats from you. Come, hug me."

It was not easy, my arms so small, his bulk so vast, but my relief made me expansive and I hugged with all my might. From the corner of my eye I saw that Princess Mary notched a further score of personal resentment towards Elizabeth for her effortless pleasing of their sire; if looks were daggers drawn...I paid no heed, and laid my face upon the padded royal belly. In close proximity, the ointments on the ulcerated leg and those that blended with the sores about his person gave off a heady rancid odour which filled my nostrils till I thought that I would retch; and yet this selfsame odour had for me the sanctity of incense, for as it enclosed me I knew that my grandsire had accepted me and here against his putrid heaving bulk was my true home.

II

Now if it be thought unlikely, nay, impossible, that a small intruder should so easily fool the monarch of the realm and all his progeny, let me declare at once that this was not the way it seemed. I never could have achieved this end had I not absolutely believed that it was mine by right, indeed I never faltered in that firm belief my whole life long. I was the son of Henry's most cherished elder son, my place was at court, this prince and princess my true kith and kin. I merely claimed what was my own. I would have preferred to receive my birthright in my own persona, but if I could only do so as Elizabeth, then so be it.

In my grand deception I was aided by circumstance. The intimate circle of the Tudor royal family was hardly that kind of social gathering which assembles round the hearth to reminisce. Indeed it was a shared desire to put the past behind which now bound them. Under Katherine Latimer's auspices we all colluded in a deception of another kind – that we were a happy family that loved one another well. In everybody's interest, references to the past with all its bitternesses, hatreds, cruelties, were not appropriate. No one said 'Do you remember how we – ? Was it not pleasing when we – ?' hoping to evoke a surge of reciprocal delight. Now all was set to change. Like a radiant sun, Katherine shone her beams upon us all and made us love each other. In other words, our life began that June at Greenwich, and whatever Elizabeth did now was Elizabeth. Her father saw her with fresh eyes, surprised – but finding the occurrence totally pleasurable – that she recalled the Duke of Richmond and that he had never seen the likeness previously; her sister Mary thought her grown more stupid than before; her brother Edward was so taken with his wonderful new mother that all else paled into insignificance. Dear Kat was ever with me, and if she supposed me weary of pretence or in any way discomfited she could with all reasonableness take me away to rest; this was entirely appropriate. At night in our bedchamber she would speak to me about the day and guide me in the prospect of the morrow.

Princess Mary I found the most difficult. Her kindnesses to Elizabeth in the past were no doubt well meant, but, I suspected, also reeked of policy, conditional upon Elizabeth's continuing regard for her. Why should she love the brat who had deposed her, spawn of the whore who had displaced her sainted mother in the king's affections? She was mischievous to me now.

"Will you not play the lute, Elizabeth?" she would invite. "As I recall, you were so skilled at that."

"I pray you forgive me," I must answer, "but my hands since my illness have been clumsy and I fear to give offence. Will you not play upon the spinet, sister?"

"Where is your sewing?" Mary asked. "Your fine cambric?"

"My physicians have forbidden me to perform close work while my eyes remain weak," I faltered.

"Yet you read."

"It tires me, but I love to learn. I grow melancholy away from my books."

"She will be a patroness of learning in her time," boomed Henry, pleased. "Much like dear Katherine here" – whose knee he squeezed. And once again I was applauded, and Mary, by implication, criticised. Her jealousy was but barely concealed, and I, that is Elizabeth, in a fair way to being spoiled and petted in that heavy atmosphere of parental indulgence.

If Mary thought me odd, or different, she was blinded by her own dislike of me, which saw fault whether there were fault or no. It was in those circumstances perfectly permissible to think 'Elizabeth has grown haughty, forgetful, indifferent', but who, in those same circumstances would in all honesty then think: 'Perhaps it is not Elizabeth? Perhaps Elizabeth died and was supplanted by a little boy from Bisley?' Who would think that, who in their right mind? It is not the logical conclusion following the discovery of small inconsistencies in a person one did not after all know well. And so for all of them. Elizabeth was here before them all; she looked like Elizabeth; she came from Hatfield with Elizabeth's attendants; therefore she was Elizabeth.

But I say this: we never could have succeeded with the substitution at any later date than this. My Lady Latimer brought me forward to the gaze of court and family. I made such impression as I might. King Henry saw his children almost as if for the first time. Together we achieved some kind of unity. Our parts in the family circle were created from that time. Lady Latimer poured love and harmony upon us all, sensing our strengths and weaknesses, drawing us out, making us relate one to another. She set herself to get to know us. I believe she was aware of every freckle on my cheek. No small impostor could have made his presence known all unsuspected after this close scrutiny. I never could have fooled Queen Katherine Parr.

Lady Latimer was wed to King Henry in July at the palace of Hampton Court. The marriage took place in an upper oratory; Princess Mary and myself were present, with many luminaries from the court, and King Henry in great good humour. After this, their majesties set out upon a royal progress, and Kat and I returned to Hatfield in the rain.

The trees hung down in sodden heaviness, the roads awash with mud. We were very silent on the journey. It was as if the trees themselves were in disguise, intelligencers that were sent by hostile means to spy on us; we preserved our dignity, aloof, impassive.

But when we were safe within the walls of Hatfield, safe within Elizabeth's own room, the door fast barred, we turned to one another, Kat and I, and all with one accord we fell upon each other, weeping, laughing, made idiots by our relief and joy.

"We have achieved it!" Kat gasped. "The impossible. It is done."

"O Kat! I could not have done it without your constant help."

"My dear young mistress – my dear young master!"

"O Kat! Sometimes I thought that I would burst or scream or swoon, or that some wicked wind would lift my skirts above my head...or that my Lady Mary would! Or that my father-grandsire would insist that I be breeched to prove his point, and I would look as once I did at Bisley – "

"O my dear, my poor sweet dear." She cuddled me, I her; but we were too pent up yet to be calm, and in the darkness we must dance and jig and fall upon the bed and hug the bolsters, nay, to tear at them and hurl them at the wall and at each other, till the seams split and the feathers flew, and all the down like snowflakes fluttered all about us, and we dancing, under it.

In the middle of the night I was awakened by I knew not what, and with a sharp awareness that all was not as it should be. There was a candle lit, and I was curiously cold. My hands moved: I was naked and my sheet and coverlet were gone, and when I turned startled eyes towards the door I found it open, and Blanche ap Harry standing there, a candle in her hand, whose light illuminating her face from beneath gave her a look of the Angel of Doom. I squealed and looked for the wherewithal to cover me.

"Who are you, brat?" she asked in a voice of stone.

I gibbered something, stupefied with fear.

"You thought to fool the folk in London, boy," she said, immobile as a gargoyle, as grim-faced. "You fooled the love-sick king, the infant prince, the sour princess. You fooled the silly gaggle gathering about the great. But you did not fool me, no, not from that first meeting. Do you think that I don't know my lady, down to every hair of her head, every fingernail and tooth? As soon as you walked in the door I knew you were not she."

I sat there, hunched and small, a blanket round me. I could not speak.

She put the candle down beside the bed. She towered above me, like a twisted tree on a wintry hillslope.

"I bided my time," she said. "I let you go to Greenwich, thinking you would be unmasked and punished. I thought the fools at court would see through your disguise, so easily did I. When you returned I scarce could credit sense. To me you are a boy as plain as I stand here – a pretty boy with auburn hair and in the half light some passing resemblance to my own princess. I must suppose her dead. Why else this curious subterfuge? You shall explain. Where I grew up, the folk believed in changelings. You are such – but how, I ask myself, by whose connivance? Kat is with you in your dissembling, and, as I must suppose, Thomas also. But you came from no fairy dwelling. Those pretty limbs are real enough, that dainty prick no ethereal illusion. Kat? Are you now here? And what have you to say?"

Poor Kat was now seen to be lurking in the doorway. In she came, and closed the door behind her. She looked beaten down, depressed and cowed. "Forgive me, Blanche," she murmured. And in whispered tones she told her all that passed in Bisley.

"And we were so afeard," she sobbed. "The wrath of the king, as God's judgement, was like to fall upon the heads of those who had offended him." She looked about now wildly. "The truth is now that the king, God save him, is grown so soft and so reformed and gentle that I know not what I feared. The queen's Grace has so mellowed him that I could now dare tell him that the princess died; and though it break his heart I doubt that he would punish me for it, as I believed he would before. He is so changed, so honeyed; he is not the wild fierce man he once was; and now it is too late. I dare not tell him now because we have deceived him. And this is worse than that we did before! He will not forgive us for so monstrous a deception."

"You are a foolish stupid woman, Kat," said Blanche.

"I own it," Kat sniffed, head in hands.

"I knew the princess dead," said Blanche. "I grieved for her. I grieved that you dared not confide in me."

"She did not suffer," Kat said. "She knew not when she died; she was asleep."

"This monk...this man who worked it all..."

"Xavier? We have not heard from him. He was the power behind it all; his idea it was, and we were persuaded by his eloquence."

"He is yet in Bisley then?"

"We must suppose it. It was left to him to make the burial more secret, to persuade those round about that John had run away to sea. He said that he would join us here when it was done."

"This monk then is a danger to us..." Blanche mused.

"But you, Blanche," Kat cried. "What of you? You are the danger, as it seems. I own my folly - but the deed is done. We throw ourselves upon your mercy. John shall go back to Bisley - we shall say he died. I will go back to Devonshire. Only keep faith with us, Blanche, keep our secret - save us from whatever fearful fate must follow a deception of such magnitude!"

"You speak gibberish, Kat," Blanche snapped. "Do you think I wish to see you hurt? No, there is but one way forward now, for all our sakes. If this vast lie be known, we all risk punishment, every one, for who will be believed that swears his innocence? You made your choice in Bisley and you shall stand by it."

"You'll not give us away?" Kat quivered.

"Not only will I keep the secret close," said Blanche, "but I shall make that boy to outward show the image of my lady. What he hides beneath his skirts shall remain concealed. But all that folk see shall be Elizabeth complete and perfect. I undertake it, I, that nursed her from her cradle. Boy!" she turned to me. "Prepare yourself to tread that path down which you stepped so blithely, for under my tutelage to save us all, you'll live and die Elizabeth. And the first thing you shall learn, come tomorrow's dawn, is how to sew. Elizabeth could make a shirt! And have you given thought as to how you will spend the seventh of September?"

"What day is that?" I stuttered stupidly.

"Your birthday, dunderhead," said Blanche.

I saw little of the king and queen henceforth, and my time was spent at Hatfield or at Ashridge with my brother at our lessons and our sports. Ashridge was a sombre place, a monastery of yore, surrounded by forests of beech, and very pure of air. This way of life was to be the pattern for the next three years.

But in the months that followed what I chiefly learnt was to forget that ever I was boy. Blanche was more stern and implacable than any beast-master. Mercilessly she stood over me and made me sew, and as I sewed she spoke to me of girls and women; thus do girls...and thus say women. In the village schools, she said, both girls and boys are taught, and the education of women is an idea highly prized – but, educated and intelligent as they might be, let them not hope to attend a grammar school or university, though their learning shine as a star. Women and girls are educated for the needs of society, and their ultimate goals are marriage and childbearing, the while proving a support to husband. Reading, writing, music, needlework and all that does pertain to home and hearth – these are their province; and since they never will be lawyers, merchants, preachers, mathematicians, what need they of geometry, philosophy, divinity and all that causes mind to grapple with the matters of the intellect? I was to think on other 'girls' less fortunate than I, who would have benefited from a superior education, and whose talents were then gone to waste, walled round about with herb garden and still-room. I must ask myself how it must seem to take second place to a boy for no other reason than that of sex, as of course I did to Edward, and as Mary did, though she was fully grown. And is this right, and is this just, she said? Think upon it.

Blanche reminded me of the learned women of our time. She spoke of Lady Margaret Beaufort, grandmother of the king. She said that Queen Katherine was brilliant as she, and would be remembered after her death for her fine mind. I must ponder whether marriage and childbearing were justification enough for one's existence upon this earth, for this was what society expected even of the clever women. And so this I duly pondered, and I came to the conclusion that for me at least it would not be enough; that as a woman I would want a good deal more than that. And then I'd laugh, for I had half forgot that these matters were all hypothetical, and it was ludicrous to suppose that anyone would ever beg me to give birth.

Daily, in the window alcove once used by the monks, while I pricked my fingers over cambric, Blanche took me through the incidents of Elizabeth's childhood. Do you remember Lady Bryan? What do you think of her? The birth of Prince Edward? How did you feel? The Imperial ambassador, Sir Thomas Wriothesley - describe them - what did you say to them at Hertford castle? Hertford, Ashridge, Havering Bower - which is your favourite residence? Catherine Howard - she cared for you, she promised she would be a mother to you, she was kind, they dragged her screaming down the gallery at Hampton Court - how did you feel? How do you feel now, remembering?

Fornication was Catherine's crime. Fornication, that sin, that lewd and filthy sin.

"What is fornication?" I asked Thomas Parry.

He tousled my hair. He should not have done so to a princess, but it was the boy he answered, sympathetic.

"Something you will never know, poor codling."

Edward was becoming dull and priggish.

"I have written to the queen at Hampton Court concerning Mary. I have been told that she goes late to bed because she dances."

"Mary? Dancing?"

He smiled a little. "Yes. They say that with her ladies she is other than she seems with us. She laughs, is merry, dances. Well, I fear for her. We know she gambles at the cards. It is not proper for a princess of the realm. The queen should instruct her and correct her. I have told her so."

"But we dance sometimes," I said cautiously.

"We dance with circumspection, to portray in movement the virtues of a good life. Mary, they say, dances for pleasure. This is wrong."

"What do you think?" said Robert Dudley picking his teeth. "Is not Ned become a prig?"

We leaned against a sunny wall. Further down the garden Edward sat upon a bench, reading the New Testament aloud to Barnaby Fitzpatrick who sat at his feet, chewing on a grass stem.

"Barnaby would rather swim, but Edward has been forbidden in case he catches a chill. In August! Barnaby is too polite to say he does not wish to hear the Holy Writ, and there he sits, and sweats; no wonder he is Ned's favourite."

"Edward likes gentle people who don't make him uneasy."

"You think that I make him uneasy?" Robert grinned.

I looked at him. "I know it," I replied.

A group of well-born boys were Edward's companions in his household. One of them was Robert Dudley. His father the Lord High Admiral was, along with Edward Seymour Lord Hertford, the most important man at court, a great general, and a man close to the king. Robert was often at court and knew it better than I. He was his father's cupbearer. He had dark hair and grey eyes and, I swear it, even at ten years old a wicked smile. He knew all about ships and sailing, and the discoveries across the seas. He knew lewd rhymes. He knew what fornication was.

"Wrestle with me," he invited.

"No!"

"What, coy? You never used to be so."

"I am too old for wrestling."

"A veritable greybeard!"

"Why do you say that?" I gasped. "Greybeard is a term for men."

"You always were more boy than Ned. I see you now with your wooden sword; you all but beat me. And last summer you sat astride me, wrestling."

"You permitted it," I guessed.

"It's true, I did. But you were monstrous fierce. I must submit; I had no choice. And by the by," he added, "will you now give me your answer?"

"What answer?"

"To the question I asked of you that day."

"I have forgot," I pouted simpering.

"I know you have not. You said next time we met..."

"Well – I have changed my mind."

"When will you give your answer?" he enquired.

"When I am ready," answered I.

"That song you taught Ned," I began, and ground the daisies with my heel. "They said it was a sin and dealt with fornication."

"So it does!" he laughed.

"Edward and I were not entirely sure about its meaning."

"You surely never would persuade me to converse with you upon such a subject, Lady Elizabeth?" he said mischievously.

"Princess Elizabeth," I corrected.

"Princess Elizabeth then. I am already whipped for teaching Edward how to swear."

"I'm sorry for it – the whipping, not the swearing."

"You need not be; it did not hurt," he shrugged. "And now you wish me further to endanger myself!"

"For my sake," I said. We were eye to eye.

"Do you really not know what it means? I am surprised. I understood your knowledge was extensive."

"I know about sodomy," I said defensively.

Robert looked embarrassed. "We are on safer ground with fornication." He put his lips against my ear and told me plain what fornication was.

"Though why you wish to hear it I don't know," he teased, "since you have told me you will never wed. You mean to take a lover, I suppose?"

"I mean no such thing," I answered blushing.

In those three years before my grandsire-father died I was a good deal in Robert's company. We rode together; he and I were faster than the rest. I watched him learn his manly skills – swordplay, tilting at the quintain, combat with pike and staff and dagger. All the prince's friends learned this, but it was plain for all to see that Robert was best.

One day at the archery butts I shot my arrow sure. They gathered round me in astonishment, clapping me on the back and marvelling.

"But who'd have thought it of Elizabeth!" cried Barnaby. "A girl, to shoot so straight and true. I never knew she had such strength in the shoulder."

I caught Kat watching me and reddened. I saw her shake her head. I ran to her and sat down by her side. She put her arm about me.

"I should not have done so well," I murmured.

"No," she answered quietly. "Once will do. A momentary flash of brilliance not to be repeated. Next time you shoot, shoot wide. Leave prowess to the lads."

That night I lay and wept. What was I about, in skirts and petticoats, parading like a doll, a puppet to the likes of Kat and Blanche ap Harry? Where was Xavier? Why had he abandoned me? What was to happen to me? I was learning lute playing, I was studying my books, I was learning how to play the virginals. But I should be there with Robert Dudley with a sword in hand, my fist around a quarterstaff; what business had I in this hideous mummery?

I became half ill with misery and guilt, tormented by the knowledge of this fearful fraud of which I was a part, which if laid bare would surely mean my death. I was a sinner. God would punish me. Sin and fornication – these words haunted me.

I made a present for the queen, a book, my own translation of a poem from the French by Marguerite of Navarre, 'The Mirror of a Sinful Soul', copied carefully, each phrase more meaningful to me than anyone might guess.

"Is there any Hell so profound that is sufficient to punish the tenth part of my sins? But thou which hast made separation of my bed and did put false lovers in my place and committed fornication with them; yet for all this thou mayest come unto me again. O poor soul! to be where thy sin hath put thee, even upon the highways where thou didst wait and tarried for to beguile them that came by. Therefore having fulfilled thy pleasure thou hast infected with fornication all the earth..."

Strange dreams disturbed my nights. I tossed and turned, confused with fear and pleasure. One so obsessed with sin and fornication as I was then was like soon to turn anchorite or whore, and in my quiet way my inclinations tended toward the latter. Therefore in an attempt to give my ravings substance I said bravely to one whom I believed my friend:

"Robert Dudley, will you kiss me?"

"I will not," he answered. We were eleven years of age and stood in a draughty passageway at Ashridge, where monks once filed to prayer.

"I command it," I insisted.

"Very well then," said he with poor grace, and kissed my cheek, noisily, with warm wet lips.

I thought kissing much overrated. I remembered then that Robert was no good at Latin either.

Kat married John Ashley, an amiable fellow, a gentleman attendant, cousin to Queen Anne Boleyn; but she would never leave me, even married, while we shared that secret that must bind us. We still believed that Xavier would come and tell us what to do and put all right.

Meanwhile I was whirled to Hampton Court and to St James's where in the bosses of the vaulting of the gatehouse I saw the initials H and A entwined and I remembered how it was said the people pointed to the letters and laughed cynically because the device read Ha Ha. I saw jousting in London; I ate at a banquet in the open air in the royal deer park of Hyde; I fled the plague to the safety of Eltham; I acquired a new tutor Master Grindal and worked hard at my books. I saw Robert Dudley grow more handsome; I saw Edward grow more pious. I loved and respected my mother the queen the more times that I saw her, and I learnt to sew as fair a stitch as ever true princess did.

Then my father-grandsire died, and there were momentous changes.

Although we knew the king to be in poor health, white-haired now and failing in his faculties, we supposed that he would live for ever. It had always been King Henry in my lifetime, King Henry the father of his people, Defender of the Faith. A man of great fame. A man of great frame. They needed sixteen of the strongest yeomen of the guard to place his mighty coffin in its vault.

It was at the end of January when Lord Hertford and Sir Anthony Browne brought Edward to me where I then was, at Enfield Manor. Not a word was said of any change in the situation as we knew it. We thought it was a New Year visit. Lord Hertford had said nothing on the journey, knowing all the while the king was dead. What a strange man, that. Some forty years old, a soldier, scholar, handsome and of noble bearing, married to a proud and shrewish wife, he was to make himself Lord Protector and Duke of Somerset, which was not, as was said, what the king had intended.

This man sent word to Edward and myself to await him in the Presence Chamber. The room dignified by such a name was small, with walls of panelled oak, leaded windows, and a ceiling ornamented with the rose and fleur-de-lys. A fire burned in the hearth, illuminating by its flame the carved portcullises and crowns, the griffins and the royal arms about the chimney-piece. Our two visitors now knelt to us and told us that the king was dead.

To see Lord Hertford kneel one would suppose the news to be of some import, but nonetheless it was a bitter shock to us. Edward gasped and turned and clung to me. He was distraught; he wept. His eyes were full of fear, fear that I found contagious, and my body trembled. I should not be here, hearing this news, I who had no right...but what base denial was I now about? I had as much right as the prince to make show of my grief – my father's father dead who truly loved us and had kept us safe from harm and made a home for us. So I held Edward, who was barely nine years old – the age when I had come from Bisley – who, like me, would need to call on the brave aspects of the name we bore to face the task ahead.

"Now fear not, sister," Edward told me when they led him hence to be a king. "I shall look after you; all shall go well with you."

We watched them go.

"Poor lamb," said Kat. "His head is scarcely big enough to hold a crown. They say the crown weighs more than a pile of books, for all it looks so noble."

It was for Queen Katherine that the changes were most painful, though she made light of them. The Duke of Somerset's proud wife demanded precedence now. She would not bear Katherine's train, and made herself ridiculous by pushing Katherine from her path in order to achieve the desired prominence. She was heard to say that Katherine was but Lady Latimer now and had tricked King Henry into marriage in his dotage. What would have become of her in her unenviable position none could guess, but Dame Fortune was a sly one, with a trick in hand.

I came unannounced into Katherine's chamber one day in February, the king but one month dead, to find my stepmother standing close to a tall man and looking up into his eyes. The couple sprang apart, so like a pair of guilty lovers that I deemed them so to be.

Queen Katherine laughed, plainly relieved. "'Tis but Elizabeth!" Her cheeks were red with blushing and her eyes were bright. "My dear," she said to me, "come forward. This is the new Lord Admiral, the younger brother of the Duke of Somerset – Baron Seymour of Sudeley, Thomas Seymour." She spoke the names with a long savouring smile. "He and I are...friends of old. My lady Elizabeth's Grace...for my sake become well acquainted."

Queen Katherine's friend strode forward and took both my hands in his. We looked at one another, I with curiosity and hesitation, he with a frank and glowing ardour. He was then thirty-eight years old, tall, handsome, ruddy, with merry eyes, a great beard and moustache, and thick chestnut hair. That much I saw from one glance. I dared look no more but I had the impression that his body was a goodly shape. His eyes ran over me quite shamelessly. He made me feel uncomfortable with his gazing, and I pulled away. He laughed. He had a dazzling smile.

"But what a beauty!" he declared. "They did not tell me that the young Elizabeth had grown to be the fairest flower in all the land. Katherine!" He reproved her playfully. "You should have warned me that there was a treasure hidden here. We shall need to set a guard about her. Men will come courting like Saul's thousands when word of her great beauty gets abroad."

"Indeed, I am not beautiful," I gasped, most ill at ease.

"I say you are, and though it be a fault to contradict a lady I must do no less. How old are you, my child?"

"Thirteen, sir," murmured I.

"And you say you are not beautiful?" he marvelled. "Are there no mirrors at your royal palaces? I am your mirror now. I see a tall and slender maiden in a gown of cherry red. I see a head of auburn hair constrained by a cap of pearls. Two fine eyes full of wisdom, and a lovely mouth, a veritable rosebud. I see a skin so white and pale, translucent almost, a waist so small it cannot be a double handspan. All in all such fairness that its radiance almost renders me speechless!"

Katherine laughed outright. "Nothing will ever do that, Thomas," she teased. "But leave your compliments – cannot you see the poor girl knows not what to think?"

It was true; I did not. Not only was I curiously discomposed by the man's half-jesting admiration – a matter which I would think on later at my leisure when I was alone – but also I was startled at the change in Katherine. I had never seen her so...so girlish, fond and foolish, she who had once seemed all-knowing, all serene. Unaware, it seemed, of any difference in her comportment, she now turned to me and hugged me.

"Elizabeth!" she breathed with shining eyes. "You and I are to live at Chelsea. We shall be together, in that pleasant house near the river, with its cherry trees and lavender and damask roses. We'll read and study and be close. And Thomas will come visiting! What do you think of that?"

As far as I had coherent thought in my head, I could not but suppose that such would please me very much.

FIVE

I

Who first reveals to us awareness of our own beauty retains forever a particular pride of place in the recollections of the heart. Was I beautiful, I asked myself as I lay on my back and looked up at my own reflection in the hand mirror that I held. I had never believed myself so.

That elfin face of pleasing pallor, the foolish freckles, those clear eyes, the nose which I considered over-large, the lips – did these somehow combine to please? It seemed so. Thomas said so.

My hair, now long and thick, I freed from its constraints and let flow about my face; it framed the pale oval in luxuriance with all the shades of autumn's brilliance in its lustre. I smiled up at myself, petulant, inviting. So...Thomas thought me beautiful, my mouth a rosebud... I watched the colour come into my face. Simpleton, I told myself in scorn, what of your fine philosophy? Were you not taught that men cajole for gain and use this perilous poison to entrap the gullible into fondness? So was I taught, I answered, laughing, winding my long limbs about each other, stroking my inner arms with long finger-nails; but it was the springtime of the year and the sun shone upon me, and the manor house at Chelsea was a fair and lovely place. Katherine, newly amorous, called love to mind, and I lay late amongst the scented sheets, putting my hand upon my prick and letting my thoughts run on unbridled. Thomas Seymour, big, like Zachary, red-bearded, loud, a man whose nearness pleased me and unsettled me.

Now there it came again, the muffled laughter; and I jumped up from my bed, my shift about me, and looked down from my window. There below me by the early light of day I saw them embracing, Katherine and Thomas, as he said goodbye at the gate that led into the fields. He came to visit her by dusk or in the early morning, secretly, because permission was not yet granted of the king. But there was no secret here at Chelsea; we all knew that Thomas was now here, now gone, and Katherine radiant as a bride.

One morning Katherine came into my room where I sat reading at the window. She ran over to me and knelt by my chair.

"Elizabeth!" she whispered. "We are wed! Tom and I are wed!" She turned to Kat who sat nearby. "Oh Mistress Ashley, give me your blessing – I am the happiest of women!"

She was thirty-three. In my innocence I considered that a little old for a woman newly wed, and briefly pitied Thomas; then the moment passed, and I felt a pang of envy. I dismissed at once this uncharitable thought and I hugged her and wished her well. "But you will be my mother still?"

"More than ever!" she assured me warmly.

When she had gone, Kat drew me close.

"What will it mean?" I wondered cautiously.

"Best not to ask," said Kat. "Poor foolish woman."

"Why so? She walks with angels."

"I know a secret," Kat replied.

"Share it then," I urged. "Indeed, I do command it."

"She was his second choice," shrugged Kat. "He asked for you."

I stared astonished; then I trembled. "But that could never be," I stuttered.

"Tom Seymour is not privy to the knowledge that you and I possess," Kat agreed tartly. "But calm yourself; we shall not be put to the test. The Council thought his offer most presumptuous. Lose no sleep on it. He is content enough to marry the queen dowager. He would have wed her long ago, but for the king, the king that is dead."

Princess Mary wrote to me. "I like not this new marriage. I cannot understand my dear friend's sudden course of action, she who was always so prudent and so virtuous. There is that spoken of the gentleman which should disturb those that profess to love the queen. You know there is a place for you with me in Essex if you find your situation there intolerable, for I know that learning and religion are not of first account with him."

This was true, and it was for the best. I had not seen it clear till now, but prior to Tom Seymour's coming we were grown a sober household, study our best pleasure. William Grindal was my tutor, but Katherine also taught me, and the many happy hours we spent in conversation of a thoughtful nature were most dear to me. And there was also with us a quiet girl, Jane Grey, some ten years old, her tutor with her, and her fervour seeming to be directed more toward Heaven than earth. We were a house of anchorites content enough in gentle ways. But not till Tom joined us did I learn that we had forgotten how to laugh.

The cherry trees were now in bloom at Chelsea and the month was May. Tom's presence filled the house. Where he walked the floorboards creaked; one always knew where he was. I could sit in my room and chart his progress through the house simply by the thudding of the boards where his great boots strode. The amount of time I spent in such a foolish pastime ought to have brought shame upon me, I who was so studious till now, and there I would sit with pen in hand and mind in other places, and the scents of springtime at my window.

Tom rarely came to morning prayers, for which Katherine often scolded him, but laughing the while; and when he did come to pray he looked about, fidgeted and yawned, and cared not who observed the same, and if he caught my eye he would wink and yawn again and work to make me do likewise; or if not to yawn, then to giggle, and the better if the merriment were unseen by Katherine, as if we two shared a secret.

In the garden where the blossom hung down heavy he would dart by Kat and me, wily as a weasel, to pinch us as he passed, and make as if it were not he that pinched. Kat and I sat on the river bank and watched him row Katherine in a little boat, and like a player he performed to the watchers, every movement of the oars a fine thing. I rolled back my petticoats and dangled my bare legs in the cold clear water, and Tom came rowing nearer especially to gaze, shading his eyes the better to see my flesh; and Kat slapped my knees for immodesty, and Katherine reproved Tom with a wagging finger; and Tom rowed closer and leaned to the water and scooped up a handful and splashed me till I squealed and ran; and then I heard him laughing loud and long as I sped for the safety of the house.

But was it safe there? And would I have it so?

Ah, how we all did love that manor house down beside the river, with the water meadows and the garden rich with roses and with lavender! It was built of old red brick which in the sun's heat was warm to the touch. It had four great chimneys and a battlemented roof and tall thin windows. Within, the rooms were small, the passageways rambling and dark, with crooked embrasures where a man might hide and jump out and pounce upon a person to surprise. The first time Tom did that to me I cried out in alarm, which pleased him mightily, and in the shadows he tousled me and brought my hair undone and left me flushed and unkempt. A wise one would have kept henceforth clear of dark corners; not I. To my shame I frequented them the more, lingering where it was darkest, hoping Tom might lie in wait. Once he but tweaked my nose, which made me angry, and once he gripped me by the arm and bent me forward slightly and slapped what would have been my buttocks had I not been well padded with my petticoats.

Naturally Katherine was not privy to these trifles and I supposed that she would remain in ignorance, for it was not seemly in a new-wed husband to behave thus and so Tom was not like to tell. But to my amazement he began to make no differences between dark passageways and daylight and in Katherine's presence took the same liberties with my person as before. Laughing he would disarrange my cap and cause my hair to fall awry, and this at mealtimes, when anyone might see; and he would seize handfuls of my gown about my arse and rub it round and round and let it go; and pull my ears if I looked sober and tweak my nose the which licence I most heartily detested.

"Ah, leave her," Katherine cajoled, amused. "It does not please her; let her be."

And Tom said, knowing it would further anger me, and looking at me, mocking, as he spoke: "She likes it well enough. Besides, what do I? These are things a man may do with wenches."

In Katherine's eyes he could do no wrong. Her gaze ran over him in rapturous adoration. She had always been a warm and loving woman, but at court her radiance was of necessity tempered, and her reputation as a learned and virtuous dame obscured that which here was self-evident, her capacity for pleasure. She was more open in other ways too. She confided in me.

"You know, Elizabeth," she said, while working at her sewing, "I always knew I would be queen one day. An astrologer foretold it. 'Born to sit in the highest seat of imperial majesty,' he said, and I believed him." She laughed. "I'm afraid that I became a little arrogant. I told my mother that my hands were ordained to touch crowns and sceptres and not needles and spindles. Being a wise woman she ignored my insufferable grandiosity, and consequently I am a fair needlewoman."

I learned that when Lord Latimer had joined the Pilgrimage of Grace, his lady had been left at Snape Hall with her husband's children, and an angry mob had hammered at the door and broken the windows; this mob demanded to be let in and threatened to burn down the house, and Katherine all alone had dealt with them, obliged to let them in to save the house and standing by undaunted as the villains rampaged through the rooms. I understood this was a lady full of prowess in her own right, not merely to be regarded as the nurse of the old king in his declining years. Kat also knew it. She warned me that the queen dowager was astute, that new-enjoyed love would not blind her to everything, that when this selfsame love wore thin, as love will often do, the queen would prove a sad sour lady. Kat sat beside me with her needlework if Queen Katherine and I were sewing. She said that over tapestry and cambric more intimacies passed, more secrets were let slip, more confessions told, than ever London's alleys knew.

"How we survived those danger days I know not," Katherine continued gravely. "We were fortunate. Not so my lord's cousin. He was hanged, drawn and quartered, that most horrible of deaths. His name was Sir John Neville... Elizabeth? What ails you? You are grown so white. I should not speak of sad things. Ah, such a tender heart, to lose all colour for a man you never knew..."

It was true – the name, the mode of death, these had much discomposed me. I forced myself to smile, to reassure, to ask forgiveness for my weakness. When Katherine looked at me so searchingly I trembled, fearing I know not what. But Katherine's probing gaze was due to quite another matter.

"Elizabeth," she said. "Have you begun your monthly terms?"

I gaped, tongue-tied and stupid. Kat pricked her finger with a noisy yelp and said in firm tones: "We do expect it any day. Your Grace shall be the first to know."

"I thought the child was looking peaky," Katherine agreed. She leaned towards me and patted my wrist. "Then shall you know the joy it is to be a woman."

Kat came into my room that evening carrying a tray with cordials for the night, the which she set down on the chest beside the bed. I sat, sullen and irritable in my nightgown, my legs apart, my hands between my legs, playing with my prick in ostentatious display.

"Well, Kat? Now that we are alone, have you to tell me tales about the joy I may expect in being a woman?"

"I am not unprepared," she answered briskly. "I knew that this would happen. And," she added, clouting me about the ear, "put that away."

I ducked and sniggered, covering my cock.

"God help us," murmured Kat, shaking her head. "Sometimes I do not understand how anyone believes in your disguise. To come upon you sitting there 'tis clear as day you are a lean and gangling lad with long red hair, no more nor less. I see it plain; why others do not is a mystery."

"I did offer a clue, I think," I smirked, and gestured to my loins.

"That priest of yours should have by rights made you a eunuch," she said huffily. "We'll have no more glimpses of Master Priapus, John. Maybe I should send Thomas Parry to you and let him give you fair warning of the merry dance that gentleman will lead you, for I know it has a life all of its own! Thank God we wear stiff petticoats and great broad skirts and stomachers enough to hide our shape! And now I am in a fine muddle, for I came to tell you how you may counterfeit a female matter and I speak to you of the male member."

Then she caught my eye and we began to grin at the ludicrousness of our predicament.

"Kat, I am certain that you have all in control," I prompted.

"I pray I do so," she answered grimly. "Or both of us will answer for it. I have here all your nightly cordials; but here," she removed a lid, "ah, no, that's elderflower. This is he," she said, and taking a small jar of earthenware she pulled back the bedcovers and cast forth the contents. A stain of blood now streaked the sheet.

"Lord, whence came that?" I asked.

"A rabbit's throat," she said complacently.

"And must I sleep there? Ugh!" I said with distaste.

"You must. Is this the thanks you give me for my pains?"

I hugged her. "Brave Kat – bold Kat – resourceful Kat. Now tell me what I am to do."

"Tomorrow you shall lie in bed," said Kat. "Then on the morrow when you come downstairs it would be reasonable to hold your belly and say you have a stomach cramp; then be prepared for the knowing glances and the arch remark about your being now a woman."

"This I can do," I mused. "But Kat – for how long, and how often? And," I demanded querulously, "will there always be rabbits?"

Then once again we caught each other's eye and creased our faces in a surge of silent laughter, born no doubt of panic and hysteria. When we had grown composed Kat answered: "Thomas Parry will provide the rabbits. And should he prove at fault here, either Blanche or I will make sure that you have the wherewithal to give the laundresses something to wash. And if there lack some regularity, no matter. You will be merely one of many maidens to whom Dame Nature is not bountiful."

At the head of the stairway Tom Seymour stood, barring my path. Mounting the stairs, my eyes on a level with his shoes, his hose, his breeches, I paused, looking up at him.

"So," he said with the advantage of one that is higher. "I hear you are a woman now."

I sniffed in scorn at the triteness of his observation.

"Let me pass," I answered coldly.

"What if I should choose to remain here?" he replied provocatively.

"Then I must hold converse with your breeches," I said tartly.

"Ho, are you grown bold with your new powers?" he laughed, and stepped back. As I reached the stairhead he caught me by the arm and pulled me into the alcove, and of a sudden caught me to him and kissed me on the lips. It was a man's kiss, hard, demanding, full of tongue. It took my breath away. I should by rights have struggled in his grasp, but I did not, and when he let me go I was as weak as water. Then I ran from him; I heard him laughing as I fled.

Secure in my own chamber I leaned my back against the door and worked to catch my breath, to make some sense of my pulsating thoughts. This was a man had kissed me, and I too was male. Yet I was faint with pleasure, giddy at the recollection of his nearness, and beneath my petticoats my prick was hard as wood. For my own peace of mind I must avoid him henceforth, my stepmother's wild husband; or I could not answer for what might befall.

Maids-in-waiting ministered to me. They were not intimate; they came to me when Kat or Blanche had already overseen my waking; they grouped themselves about me as an ornamental backcloth, sewing, gossipping, gathering flowers, combing my hair. It was my care now to be always with them, never to be alone where Tom could come at me, and I guessed that he was cognizant of my intent; his eyes were very merry.

Our household moved to Seymour Place, Tom's London house, with London's streets about its walls. It was while we stayed there that Master Thomas Parry took me on a strange escapade of his own devising.

Conversing in a low tone while we stood together in the stableyard he said to me: "I could procure you doublet and hose if you so wish it, and if you hide your hair in a small cap you might come with me on such a venture as a man might undertake, by night. As I say – if you so wish it."

"How will I leave the house unseen?"

"Tie a rope to your window; I will contrive the rest."

I told Kat that I wished to sleep alone. I did as Master Parry said, and for the first time for five years I wore a boy's garb. How strange it seemed! How curiously immodest to reveal my legs! I could not help but note the unaccustomed freedom of the lack of petticoats. As I swung my thigh across the window ledge and wound my way down the rope it crossed my mind that mere fashion alone might well be the cause of the divergent achievements of male and female. Master Parry waited for me below; we slunk away into the night.

"All this craziness," Master Parry muttered. "Trapping rabbits, hiding pots of blood like some hedge wizard... A boy has certain needs – and boy you are – and you will thank me for this night's work."

I cannot pretend I did not understand what we were about. We made our way through the silent streets, where lanthorns glowed above each doorway, and Parry's own lanthorn illuminated those dark crannies where no light reached. Parry was a broad and bulky fellow and bore a cudgel in his fist; we did not fear attack. As we passed between the dark exteriors of tall and timbered houses I recalled that time when as a boy I quit the company of Zachary and Ambrose and wandered off alone into the city. Where were they now? What would they think about my change in circumstance? Had they ever returned to Bisley? What would Xavier have told them about my disappearance? And then I grew despondent for I knew he never would have told the truth, and they would surely now believe me dead.

At the open doorway of a house a woman waited, looking out for us. With a glance behind us, Master Parry hustled me within; the woman closed the door. There was a smell of beef broth, and I was sharply reminded of a way of life where folk lived close to cooking. We went up a narrow stairway; at the top a latched door opened. Master Parry cast a glance within, was satisfied, withdrew, and in a moment I was left alone in the little room where a girl lay on a bed.

This was no street whore, I knew that. I supposed a mother and a daughter fallen upon hard times. The room was clean, the girl about my own age, pleasing in her way, half innocent, half knowing. She took off her shift, she moved in such a way as would invite, and when I hesitated she became more lewd and showed her parts. Still I remained beside the door, unfeeling as a post. She then came to me, put herself against me and reached between my legs; I gently eased her from me.

"Forgive me," murmured I. "The blame is mine, not yours."

I came down the stairs, surprising Master Parry who sat at a table with the dame, a jug of ale between them.

"What, lad – ?" he began.

"See they are well recompensed," I said, and quit the house.

Master Parry caught me up. "Oh John," he groaned, "now was that wise? There never will be such a chance again. And the mother swears the girl a maid."

"And so she would," said I.

"What is it with you?" he enquired more kindly. "Were you afeard? There was no need."

"Make me no more assignations, Master Parry," I said. "You meant it for the best, I know, and I am glad of it. I learned a truth tonight, and if I had not come with you I never would have been so sure of it, therefore our night's adventure was not wasted, though to you it must appear so."

Master Parry remained unconvinced. "I say you are a fool, John," he decided.

Kat Ashley was half senseless with fear and alarm when I returned, heaving myself carefully over the sill and safely to the floor. She beat me about the head with a leather glove, and as my cap was dislodged the tresses of my hair came cascading down. I crouched groaning at her skirts, my hands warding off her blows.

"Never – never do that again!" she squeaked, her words tumbling over one another in her distress and fury, and swishing with the glove the while. "What kind of caper was that, to risk our lives by chance discovery? Are you mad? Would you throw all away? May all the saints be praised you were not seen! Are you so eager for the gallows? Idiot boy! Numbskull! Is all our work to be for nothing?"

"Leave off, dear Kat, I shall be black and blue." I crawled from her and clung to a chair's leg and I began to weep.

"What, did I hurt you?" she cried in alarm, and crouched down with me, plump and panting, all contrite.

"Yes! But it is not for that, my snivelling." I sniffed and brushed my tears away. "Kat, I was given an opportunity to love as fair a wench as might be and all I could think of was how much I lusted for the strong arms of a full-grown man, and the tickle of his beard and his moustaches – and how much I do desire Tom Seymour."

II

I awoke from sleep, warm and content, dozily aware that it was day. Even through the thick brocade of my bedcurtains I sensed that the sun was shining and the pleasures of a summer morn were awaiting me. I stretched langorously, lying like a letter X beneath the sheets, my prick aroused and like to emit. Of a sudden my bedcurtains were thrust back, and Tom Seymour's face appeared in the space between, his mouth a laugh, his eyes glittering with mischief.

I shrieked. I pulled the bedclothes to my chin. He leaned towards me, each hand holding the bedposts, savouring my discomfort.

"W-what do you here, my lord?" I stammered through dry lips.

"I look on beauty," he replied.

"You have no business to do so here," I gasped, "in my bedchamber."

"Does not every worshipper seek the holy of holies?"

I knew not what to say. I was the further startled to see that he was in his nightshirt, this loosely covered by a dark brown velvet robe, the hairs upon his chest clearly visible. Lord save us, I thought, he is almost naked!

"Be gone, my lord," I murmured. "The queen will be displeased."

"Not she," laughed Thomas cheerily. "For what is there to give displeasure? I have but come to say good morning. This done, I withdraw."

"Kat!" I shouted as the door closed after him. "How could you permit this? How dare you let my lord into my chamber?"

But Kat was dimpled, merry, unrepentant. "He has such a wicked way with him, and what harm can it do to peep at you?"

"You are a fool, Kat," I scowled. "You are silly as a goose girl to be swayed by his bright eyes when all the world knows him to be lickerish as a goat."

"I trust you will remember your own advice, pet," retorted Kat with something of a flounce.

That evening in Tom's company I was on the river in the richly ornamented barge. Queen Katherine, being out of sorts, did not accompany us, and though I was accompanied by my maids, it was as if Tom and I were alone. He had brought a lutanist who strummed the while, and I lay back on velvet cushions while our barge glided along the Thames, its torches glowing, leaving trails of glimmering amber light in the dark water. Tom caused the minstrel to sing songs of love, and Tom himself said no words, but looked deep into my eyes with such an ardent gaze as made me breathless. He pressed my hand, and by such motions gave to understand that the words of love within the song came from his heart. And for all his assurances to the contrary, I could not help but feel that Katherine would not be content at this, nor would Tom act so if she were here.

That night I was the lovesick fool of which the poets sing – he who believes the flattering attentions of the practised libertine, the gullible buffoon about whom Vives warned his pupils. And when I lay in bed I thought of Tom's face. I traced its shape in my mind's eye – the lovely eyes, a little close together (the sign, they say, of a deceiver), the long lashes and thick eyebrows, the full sensuous mouth, the slightly crooked nose, the russet beard and moustache, the thick manly neck... I saw us riding to a far-off place where we could be alone. I knew he loved me. I knew he would rather lie with me than Katherine who was nearly forty and so old. Kat had told me as much. I was his first choice. It was me that he preferred. I drifted off to sleep in dreams of ecstatic fancy.

Next day he rudely brought me back to earth. I met him in the passage near my bedroom door, that ardent lover from the torchlit night. I blushed, awaiting compliment. He lunged at me and spread his hands upon my chest.

"Ha! Woman you may be, my sweet," he chortled, "but you yet lack tits."

Catching sight of Kat behind me he added insult to injury by his next remark. "She has no tits yet, this young wench of yours. Now grow yourself a big round pair like Mistress Ashley's and no man shall say you nay!"

"Kat!" I gasped. "Tell him – scold him for his boorishness!"

But Kat all stupid would not, laughing like a Cheapside serving wench, with all appearance of his coarseness pleasing her.

I thought that Tom had come to try me further when the curtains of my bed were pulled apart in the morning. But though he was yet in his night clothes, Katherine was with him.

"I have told my wife how modest and timid you are in your manners, my sweet girl," said Tom as brazen as could be. "And she has come with me to tease you into mirth."

"Indeed I am not melancholy," I replied alarmed, burrowing deeper into my blankets.

But they were here for sport and would not be gainsaid; they pulled the bedclothes from me and began to tickle me. Encumbered by the great nightgown which I always wore I turned this way and that, my hands about my prick, squealing for Kat to come to my aid. She did so, the good woman, pulling Thomas from me, crying out: "For shame, my lord, my lady, leave the child in peace!" and, laughing all the while, Thomas and Katherine stepped back, well pleased with their shared foolery.

"'Tis true, the maid is modest," Katherine said, wiping tears of merriment from her eyes. "See how she holds herself!"

"As if we meant to look between her thighs," laughed Thomas scornfully, as if the notion were the oddest in the world.

But, safe yet, weak and gasping as I lay there and looked at them I thought: poor Katherine – how she is duped. He brought her to bear witness to his innocence, but he is devious, and in his seeming artlessness most devious of all.

On the following morning Thomas sneaked into my chamber, softly padding over to my bed. He paused there for a moment listening; then pulled aside the bedcurtains with a shout. Had I been yet abed I daresay I would have been as startled as he hoped; but this time I was dressed and ready, half hid by the linen cupboard, and I laughed outright to see his disappointment and confusion. I could tell that he was vexed to be discovered thus by me, in his nightgown with his calves and ankles bare; and my two maids-in-waiting, lurking in the nearby chamber, came and stood about me, their girlish giggling no doubt adding to his pique.

"Very well, young mistress," he chuckled and wagged a finger. "So, and would you beat me at my game? We shall know more anon!"

A pleasurable quiver flickered at my belly as I wondered what he might do next.

Some sickness in that part of London caused our household to be moved to Hanworth manor in the autumn of the year.

This country house was possessed of a fair garden, with a hedge of brambles beyond the herb border, where it was my pleasure to pick the blackberries. Tom learned of my predilection. One day I found him waiting there for me. I should have turned back, fled back to the house. I did not. Instead we picked the berries. As he placed one on my lips he murmured: "Let us have done with teasing."

"Teasing, my lord?"

"You know what I mean. I love you: I believe you feel the same for me."

"Have a care, my lord. You are wed, and wed to a lady whom I hold dear."

"And so do I, that is not in question. But you, how you unsettle me – your youth, your long limbs, your body slender as a reed, your wild red hair – I long to twine it round my fingers."

"My lord, I do permit it," murmured I, and stood unmoving while he unpinned my hair and let it tumble loose. He bent his head and kissed my hair. Taking it between his fingers he pulled me closer to him till our mouths touched and his tongue probed between my parted lips. This long sweet kiss amongst the blackberries weakened my knees. I put my arms around him.

"Elizabeth! At last!" he breathed and held me close. "How your nearness has tormented me! From the first day I beheld you I have longed to hold you close." His hands moved up and down my back and settled lower, on my skirts, pressing my buttocks and no doubt finding some hindrance, for it was all velvet and skirt. I giggled.

"I long to undress you," said he, panting. "I long to see you naked."

"That may never be," I gasped and pulled away.

"Don't be afraid," he cajoled, preventing my escape. "I would not harm you and no one would know. It would be our especial secret."

"My lord, I am not ready."

"But you will meet me here again and let me embrace you."

"Yes my lord, I will permit that."

"Dearest girl..."

I smiled. He shook his head, baffled, having, as he thought, said nothing droll. We kissed again. I licked his beard. Beneath my skirts my prick thickened. I drew back.

"Still timid?" he surmised. "Trust me; I am a man upon whom you may depend."

Dear Thomas, how truly he spoke, as I was to find.

We met amongst the blackberries each day, and kissed, and murmured sweetnesses. Virgin as I was, I knew well enough that he was roused, that he would not for long be well content with decorous embraces. When his hand reached for my loins I must repulse him, and he grew morose.

"Not yet, not yet," I pleaded, and I knew it cost him dear to give way to my scruples.

Then one warm bright afternoon we were surprised – that is, not exactly surprised, for we heard the queen dowager's attendants laughing and talking as they approached, and Katherine in crimson velvet with them, bright as the sun.

"Why, here they are, amongst the brambles," she cried, pointing, "and my lady's hair is down."

"Your stepdaughter has an inordinate fondness for blackberries," Tom said gaily. "Watch how I feed her as the mother phoenix feeds its young. Pucker up your lips, my little girl, and take my juicy fruit. Like a babe, Kate, look at her, and she turned fourteen – what an innocent!"

"I think we would all like blackberries, Tom," said Katherine with some acerbity, and suddenly like roosting starlings she and her ladies were descended upon the hedge, all plucking at the ripeness there.

"So, is our maid more yielding?" Katherine asked. "Or must we tickle her again?"

"An you help me, madam, I will gladly tickle her," said Tom.

"We want no cold maidens here," Katherine said. "And wenches that come seeking blackberries must learn that rooks lurk in the brambles. Eh, Tom?"

I looked from one to another, puzzled, apprehensive. I guessed she supposed I had been making large eyes at Tom Seymour, but that he had not been stupid enough to give encouragement and like a naughty child I must be put in my place. How else may I explain her strange behaviour? She laughed all the while throughout that which followed, but I found her joviality false and grating. I did not know what to do for the best and therefore I did nothing. She held me by the arms and, standing behind me, made me her prisoner.

"Now Tom, to it!" she commanded, and Tom, perplexed as I, paused, as if awaiting her instruction.

"Well, tickle her, man," said Katherine. "Why do you hesitate?"

"I may not come to her," smiled Tom. "She is fully clothed. There is no joy in romping when the maiden wears a velvet gown."

"Then cut it off," said Katherine comfortably.

Tom blinked, then, being a man of action and no coward under orders, drew his dagger and attacked my sleeve. I stood frozen, held in Katherine's grip. I should have pulled free, but I was like one enchanted. I wanted nothing better than that Tom should cut my clothes from me and strip my body to his gaze. A sensuous excitement overcame me, sending reason to the winds. He must have sensed my yielding invitation; he too behaved like one possessed. He cut my sleeves from me and the black velvet drooped and showed my arms; he held the bodice of my gown and snipped with care. My stiff white stomacher edged with lace was now revealed, and the pale skin of my shoulders. He slit the waist band, and, discarding dagger then, he seized the velvet in his fists and ripped it wide asunder, to my petticoats. I shrieked. Behind me Katherine was chuckling in my ear, but Tom was not now laughing. With an effort, as it seemed, he forced his face into habitual good humour and replaced his dagger in its sheath. Then he ruffled up my hair.

"Enough, I think," he said. "And Katherine my dear, now we have had our sport let us be merciful and let the wench go, eh?" Her hands grew slack upon my arms. I ran from them, gathering the tatters of my gown about me. I turned once, and saw Tom had his arm slung about Katherine; he was nuzzling her and leading her into the cultivated part of the garden, where all grew to order and without luxuriance.

"Lord save us," Kat wept, encountering me at the sundial. "What are you about? What will folk say? You must be mad – your gown cut from you – one would think you set upon by rogues who took their turns upon you..."

"I had no choice," I whispered shaking. "Katherine held me and Tom cut."

"Come into the house, my pet," she crooned, all sympathy now. "Let us get you to rights."

I had not thought that Tom would come to my room again so soon after that performance an he wished to retain his wife's regard; but when I opened my eyes and peered beyond the blankets, there he sat, upon my bed, in dressing gown, surveying me with a preoccupied and probing stare.

"This is not wise," I murmured wearily.

"We are alone," he interrupted swiftly. "Kat Ashley has undertaken to keep your maids away and I have locked the door. We are quite private."

"To what purpose, my Lord Seymour?" I asked warily.

"Conversation," Tom replied.

"We may speak anywhere, without this secrecy," I shrugged.

"But not upon this subject," Tom said meaningfully.

We waited, silent. I had never seen him thus, all jesting gone from him, a frown upon his brows.

"I am come into the possession of a secret," he began then.

I pulled the bedclothes round about my chin.

"When I so foolishly took part in your stepmother's romp amongst the blackberries and cut your gown from you," said Tom, "I own I acted out of lust. My prick was up. I did suppose that you also, by your remaining, did derive some pleasure from the foolishness. I saw that it was so." He looked at me now, full in the face. "I saw in you reciprocal delight. I all but died with what I saw...boy."

For a stupid moment I hoped I had misheard him. Then I knew I had not. I was numb, nor moved, nor spoke.

"Now pull those bedclothes back and let me into bed,"said Tom. "You have no longer any need to play the lily."

He climbed between the sheets and settled himself against me. With a rapid lurch he had his arm across me and his hand between my thighs. With a sure and certain movement he now gripped my balls and closed his hand about them. He gave a grunt of satisfaction. "Yes," he said, half to himself. "I half began to doubt it. I began to think I dreamed...you fooled me, boy. You fooled me to the hilt.

What punishment? What does such admirable deception merit at the hands of one deceived?" His grip now tightened, twisting, tugging, till I writhed upon his hand and my eyes watered. He laughed into my mouth. "The first display of true emotion you have ever shewn with me, I believe."

"No, no," I gasped. "All I have said to you was true."

"Love, I recall, was spoken of?" he prompted disbelievingly.

"Yes, love!" I answered heatedly. "It's true. I love you. I longed to give myself in a complete embrace but I was in terror that my lust would give my true self away, so I held back. I think about you day and night. I am awash with guilt because you are the husband of my dearest Katherine. And when you ripped my gown I wished that you would strip me to the skin and love me, there and then, before all folk. But it can never be, because you love a maiden princess, not a hapless lad, the which I am."

His mouth sought mine, stopping all protestations, and he lay upon me and half choked me with his probing tongue. He held my head between his hands, hurting me as he twined my hair in his grasp, moving on me in the rhythm of his lust. I held him tightly to me, winding my parted legs about him, daring to use my own tongue, savouring the wetness of his mouth. Suddenly he seized me by the hair and pushed my face down to his belly. I smelt the male scent of his crotch. My cheek was pressed against his rampant cock.

"Get your lips about it," he ordered and I obeyed. He held me there and would not let me move thence until I had swallowed all that gushed from him.

"Well, that will do for a beginning," said he, gratified. "And now let us be hearing who you are."

I told him, in low whispered tones, my mouth still flavoured with the taste of him.

"Who knows?" was his response.

"Kat, Blanche and Thomas Parry; none other, save the monk that planned it all."

"And now I," he mused. "This is a secret which would rock the edifice of government. A jewel beyond price."

"I have to point out," I said unhappily, "that if it were revealed we all would die – Kat, Blanche and Thomas and myself, and even Katherine would be suspect."

"Revealed?" he snorted. "There's no cause for that. This truth is for concealment. How we may turn it to advantage I am not yet certain, but whether male or female, Princess Elizabeth must live and thrive. No, sweetheart, rest assured, I shall not blab. Your secret is yet safe. I told you that I was a man of honour. You may believe my words. And Katherine does not know? This does astound me. I congratulate you, minion mine. You played your part to perfection. And you fooled me..." He shook his head and laughed. "A fine blow to my pride. But do not fear that you are any less desirable to me male, my lady! I've travelled in my time. I've been to places where men fuck boys in preference to wenches. Believe me, I can handle such as you and treat you as you well deserve!"

I was to find that this was so. We returned to the manor at Chelsea for the oncoming winter, settling ourselves in with great enjoyment, for it was the favourite of our present dwelling places.

I believed Tom when he said that he would keep my secret. It was in his interest to do so, if for no other reason than to play for time while he decided what to do. And of course, while he decided, there would I be, helpless, malleable, and in his hands, which in the truest sense was where I was content to be.

My room was on a higher floor than his, and for that the manor was a dark and rambling place, it was easy enough for him to dodge about, particularly as he seemed now to have an understanding with Kat who readily contrived to whisk my maids away to their own rooms when such shift was required.

And thus he still came calling in the mornings to my chamber and whatever he demanded I might not refuse. He dared not long remain, but in his lovemaking as in his outward actions he was brisk and self-assured, took what he would, and left without a backward glance. This was a man who had lain with boys before – "All seafarers do so," he said carelessly, "what else is there to do so far from wenches?" – and took the pleasures of the flesh as part of nature's generous bounty. I learnt from him that what Xavier had told me so long ago was true, that sodomy could, its first pains past, prove pleasurable, and afterwards I sometimes was obliged to pretend an onset of the flux.

Immense was my personal satisfaction knowing him to be my

lover. I experienced a wicked thrill to be in his company at meal times and with Katherine present. I would sit in modest silence while my stepmother conversed and laughed with Tom, thinking herself secure in his affections. I would recall that this strong man had been naked in my arms that very morning, that I had had my mouth about his cock, that he had grasped my buttocks in his hands and praised them; that he had turned me on my belly and had taken pleasure on me, biting my ear, tangling his face in my hair, calling me his darling. My vanity was monstrously gratified to know that I could have such an effect upon a hero of our time, a man respected by the world, a man moreover famed for his past encounters with fair women. I, a boy, could bring him to my bed, eager for my body, panting for my favours. On many mornings now he came to me and had his will of me, which was my will also.

These matudinal encounters left me both elated and afraid. I loved the touch of his strong hands upon me, his blatant maleness, his perfume and his sweat – but I knew that we played with fire and risked discovery, and I knew that he would never willingly relinquish his hold upon me. I dreaded that my fear might make me stupid and less able to pursue my chosen course. I was excited and confused, a little boat upon a turbulent sea.

It was thus somewhat of a relief to me when I was invited to spend Christmas with my brother at court, though I was astonished to discover how very glad I was to be well quit of Tom's close company once I was clear of him. I found a curious peace amongst the rigorous formality of Edward's modus vivendi, where no one pestered me but treated me with great politeness, never doubting that I was Elizabeth, never making me uneasy and on guard.

Kat of course was with me. In our own rooms we were merry as we always were, as if a burden had been lifted. We both shared this odd sensation, as folk breathing clear air, released from an enclosure, and this puzzled me, since Chelsea's air was clear enough and court life by its very nature close, restrictive and confined.

"I love him, but I fear him," I confided. "A man that would so cheerily deceive his own wife whom he says he loves, and this in the very room above her head. And though he says he loves me he does not, for he was very angry in his passion when I so fooled him, and his lovemaking has in it the trappings of a certain rage, controlled, but ever present. Oh Kat – I am glad to be here where he cannot come to me."

"He is a rough and lovely man," said Kat, and added sagely: "And such are never comfortable."

I had forgot how out of touch I had become at Chelsea. Utterly obsessed by Thomas Seymour I had given little thought to policy and personality. I thought Edward, though well in health, looked a little strained and preoccupied. I was naturally aware of the Duke of Somerset, Tom's elder brother and Protector of the Realm, who was ever present with the king, and of Robert Dudley's father, now created Earl of Warwick and a member of the Privy Council. If I had missed the undercurrents, Robert Dudley told me soon enough.

Robert was still one of Edward's close companions. During the festivities we danced together and had opportunity for converse beneath the great boughs of greenery and garlands bright with candles, while the minstrels played loud jocund music from their gallery. He explained to me:

"The Duke of Somerset still works to bring about a marriage between Ned and the little Queen of Scots. He has a grand design, England and Scotland united. But he has grown greatly misliked. He is thought to be aspiring beyond his means. He has built himself a great house – Somerset House – and he has had two churches knocked down to make way for it. Ned fears him. Do you know who is Ned's favourite now?"

"Other than Barnaby Fitzpatrick?"

"Oh, Barnaby," laughed Robert easily, dismissively. "No, I mean one with influence. 'Tis Thomas Seymour."

"Thomas? What of him?"

"Ah, that makes you uneasy, does it? That is a dangerous and stupid man. He has bought Edward's favour; Somerset is mean with Edward's spending money. Tom Seymour knows as much, and leaves Ned money hidden in odd places – under carpets, under tankards. Ned is much in his debt. And in return, our Lord High Admiral has asked Ned for a little gift – the Protectorate."

"I don't believe it."

"Such a bold and open fellow he appears," said Robert. "That is his outward show. Beneath, he is all intrigue, all deceit. And many have suspicion of him, yet because he is a stupid man he does not guess it, but continues with his tricks and deviousness. He will have Ned wed Jane Grey, and he himself the man behind the match, the source of power. But being stupid, as I say, he never will achieve his ends, and everybody knows it."

"Your judgement of Tom Seymour is at fault," I protested. "I know him for an honourable man."

Robert shrugged. "I did not say he was not so. Therein lies his strength. For all it is supposed he works against the peace of the realm, no man is more universally applauded for being a good fellow. The rumour goes," he added slyly, "that you think the same yourself."

"I? What have I to do with this?" I gasped.

"They say he looks cow's eyes at you."

"Why should he not?" I answered with an attempt at archness. "I am not the ugliest of maidens."

"You are monstrous plain, as you were ever," Robert answered devastatingly. "I thought to find some change in you; but you are thin as any post, and much as I remember you."

"I may not be to your taste, Robert Dudley," I said with dignity, "but it is common knowledge that Tom Seymour asked for me in marriage."

"Aye and for the Lady Mary also," Robert retorted scornfully. "First she, then you, and the Council would grant neither."

"What? He asked for Mary?" I blanched, horrified. I did not doubt him; Robert was ever honest.

"He did so. Had you and she been ninety years of age he still would have done so. You and she and Katherine also, I believe, are merely stepping stones for him that mark the flow of his unstemmed ambition."

"It is not so," I answered weakly. "Katherine at least he loves. And for myself – I think he cares for me."

"If you are minded to give your heart, Elizabeth," said Robert kindly, "hold back from Thomas Seymour. I believe him dangerous, and stupid...and though I called you plain, you are not without a certain forwardness which a practised seducer might take for invitation; and therefore you may be at some risk from his attentions. I speak as a friend," he added not without pomposity.

"If we were elsewhere I would slap your face for your presumption," I hissed furiously.

"Forgive me," he replied, though I believed him unrepentant. "But there are sycophants about you saying what you wish to hear, and one at least should speak in plain terms. And I would not have you admire one whom they say is hand in glove with pirates."

"They say that, do they?" marvelled I. "And nor would Thomas Seymour fall in my estimation of him, were it so."

"I had forgot your perverse adoration of the wicked," Robert grumbled. "You always did admire the reckless, the adventurer. Then Seymour should well be a hero to you, since in his capacity of Lord Admiral he joins with the very pirates he was commissioned to suppress and gives them haven in return for a share in their pickings. I hope you are best pleased to learn what manner of man it is whom you defend."

"I suspect you, Robert Dudley, of some envy," I surmised, glancing at him sideways. "This is a man such as you would wish to be, and one moreover whom I cherish, as the husband of my stepmother, and you are eaten up with jealousy for that he is grown dear to me and once asked for my hand in marriage."

"For a wench lacking in beauty," Robert answered, "you are the vainest creature ever I set eyes upon."

I turned my back on him, losing patience; and vastly irritated I resolved to have no more to do with him. But for all I vowed to put him from my mind, I found the warnings offered me by Robert Dudley added to my own disquiet. Any rumour Robert knew was sure to be the truth for he would have had it from his father the Earl of Warwick. As Kat said, Warwick was as great an intriguer as the best of them and knew all there was to know.

In January I heard that my tutor Master Grindal had died, he being but a young man, and his fatal sickness the plague. That grim headsman being thought in general a summer or an autumn visitor, and coming so near to home, I felt a certain vulnerability; as I believe we all did. And it was with a heart heavy with dread and apprehension that I set out in the spring for Chelsea. But I cast base fear firmly from me as we approached the manor house by the river and I set myself to receive well whatever it should be that there awaited.

We were quiet at Chelsea as the season turned, for Katherine and Thomas were away from home, and I settled to my studies with every hope and intention of self-betterment and instruction of the mind. My new tutor Master Roger Ascham spoke Latin and Greek to me with the accent of a Yorkshireman, and loved archery as much as he respected Demosthenes and Livy. In his pleasant company the ever-present joys of learning were magnified a hundredfold and I believed I could be well content to pass my days so henceforth, godly as Jane Grey and free from worldly toils as any hermit, but that I knew this was a false quiet, as that same silence of expectancy when the firework torches are first lit before explosion.

SIX

I

The spring was well advanced when Katherine and Thomas returned from London, and my first surprise was that my stepmother was visibly with child, expected in the summer. She looked bonny, and the first meeting between the three of us was warm, affectionate and public. All saw how much we held each other in regard. Later, Katherine enquired of Master Ascham how my studies went, and he, after recounting in some detail my various achievements, added: "Indeed, I cannot pay a greater compliment than this: the princess shows in judgement and in understanding the mind and temper of a man."

Tom gave a great guffaw. Master Ascham laughed also, explaining: "It is not common for a young girl to show such a fine grasp of language, style and doctrine; that is, not within my own experience."

"Then I suggest," said Katherine sweetly, "that you did not know myself when young, nor Princess Mary, nor my own sister Ann."

"I count it my misfortune," replied Ascham contritely.

"We are pleased to hear Elizabeth does well," said Thomas smoothly. "I freely own she is far cleverer than I!"

I could not credit his rashness when he came to me that morning as of old, in his nightshirt as before, and his wife below us in her own room, and she great with child. Yet notwithstanding my astonishment I was very glad, and indeed that vanity of which Robert Dudley had accused me was much increased to think that Thomas took such risk for love of me.

"It seems I must congratulate you on your potency, my lord," I murmured archly, nestled in his arms amongst the sheets.

"Oh, I was ever potent," he agreed tersely.

"You cannot have much missed me then," I said, "since all the world now sees you have been busy."

"On the contrary," Tom answered, "you are more than ever in my mind, Master Mischief, and my need for you, if anything, has grown. Since Kate has been with child I have not touched her carnally. She is not a young woman as regards the matter of childbearing. I fear that I may cause her harm. And therefore, sweet boy of mine, I am all but bursting for that which you alone can offer me. And so, about it."

"Wait – first I must be assured that you have not told her," I began.

"Told her? About your true sex? What do you take me for?" Thomas spluttered. "Of course I have not told her. At home if not abroad I want a quiet life! All Hell would erupt here if my dear wife learned our secret. Now part your arse cheeks for me and have done with talking. Thank God I may treat you as a man may treat his boy, and not as a doll I am afraid of breaking!"

He was rough with me, but, so help me, I was glad of it; and my pleasure was as great as his as I writhed beneath him, stuffing the pillow into my mouth to stifle the wild noises of my satisfaction. When he had done he bit my ear and tousled my hair and then was gone. I lay in the crumpled mess of sheets where he had left me, weak and ecstatic, happiest of boys, knowing my lover to be such as many might wish for, alone, unsatisfied, making their own pleasure, far less fortunate than I.

Business at court took Tom away from home in April, and I settled to my studies. But in believing I had been given respite from alarm I was to be proved entirely wrong.

One sunny morning Katherine sent for me. She was in her chamber. I knocked and entered in all innocence. I saw that she was alone. She was sitting by the window, large of belly, buxom, dressed in her favourite crimson, the sun upon her, and the room a little close, for a fire had been lit so that she should be always warm and at her ease. Between us, on the floor, stood a bath tub, already filled with water, its surface covered with a welter of floating leaves and fragrant petals.

"Close the door, Elizabeth."

I closed it. Katherine began with inconsequential idle chatter to which it was simple enough to respond. Then she said: "My maids have prepared a bath with a new receipt for sweetness and softness. But I am not disposed to bathe. Rather than waste a fine perfume I thought of you, child. As you see, we are alone; no one is by to offend your modesty. You may bathe here. It is a long time since we talked, woman to woman."

I gulped. "Forgive me, Your Highness, but I myself am not disposed to bathe; I am unwell, and shall retire, with your permission."

"But I insist you bathe," said Katherine steely-toned. "I will take no refusal. An you will not undress I shall call in my maids to aid you – all in merriment, of course. And now what do you say?"

My mouth opened and closed like any fish.

"I do command it," Katherine said.

"No, no, I will not!" answered I in great distress.

"Is there any reason," Katherine asked, "why you should wish to hide your nakedness from me?"

She knew. He must have told her. He had betrayed me after all. His promises meant nothing. I was lost.

"Madam, is there any reason why you would have me strip?"

"If you do not," she answered, frighteningly calm, "I shall assume my curious suspicions true."

"What is it you suspect?" I whispered.

"Something so incredible that I almost dare not put it into words," she said. "Ever since I first became convinced of it I yet have not been able to believe it. I have known you well these past five years. Must I doubt what my reason tells me to be true? And yet I must. Whoever you may be that live with me and share my way of life, I do not think you are the Lady Elizabeth. Yet when you ceased to be she I know not. I believed you to be she when we first met...and even now I know not what to think. Some conspiracy – and yet some vast conspiracy, since such a secret could not with all sense be kept from such as Mistress Ashley, Mistress ap Harry, and your maids perhaps. I am confused. Is it simply Thomas and myself that are kept in the dark?"

I started at those words. Thomas? Did she believe that Thomas did not know? Had I been wrong so hastily to condemn him?

"When was it, madam, that you first supposed I was not as I seemed?" I asked, heartened by her tone, which was not hostile but merely perplexed. I recalled again what manner of woman Katherine was – strong, fearless, and unlikely to be laid low even by so startling a discovery as she had made. "Your Highness has always been so good, so kind to me. I have not been aware of any change in your affections."

"Sit down, Elizabeth," said Katherine, adding with a half smile: "Yes, even at this moment, it does not seem untoward to call you so."

I sat upon a stool and waited, hands loose on my lap, head bowed.

"I am not a stupid woman," Katherine said. "I have known well enough that my husband found you pleasing. Thomas was ever thus. I have known him many years and he was always one that had an eye for wenches. The kind of man that Tom is – well, they are all the same, and more so as they grow older, needing reassurance that their prowess is in no wise diminished with the years. I know he has been coming to your chamber; he always told me; and he told me of his displeasure that your maids kept you from him, and that try as he might, he was ever thwarted by that demon Mistress Ashley, as he said." She laughed. "I knew that, having respect for your own honour, you would never permit intimacies. That is, when I believed you maiden. I know that as a..." she faltered, then went on, "as a boy you cannot. Therefore I did not overmuch distress myself. We laughed about it, Tom and I. He said 'I do declare, that wench is harder to come by than the Philosopher's Stone! A wall of maids surrounds her, and she teases me with her eyes from beyond the safety of their protection. She will come to no good, that one – a temptress, promising I know not what wonders, and then withdrawing all she promises!' If you were maiden, it might well make you vain to hear Tom talk of you thus!"

She laughed, but mirthlessly. I raised my eyes and offered a wan smile in return.

"It was Tom's interest in you that caused me to look at you with more than careless observation," Katherine said. "What is it in this girl that so appeals, I wondered? Is it youth? Slenderness? Virginity? The Tudor blood? I watched you carefully, with the eyes of a suspicious wife. Only one such as myself would ever have seen those things I saw. I cannot even say what they are, so intangible are they. And the unthinkable occurred to me, as if a veil were taken from my eyes. I had to suppose that you were not Elizabeth – that you were male. It is so, is it not? You are a boy."

I nodded. "And at your mercy, sweet Your Highness."

"Yet I would swear upon my life that you came of Tudor stock!" said Katherine.

"It is so," I answered soberly. "Nor would I ever so presume if I had not believed I had some rights to be where I now am."

Then in low tones I told my stepmother of my early years, of Kat's fear of the rage of King Henry, of our bold venture, of the strange shifts we were fallen into. Katherine listened carefully and not unsympathetically. We talked about it further, while she established in her mind all that she might.

"You have not, of course, said anything of this to Tom!"

"Oh no!" I gasped with every show of horror.

"It has amused me," Katherine smiled, "to see him in pursuit of you, believing you a virgin maid; and I would chuckle to myself, knowing you a boy. I never would have permitted his attempted romps if I had thought you female!"

"I would prefer," I said quickly, "that Lord Seymour did not share our secret, madam."

"I shall say nothing to him, rest assured," said Katherine.

"But I must ask you then, Your Highness, if I dare – what will you do? I beg you, please be kind, as I well know you to be. Nothing has changed between us now the truth be out – I love and honour you as I have ever done, the only mother I have known in the true sense of the word." Tears fell from my eyes then, and the dear good lady touched my hand.

"Be still, dear; calm yourself. What will I do? At first, nothing at all. I must think...I must consider. Morally what you have done is very wrong; but you yourself are less to blame than those about you, and I shall speak to those three who abetted you. As you say, in a way nothing has changed; I find I do not love you less, though I am sad our friendship has been grounded on a falsehood. But while I wait my child's birth all my thoughts tend to that end only, and therefore even your miraculous confession pales in the comparison. Let us continue as before, and when my child is born we shall think more upon the matter. It is fortunate for you that I did not learn of it while

I was yet wed elsewhere, for believe me, I would not have kept this matter from the king!"

I kissed her hand, and when she gave me leave to go, I fled.

Tom returned before the week was out, and on the second morning Katherine discovered us in bed. There was no room for denial, explanation. Lying beneath Tom I heard the door open, I heard Tom's gasp. I twisted round to see my stepmother. I saw her face. I saw her clutch her heart. I buried my face in the pillows. Tom got from me, clumsily. I heard his lame and noisy protestations. Then Tom and Katherine were gone; and Kat was with me, and her arms about me.

"Naturally you will remain in this house not a moment longer than it takes to move you hence," said Katherine to me.

We faced each other in her chamber once again. I thought that she would speak of Tom, of her betrayal, of her rage; but she did not. She was serene and calm, her voice almost without a tremor.

"When you began your monstrous deception," she said, "it was an act of panic. You gave no consideration to the future, did you, any of you? It was enough to save Kat Ashley from King Henry's wrath. And afterwards it seems you moved from day to day, content merely to remain undiscovered. I have said that I will keep your secret for the moment. Princess Elizabeth shall live, quietly and far from court, and a blameless life, if she has any wisdom. But should it come about that she is brought nearer to the throne – if by illhap His Majesty, God save him, were to die, and in the course of time if Princess Mary also perished, then I would speak out, I swear it. If it lie within my power no impostor ever shall sit upon King Harry's throne; no brat from Gloucestershire rule England."

"You speak of that which shall never come to pass," I trembled. "My brother is hale and like to grow and wed and in God's time bear sons; and Mary also."

"I pray so," Katherine answered fervently. "But you know well enough, as I do, that there lurks the spectre of a slow consumption in the young men of the house of Tudor. If I speak treason, may I be forgiven, but it is so." And then she added – and it was the only truly vile thing I ever heard her say – "A matter, boy, which you might do well to heed."

My exile was to no accursed place, but to Kat's sister's house. Joan Champernowne, the beauty from the days of Katherine's youth, maid-of-honour to Queen Anne Boleyn, was married some ten years ago to Sir Anthony Denny, a gentleman of the Privy Chamber to King Henry, and a Cambridge man. They lived at Cheshunt, and to that place in the month of May went I and all my household. Both Tom and Katherine wrote to me while I was there, Katherine in order to persuade the world and me that she was not a jealous and affronted wife and yet retained her dignity; but Tom's letter contained words of love; I burned it. I heard that they had removed to Gloucestershire for the birth and had taken up abode at Sudeley Castle.

I was nervous, constantly ill at ease. I feared what Katherine might do once the child was born. I did not eat; I grew thin with dread and apprehension. The king's physician was sent to attend me.

It can be imagined with what dread and panic I received the news of such a visit.

"Peace, peace," said Kat comfortably. "He will but take your pulse; and I will never leave your side. You will be well clad in his presence."

I was close questioned by the man about the onset of my female condition. During our conversation he laid hands upon my forehead and pronounced it hot, for which he prescribed a cooling distillation. But after consultation with Kat, who never left my side, and prompted by her, he agreed that my weaknesses were due to the onset of that same female condition, which Kat said was proving most erratic. He pronounced my piss of excellent quality, my pulse strong; he ordered quiet and rest, departing with our thanks and gratitude.

But when news came to us in September that Katherine had died after the birth of her child, my distress was increased a thousandfold and I became so weak and ill I must take to my bed. I understand it now – the guilt, the sorrow, and the both so overlaid with a relief I dared not own, causing my mind so great a disorder that my frail flesh must succumb. Had Katherine lived she would have thwarted me. But she was dead, by natural causes, as if in answer to prayer; and for the moment I was spared. Yet what kind of force was it that answered such a prayer, to kill so warm and generous a servant of the Lord, and leave to prosper one engaged in great deception? Was there a devil at my back, an occult presence keeping me from harm, slaying the good and the gentle? I dared not voice my terrors, and I remained in poor health, so much that Kat confessed to me afterwards that she had feared for my reason.

In October we returned to Hatfield, and in that most favourite of places as I walked amongst the trees, I tried to make sense of my thoughts. The queen dowager's death had much disturbed me; but there was more. *No impostor shall sit upon King Harry's throne...no brat from Gloucestershire rule England...* Maybe in my idle fancies I had wondered what would happen if the world turned and my brother and sister were to die; but almost with no more application than does any man who thinks 'if I were king...' Now for the first time I must look the prospect in the face: it could be – it was not inconceivable – that I could become king; that is, queen. I thought it most improbable, as I had always done. But this was not what we intended when we took that fatal step at Bisley. We were merely marking time, staving off the anger of the king, looking no further forward than next week. Now I was fifteen years of age. Now here we were, upon a course that took us further than we ever had guessed possible. What were we to do? No – what was I to do? – for I must bear the burden. Myself was become Elizabeth; I could only lose her now by death. Or if I dared, I could cut my hair short, don doublet and hose, sneak away in my own sex and live in obscurity. I had heard a rumour that the younger son of King Edward IV had done as much, escaping from his place of confinement and living to old age, a carpenter or cobbler or some such menial trade, he who should have been King Richard IV. But once away from palaces I feared what would become of me. I had no trade, no manual skill, and from my own knowledge of the turbulent and lively London streets I had some suspicion what was like to befall a pretty boy alone and aimless, without friend and protector. My childhood dream of running away to sea I now saw as mere fantasy; I had been cheated of manhood – I was untrained at male sports, camaraderie and weaponry. Neither boy nor girl, I had no place in the restless and uncaring world. No place but here, where I now was, no skill but that of being Elizabeth.

I think it was no wonder that I wasted, shrivelled, wept. I believed that in the world there was no fool more solitary than I.

The ravages caused by my earlier distress were succeeded by a crippling lethargy, from which I was at last roused by a very odd proposal.

Master Thomas Parry had been sent to London, one of his commissions being to arrange for a town house to be put at my disposal, and, Seymour Place being offered, a meeting with Tom Seymour the natural outcome. Having intimated that he wished to speak to me alone Master Parry let me know the business which they had discussed.

"The fact is, John, that my lord would marry you."

"Master Parry! You must not call me that – after all this time, and having told you so often – you must be careful!"

"But we are alone," protested he, affronted.

"Even alone. You must believe me female. You must think it in your heart. Begin again, and circumspectly."

"How you maintain so severe a stance, my lady, when I bring such news, amazes me, my lady. I said: Lord Thomas Seymour would have you to wife. Knowing your true condition."

"Master Parry, you had best tell me what was said."

"And such is my intent, for after all, this news is such that may not be written down. Here it is then: in greatest secrecy, my lord the admiral says that the love he bears you has grown to such proportion that it must be satisfied within the lawful bounds of wedlock. He bids me tell you that he will protect and love you and offer you the name of wife. He says that in the security of his name and patronage your secret will be safe as any little boat in harbour."

"I thank you for conveying my lord's message," I said smoothly.

"And your answer, my lady?" Master Parry wondered. "I must say, it would be a matter to be wondered at, my lord to wed a lad, knowing him a lad, and pass him off to all the world as his true and loving wife. Of course, there would be no children of the marriage, and the world would pity you. But that need be no hindrance; he is a fine man and would treat you well, John..."

"Oh cease your prattling, Master Parry! The notion is ridiculous, and in your heart you know it!"

But Master Parry had a firm ally in Kat. She combed my hair that night possessed by a strange ecstasy.

"Oh my dear lady – my dear child," she cooed, "if I might see you wed! I never thought it possible! Who could have her, I thought, she being what she is? But this suggestion of the Lord Admiral's would answer all our problems. You would have a husband and hold your head up in the world – and such a man! So big! And a cock to match, I daresay! Ah, he would keep you in your place; he'd soon slap your bum and make you squeal if you would be so bold as to answer him back; he'd master you! Ah, what would I give for such a one! And the beauty of it is that in the privacy of your bedcurtains you would share those pleasures which you have already shared, and both have gratification. He must have that in mind, in his proposing marriage. It's your sweet arse he's after...my lady!"

"We should not speak so," I said, strongly attracted by the picture she presented.

Kat chortled. "Have I struck home, sweeting? It would please you, life with Tom, I think! Kissings and cuddlings, and the fooling of the whole world with your saucy secret!"

"And Tom to lie with every night, and pleasing him..."

"And the tickling of his great beard all about your body!"

"It is a wondrous proposal he has made to me...he must love me immensely, to give up hope of more children, to want me more than womankind..."

"You will say yes?" beamed Kat, combing placidly.

"Kat!" I gasped, pulling away. "What are we about? We are quite distract. It can never be, and you know it!"

"But why not?" she said reasonably. "He knows your secret; he would never blab – he is a noble creature."

"Why not?" I answered slowly. "Because of policy."

Kat blinked at me. Plainly she had given no thought to something so irrelevant, so dull...

"There is more to Tom than the lover, Kat, and that more is dangerous. I know not what Tom's plans are, but believe me, he has plans, and they concern the kingdom. Who hitches himself to Tom's star risks a rough ride. We shall stay clear of him."

"My lady, you will never again receive such an offer," Kat said soberly. "A man that swears he loves you and offers marriage, knowing your true sex."

I suppressed that swift surge of despondency that rose within me. Oh yes, I was tempted by the prospect of that merry wicked life with Tom; no one could guess how strongly. But stronger in me was the instinct to mistrust him. Maybe my reason prompted it, or perhaps it was the warning given me by Robert Dudley. Indeed, so cautious was I, that I sent word back to Tom that I must refuse his offer at this stage, implying there might come a time when I would change my mind. I dared not cause him even the mildest annoyance by a direct refusal, for he might in pique undo me. He answered that at another time he might not take no for an answer, a response which I found ominous. Yes, I much mistrusted him, and events now proved me right. His folly near destroyed us all.

I awoke one bitter January morning to hear the sounds of shouting in the rooms below, the clink of weapons, a sudden scream. I leapt from my bed and flung my robe about me. I called for Kat; she did not come. Blanche ap Harry joined me at the stairhead, white-faced, in her nightgown. There were men-at-arms below. At the bottom of the stairs stood Sir Robert Tyrwhit, who had been sent by the Council to prove me guilty of treason. And all because of Thomas.

"Send Mistress Ashley to me," I said.

"Mistress Ashley has been taken," I was told. "And Master Parry also. They will answer in the Tower the accusations put to them."

My heart went out to poor Kat, to poor Master Parry. "They have done no wrong," I protested. "They are both good kind folk whose interest only is to serve me."

"We shall discover the terms of that same service," answered Sir Robert grimly.

Now I learned that Lord Seymour was arrested. He had attempted to get possession of the king, entering the royal apartments by night, killing Ned's dog, which had barked – this I knew Ned would not willingly forgive – and using a master key. At Sudeley Castle they had found a stock of arms against the day when Tom would lead an army, and two hundred thousand crowns' worth of silver. He had worked with the master of the Bristol mint to turn plate into coin. He had openly spoken of the need for the death of Somerset, of widening Ned's personal power, with himself at his right hand. His offer of marriage to myself was part of his great scheme of things, and thereby I was implicated in his monstrous fantasy.

By trickery and menace Sir Robert Tyrwhit sought to wring confession from me. When I replied with all the dignity of my position he reminded me that I was but a subject. He hinted to me that if I would consent to put the blame on Kat and Thomas Parry, my crimes might be forgiven me because that I was young. I could not, even if I would, for there was no crime for which to answer. I knew this. I knew my innocence and I protested it in strong terms. I insisted – and I wrote as much to the Protector – that I would never marry, nor would Kat so advise me, without the consent of the King's Majesty, of the Lord Protectors, of the Council. Tyrwhit did accuse me then of being rumoured to be with child by Thomas and I laughed him to scorn, though I quaked within for fear they might pursue this matter beyond the bounds of propriety. But Sir Robert was himself embarrassed at the notion, and seemingly recounted this rumour but to test me.

He was still at Hatfield in February, and now introduced his odious wife to be my governess. He said that Mistress Ashley was not deemed fit. I raged and stormed and I demanded Kat's reinstatement. He showed me papers writ by Kat within the Tower, in which she had recounted how Tom came into my bedchamber for sport against my modesty; she told about the cutting of the black velvet gown; she specified that Katherine was present, that all was done with Katherine's cognisance. I was ashamed and angry to know that my foolishness was become common knowledge. And yet it was but foolishness – how else could it appear? For no one ever thought to ask nor Kat nor Thomas Parry that one question which would have damned us all: tell me, is the Lady Elizabeth a boy from Bisley? – answer truly or meet those shall force your answer from you!

Many a night I wept for Kat and Thomas, dear friends frightened and abused for my sake; but reason told me that folly alone was our communal crime, and reason is a wise counsellor. And it was Tom whose life they sought, not mine.

But what of Tom? Imprisoned and accused, at bay, should he resort to spite and vindictiveness we were all undone. Thirty-three charges were his to deny, and of one at least he could well clear himself: 'I never did intend marriage to the Lady Elizabeth. How could I? She is a boy.'

"What does he answer?" I asked tremulously.

"It is a charge of treason," they said shrugging. "How may he answer? He says nothing."

And thus it was with Tom. An honourable man unto the end, he answered nothing. He who might have brought me down with his own fall went to his death on Tower Hill, and they said he joked upon the scaffold, and, much offending Bishop Latimer, died laughing.

Sometimes my body shook to think how close we all had come to ruin, Kat, Blanche, Parry and myself. Illness became a way of life with me – head pains, aching eyes, dazzling lights with jagged edges at the outer rim of vision. I believed myself spied upon, watched to see if I wept for Tom, therefore I showed no sorrow; but my body spoke for me.

In good time Mistress Ashley was restored to me, subdued as I; and Parry also. We lived very quiet. When my health did permit, I found relief in study. Master Ascham was become most dear to me. This wise man said I worked with dignity and gentleness, I had no womanly weakness, my perseverance was equal to that of a man.

I began a little to recover my good health, and sometimes in our relief we laughed about our danger passed. I said to Kat: "The one thing that I feared above all else was that poor Master Parry in his fright should say 'The Lady Elizabeth? I swear it, he is as loyal a subject as you or I!'"

Sixteen years old now, I am come to London. My resolve is to have nothing more to do with men, to eschew all talk of wedlock, to make plain my resolve never to marry. My clothes are sombre, almost unadorned. Few jewels about my person gleam, no trace of gold but that which shows in the auburn of my hair. "She would have us think she never tempted the Lord Admiral," they say of me. I am unmoved, my dignity unruffled. I ride through the streets of London, my household about me in a great procession. The people stare and cheer; they cry: "God save Your Grace! God save the Lady Elizabeth!"

I find this is most pleasing to me.

II

Robert Dudley's father was the new-risen star. In the summer he had put down rebellion, and on his return, triumphant, he had outmanoeuvred the Duke of Somerset. Persuading Edward that his uncle was a treacherous enemy, Dudley had won Ned's affection and become supreme in power.

Edward had not grown tall. Through overworking on his prayer book he was become short-sighted, and his face was grave and pale. It had been said that Somerset had kept him at his studies to keep him from statecraft, and that Dudley, by correcting this, had flung him into manly sports the which were equally demanding of his now frail-seeming frame. I spoke with him; I tried to make him laugh. I reminded him of his singing that lewd ballad 'Cherry Lane', and how he once wrote 'great eggs' when he meant 'great works'; but he was grown so solemn and would speak only upon religious matters, questioning me closely as to what it was that I believed.

Robert Dudley, on the other hand, was grown even more handsome than before. We were wary of each other, even hostile. I did not wholly trust his father, and I thought that Robert himself seemed a little uncomfortable about the prominence into which the Dudley family – for Robert had many brothers and sisters – had been thrust. Robert, fiercely loyal to his father, would hear no word against him; moreover, having been correct in his assessment of Tom's character, he was hard put not to say he had told me so; and though he did not say it, he all too clearly thought it.

Robert, since I last beheld him, had seen military action. He had been with his father and his brothers riding from Warwick Castle into Norfolk where the rebels lay; he had slept in the camp and been amongst the fighting in Norwich, when they put the rebels down. I longed to ask about it, wishing I had been there also, and not wishing him to know how much I envied him. Indeed, I hated him, because I had vowed never to find man fair again, and Robert was more than a little beautiful.

"I have to speak with you upon a certain matter," he said to me in an urgent tone. "Stand aside a little with me."

Ridiculous the way my heart jumped, how swiftly I acquiesced, I who so misliked him. He will speak to me of the way his affections tend, I thought; how he wished I had been with him in Norfolk. We stood together in a narrow embrasure, and a small wind came in cold, shifting the arras with a rustle.

"There is a rumour current," Robert said without preamble. "It is said that my father intends to make you his wife, and thereby grow closer to the throne. It is insufferable...the spread of whisper. On his behalf I strongly deny it, and if you should hear the same, know it for rumour only, and deny it also."

Rage flared in me. "I need no privy word of warning from you to deny so vile a rumour, Robert Dudley. Your father has a wife; and even were he chaste and at liberty and on his knees before me begging for my hand I would not have him!"

Robert was now incensed in his turn. "Any woman courted by my father would be fortunate. But as I say, the matter does not arise. It is a rumour and no more, and we were angry when we heard of it."

"You have grown much above yourselves," I glowered, "in taking offence at that which is offensive only to myself, a princess of the royal blood."

"Then I heartily repent me of my words," said Robert passionately, suddenly contrite, "for I believe you know, Your Grace, I never would offend you for the world."

And with these words came a look from his eyes that took all my rage from me in the instant and caused my face to show it, whether I would or no. He bowed and kissed my hand and left me, and I hated him the more, for I believed he knew his own power and his beauty, and had used it with effect on foolish women, and believed me one.

"It is a marriage of policy," Kat soothed me.

"How may it be?" I seethed. "What is Amy Robsart? Nothing at all. Her father is a nobody – merely a knight with some fields in Norfolk. Could he have – no I won't believe it! – could he have fallen in love with her?"

"Be still, my pet," cooed Kat, retrieving the pieces of the torn letter from my grip. "What can Robert Dudley be to you? You never could have wed him! You never can wed, sweetheart, and I think that sometimes you forget as much! If news of others' marriage reduces you to tears and tantrums you had best learn fortitude, and swiftly, for marriage is the way of it."

Her reproof was fair, but so also was my anger. John Dudley made no secret of using his offspring as pawns in the game of power and influence – Mary wed to Henry Sidney, Edward's closest friend, Catherine to Henry Hastings a descendant of the House of York, John to Ann Seymour, and the odious Guildford to poor Jane Grey. So why did he permit this marriage between Robert and this obscure country girl of no repute? Was it a love match? I heard that she was but sixteen, my own age, Robert's.

"Why should you care?" said Kat. "You are well at your ease. Hatfield is your home; you are high in favour, and all care lies behind you. Attend this wedding; they wish it. Your presence will much grace the occasion and you do the Dudleys honour by acceptance. You have no need of Robert Dudley. He is not even handsome. Why, he's dark as a gipsy. He'll never be the man that Thomas was, a seafarer, a hero. So he will wed some wench – why should you care? Be there, and show that you do not."

I regarded her dubiously. "Is it possible? Is it possible, Kat, to be a boy, and yet more beautiful than any woman, moreover, than one who is to be a bride?"

"If anyone may do so, dearest," Kat said, "it is you."

It savours somewhat of vainglory to admit to the possession of surpassing radiance. I know it, I who do possess it. But I do recall the words of one who was there on that day in June at Sheen down by the Thames, when Robert married Amy, and his brother John wed Ann Seymour, and I was their most renowned guest.

"You were the embodiment of what our age holds to be most excellent. Your white skin, your resplendent hair, your high smooth forehead, your pale brows and fair eyelashes – these combined with your natural dignity and your gracefulness made you the cynosure of all eyes. All paled into insignificance beside you. You were like a young goddess come amongst us, the splendour of the sun about you. Every man there ardently desired you and wept to know you were so far out of his reach. Believe me, you were the most beautiful of all."

Yes, Robert never lied.

Those last summers spent at Hatfield, while Edward yet reigned, and the pain of Thomas fading, were a peaceful time. Hatfield was now officially my home, and a man I trusted, William Cecil, kept my affairs in order. I had now, as it were, a space to give some freedom to my thoughts, to permit myself to ask myself what would become of me.

I rode out by myself amongst the green parkland and dismounting, sitting in the grass beneath the oak trees, pondered my fate.

It had been stupid of me to give way to passion on learning that Robert Dudley was to marry. What was he to me, after all? He was of an age to wed and it would be surprising if he did not so. But what of me? I also was of an age to wed. I had exacted a promise from Edward that he would not force me to marry. I had impressed upon him that I proposed to live and die a virgin, eschewing fleshly desires, and he, now grown religious, heartily approved of this, and said he wished all maidens were as virtuous as myself. Therefore I did not fear the sudden onset of a suitor. But I was seventeen – where might I turn for love?

There was a stable lad at Hatfield who admired me, a long-haired brown and dusty youth with a square jaw and strong arms. He would help me from my horse, holding me a little longer than was necessary. Once in such circumstances, our eyes met, and we by a sudden mutual impulsion, fell into a violent embrace. I was startled at the strength of my own hunger. I pressed my body against his, I half devoured him in my eagerness, my mouth a-slobber, my tongue twined about his, my hands gripping tufts of his hair, awakening in him a lust as rampant as my own. Gasping, we untangled ourselves, each bewildered as the other, and both now wary and ashamed. We were henceforth most proper and correct with each other. There may be even yet an aged greybeard stable-man somewhere in Hertfordshire who recalls receiving in his youth a kiss that was no maiden's kiss from Elizabeth, princess.

My face showed me no cause for concern. The legacy of Ambrose's family gave me a clear smooth skin; I had no trace of beard or stubble, and my neck was slender. The odd small hair I could pluck easily enough; it seemed that in my physical persona I was safe enough. Seventeen...the age at which my father died. But I was hale.

True, I was troubled then by the recurrent megrims and the head pains which were brought about by leaning over my books and reading all hours of the day and night; but there was no hint of that wasting consumption to which Tudor males were prone. I was thin but not ailing. Therefore what had I to fear? I would grow old, Elizabeth, a virgin, living quietly as any nun, with study and needlework and horseriding to pass my time, and in the peace of Hatfield see out my days in honour and tranquility.

Needless to say, the prospect filled me with depression of spirit – I, who as a boy had longed to sail the oceans in the company of a strong and handsome sea captain. I laughed to see the irony of it, for in all honesty and in despite of common sense I knew that this was my ambition still.

I wondered sometimes where was Xavier, that one soul who could bring about my downfall if he chose – or if he did not choose to do so could live handsomely at my expense, myself a pawn in any game he wished to play. Into my dreams sometimes his image floated, disembodied, like a severed head, his eyes a-glitter and his teeth bared as he said to me again what he had said at Bisley: 'Mayhap I shall come to Hatfield and see you in your fine surroundings and pay court to you and you shall learn of me that sodomy can be pleasurable...' Well, another had taught me that! But Xavier yet lived, and while he lived he was a threat. 'And you shall not refuse me,' he had said, 'for fear I give away your little secret.' I shuddered at the prospect.

But the months passed by and yet he did not come, and I was left with my precious empty tranquility. Tranquility that, had I known it, hung by a thread that was about to snap. Tranquility dependent on the life of Edward.

We knew that Ned had been ill the preceding April. Measles and smallpox were the cause, but there was also sweating sickness about and the first fears for Ned's safety were voiced. He recovered from these perilous diseases, and we gave thanks. But now he had a congestion of the lungs and was grown weak and ill, and it was Robert Dudley's father who was ever present at his side. John Dudley was now Duke of Northumberland, and having persuaded

Edward that the Lord Protector Somerset was treacherous, had had the man beheaded, and now governed solely, and, as we were to discover, deviously.

I wrote several times to Edward but he did not reply. It was, however, through Robert Dudley that I learned that all was not as it should be. He wrote to tell me about the great sight he had witnessed, of which he knew I would be pleased to hear. Sir Hugh Willoughby's three ships were embarking to discover a Northern Passage through the Arctic regions to Cathay. "I was there upon the quayside," he wrote. "There was cannon and shot, and cheering from the crowd. The ships were hung with sky-blue damask. If one should send you word to come, go not with him."

I thought at first that Robert must have made an error, for it was not likely one should ask me to have aught to do with Willoughby; but when I had done with smirking I perceived his meaning and was quick to act upon it. The month was then May; in July a messenger from Greenwich came to Hatfield with the news that Edward was on his deathbed and I was summoned to be present when my sister was proclaimed queen. I counterfeited swooning, and Kat took me to my bed. We gave out that I would attend upon Northumberland when my health was recovered.

Omens and portents enough had warned the realm of my brother's fate. On the day before he had set out for Greenwich, two had drowned, and on Ludgate Hill a dog had been seen with the limb of a dead child in its teeth. On the night of his approaching death there had been a monstrous storm in London, with the rain so fierce it made a flood, uprooting trees, destroying houses; and a church spire in the city crumpled like a toy,and afterwards came hailstones red as blood, and all this in July.

We waited news of the proclamation of Queen Mary's reign, but it did not come. At Northumberland's instigation it was Jane Grey named queen, that quiet devout mouse whose life was governed by the Word of God, and what good, I asked myself, would she be for the realm of England, with its roisterers and sailors? Certain it was that we would not remove from Hatfield at this juncture, for we well supposed that Mary also would have some thoughts on this. Where was she?

Like myself, she had been warned. She was in Norfolk and, I later learned, pursued in her flight by Robert Dudley and his troops, sent out by Northumberland to capture her; but they missed her, and she made her stand at Framlingham and all the loyal of the land flocked to her.

Nine days after Edward's death, Princess Mary was proclaimed queen, and there was dancing in the streets, and bonfires, and the ringing of bells; and rightly so, for she was King Henry's elder daughter and the lawful heir. Now we might come from Hatfield.

I had not seen Mary closely for some six years. I was elated to be coming once again to London, which was decked for celebration. My heart was light that day in late July as I rode towards Aldgate with a great procession of my own, there to meet with my sister's triumphal procession and to join together and enter the city. Nor did I at first see any reason to feel anything but joy in our reunion. But as we rode in majesty amongst the cheering citizens, the gaudy decorations, the garlands and the high-held bunches of flowers, to the sound of riotous peals of bells and the braying of trumpets, I was beset gradually with unease.

Mary looked so old, so worn. Her purple velvet was too bold and dark a colour for her visage, which had a yellow tinge and was lined about the eyes like wrinkled parchment. I saw the faces of the crowd that cheered because she was their queen, as she passed on before me; but I saw in those same faces as they turned to me a different kind of welcome, a pleasure and surprise. "God bless Your Grace!" they said to me – not because I was queen, but because I was I.

An older woman, past her prime, followed by, as it seemed, a younger, pale and fresh of cheek, a maiden moreover reputed to have been loved and pursued by the most handsome rakehell of his day, a maiden of nineteen... It was a contrast I saw plain enough, and when the euphoria of her present situation had a little modified, I thought that Mary would begin to see it also.

And so to Richmond, that loveliest of palaces, to await the coronation.

Ah, this is a beautiful place – who could not be well content within these walls! Placed at the river's edge, ensconced in water meadows beside a garden rich in flowers and orchards of pear and apple trees and sunny walls of peaches, the palace glittered in its intricate perfection. Topped by towers and pinnacles, each with its onion dome, its gold and silver vane upon which the wind played and made music sweet as any harp, the palace was full of light, and the sun poured into the long galleries. The scents of summer floated in the air.

I was most joyous to be there. Caught up in the great excitement I turned back from the window and hugged dear Kat, shining-eyed, all doubts and apprehensions dissipated in the all-pervasive pleasure of the moment.

"Who would have thought it?" I breathed. "Whoever would have credited it that I should be here, now, at the heart of it all!"

She hugged me in return. She did not need to speak; she understood. I moved about the room.

"This is a fine chamber," I murmured, touching the bed, the chairs, the tapestries. "Ah, Kat!" I said and paused, stricken. "What a vile ungrateful wretch I am..."

"My dear?" she frowned.

"Robert," I said helplessly. "What will become of Robert?"

Robert had been captured at King's Lynn. They were all in the Tower, the Dudleys – Northumberland and his five sons, all under threat of execution, dependent upon Mary's mercy. Northumberland must be condemned; what else for one who tried to thwart the wishes of King Henry and the natural succession? And Guildford, for that he wed Jane Grey and would be consort to an usurper – not much was given for his chances. But the others, they were only loyal sons, obedient to their powerful father. Surely this was understood?

Amy Robsart was permitted to visit Robert in the Tower. I winced to think of these brief poignant meetings – the swift embraces while the guards looked on, the emptiness that followed. But she was not with child, Amy. Three years wed; no infant. That did not sound like a love match to me. But then, I wondered cynically, what did I know of such?

From a life of agreeable seclusion punctuated by brief intermittent visits to London, I was now thrust in the public gaze and very much spied upon, so much so that I scarce believed myself secure within my chamber and never even with the doors locked dared stand naked. I took my bath with a voluminous nightgown about me, and Kat and Blanche at hand, and all ears pricked to catch the rustle of the arras, all eyes strained for the glimpse of spy hole in the wainscoting.

My sister worked on me to seek out my religious leanings, a matter of no more concern to me than was entirely reasonable; but a matter of great urgency to her. Dreary scenes of my hoped-for conversion to the old faith followed, much of conscience and doctrine and regular attendance at Mass, while I trod a fine line between acquiescence and hesitation, which gave me more headaches than my studies ever did.

While this continued I was pestered by the sudden emergence of a rich and varied list of possible bridegrooms and requested to make comment on my preference. A thousand times I must have repeated my earnest plea to live and die a maid; nonetheless I was invited to consider amongst others Don Carlos of Spain, a child of eight; Emmanuel Philibert, Duke of Savoy, who would take me well clear of England; and a bevy of Italian dukes.

If I was not minded to travel far from home, there was one near at hand that some would have me favour. This was Edward Courtenay, a true Plantagenet, descendant from King Edward IV, imprisoned in the Tower for fifteen years and now released, and strong in popery.

He was there at Richmond, this scion of the old stock, a pleasant-featured man, pale, fair, and stupid.

"Women!" he said to me, licking his lips. "The most wonderful creatures on God's earth, and made for man's delight and comfort. I've been deprived of man's due rights for so long that I'll need a lifetime to find recompense. I'll prove a lion in lust; the world shall see..." He squinted at me over the rim of his goblet. "They say you're learned. They say you read and write as well as any man. That's not my way. I like a maiden to be simple – to look up to her lord..."

Ambassadors moved amongst us, casting nets for the unwary, noting all we said or did and spying on each other – Simon Renard for the Emperor Charles, always at Mary's ear, plainly suspicious of my good intent and weaving I know not what web of rumour against me; Antoine de Noailles for the King of France, who tried to make me say I longed to be in Mary's place. Mary was crowned now; we had witnessed it, I in a gown of white and silver with a coronet too heavy for my head, the first to vow allegiance.

And indeed I was become a figure of some import. Heir to the throne by rightful succession, and moreover, heir to the throne of a woman already old, a woman without sons, a woman who was beginning to make every effort to foist upon the people the old faith which they had already well rejected. I on the other hand practised the established way. Small wonder I was marked. Staunch Protestants came privily to me, demanding reassurance that I did indeed propose to follow Edward's faith; staunch Catholics hinted to me of reward if I would turn about. One came to me with a plot already hatched to displace Mary and hurry me to the throne, would I but give the word; and this all in a crowded room with Mary's eye upon me. Every day for me was a field of snares and I walked warily, never in repose, testing each step before I placed my toe. I longed to quit this place I had at first found fair.

I begged leave to withdraw to Hatfield; Mary refused. She no doubt wished me to be where she could see me, and those who buzzed about me. But I could not withstand the pressure of this communal cat-and-mouse game in which all seemed to indulge, and I lurked in my apartments as much as I dared; yet this also was seen as suspect, for those who could not see me supposed that I was entertaining those that worked against them and I was obliged to show myself merely to prove I was not plotting with whoever was not present.

Finally I was permitted to depart from court, not to Hatfield but to Ashridge. It made no difference to me by then, I would have gladly gone almost anywhere. Mary gave me stern injunctions to pursue the Faith, to listen to the voices of the priests that she would send and to open my heart to the true Word of God. I pledged in return my true devotion to her and asked that she give no credence to those who spread false rumours about my intentions, but to give me the chance to prove all slanders false.

Sober gentlemen came to me with warnings to stay on the straight and narrow path and steer clear of all heretics and Frenchmen, and I vowed I would do all in my power to please the queen. We said these things, we swore our good intent, but it was clear enough none trusted other, nor believed in any protestation given.

It was December when I came away. Never had those gloomy beechwoods seemed so beautiful, those dark and ancient walls so hospitable, those draughty passageways so full of cheer.

But it was not a happy Yuletide. So insidious was the influence at court it seemed its tendrils yet pursued me, with the whisper on the stair, the covert glance from servant to servant, the unease whenever messenger approached. Was I still watched? Which of my household was suborned? And though I was yet free, it could only be a matter of time before my froward sister thrust some vile suitor upon me and I must once again repeat my vows of chastity.

"And Courtenay," I said to Thomas Parry, "has told me himself that he intends to be a womanizer of the greatest magnitude; therefore any notion of coupling him with me must be out of the question."

"Bombast," confided Parry in return. "Edward Courtenay's boasts concerning women are false and full of wind. I have it on the very best authority that, confronted with a woman, he could never raise his lance."

Ascertaining the source of his information and judging it to be a viable one, I pondered this.

"His years within the Tower," continued Thomas, "with his boy servants for his companions, have prejudiced his leanings in favour of his own sex. I have heard that if all does not go well for him in England he purports to travel overseas...to Italy, where boys are most voluptuous and cheap."

I recalled the vacuity of this man. There was no denying his beauty. He was of that fair and florid nature such as the fourth Edward had been, and he was Plantagenet, therefore of worthy ancestors. Ah, but they said that he was weak and spineless. Was this so? And would it matter? Yet I myself had judged him stupid. If he were my consort, would it be enough that one of us were strong? He was personable. And it was possible that I might grow to love him. He had to all appearances a fine well-shaped body. It was not inconceivable that, each with a predilection for the male, we might enjoy a marriage of some satisfaction, sharing our delicious secret and presenting to the world an image of conjugal felicity. Yes, this was possible.

The notion pleased me. But we must tread so cautiously. Sir

Thomas Wyat's plan was treason of the first magnitude, and, moreover, financed by French gold. Sir Peter Carew and Courtenay were to raise troops in Devonshire, Wyat himself in Kent, Sir James Crofts in Wales, and in Leicestershire the Duke of Suffolk, all moving towards London, to save England from the yoke of popery and vile dependence upon Spain, and to make Edward Courtenay Earl of Devonshire my bridegroom, a man that loved his own sex. Consideration of the matter was preferable to warding off a swarm of suitors of my sister's choosing.

"Inform Sir Thomas Wyat that I give favourable consideration to his suggestion – but consideration only, and no more than that."

Late in January Master Parry came from London with news that took all other thought from my mind and caused me turmoil such as I had never known.

"Lord Robert Dudley tried and condemned..."

"Condemned?" I blanched.

"To the traitor's death," said Master Parry. "To be hanged, drawn and quartered."

I all but swooned. If ever I had needed confirmation of the truth about my sentiments concerning that youth I had it now. Recovering my composure with all the skill at my command I set about to make my preparations for a journey to London. I hunted out the holy beads my sister gave me, discarded in a drawer, and all the many crucifixes. I was about to promise to turn papist on the instant, if in return my dear and generous sister would consent to spare his life.

SEVEN

I

No such sacrifice was required of me.

Robert was reprieved, or simply overlooked; for suddenly the world changed, events taking such a turn that Mary must put all other matters from her and defend her new-gained throne. Within the month it was I the one in need of clemency.

"Lord save us," Thomas Parry moaned, and, in the manner of those receiving ill tidings, added: "We are lost."

We were not lost, but we were patently in danger. The rebellion had broken out too soon. The messengers whom we received at Ashridge spoke of collapse, of plans revealed, and Courtenay himself suspected of betrayal. Now not for all the world would I have quit Ashridge. I was advised to make for some castle that might be fortified against attack, but that were to admit myself guilty of treasonable intent; best brave it out; best to know nothing. I took to my bed when Mary wrote to me and asked me to return to court for my own safety's sake. I gave answer that I was too sick to travel.

Outside the walls of Ashridge the January winds rattled the bare branches in a dismal dreary noise, and I lay beneath the blankets listening to that encroaching storminess which in itself echoed the turmoil of the realm.

Notwithstanding the disintegration of his well-laid plans, Sir Thomas Wyat had raised rebellion in Kent and marched on London; many flocked to join him as he went. I tried to picture him triumphant, but his throw had depended upon the rise of Courtenay, and I knew well enough now I would want nothing to do with that gentleman. My initial judgement had been correct; I would have done better to have given no encouragement to Sir Thomas Wyat. I had been swayed by my emotions, by my hopes, the foolish notion of myself and Courtenay living as lovers. I had been wrong so to indulge, and now I might well pay for this lapse.

But might he yet succeed? Did hatred of the Spaniard so prevail that God's Anointed could be displaced? The people would decide it. I believed they would stand by their sovereign; I was proved right. There was fighting in the streets of London; the rebellion was quashed, and largely, I must in all fairness add, by Mary's own bravery. Unfortunately she now had leisure to attend to me.

"My dearest lady," Kat whispered, shaking me awake. "There are men below..."

"Oh no, not that again...," I gasped, angry and afraid.

"They are physicians..."

I sat up in bed, monstrous fearful. "I will not see them."

"They will not be gainsaid."

Indeed they stood there in the doorway, Doctor Owen and Doctor Wendy, physicians to the queen. I must have looked diseased enough to satisfy the most mistrustful, for, ironically, since I had taken to my bed my limbs had swelled, especially at the ankle, also my eyelids; my natural pallor had increased till I was ghostly white, and, with my hair down and dishevelled, I was a sad sight and fearful to behold.

"We are to escort you to London, my lady."

"I am not well, as you may plainly see."

"We are to judge the same, Your Grace permitting."

"What would you do?" shrieked Kat. "What more is needful than to see my lady's condition with your own eyes? She is ashen pale and faint; her face is swollen – "

"My ankles also," I added, "and my throat aches. It pains me to speak. I could hold no converse. Indeed, any journey that I were obliged to undertake might be my last. I beg you to consider, sirs, your personal embarrassment, should I die under your ministrations!"

Alas, the learned fellows were bold enough to take that risk. The sheets and blankets heavily about my midriff I permitted them to press my ankles and to prod my face and neck. They then retired and muttered together. They pronounced me suffering from watery humours. They requested me to stand. Kat brought my dressing robe. I cautiously removed myself from bed, and stood. Lord, but the room was cold! They would have me walk up and down. I could do so; therefore it was adjudged no hazard for my condition to quit this place and travel by litter to London.

"But the month is February!" Kat protested. "One does not travel in the snow!"

"There is no snow," they answered patiently, "and you will see to it, Mistress Ashley, that the lady is provided with all necessary for her warmth."

Gentlemen from London now descended upon us, adding the weight of their authority to the opinion of the physicians. There was nothing for it, it would seem, but that I must make the journey and that right soon.

"There is nothing I would sooner do than go to Westminster and present my humble greetings to my beloved sister," I maintained, with chattering teeth, "but you see for yourselves I am not blessed with health. I do fear the rigours of the journey. If I might wait till spring brings clement weather..."

I might not. Protesting, swooning and stumbling, I was led unto my waiting litter. I was not well, I knew it, but it was impossible to separate my physical condition from my state of mind, for I was in a cold sweat of terror, knowing I must answer to those who would judge me with hostility, and knowing also that they had cause.

But Mary would be merciful. Or would she? For we learned as we entered London that poor Jane Grey was executed, Guildford also; and we passed gallows newly standing, with the corpses of the rebels hanging there. A terrible foreboding came upon me that before the week was out my own would join them.

I was taken to the palace of Whitehall, which at that time seemed to me a dark forbidding place. King Henry had died here; this was in my mind as I stepped from the litter, in so desperate a dread I scarce could stand.

"I wish to see my sister." They ignored my tremulous request and escorted me to a dark part of the palace, very strait, with guards at every turn. Low-ceilinged, with a maze of narrow passageways, the buildings that made up the palace sprawled in rambling fashion along Thames side. With crenellated roofs, small courtyards, stone gatehouses straddling its walkways, its rooms small, dark and wainscoted, it covered over twenty acres, space enough for Mary and myself to live in separateness and never to meet, as was her intent.

Her aged chancellor Stephen Gardiner, Bishop of Winchester, was instructed to question me and find me guilty. This vile old man received me for questioning, no benign disinterested judge with mandate to discover innocence, but one so full of hatred for me that his eyes glowed with a horrid light as if they would pierce through me.

"Your only course," he told me, "is to throw yourself upon the mercy of Her Gracious Majesty. Your guilt is proven; you are lost."

"My guilt is not proven," I replied. "Suspected only."

And he knew as much. He loathed me, but he could prove nothing.

"I advise you to confess," he said. "Your fellow conspirators have confessed. You are doomed. You will suffer the severest punishment. Confess; and pray that the mercy of the queen will save you from certain death, for nothing else will."

"My innocence shall save me," I maintained. "And innocent I am, and loyal to the queen and ever like to be."

He almost gnashed his teeth, for nothing could be proved, though he would surely work for it.

"You shall say different when our evidence is gathered," promised he. "Nor think that who you are shall save you from God's justice."

"God's justice I do not fear," I answered stoutly, all this the more marvellous, for my nose and eyes were streaming from a head-cold and my answers given from behind a handkerchief. "And while I lodge here this I strongly will maintain."

"May I remind Your Grace," he said ironically, "that your lodging here is like to be a temporary matter, and that apartments for the proven guilty wait for you...elsewhere."

The Tower! Here Thomas Wyat lay, and Courtenay; here had Jane Grey and her husband Guildford Dudley stayed, in that brief time before their execution; and the wretched Anne Boleyn. I was frightened now. Satisfied that he had got the measure of me, Bishop

Gardiner gave me respite; but when we parted it was understood between us that his intention was to bring me to the block.

I never did believe they would dare to take me to the Tower, my guilt unproven: I was wrong. They came for me and told me to make preparations – I might bring six ladies only, and three of these were chosen by the queen. I must make no delay. My protests were in vain. I was permitted to write to my sister, but was ordered to hurry, so that our boat might catch the tide. I wrote the letter slowly, and more slow as I continued, while they fidgeted about me, urging speed. With my delay and carefulness the tide was passed; we could not leave until the morrow.

That night I did not sleep. I lay upon my bed, Kat with me, and we whispered our fears.

"I shall never leave that place alive," I said and shivered.

"They will not dare mistreat you," Kat replied, bravely but unconvincingly.

"I pray you may be forgiven, Kat," I wept into my pillow, "that ever you took me from Bisley."

"That were unkindliness to speak so," Kat said reproachfully. "I never wished you harm, no, and I've done my best at all times to make things well."

"I know it, Kat. Forgive me for my ungratefulness." I said contritely. "Will you come with me tomorrow, Kat, and be with me?"

"I will, God give me strength."

"Had we guessed what would befall us, would we yet have done as we did, Kat? How could we have foreseen, so long ago at Bisley, that time would bring us to this fearful moment?"

"But would you wish, my dear one, to be back there now, a wool merchant – for so you would have been, I understand – and never to have seen palaces and princes, nor known my lord of Seymour's wicked ways? Would you sooner have remained a country boy and lived a quiet life? Now answer me truly."

"God help me, but I would not, even now," I answered soberly.

And in the morning, in the rain, we were taken to the Tower as prisoners.

Lord! how silent was that place by night after the last sounding of the bell, save for the slithering of water down the weeping walls somewhere in the passageways! All night, as it seemed, this water trickled, and the stone gave off a foul and mossy vapour.

We were housed in an upper room, a vaulted chamber with three narrow windows and a grim door with a lock upon it. We had a fireplace, but we were never warm in spite of flame. There was a monstrous chill about that place, part emanation from the thickness of the stone, and in part the dank air heavy with the stench of fear, and of much else besides: in the passageway outside, three privies gave on to the river.

Yet my lot was not such an evil one. Sir John Brydges, the Lieutenant of the Tower, was kind, and when we ate our meals it was to his own lodging we repaired; and he permitted me to tread the walkway along the battlements for recreation. Although our lodging was small and cramped, both Kat and Blanche were there to protect my person, and about my bed I had a curtain hung, where I had the illusion of some privacy.

I was not to be left in peace, however, for I was sent for by the Councillors under Stephen Gardiner, to be close questioned on that same subject as had been begun at Whitehall.

"Sir Thomas Wyat has confessed...he writ you letters. Your Grace was visited at Ashridge. You were advised to move to a fortified castle...to what purpose? Sir James Crofts...you know this man, you had converse with him, you knew he undertook to lead rebellion in Wales..."

I heard my own replies – my straight denials, my question why I should not remove to another of my houses if I so chose, my inability to prevent Thomas Wyat that great traitor from writing to me if it was his intent, my insistence that I had received no such letters. I heard my voice – and grew alarmed. It was a boy's voice, low and hoarse. How could my accusers not be cognisant of the same? How was it they could not see through my dissembling? I lied, all that I said was false, but I myself was false – how could they not guess as much?

On the contrary, the Earl of Arundel fell to his knees and begged forgiveness for distressing me with these vain matters. It then occurred to me that something in my bearing or my helplessness had touched him. Kat said: "Some men there be that cannot bear to see a lady ringed about with foes, and needs must give her succour; of such is chivalry." This selfsame chivalry did monstrously affront my enemy Gardiner, whose glowering look proclaimed that he was not like to be softened by my weakness and quitted me but to work further for my downfall.

The winds of March blew about the battlements where I walked upon the leads atop the curtain wall. This yard-wide walkway from the tower of my imprisonment to the next tower was my parkland, hunting ground, long gallery. Below me, to one side, were the roofs of the houses built within the Tower; far away to the south, the distant Essex marshes. Guards followed and preceded me at first, but sometimes when it rained they waited in the doorway, watching; after all, where might I go?

At the far end of the walk, there was a small locked door which led into the further tower. One day I paused there as was my wont, and leaned my back upon it, and a voice behind the door whispered my name. That is, it said:

"Elizabeth!"

So practised in impassivity was I by then that I betrayed no emotion nor surprise, but with my handkerchief about my mouth I asked who it was that spoke to me.

"Elizabeth! Thank God! At last you hear me. Don't you know my voice? Who else but Robert Dudley?"

God's truth, but in my own misfortunes I had forgot that he was here, nay, had been so for many months. I was so moved then that I could not speak.

"Elizabeth? Are you still there?"

"I am; but watched. How did you know that I was here, upon the leads?"

"They said you walked there. So I stand beside this door and speak your name upon the chance. I must have said 'Elizabeth' a hundred times. At last you hear me – the reward for my endeavour."

"Robert, how do you fare? Are you well treated?"

"Is any, lacking freedom?"

"My own imprisonment is sweeter, hearing you."

"I wish that I could see you."

"I am glad you do not. I am not well. My face is foul, my eyelids swollen like one stung by a bee. I am grown ugly."

"You were never beautiful," he said reasonably.

"I had some charm," protested I, affronted.

"Yes, you did, indeed you did!" said Robert warmly.

"I must go. My guards are waiting, gesturing."

"I will wait...I will speak to you again."

"But take no risks for my sake – promise me."

He did not promise; and my heart was almost light as I returned to my imprisonment.

Like Pyramus and Thisbe, we conversed on each side of that wall. We talked of horses and astrology, music and dress, anything but policy; and all this in brief snatches, while the guards lurked further off. We wondered whether they permitted us to speak, hoping we would speak of the rebellion, but we said nothing of that, nor of Northumberland, nor Jane, nor Guildford; one would have thought we met in some long gallery, with time to spare and nothing on our minds, yet both of us, as we then thought, under threat of execution.

And neither did we talk of Amy. We talked of Robert's tutor Doctor John Dee, whom the unlettered thought to be a sorcerer, for that he knew mathematics.

"He has been known to play upon the gullibility of those that fear him," Robert laughed. "And certainly he knows some tricks – sudden lights and sparks, papers that change colour, objects made to disappear; all things which have a rational explanation, but which, without the explanation, seem arcane. When he was at Cambridge he used magical effects upon the stage. He owns as master that Henry Cornelius Agrippa, the archmage of Louvain. He is the most widely learned man that ever I have known."

One day, my face close to the door, I said: "But Robert, are you well? And do you look as I remember?"

"I don't give much thought to appearance," he replied. "But since you saw me last, I have a fancy little beard."

"Brown, as your hair?"

"Of course! Not marigold-coloured, as yours would be!"

"Robert Dudley! How dare you speak so, to a woman!" I said, flustered and alarmed.

"Lord save us, how you do protest!" his voice came through the thickness of the door. "I know you are a woman, but you have not some of woman's sillier ways. Believe me, I know something about those! I intended it as a kindness when I said you were not womanly."

"I do not take it as a kindness," I sulked.

"Yes, I understand as much. But when I say that in my small knowledge of the ways of women, to be womanly means to simper, to withhold, to speak of meaningless matters, to wait upon compliments and abuse the while, then you will readily surmise it is no fault in you to seem unwomanly. And besides, your voice is low, not high and querulous, and since I cannot see you, I might in all good faith be talking to one of my own sex when I talk with you."

"But you are not," I answered blushing.

"No, I know it," he replied.

"And I would thank you, Robert Dudley, to refrain from such praise as is seen by its recipient as insult. My voice is low because I have a sore throat. And some have thought me beautiful though you do not. But when were you ever known for fine discernment? Others have more grace, more wit, more courtliness. You know much upon the subject of horses, but nothing of the hearts of women. And if you could but see me, you would find me fair enough. I wear a gown of crimson velvet, which does much become me!"

"Peace, peace," he laughed. "I see that you are very woman."

"Am I forgiven, dear Elizabeth?" he asked me through the door.

"For what?" I asked, startled and delighted at that which had preceded my name.

"I thought I had offended you."

"No, it was nothing," I said graciously.

"Then, may I request a favour of Your Grace?"

"Dear Robert, in this place I own nothing and may therefore give you nothing. In other circumstances..."

"This gift is yours to bestow, if you so wish it."

"Whatever can it be?"

"Do you remember when we were children and we played at Ashridge – Edward, Barnaby, and Harry Sidney?"

"Of course I do."

"And one day you and I were separate from the rest, and I asked you a question, and you would not reply."

My heart sank. It was not I of whom he asked the question. He had been eight years old, and so had she.

"Do you remember?" he persisted.

"No," I said unhappily.

"You do remember! I asked you about it once, and you said you would tell me when you were ready."

"I did?" Yes, that I recalled well enough.

"You did. I know it was a childish question. But – as if we were children still – give me the answer now. What better time than this? When may you be ready, if not now, when both of us may never..." he broke off. "Elizabeth...it would mean much to me."

A stupid tear coursed down my cheek. What would I not have given to have satisfied his so reasonable request?

"I am not ready," I repeated miserably, and I turned and stumbled from him, cursing the plight of all impostors.

Henceforth I was forbidden to walk upon the leads; perhaps they had observed my obvious distress.

But I might walk in the small walled garden, which was a joy to me. The month now being April there was birdsong all about, and primroses and violets growing. Three children of the Tower, one the son of the Keeper of the Wardrobe, played in that same garden, staring at me, smiling shyly as I passed.

One day the boy brought me a bunch of primroses, the dew yet on their petals. Their perfume recalled the coney warren at Hatfield, where flowers such as these grew in a little grove of trees. I thanked the boy; he was some four years old; we had converse. Another day he brought me violets; and one triumphant day a fistful of cowslips, wild flowers from a meadow without walls.

My pleasure at this coup was the more intense when I discovered deep amongst the flowers a folded scrap of paper, which I read by pressing the nosegay to my face.

"Yours unto death," Robert wrote. "I was wrong to trouble you. Tell the boy yes if I am still permitted to call you friend."

Tears came to my eyes. I bent down to the boy. "Tell the gentleman yes."

The boy sped off.

He came again another day with more cowslips; their bulk made it easier to hide the folded paper. "I am the happiest of men," wrote Robert.

No, thought I in great content, there is one happier.

Next day the boy came not by me, but pressed his face between the bars of the walled garden's gate.

"Psst! Mistress, I may bring you no more flowers..."

Thomas Wyat died the traitor's death. With his last words he made it plain that Courtenay and myself were innocent. Courtenay was set free; not I.

My captivity now grew more strait and I feared more for my life than ever I had previously; and not without cause. Sir John Brydges told me that he had received a warrant for my immediate execution.

"Fear not," he told me gruffly. "It was not signed by Her Majesty. It was a ploy by certain members of the Council to achieve your final removal. Another than myself might have obeyed its order; but I know there be those that wish your death, and I was wary. Yet we must be on our guard. They failed; but they will try again."

I understood him – the assassin's knife, the poisoned bread... How many secrets of that nature did these walls hide? Those little princes, as was generally assumed, their bones buried somewhere in this place... What if there were a secret entrance to my chamber? What if by night one came from Stephen Gardiner, who wished me dead? At night I clung to Kat; we listened, and we did not speak. We heard that ooze of water dripping down the passage walls and thought it footsteps.

It was one of my ladies who shrieked that the courtyard was full of a hundred armed soldiers; and rumour spread like plague that there was come a new Constable with particular instructions.

"God's truth," I gasped. "He comes to murder me."

It was plain that all believed the same.

"The scaffold of my Lady Jane," I breathed, "does it yet stand?"

"My lady," said Sir Henry Bedingfield. He was a ponderous slow man, some forty years of age. I found him ugly. He had a gross neck, a beak of a nose, flaccid hair, three chins, and a coarse face. "My first task," he said, "is to scotch those most malicious rumours of the purpose of my coming here. You do not know me yet. Lord save us, but what do you take me for? Indeed, I bring good news – the news of your release from this captivity."

"What, am I to be freed?" I cried in disbelief.

"That is, not exactly," answered he. "You are to be taken to a place of safety..."

"And after, murdered?" I demanded.

"Not at all," he answered irritably. "We are to proceed by river to Richmond; thence into the country."

"To another Tower perhaps? To Pomfret maybe, where I hear murders may be done quietly?"

"My lady! My task is difficult enough without this talk of murder. We simply go into the country, to your royal palace of Woodstock. My purpose there is to protect you."

"But I am to be yet your prisoner."

"Madam, that is an unavoidable truth. But given that much, if we both comport ourselves with dignity, we may yet weather all that is to come."

"You swear you have no order to dispose of me by secret means?"

"I swear it."

"Then I will go with you."

"Your Grace has no choice; but I thank you for your trust."

"I do not trust you, sir; I said that I would go with you."

"Sir John Brydges," I said, parting from him. "I am well aware of all that I owe you, for as I understand it, I am in your debt for life itself."

"I was vigilant," he said modestly.

"May I ask a favour of you? When I am gone from this place, to what end I know not, you will lack company at meal times. Be kind to those poor Dudley brothers – Ambrose, John, Henry...Robert. I believe they are incarcerated somewhere in this place."

"Your Grace has grounds for more than supposition, I think," said he with gentleness.

"It was with your contrivance then, Sir John, that I spoke sometimes to Robert, and I thank you for it. You will be fair then in my absence, with those hapless sons of Dudley?"

"I shall, for Christian charity's sake alone," he answered pleasantly. "Much like Your Grace's own self."

"Mistress Ashley may not accompany me?" I said tight-lipped. "Why not?"

"She is not deemed a fit companion for you, my lady," replied Sir Henry Bedingfield.

"And why not, pray? She is my governess and has attended me since I was a child. Moreover she is my dearest friend. I will not go if she may not."

"I understand there has been some negligence on her part. She should have kept close watch upon Your Grace."

"Close watch? As gaoler, do you mean?"

"By no means. But converse with young Dudley never should have taken place, and Mistress Ashley is held blameworthy. She shall not go with you to Woodstock."

"Never fear," said Kat, and hugged me, laughing like a fool, as if we knew no care in this world. "I'll be waiting for you when you are permitted to return. And you'll have Blanche to watch over you at Woodstock." I understood her meaning well enough: to be beside your bed, to robe you and disrobe you, to fend off any who might come too close...

"Safe journey," whispered Kat. Her eyes were full of fear.

II

All the waysides bloomed for us at our sally forth; it was the month of May. On such a morning, in despite of reason, it was impossible to believe that death awaited me at my next place of imprisonment.

From my open litter I saw waysides thick with cow-parsley, hedgerows luxuriant with blossom white as snow, red as strawberries; meadows starred with daisies. Folk from their cottages came, strewing flower petals, reaching to me, handing me posies of the wild wallflower, the emblem of fidelity in misfortune. Sometimes they followed us and played music on pipe and tabor till the guards drove them away. Then folk gave us cakes and biscuits and piled my litter with such till I must ask them, laughing, to desist. Bells rang for us in churches that we passed. "Good people," I cried, holding out my hands; and some clasped my fingers and kissed them, and some waved from the waysides; and I heard time and again the shout: "God save Your Grace - God save Elizabeth!"

At last we came to Rycote, our last resting place before Woodstock. By this time Sir Henry Bedingfield was in foul humour and glad to be in part relieved of his command by Lord John Williams, master of Rycote.

Sheep grazed in the parkland, raising pensive eyes to watch us pass, and a sweet wind blew over the long grasses. Rycote stood amongst its trees, a house of mellow brick with stepped gables and cupola-crowned turrets, and nearby, beside a young yew, the chapel with its buttressed tower.

At the steps of the house, the whole family, as it seemed, were gathered to receive us. Lord Williams, an elderly man, made a speech of welcome, introducing to me his daughter Marjorie, a black-haired, black-eyed woman, and her husband Henry Norreys of Wytham, that same whose father had been executed as the lover of Queen Anne Boleyn. Cherishing a fondness for the memory of Anne, they took her daughter to their hearts. They greeted me with palpable warmth; and as for me, it was a wondrous and novel thing to feel I was amongst those that wished me well. Out of the corner of my eye I saw my keeper Bedingfield much discomposed, and I was glad, and went into the house with them, well content.

All was done for our best pleasure. In the garden where we walked, musicians played sweet airs; a banquet in my honour was awaiting us, neighbours invited, and much merriment. At night I slept in a great bed with scented sheets. After my close confinement at the Tower, this was a paradise to me.

Beyond the open latticed window, in the morning the birds sang, and the sun shone warm upon the pillows. I heard, below, the tail end of a heated discourse.

"You have much overplayed the host, Lord Williams," said Sir Henry Bedingfield. "The lady is after all but a prisoner, neither more nor less. You did wrong so to favour her. You were required to give her lodging, not to make your home a sanctuary, nay, a palace in her honour."

"That is the daughter of the king," Lord Williams replied, "and shall receive all honours that my poor home may provide."

Before we left this pleasant place I went into the chapel of the house, a building set apart, a hundred years old, all of Taynton stone, and framed by trees. And here I sat awhile in solitude upon a backed bench, praying that all prisoners might soon be freed.

Even as I sat, I heard without the neighing of the horses and the shouts of soldiers – sounds that emphasised the briefness of my respite, the inevitability of what must come. With a great unwillingness I left that sweet retreat, bade a sad goodbye to those kind people, and set my face sullenly towards Woodstock.

Leaving the village of Woodstock we turned to the marshland beyond, where the river Glyme flowed between reedy banks. A narrow causeway led across this swampy waste to where the ancient palace stood upon a small incline. Behind and to the left, great vasty oaks grew, that forest rich in deer beloved of monarchs of a bygone age, but inaccessible to me, a mere dark gloomy frame for the place of my imprisonment.

This palace was in a state of disrepair – but what was that to me, since I was close confined in four rooms in the gatehouse? Sir Henry wrung his hands and said there was no way to keep me secure nor prevent those that might come against me; this he soon remedied with many locks upon the doors.

Blanche and myself slept in one upstairs room, the maids in the other. From our window we looked out on desolation, a nothing, an expanse of wetness with that dark jut of the causeway whence all visitors could be seen long before they drew near. Despair engulfed me.

"I see I am to be forgot," said I.

"Your Grace shall make it certain you be not so," Blanche answered briskly. "And you may trust Master Parry to work for your interest from his rooms in Woodstock."

"He is at the inn, I think?" I smiled. "He will be better served than I."

However, I now had books, and might walk in the garden. But when I learnt that Bedingfield must accompany me on such walks I thought myself much put upon.

My maid Elizabeth Sands was always there beside me to listen to my grumbles; and there were many.

"I am treated worse than any prisoner in Newgate! No visitors except those Bedingfield approves, no letters writ nor received, all about us a great park and forest and I may not tread in either."

She put her hand upon my arm and looked at me with such a gaze as made me look again at her.

"Your Grace is all fortitude," she said. "So many tribulations, and always so brave."

She was a pretty fair-haired girl, small and dainty, yet with the kind of breasts that Tom Seymour would have well commended. Beside her I felt tall and straight as a post. This sweet girl, one of my sister's choice, seemed to admire me. When we walked she was ever at my side. I almost would have supposed her a little in love with me.

The curious truth became apparent to me as the days of our captivity passed by, that this was so indeed, yet she believing me a woman. I did not dream it, for she said as much to me. "I am honoured that we bear the same name. But I am unworthy. Oh Your Grace...if I might prove my devotion to you...if I might prove my love..."

What might she hope for? She seemed happy to be close to me and I was touched by this. Sometimes when we walked in the garden I gave her my hand and I kissed her on the cheek. This was no doubt observed, but nothing was said – why should it be?

I found our friendship piquant. Its pleasure was, however, tinged with some uneasiness. I feared that there might come a time when she would hope for consummation of our growing intimacy. And then one day I awoke to find she was dismissed.

"Blanche! He has now removed Elizabeth! Is there no limit to his villainy and spite?"

We stood together at the window, watching Mistress Sands riding away, escorted, tearful, to return to London.

"Enough," said Blanche in low tones. "It was not Bedingfield. It was myself arranged that she should leave. I told Bedingfield she had become an embarrassment through her immoderate love for you."

"You knew she was my favourite," I protested in surprise.

"I knew it; I also knew that the poor fool was besotted with you."

"You surely do not think I would have been so stupid as to accept her love in any form that might have compromised my dignity? Master Parry must have told you that the love of women does not move me. Where was the danger?"

"You could not see it. The observer sees more plainly. When Mistress Sands stood by your side she caused you to seem male."

I was angry to be so confined. Four rooms and a garden, and the bolting of many doors, with complete restriction upon my personal freedoms – this was my lot. A prisoner no more nor less, yet nothing proven of me.

When I wrote a letter to my sister it enraged her; meanwhile, my simplest requests were referred to the Council, Kat was kept from me, and health also in that vile swamp far from palaces and pleasures. Meanwhile Mary married her Spanish prince, and the odious Bishop Gardiner officiated at the ceremony.

It was William Cecil who brought this news to me, in his capacity of surveyor of my properties. He told me that Queen Mary was ecstatic, like a maid new in love, and confident that she would bear a son. The prospect filled me with desolation. What of me? What would become of me? Was I to grow old here at Woodstock, until sickness or the hand of an assassin brought me low?

There were many at court that worked for my downfall, the worst of such being Bishop Gardiner. What if he persuaded Mary to disinherit me, and leave the way open for this popish heir that she so firmly believed to be her destiny?

In November Cecil told me that she was with child. Cardinal Pole had come hotfoot from his master the pope to bring absolution for the realm of England, and the country was returned to popery. Those who did not conform were to be burned to death, whomsoever they might be – the humble and the great, bishop, archbishop...princess...

I sat with Blanche at our little window, which looked so drearily down upon the marshland below. The river Glyme had overflowed its miry banks and made a scene of watery desolation. The rain coursed down the window pane, blurring the grim image with a dull grey wash.

"All hope is gone," I said to Blanche.

She turned to me. Tall as myself, she put her arm about me – not as Kat did, warmly and lovingly, but hard; her grip a vicious clamp.

"God strikes down those that falter on the way," she told me fiercely. "He has no use for weaklings."

"Don't threaten me with divine wrath. It touches me not at all," I said irritably. "You speak so because you know I am right. The queen is with child. A healthy son and I am doomed. The might of Spain and the authority of the pope are with her, and now Parliament is won to popery. I am forgotten. If I live I shall grow old here; if I am become a trial to them they will find a way to rid themselves of me. And I have had enough."

"You are brought to low spirits, that is all."

"No; it is more than that. I have had enough of taking someone else's punishment. This gloomy fate by rights has fallen upon the Lady Elizabeth. She had the misfortune to be Mary's sister and heir to the throne and of a different faith. But I am not she."

"You are," she hissed. "You must be."

"Why should I?" I shrugged. "I only ever did it to please Kat. It was pleasing enough when all went well. Even the dangers concerning Thomas were not without their curious joys. But this...this tedium, this wearisome staleness, this wastefulness... I cannot bear it – and I need not," I said stoutly. "All I have to do to be quit of it is to be my true self. All I need to do is to present myself before Bedingfield and say 'My lord, you have been misinformed... The Lady Elizabeth is dead; there is nothing to fear. Merely a boy from Bisley.' Bisley!" I smiled scornfully. "Who has ever heard of such a place?"

"This is foolish talk," Blanche whispered. "They would never permit you to live. You would merely exchange captivity for death."

"Maybe not," I shrugged. "I might be seen as a curiosity. Exhibited, like an ape or an Indian. Made to work in the kitchens, like Lambert Simnel. Then released. Free to run away to sea. Free to find Ambrose and Zachary and voyage to the islands of the west. I tell you, Blanche, it is a risk I do not fear to take when I look out on Woodstock marsh and know that Mary has won all and I have lost, my enemies triumphant."

"You have not lost," said Blanche in a low voice. "Where is your grasp of logic? The queen is with child, yes, but she is not a young woman. Anything may happen. Remember Katherine Seymour. Yes it is true that popery reigns, but it reigns only in the person of the queen, and without her it will disperse as any mist. Then what? What comfort will it be to you, in the kitchens of Whitehall, to see that silly ninny Catherine Grey ascend the throne – for by King Henry's will 'tis Jane Grey's sister that must follow, if not you? Have you so soon forgot the common folk that cheered you on your way to Woodstock? 'God save Elizabeth!' was all their cry. And God has saved you. Whoever you are, it is you that must be there to bring the country to its proper course. Nobody else can do it; and for that reason you shall not quit your post through weakness. Rather than permit it, I would first slay you myself."

I laughed in spite of myself. "And Blanche, where is your logic? Am I to be the saviour of the realm if you should stick a knife in me?"

"Nothing so bloody," said Blanche huffily. "Give me credit for some subtlety."

"Ah, Blanche," I murmured then, "I think that I may be permitted to be weak sometimes. If truth be known, I have a horror of the block, whereon so many in these times have perished, all bravely. I fear that I would not be brave. It is too sudden, do you see, one moment living, one moment dead. I could not raise a jest nor speak composedly to those assembled. I would make a poor and shameful end. The fear has been my constant companion day and night. I used merely to fear discovery. Now I would welcome something so simple. If one had told me, long ago at Bisley, that to put on the skirts of that princess would bring me to a constant fear of the tickle of the axe upon my neck, I would have run to Master Dutton, begging to drive sheep to Mynchen Hampton."

I heard what I had said, and made a noise of irritation. "What am I about? It is not so. I quit Bisley gladly."

"You are not yourself," Blanche soothed me.

I smiled at the aptness of her observation. "I fear this grey dull place has worn me down more than the erstwhile danger did. Maybe danger stimulates even as it terrifies? I moulder here like a corpse. When will I ever be set free?"

Thomas Parry, persona non grata for that he was suspected of masterminding plots for my escape at his bolthole in the village –

supposedly a hotbed of intrigue – must nonetheless attend me to discuss the management of my affairs. Always Bedingfield sat by, mistrusting his intent, listening for verbal cipher. But Parry's news was more direct.

"One of the Dudley boys is released."

"Lord be praised! But which one?"

"That I do not remember. But no praise is due. He died on his release; and he a young man. His mother the duchess was so distraught her own death came soon after. It is a sad thing for so great a family."

"Which brother?" I cried, reaching forward, shaking him.

"Indeed I do not recall. There are so many in that brood..."

"Leave me, Thomas... I cannot think about accounts and addition...of a sudden I am not well..."

Master William Cecil was a different proposition. Admired by Bedingfield as a man of sober and trustworthy nature, his news was ever concise.

"John Dudley it was that died; and but three and twenty years of age. For the remaining brothers, some change in fortune. Henry, Ambrose and Robert are released, but to small purpose; they are penniless and malcontent. I spoke with Robert Dudley. 'Get you to the country,' I said, 'live a quiet life and cause no rumour. God's protection was upon you; but His patience stretches so far and no further.' Needless to say, he did not take my advice, and may be found among the wastrels and the dispossessed in Paul's Churchyard, as plainly hatching plots as if the same were writ upon his brow. But naught will come of it, for he is watched and knows it. I think it likely he will turn soldier – what else is there for such as he and of such ancestry?"

And in times like these, he might have added, for I guessed he thought as much.

"It grieves me that the queen can find no place for his most particular talents," I said angrily; and when Master Cecil eyed me narrowly I added, by way of explanation for my outburst: "I have always lamented waste."

It is April and I am commanded to present myself at Hampton Court.

Our preparations for the journey were fraught with febrile tension. Why were we sent for? Was it merely to be subjected to the humiliation of dancing attendance upon Queen Mary's new-born son, whose arrival would cast me back once more into obscurity? We understood that the palace was become a shrine to Mary's expectation of the birth of a healthy son. What place had I in this?

Elated as I was to be quit of that vile gatehouse I was filled with unease at the contemplation of what might await me now. In London they were burning so-called heretics at the fires. Never had I been a more vociferous and fervent communicant, receiving the Sacrament and confessing those of my sins which were not treasonable, and this before as many onlookers as my situation might provide; and I had every intention of continuing so to do when we arrived at Hampton Court. Why had she sent for me? Why now?

The blustery winds gusted about us as we travelled eastward. Always as we made our way along the waysides yellow with spring flowers, the people gathered, cheering, waving, vigorously calling out good wishes. However Bedingfield might frown, it was plain enough that in this pale-faced person with the wild red hair that blew so waywardly about the face, lay passionate hopes for something other than did now exist. It was heartening to me, having thought myself forgot; but yet it frightened me. Mary must be aware of it; and she misliked me. Therefore why was I now sent for? I knew I would once again be questioned, harried, forced to swear my innocence of charges about which I had yet no knowledge, and my false attempts at sincerity while attending Mass subjected to a rigorous examination. Would it not have been better to have remained confined at Woodstock? And what of Philip, Mary's Spanish bridegroom? Had he some odious plan to send me from these shores, to wed his young son, ten years old, or some foreign duke, his creature? My presence could be no delight to him. What did they want of me?

On our last night before arrival at the palace, we put up at an inn near Windsor, and, the meal done, I was sitting in the parlour on a high-backed settle beside the hearth. I stretched my hands out to the generous blaze and breathed in the pleasant scent of burning apple boughs. The servants tidied away the platters, and in the general bustle and confusion Thomas Parry handed me his account book for my perusal, a common enough occurrence. Betwixt the pages lay loose sheets of paper, lists of purchases for me to verify. Parry remained beside me, so that his bulk masked the expression on my face, for he supposed that I would blanch when I observed the letter from Robert Dudley; I did not. I read it with all appearance of serenity, although my heart spoke otherwise, for this epistle – mere kind words from one friend to another – was treason pure and simple.

"...Many designs there be abroad to bring Your Grace to a better circumstance, for I have met with none that is content with what now is; but any plan that links your name with that of Courtenay I find little to my liking, for he is a ninny; therefore I have held back, but not from any disloyalty or want of courage, as I think Your Grace knows well enough. If the world were other than it is I would ride boldly to you on a brave white charger and offer you my service in whichever way you chose; or take you with me to where we might work our will upon these troubled times and change them. Until such time, be pleased to rest content in the certainty of the devotion of

your servant Robert Dudley."

Dear fond vain hopes; but ah! so welcome to me at this time of trial.

I folded the letter to a taper's width and put it in the flame and watched it burn away to nothingness.

EIGHT

I

"It was I that caused you to be sent for," said Philip, Prince of Spain.

He was standing on the first two steps of the dais, half turned away from me. He had arranged himself thus to add inches to his lack of stature, and I perceived as much. He was stocky of build, but so thin of shank that he appeared ill-proportioned, and his choice of tawny stockings called to mind the scrawny legs of a chicken. Momentarily I experienced a passing pity for such gentlemen whose lack of thigh muscle was so mercilessly exposed by the fashion of our day. And now he turned towards me, my sister's husband, suddenly, and directed a most searching gaze upon me.

We were alone. I had been three days at Hampton Court, and had not yet seen my sister, nor any of her ministers of state. I lived in my apartments, with guards upon the stair. That first evening, Blanche and I had gone about the rooms pressing our palms over every inch of wainscoting, searching for spy holes. One indeed we found, and stuffed a handkerchief into it, but we assumed others. We rested from our journey; but we were not comfortable.

And then we were visited by Mistress Clarencieux, my sister's friend and lady-in-waiting.

"You are commanded to attend upon the king, my lady."

"The king?" Such was Philip's title by right of marriage. But we had expected the command to come from Mary.

"Her Majesty so wishes it. And it is her express request that you wear your finest clothes."

"I have not a vast array of clothes," I answered irritably. "We lived a quiet life, in the country, where I was."

"Your crimson velvet is tolerable," Blanche said firmly.

"Convey to His Majesty my humble thanks for his graciousness. It is my pleasure to attend him."

Needless to say, we speculated upon the unforeseen summons as Blanche helped me to attire myself for the occasion. My ladies gathered about me, putting the final touches to my appearance. I surveyed myself thoughtfully in a small hand mirror. I was twenty-one. Now that my sicknesses were gone from me I was personable enough. Indeed, far from tiring me, the journey had reanimated me. My eyes seemed more alive than they had done while I was kept close at Woodstock. As always, I peered carefully for any sign of coarseness about my chin; but all was smooth. My face was oval and well-balanced, my mouth firm. My neck was slender yet, the gold of my necklace answering the red-gold of my hair. I was as fair as any. I might present myself with pride before this stranger king.

Philip, Prince of Spain and Sicily, Archduke of Austria, King of Naples and Jerusalem, Duke of Milan, Burgundy and Brabant, Count of Habsburg and Tyrol...he exuded power, this short-built man with scrawny thighs. He was dressed in black and gold. Now that we were close I saw that his face was unnaturally long, with a large jaw in no wise disguised by his beard and moustaches. His brows were dark and well-marked, his eyes dark and bright, his lips thick, and, I thought, sensuous. Where had I heard that this was a cold unfeeling man? My first impression was of a deep passion, rigorously controlled.

"It was I that caused you to be sent for," he said. "It is time that you and I made each other's acquaintance."

"I am honoured by Your Majesty's attention," I replied, the words a formality as we assessed one another, each making no secret of the fact. "My dearest wish is to please Your Majesties and to show by word and deed my loyalty, obedience and devotion."

"I know it," he replied. "I have never believed those that spoke against you."

"I am completely innocent. I maintain it before God. I have never acted but in faith and honesty."

"I believe it... I see it in your eyes."

Indeed, he was now close enough to do so. We were much of the same height. I blushed. I knew this man to be subtle and astute. I feared his penetrating gaze. What if he, who had not watched me grow from infancy, now coming to me with unclouded vision, saw me straightaway for what I was? He was not much older than myself, I judged, some seven and twenty years. His first wife had died; they said his son Don Carlos was of unstable disposition. They said that Philip was entirely motivated by a sense of duty, that this alone had brought him to my sister's bed. She had permitted, nay, commanded this meeting. Did she know that he was now in such proximity to my person that I could see the movement of his tongue as he licked his dry lips?

"I shall speak kindly of you to the queen," he told me.

I murmured humble thanks. Our first meeting was at an end.

Our second was much closer than I had anticipated. That evening as I sat with Blanche in my apartment, we were astonished to see one of the wall panels in the wainscoting slide back. There stood Philip, Prince of Spain, smiling like a cat with cream to have caught us unawares.

"Don't be afraid," he said, and stepped over the threshold. Afraid I was not; affronted, perhaps, to find my privacy held in such scant regard. It seemed that he mistook my blushes and my silence for mere maidenly modesty. To reassure me of his good intent he knelt now at my feet, and took my hand and kissed it. His lips remained upon my fingers long enough for me to feel their warmth; also their moisture.

"Please rise, Your Majesty," I murmured discomposed. He did so soon enough, for now he became taller, I yet seated.

"Elizabeth," he said. He had a droll way of speaking my name. He began it with a guttural sound, as if it began with H, and continued as if there were none at the end. "I came to tell you that you have a friend. You have not been well treated. The queen now understands that you have been much maligned. Be at your ease. In me you see a prince who knows well how to be a friend."

His eyes were on me, indeed, all over me, threatening my equanimity, and my trepidation plainly pleasing him. What did he want of me? Was I mistaken in my interpretation of his behaviour? This seemed to me the outward manifestation of no more nor less than lechery.

"You are a princess of surpassing beauty," said he then. "This, I confess, was a surprise to me. I look forward to more converse with you; there is no more gracious ornament to the courts of princes than a woman fair of face and yet possessed of wit and learning. I presume, in paying compliment upon so short acquaintance; and yet I hope, Elizabeth, that you find my poor praise pleasing."

Nothing ever was more like to please me. The full force of my smile I now turned on the prince of Spain. He believed me woman, and he thought me beautiful.

"Your Majesty," said I composedly, "I too look forward to the ripening of our amity."

Something had passed between us, some understanding, a mutual attraction of a fine and subtle nature.

Sure of me, having received what he had come for, Philip now bowed formally and withdrew.

I was aglow with pleasurable disturbance. But why, I frowned? I who admired muscle and strength, unsettled by a man with concave inner thighs! Ah, but no, it was his power that excited me. This dark-eyed man who found me beautiful was heir to half the thrones in Europe.

My sister stood in shadow. The great curtained bed half hid her from me. The candlelight revealed partly discernible shapes in the darkness, the dusky red of tapestry, the gilt of chalice, the carved oak of the coffer, the velvet of cushions. Upon my knees I waited.

"You will not confess your offence," said Mary in her gruff voice. "You keep stoutly to your truth. I pray God it may so fall out."

"If it does not," said I, "I request neither favour nor pardon at Your Majesty's hands."

"I suppose that you believe yourself wrongfully punished," she said tartly.

"No, Your Majesty; I have borne the burden and must bear it. But I humbly beseech Your Majesty to have a good opinion of me and to think me to be your true subject as long as life shall last."

She had sent her councillors to me, and once again I had found myself protesting innocence to Chancellor Gardiner. I had told him I would rather lie in prison and maintain my honesty and truth than go free under a cloud, suspected of disloyalty. Now I was sent for;

now at last, in the gloom of her bedroom and at dead of night, we faced each other, bathed in shared mistrust and personal antipathy. But I was not afraid, for I possessed that secret trump, the avowed goodwill of her enigmatic husband with whom Mary was besotted and whose wishes she would obey.

She now moved forward and she bade me rise. I found I had grown taller than she; this was inevitable, of course, in the way of it; but it seemed to me that she had somehow shrunk even from her natural height. Her face was wizened, lined and old. Her teeth were vile, and some were gone. It was all I could do not to show surprise. I had expected a woman bonny, great with child, in good health, well content as her time drew near. I cast a glance to her belly; Katherine Seymour had been bigger than this when she had been but a few months gone. This child of Mary's would be very small; sickly, I hoped.

It occurred to me that Mary was eyeing me likewise, as if possessing thoughts of a similar nature.

"You are well?" she asked me tentatively.

"God be thanked," I answered.

"They tell me," she said with some malevolence, "that in all your time at Woodstock – some ten months, I think – you never had your monthly terms. That seems a little strange to me. I understood you had begun when you were at Chelsea."

This was the first time that it came to me how thoroughly I had been spied upon. My maids? My laundresses? How right had Blanche been to stay beside me constantly, her shrewd eyes watching while she seemed about her books. How right had I been never to stand naked!

"My physicians tell me that this sometimes happens in a young girl when her life is...difficult, and she lives in fear," I answered, composedly.

"Perhaps," she answered, and with complacency she laid her palms about her midriff. "Or perhaps it will be your lot never to know the greatest fortune ever to befall woman."

"Indeed I truly hope so," I answered stoutly, "since I intend never to marry. I am well content in my virginity, and I have no wish to bear a child."

"Then you are a fool," she answered, "for I tell you plain that I have known no greater happiness since my lord got me with child. I pray," she added piously, "that you may one day know joy such as this."

"I doubt that Heaven will grant your prayer," I said, "but I give thanks to Your Majesty for your kind consideration of me."

"It seems that upon all matters," Mary said soberly, "we are content to differ. It never could be otherwise."

"I have heard much spoken of you, Doctor Dee," said I to the tall thin young man who sat opposite me. "You are a Cambridge man, a mathematician, and a traveller. You have lectured in Paris; I hear they flocked to you there. You were in the service of the Earl of Pembroke and the Duke of Northumberland, and you were tutor of sciences to Lord Robert Dudley. It is from Lord Robert that I have heard about you and he speaks most highly of you. I hear, also," and I smiled, "that we are related, you and I."

"It is true, Your Grace," maintained he. "Genealogy has always been my passion. I am descended from Rhodri the Great, Prince of all Wales. If we had time I would draw you a family tree to show where my ancestors conjoin with yours."

"I do not doubt you, Doctor Dee," I laughed, "but you are here to calculate my nativity, as you have done for my sister and her husband."

That he was permitted to do so made me understand that Mary knew of it and that she wished to know the result of his casting. This brilliant and astute scholar would certainly guess as much. He would play along. He would cast such a nativity as would reassure the queen. We smiled at one another. I gave him all the information he required concerning the unfortunate princess. He would retire and work on it. But maybe he had other knowledge to impart? He nodded.

"For our eyes only," murmured he. He began to shuffle a pack of cards.

"The Tarot of the gypsies," he said. "It comes from the east. The cards bear the names the gypsies gave them – Pal, Pohara, Spathi, Rup; in our tongue Wand, Cup, Sword and Coin. These are the four elemental tools of magic: Fire, Water, Air and Earth. They are the four letters of the Divine Name, the Tetragrammaton. Arranged in a certain way they will form the figure of the Qabbalistic Tree of Life. What I tell you with these cards is true."

I leaned forward and watched his hands at work. He spread three cards. The strong man, the two of coins, the Wheel of Fortune.

"The unsheathed sword," he said, "shows your use of mental skill to overcome obstacles in the past. You made a choice. You knew what you wanted; you applied courage and patience to attain your heart's desire. You are a juggler. You wear a mask. You tread a fine line, always aiming for balance. Pleasure and merriment, yes, but always flexible, always changing, as new obstacles present. Behind you the sea is rough. Fortune and success are indicated, the manifestation of something anticipated." He looked up at me. "I would like to cast again," he said, "to shed more light in some dark corners. You permit?"

"I do."

He shuffled, cast, and spread; this time using many more cards, making a mathematical shape upon the table. Sometimes he paused, frowned, cast again. The coloured cards with their strange images lay before us like a vibrant mosaic.

John Dee laughed, like one that sees a joke against himself.

"The Emperor – well, that is clear enough, I think, and needs small interpretation. An influence upon Your Grace's life, a man of authority, used to controlling others. And this, the Knight of Swords, perhaps, is not so hard for us to understand...a strong young man, impetuous, self-willed and discontented; a fighter, proud, determined. And here, the Knight of Cups, the seeker after perfection, the lover who brings himself as a gift. The Knight of Rods – generous friend and loving heart, purposeful, again, blocked in his endeavour. That I could interpret in like manner. But such a plethora of gentlemen! I wonder whether you see my drift in all this, my gracious lady? When I cast cards for you I ask myself 'and where in all these gentlemen is she?' I look for Elizabeth. I find knights and pages. It is...unusual. Somewhere in all this richness I would expect to find a Queen, either a Queen in power or a Queen in prospect. I look and once again I look. There is a King, here, at this right-hand side. Who he may be I know not, since he represents the future. A dearth of female influence. Yes, this is odd."

"And therefore what do you surmise?" I whispered.

"What I surmise is quite impossible," he answered firmly. "My final interpretation, therefore, is this: Your Grace, though female, is possessed of many princely attributes, commonly associated with the male. These will stand you in good stead throughout your life. Moreover, you will always be surrounded by a troop of knights desirous of influencing you, of serving you...and of loving you."

We looked at one another. His glance was veiled: I could not read his expression.

"I would count myself honoured to be amongst that number," he said then.

"An you were so, I tell you, you should never lack," I said.

"Your Grace is kind."

"Always, to my friends," I answered.

"I am one such."

"I thank you," I replied, "for much more than the reading of my cards."

Within a week or so, they had arrested him for treason.

That summer it rained ceaselessly. Mary shut herself in her rooms, to await her confinement, it was said; but no babe was born. May turned to June, June to July, and folk whispered. What kind of child was this, that grew a twelvemonth within the womb? Where was the promised heir?

Myself I hardly dare believe in my good fortune. Could it be that there was no child at all?

"I think you can imagine the extent of my humiliation," Philip said to me as we took shelter under the trees. "She will never bear a child. Somehow she did persuade herself that she carried an infant; somehow her body did contrive to make it seem so. The physicians swore it. Ah, how sacrilegious seems it now, those cries of 'Ave Maria gracia plena' that greeted her so welcome news! Myself so deluded, believing in that monstrous falsity. No, there is nothing for me here. At least..." he added, and he looked at me. "Elizabeth," he said, "my anger dissipates when I look on your face."

He leaned to me, and kissed me. All around us, the leaves shivered in the rain, and spewed their waterdrops upon us. A bead of sweat appeared upon his brow and trickled down his temple.

"She is not in good health," he panted in my ear. "If I were at liberty to take a wife again I see no reason why I should not continue to remain in England, furthering my policy of friendship between our two countries, by a marriage with yourself, dear sister." He raised an eyebrow in enquiry. I replied by inclining my face to his and kissing him once more, with as much passion as I could muster from a heart that felt no physical desire. I knew he lusted for me, down beneath his gilt and his black velvet and his pedantic words; and I knew it was through his lust that I would reach him and retain his interest. He responded greedily, a man who did not hunger for his wife. And then as suddenly he ceased, and lightly cleared his throat. He brushed the raindrops from his sleeve with a movement of distaste.

"We will not speak of this again," he said, "but the matter is now understood between us. We shall ride together, we shall walk together; we shall begin to know one another a little better."

It was on one such occasion, as we rode in the parkland, ever with an eye upon the lowering clouds, that I was able to persuade the prince of Spain to take into his entourage a gallant man who longed to serve the throne, one Robert Dudley, who for want of good employment was languishing to death, his talents wasted and his loyalty denied. The prince of Spain agreed to use him as a messenger.

Prince Philip's interest in me was my salvation. Such was poor Mary's love for him that even after he returned to Spain she obeyed his instructions to treat me kindly, or at least with as much kindness as her nature and our situation did permit. No child was born to her, and at the end of summer it appeared that she accepted as much, for she and all her household moved from Hampton Court, the place which she had chosen for her confinement. By October I was once again at Hatfield.

And here to my great joy Kat Ashley was restored to me. We rushed to one another in a warm hug. How different she was from Blanche! Blanche, tall, severe, iron-willed, utterly dependable, always at her books, rarely showing emotion, would never run to me in such a spontaneous display of affection. How wonderful to be with Kat once more, and in our favourite place!

That night, however, her plump face was troubled as she made me ready for bed. When I was ensconced beneath the bedclothes, she curled up beside me on the counterpane, and put her mouth close to my ear.

"My dear," she whispered. "We are not yet safe, though we seem so."

"I know that who comes here does so by permission," I agreed morosely, "and any who come on their own account do so at risk."

"Worse," whispered she. "We may trust no one; those who seem friend are not so; and I myself was instructed to bear news of you back to London. Only on that understanding was I allowed to return to your service."

"Oh Kat," I sighed wearily. "What would they? I do nothing. What would they find? You don't think, do you, that they suspect...that after all this time, someone has guessed...?"

"No, no," she said dismissively. "That, after all, my dear, is very easily proved. No, we are in far deeper waters – the shifting world of policy. What they seek is a reason to bring you to trial. They say at court that Her Majesty is working to have the prince of Spain made King of England in his own right, so that, should she die, you will be forever excluded from the throne. He might then marry and bear sons. It is unthinkable!"

I giggled stupidly. "Indeed it is so, since he wants to marry me!"

"He does? The rumours have gone so. Lord save us – what a muddle!"

Then, because she was Kat, her mouth twitched, and she chortled: "He wants to marry you! That grim-faced icicle? And give you sons, no doubt!"

"No doubt," I smirked.

We lay together, heaving in silent mirth. Then Kat grew sober.

"What are we about, my dear? It is no laughing matter. Look at you, your skin is smooth as satin, creamy as fine parchment. No sign of hair, no roughness. A strange business. There is nothing about your face to show that you are other than you appear to be. I half feared to see you; after all this time, I thought there would be changes. I thought perhaps some fault would show, some hint of... But no, you are become quite beautiful. I'd almost swear that there was witchcraft in it. Small wonder that the prince of Spain lusts after you. They say he is a secret lecher and no maid is safe from him. It would be better were you ugly."

"Not at all," I protested. "What man would look at me were I ill-favoured?"

"Fool! What can you offer any man who looks at you? And sooner or later you may be called upon to show your wares upon the marriage bed! Listen, dearest chuck, they questioned me. They said you have a secret, Mistress Ashley, you and the Lady Elizabeth. What is that secret? Secret? I know not what you mean, I answered. But you are very close, she and you. They say you share a secret which you have sworn to keep till death. What is that secret, Mistress Ashley?"

I stared into Kat's wide bright eyes, appalled.

"What do they suppose?" I gasped. "What do they mean?"

"I think they half believe you bore a child by Thomas Seymour," Kat whispered in reply. "I guess that is their drift."

"Oh that!" I said contemptuously and in relief. "Is that all?"

"We may not rest," said Kat and shook her head. "It must concern us that they believe we share a secret. They will try to keep me from you. They think our closeness is born of guilt."

"Then let us be a little cool toward one another," I said, "and suspect every inch of wainscot, even here."

And thus, even there, our procedure was as ever – that Kat or Blanche saw me to bed and bath, that when my tub was brought a screen of arras stood about it, that when I took my nightgown off, my shift was already in place beneath it, that never stood I naked.

II

"Leave your books, dear lady! Lord Robert Dudley is below!"

He was waiting for me in the great hall, illumined by a fine sliver of winter sunlight. Tall, graceful, muscular, upright of build, he stood, bareheaded. He wore a doublet of dark green, edged with black fur, and a short dark cloak, and ah! long leather boots begrimed with mud. He carried his gloves in one hand.

His cheeks glowed from the wind and weather. His eyes glittered. I thought I had never seen anything so beautiful.

I stumbled over my petticoats with an oath. My eagerness to speak with him had made me clumsy.

"Your Grace! My lady! Elizabeth!" he said, with a smile of warmth that melted all my bones to water. We clasped each other's hands, equal in misfortune, dispossession, hope; then he dropped to one knee; I raised him.

"You have grown taller," I admired.

"Than you? So I should hope!" he laughed. "That is the way of it between men and women."

"What do I know of such?" I shrugged. "But you, perhaps, know something more?"

"All that I know upon the matter," he answered ardently, "is that when he regards one certain woman, this man forgets all else."

"And which woman is that?" I asked him archly.

"The vainest in the world," he said, "that ever fishes for more praise," and then stepped back smartly, ducking as if he feared a buffet on the jaw.

"What is your business here, Robert Dudley?" I asked with dignity.

"I bring gifts from Philip, prince of Spain, and good wishes for Your Grace's health and happiness."

He gestured to the table, where the bounty lay.

"I may not stay," he added. "I am to return at once. But there is time for you and me to take a ride in the parkland."

He could not have been in need of exercise and I almost said as much, the tart rejoinder ever present with me in the company of Robert Dudley.

"I will be pleased to ride with you," I answered swiftly.

Some of my ladies began to protest, pointing out the inclemency of the weather. Laughingly I parried their objections. Kat wrapped a cloak about me.

Under a sky of heavy blue-grey cloud shafted through with silver and amber light, Robert and I rode off to where amongst the oak trees and the wide bare fields our conversation could not be overheard.

But first we simply rode, at speed, saying nothing, riding for the joy of it, in shared good humour, almost as if we were free from care and suspicion; and when Robert turned and grinned over his shoulder in bravado because he went the faster I muttered an oath, knowing that it was purely due to his riding astride. Truly petticoats were an impediment.

That first elation past we slowed our horses and dismounted beside an oak tree. A strong emotion kept us silent. I sensed that we were both remembering the barred door in the Tower, the cold rains of March, the stench of imprisonment, our snatched converse without sight of each other. Suddenly he took me in his arms. He held me, saying nothing; but I felt his heart beat.

"Forgive me," he said in a low voice. "I may have overstepped what is permissible."

"No...you have not," I said, most agreeably weak from the touch of him.

"I bring news of one kind and another," he said, swiftly recovering his composure. "None of which I wished to speak of before a crowd. It is well known that half your household is in the pay of somebody or other."

"But which half? If only we knew," I said ruefully.

"Precisely," he agreed. "Indeed, I half suspect these mighty oaks, so wary is my nature grown. First, had you heard that Doctor Dee is released?"

"I am most glad of it. You could have told me that before folk."

"This also – but I guessed that you might want to dance when you heard it, and so alarm our spies: Bishop Gardiner is dead of apoplexy."

"Yes! I do want to dance!" I squealed delightedly, clapping my hands. "But," I added most demurely, "I shall refrain and keep my dignity, as becomes a princess of the realm."

He looked at me oddly, speculatively. "I wonder what you truly are," he said.

"I am what you see," I answered at once, uneasy.

"No," he answered measuringly. "You show an image to the world, that's all. Out there," he gestured widely, to include all that lay beyond the confines of Hatfield Park, "men are prepared to die for you, to risk their lives to place you on the throne. But whom will they be dying for? You are a symbol of hope. A symbol, yes; but what, in actuality?"

"A stupid question, Robert," I snapped. "You know how it has been for me since Mary became queen. I cannot afford to let the mask slip for an instant. An image, you say. Yes, I am an image. I dare be nothing else. I doubt whether I, no more than anyone else, know what I truly am. My energies are spent in simply seeing out another day without discovery."

"Discovery?" he frowned. "An odd word. Discovery of what?"

"Of my true self," I answered flustered. I had not meant to speak so honestly. "Of my true thoughts, my fears, my hopes."

"Yes, yes, I understand," he said. "I did not mean to vex you. I ask because... Elizabeth," he began, "what if there were in existence a plot which I believe like to succeed...to send the queen to Spain where she would be well content beside her husband...leaving yourself Queen of England, wed to the Earl of Devonshire?"

"Oh, not those old tales once again!" I groaned.

"No, this one has a chance. A kinsman of mine has worked out a plan...and we have warm support from France – an army – money – we cannot fail. Myself I am inclined to take a part in it, but I would not take one step without first assuring myself that, should we succeed, Your Grace would be content to marry Courtenay; which is the nub of the matter."

"You have told me yourself that any plan allying me to Courtenay was antipathetic to your nature," I protested outraged. "But now you are become content to barter me where it best suits you."

Robert scowled and looked away, his boot heel stabbing at the ground. "It is because I am so dashed by what I must endure – what England must endure. I grow daily more malcontent. How long, I ask myself, will misery persist? And many good men with me ask the same. Hundreds burned for their beliefs, hundreds fled abroad, the pernicious influence of Spain – this is not what the true-born Englishman desires. We live in fear and dread. This should by rights be a time of knowledge and discovery, a time when youth is tested to the utmost in the service of the realm, not thwarted and held down at every turn. The old advise be patient, wait for time to take its course. But I say time needs somewhat of a nudge, or else a kick. And therefore," he said, turning back to me, "if you agree to wed with Courtenay, give me the word, and I will set in motion that which shall bring comfort to us all."

"Oh Robert," I breathed. "Have you learned nothing? Forgive me – but what of your father? Your grandfather? Remember what was their fate! What of your own misfortunes? Conspiracy is not the answer. It never is. I take the part of those ancients you despise. I say wait. Be patient."

"Till I am old and grey?" he shrugged.

"If needs be. I recall you wrote a letter to me, swearing you would take no part in any plot that bound me to Courtenay. That pleased me, Robert, and I would you were yet as scrupulous. I will not marry Courtenay. I will not wed. It is my clear intent to rest in that state in which you now behold me. Tell your friends. I want no lives lost in a vain attempt to change the order of things. And if I possess any power over you yourself by virtue of my birth, when I order you to shun these malcontents you will obey."

"Do you so order it?" he glowered darkly.

"I do."

"This is unfair," said Robert angrily.

"Nonetheless," I countered, "you will do as I say."

"I will be accused of cowardice amongst those with whom I have been close."

"Your reputation should not hang upon an act of folly."

"It is monstrous that I should be forbid by you in a matter concerning men," he seethed.

"You came here expressly for that purpose," I protested. "You sought my approval for a hare-brained scheme and promised to abide by what I said. Do your promises count for so little? What of the vows of loyalty? And the white charger upon which you were to carry me away? Mere words, Robert? Am I to believe anything you say?"

"Ah," he groaned, dropping to one knee. "I would die for you, Elizabeth, and you know it."

"And this is what you will do, by joining in this foolishness! Robert, Robert, what good would you be to me dead?"

I leaned and put my arms about him. Ah! He had wonderful eyes! A man possessed of eyes like those would always achieve his desires!

"Promise me – no part in any plot on my behalf."

"You have my word," he said reluctantly.

"Stand up – have done – let us be as we were," I said cajolingly. He stood.

"The French are not our friends," I said. "If your companions receive French gold they may be sure that they are victims of a greater plot."

"Ah, now you would instruct me in the ways of policy," said Robert huffily.

"It seems necessary," I replied.

We faced each other in a hostile silence. I saw anger and frustration smoulder in his eyes. Then he seized me by the shoulders and shook me, and when I gasped and opened my mouth to upbraid him for his impudence, he reached down and kissed me hard upon the lips. Then he strode towards his horse. I followed. I caught a glimpse of his expression. I thought that he regretted what he had done. He assisted me to mount, then swung himself into the saddle.

We rode slowly back towards the palace. Myself I was in a certain turmoil. I knew that he had kissed me more in rage than wantonness. This did in no way lessen the shock of pleasure I had undergone. The imprint of his mouth yet burned my lips. What Robert's thoughts were now I could not guess. There had been force and passion in that kiss.

But I suspected that he might not be best pleased to learn that he had kissed a boy.

I had been right to counsel Robert against the plot. In the following spring the whole sad business came to light, and many were arrested. I myself was spared questioning, but some of my servants were withdrawn from my household, and amongst them Kat. I believed this a mere act of spite. In answer to the letters of protest that I wrote, they told me she was accused of sedition and the possession of contentious books. They sent Sir Thomas Pope to live with us at Hatfield to watch what we did; but if they thought to anger me by this they were mistaken, for he proved a likeable gentleman. He had a big long nose, a double chin and pleasant eyes, and seemed to be content with me. But plot and rumour hung in the very air. I missed Kat's presence. I grew skilled at writing long letters of convoluted prose unto my sister, protesting loyalty and devotion, and I ached with tiredness at the repetition of it.

The summer came on apace, hot and arid, so that folk were irritable and smelt prodigiously of sweat. One day I gave express command that I was not to be disturbed or followed – "By no one, do you understand, upon whatever pretext!" – and I rode out alone as far away from the house as it was possible to go.

The sun beat down upon the dry bleached grass; the dusty leaves drooped in the heat. I rode to where the meadow dipped and hawthorns grew. I dismounted. I was quite alone. I walked amongst the trees, always looking about me, still finding it hard to believe that I was alone and unobserved. I suspect the very oak trees, Robert said. And hawthorns? I took a leaf between my fingers; I believed the hawthorns friendly.

Carefully I began to undo my clothes, having chosen a gown that I could lace and unlace on my own. Slowly the cumbersome garments fell from me; I let them pile up in the grass. I shook my hair free. I stepped clear of all constriction. I cried out with the pleasure of it.

Naked. A nobody. Mere flesh and bone and hair; not a prince, not a queen, not a nobleman; these titles come with the clothes and the adornments. Such homage as I now received would not be mine were I to don a servant's gear or the rags of a beggar. It was the mask, the outward image to which men responded. Without these trappings I was – what?

I looked down at myself. A man. A man of two and twenty. Fair of skin, smooth of body. Along my arms, some golden hairs, some on my legs also; about the crotch a bush of the same. A prick and balls. A neat, firm arse. The entirety a slender shapely personage, one who would grace doublet and hose. Certainly a man. Yet this man had long auburn hair in lush abundance. Beautiful as any found on woman's head, its strands a-glint in the bright sunlight. No trace of beard upon the chin. And yet a man, no doubt of it.

In sudden sharp acceptance of the fact, I spread my thighs, and took my cock between my fingers and I pissed. I let the liquid arc spurt forth, and relished with a childlike delight the clear bold flow. Irreverently I wondered whether I could better Robert at this skill; I wondered how his prick compared with mine. The thought of Robert made me sensuous. I lay down in the grass and rolled and stretched, above me the blue sky and the amicable hawthorns. Later, with my hands about my cock I eased my pleasure from me, lying on my back, and watching as my juices spurted in a joyful and rhythmic emission. For that moment it occurred to me that I had forgotten who I was.

Who I was? What a jest! I did not know the answer. I cast a glance towards the heap of clothes. Whosoever I might be at this small moment, I knew well enough that by the act of dressing, I would become the Princess Elizabeth. But without the clothes – a naked youth, with long auburn hair, and his belly covered in the fluid of his lust.

When I returned to the confines of the palace at the close of day – somewhat dishevelled, it is true, for it is not easy to dress unaided in the fashions of the day – they told me that Prince Philip's messenger, Robert Dudley, had been there, had waited, grown impatient, and departed.

"I am to inform Your Grace," said Sir Thomas Pope, "that Robert Dudley has decided to turn soldier, and is gone to fight in the Netherlands, his brothers Ambrose and Henry with him. He says that there is nothing for him here; and, all things being equal, I was inclined to agree with him."

"He left no other message for me?" I asked, struggling with my disappointment.

"He left a message," said Sir Thomas. "He wrote it while he waited. He did not seal the paper. I could not help but read it. It is scarcely a letter; it has little meaning. It is merely his device."

I took the paper writ by Robert as he waited, and I read his words: "Droit et loyal."

I smiled. "Meaning enough," said I.

"Sister! I am so pleased to see you," lied Queen Mary with a ghastly smile. We embraced. As I drew close to her and felt the curious rigidity of her shape – more than mere stomacher – I understood that what I'd heard was true; she did wear armour underneath her clothes for fear of an assassin.

"I am glad to see you well," continued she; another lie.

"As much as I am to see Your Majesty in such good health," I responded; a double lie here, for she plainly was not so. A fine grey sheen seemed to colour her skin.

"No doubt you, my dear sister, much like myself, were both saddened and relieved to hear of the death of Edward Courtenay in Padua last month."

"A fever, I understood, in the Italian heat."

"Finally now, perhaps, your friends and servants will cease plotting to establish you and him upon the throne," she said with a curl of the lip.

"Your Majesty!" I cried. "The rumours of such vile conspiracies distress me as much as they do yourself. My views on wedlock are well known. I would never have allied myself with Courtenay."

"However," continued Mary imperturbably, "Emmanuel Philibert, the Duke of Savoy, is another matter altogether."

"In what way, Your Majesty?" I enquired uncomfortably.

"I have good news for you, dear sister," Mary's voice grew lower, gruffer than before in her intensity. "All maidens long for marriage. The Duke of Savoy is a fine match. You are well suited. And most important of all, my husband approves the choice. It was to offer you this good news that I invited you to court. I look now to see earnest of your gratitude. Philip and I wish only the best for you, as this must show. Your wedding will take place next spring."

"Indeed it shall not," I protested, white-faced.

"I beg your pardon?" Mary said politely.

"I refuse! I want no part in this. I cannot understand how Your Majesties would even have considered such an inappropriate notion. I have sworn never to wed. The world knows it. I absolutely and entirely refuse to wed the Duke of Savoy, or any man – prince or king."

"I knew you would prove obdurate," Mary growled.

"I have a fear and dread of men," I confided in a low voice. "A fear of submitting my body and soul into the power of another."

"I understand this," Mary answered, and here at last I believed she spoke the truth. "But if you are fortunate, as I am, a kind husband will lead you gently in the ways of love."

"I am not yet ready," I said then.

"It is a woman's duty," Mary told me firmly. "And in this respect you are no different from any other, and must follow God's ordinance."

"God has ordained for me a virgin state," I answered piously. Tears came to my eyes. "I cannot – will not – marry. Never ask it of me, dearest sister; it would be too cruel."

"Oh get you gone," said Mary wearily. "You try my patience to the utmost."

I snivelled loudly in reply. Suddenly she bellowed at me: "I know you sit there in your den at Hatfield, like a monstrous spider, waiting, waiting, praying for me to die, so that you may ascend the throne. I tell you, you shall never have it. I shall have you declared illegitimate by act of Parliament – and so you are, and your mother a whore and your father Mark Smeaton the lute player. You shall never sit where I do now. Go from my sight!"

I fled.

Lying in my bed at Hatfield, I carefully considered what the queen had said to me. It was true, God help me, that I wished her dead; but this wish was not born from spite, but simply from a need for self-protection. I had hardly dared consider the implications of her death. I did not ask myself whether I wished to rule England, with all that that entailed. By now it seemed the logical progression from all that had gone before; and though I was Bisley born and bred I believed that I could play the part of queen as well as anybody. God's breath, the alternative was Catherine, the silly sister of Jane Grey. I was familiar now with palaces, with ceremony, with diplomacy; and it was plain for all to see that there must be an end to the burning of the wretched so-called heretics, and peace throughout the realm: this would be my endeavour. But during that winter, frighted by the threat of marriage, knowing that such was a constant likelihood, I did wish for that woman's death, yes; because only thus would I know that most cherished of possessions: peace of mind.

From Hatfield we kept careful eye upon the troubles in the Netherlands, where Robert Dudley was a soldier. Prince Philip was planning to invade France from his lands in the Low Countries, using his Spanish and our own English troops. In July they marched on Saint-Quentin, where Admiral Coligny held the garrison, and there laid siege. Our armies won a great victory and Saint-Quentin was taken. Robert was amongst those who came back to England.

He carried dispatches, and a change in fortune, for he was now restored in blood, which meant that he could once again claim the rights of his rank as the son of a duke. He came to England, yes, but —

"To Norfolk!" I spat. "To Amy!"

Why not? She was his wife. She had presumably made a home for him. Syderstone. Certainly it would be a pretty house, with herb garden and rose bushes. I pictured her standing in the doorway – running to welcome him. 'Oh Robert! You have been away so long!' I squirmed. They would embrace. Upon a rustic bench they would recline while she would tell him all her paltry news – the gowns that she had had made, the neighbours she had seen, the rising cost of her huswifery, the petty problems of her dairy and her still-room. Later, they would go to bed... I strode about my chamber, kicking at the petticoats that impeded me. I paused. Perhaps she had a frigid nature. 'Oh Robert, I have such a headache...' I sniggered. 'Perhaps tomorrow?' 'Amy, this cannot continue, night after night you refuse me.' 'But Robert, I am not well...'

"Villain! Coystrel! Beast!" I muttered. "What do you there? You will grow fat and red of face. You never were a youth that loved his books; you have not even that which I enjoy, pleasure in study. You will never be content in the country."

Then I received communication from him; a messenger brought me a gift of money. "I know you live in straitened circumstance," he wrote. "From sale of land I have acquired these monies. Use the gift as is most useful..."

Ah, dearest Robert...restored to rights; and his first thought is all of me...

My sister honoured us with a visit to Hatfield. I had no doubt but that Prince Philip had asked for a positive demonstration of her continuing goodwill towards me, and almost certainly she would be glad of any opportunity to seek out the lurking malcontents whom she suspected of hiding behind my wainscoting.

Sir Thomas Pope and I laid on fine entertainment for her, culminating in an evening of musical delight. We had the choirboys of Saint Paul's to sing, and one of them – Maximilian Poynes his name was – gave us a fine solo while I played upon the virginals in accompaniment.

As I played, I smiled. I recalled how when I first came to the court, expressly to deceive the old king and his children, it was always Mary who gave me most difficulty, with her requests to play at cards, or upon those instruments with which I was not then overly familiar. Now I could play the virginals as well as anyone, indeed, much better than most; and as I let the sweet notes out I wondered whether Mary ever thought back to that time.

Her face was haggard now, and, in repose, that of an old woman. She sat there, in her place of honour, looking straight ahead. Upon her finger gleamed the black and gold betrothal ring which would never leave her hand while she yet lived. Earlier that day she had confided in me that she was yet again with child. I told her of my joy, and promised to sew baby linen. This time I did not fear her confinement. I could not believe that, even were she like to bear an infant, her gaunt frame would survive that perilous ordeal. They said she did not enjoy the blessing of good health, nor had for some time. I could well suppose it.

My long white fingers moved upon the keyboard in time to the boy's sweet voice. I watched him. He was very young, and very pretty. He had wide blue eyes and a mouth small as a button, with downy pink cheeks. His voice was high and most melodious. I wondered what would be his lot when that fine treble broke. I hoped he would fall prey to no fierce music master who believed in prolonging the musical life at the expense of the amatory. I thought of Ovid's warning:

> Qui primus pueris genitalia membra recidit,
> Vulnera quae fecit debuit ipse pati...
>
> Who first deprived young boys of their best part
> With selfsame wounds he gave he ought to smart.

How very true, I thought; and after, unbidden, came a most sweet postscript: should I become queen I may have choirboys such as this to sing before me when I choose.

And therefore, as I played I smiled, not this time at the recollection of the past, but at what I hoped for from the days to come.

Although my sister Mary found no trace of malcontents at Hatfield, yet they came. Throughout that winter, and into the spring, came folk, some from across the seas, some from near at hand, to sound me out, to speak of their fears. When Calais fell, such sympathy as yet remained with Mary seemed fast to evaporate, and there were ballads made about the good old days of Agincourt and Crécy, and sung openly. They said that these grim tidings tipped the queen's precarious state of health into a sharp decline, that she had sunk into a melancholic fit and a debilitating and recurrent fever.

Now along the road from London came more than had previously. William Cecil told me that at Smithfield martyrs to their beliefs were burned as much as seven at one fire. That love which once the wretched Mary owned had turned to loathing.

Early in November they informed me that Queen Mary had at last agreed to my succeeding her if she should die, and had asked me to maintain the old religion; I said I would, one more of the many falsehoods we exchanged. But would she die? But would she ever die? And where, amongst this garboil of well-wishers, the nest featherers and those mere rats that quit the sinking ship, was Robert Dudley?

But of course, he did not know...far away in Norfolk...

"They will come to you with the news," murmured Blanche, "and all will watch you – how you heard it, what you said. Best have a prayer ready. Best speak of God. Piety is a great concealer of inappropriate joy."

We took to walking beneath the trees, prayer books in hand, with plenty of time to compose our features as we watched messenger or noble approaching from the house. There was suppressed excitement, nervous anticipation amongst high and low. Numbness also, as if we lived frozen in time, waiting for the signal to begin the act of regeneration.

We heard the news by rumour many times over before we heard it in truth. It was the Earls of Pembroke and Arundel who brought the confirmation of it, and it was Sir Nicholas Throckmorton who knelt and offered me the black and gold betrothal ring from off the dead queen's finger. I had the wit to speak my prayer.

I was surrounded now by gentlemen come to advise me. In some relief I turned to William Cecil, that most friendly face and constant counsellor.

"Messages must be sent...to the Emperor, to Sir William Pickering, to the King of Spain, to Sir Peter Carew, to the King of Denmark, to Lord Robert Dudley..."

He came riding up to the door upon a white charger. Darkly handsome, in a doublet of crimson and long boots of black leather, he knelt at my feet and looked up at me with those wondrous eyes.

He said: "I offer you a true and loyal heart."

NINE

I

I was never modest, and I must confess I took most readily to the matter of becoming Queen of England; I found it a considerable improvement upon what had gone before.

So many folk had flocked to Hatfield that the roads were quite blocked with their passage, and when we set out for the city we were a procession of some thousand strong.

Certain appointments had been made before we left – William Cecil as my chief Secretary of State, and a certain Mistress Ashley as First Lady of the Bedchamber, her husband John the Keeper of my Jewels. Thomas Parry became my Treasurer, and Blanche the Keeper of my Library. Lord Robert Dudley was my Master of Horse. Lord Robert was the best horseman in the land, hero of many tournaments, connoisseur of horseflesh. Now he would of necessity be near me, since the position I had given him made him responsible for every journey I would undertake, with licence to purchase horse and coach, to stock my stables with the best that might be found both here and beyond the seas, and to procure horses for carting and hunt; and having done all this, to ride behind me wherever I might go in progress. I found it most agreeable to possess the power to reward my friends.

We entered London in triumph; Robert arranged it all. The waysides, then the streets, were thronged with cheering people. As we rode towards the Tower the guns thundered salute. I wore violet velvet. Lovely little boys made speeches and sang songs of joy, pressing gifts upon me.

"She is her father come again," I heard a voice cry, and though this unsettled me a little, I understood it simply to mean that I compared with him in colouring and bearing. When I cast a glance behind me, Robert was always there, almost as dazzling as myself, upon a fine black horse – this of necessity, since I rode his white charger, it being the better beast. He had been a little peeved at that; but my violet velvet showed to best effect against the white.

Now the cannons were silent. We entered the Tower. Together Robert and I regarded the grim walls of our respective prisons. I mounted the steps that led to the room where I had been imprisoned. The remembered stench filled my nostrils. I moved across to the window. I shivered. My own fear haunted that room, as the fears of other prisoners had done before me. My fingers traced the contours of the stone. A ring of glowing emerald burned with a bright glow against the cold stone, emphasising my change in fortune.

"No one," murmured I, "shall have power over me again, I swear it."

A boy from Bisley now set out upon a great progress through the streets of London. He wore a gown of cloth-of-gold and a mantle of gold lined with ermine. His long hair hung loose. He wore shoes of gold and silver, lined with crimson satin, and gloves of fine white thread. He rode in an open-sided chariot upon crimson velvet. He was very cold indeed. From time to time, light snowflakes fell. Behind him rode Lord Robert Dudley.

This Bisley boy was carried first to Fenchurch, where a child spoke verses in his praise; he passed along Gracechurch Street to Cheapside, where an aged man and a little girl represented for him Father Time and his daughter Truth. He received a purse of a thousand gold marks from the Lord Mayor; he made a gracious speech. At Little Conduit an English Bible was lowered to him on a thread of silk; he made a great show of kissing it. He saw six pageants heavy with meaning; he saw Deborah dispensing justice and understood a reference to himself. At St Paul's a schoolboy with a reedy voice compared him to a philosopher king. He returned to Whitehall in the dusk. A brilliant eruption of fireworks cascaded into view and showered stars of light into the misty river.

He lay that night in the bedroom which overlooked that river. The bed was an immense affair of many-coloured woods, the quilt of silk and velvet, threaded with silver. The sharp cracks of the fireworks sounded yet, and darts of bright flame stabbed the darkness.

"Kat – oh, Kat – what have we done?" he whispered. "Whatever will become of us?"

It was the eve before his coronation.

Now he wore crimson velvet with an ermine cape and he sat on cushions of cloth-of-gold, a white damask quilt about him, in the open-sided chariot which brought him to Westminster Abbey where a purple carpet had been spread for him. Always Robert Dudley rode behind, now leading a white palfrey, his brother Ambrose to one side. Robert wore carnation gold, and his horse was caparisoned in purple and gold. There was music from organ, pipe and drum. For the ceremony this same Bisley boy wore cloth-of-gold and purple velvet and a mantle of crimson. He wore a tabard of white sarcenet to spare the rich robes from the anointing oil. He found that the anointing oil stank. Then he received the crown. The Black Prince's ruby glowed amongst a welter of pearls, diamonds and sapphires. A myriad bells rang out. *Will you have Elizabeth for queen?* They roared approval. In purple velvet I emerged, holding the holy orb and sceptre, and my face wreathed in smiles. They loved me! They wanted me! They would have this boy to rule them, and he would do it gladly. This bargain made betwixt us was now ratified by Holy Church.

And so to feasting in the Hall at Westminster, two hundred people seated at long rows of tables. Arundel in silver, Norfolk in gold rode up and down to announce the arrival of each fresh course of the banquet. We drank to one another, and the trumpets blared. Lord William Howard stood to one side of me, the Earl of Sussex to the other. To my chagrin I found I was possessed of a vile head cold; I blamed the open-sided chariot. Tomorrow Robert was to joust for me, and my nose was streaming and I should not look my best. Till the other side of midnight our celebrations continued. My eyes and throat ached, but by some strange alchemy I thrived and glowed, unwilling to be quit of this most wondrous day.

And now the bed curtains are drawn about me, and the warm and welcome darkness encloses me.

"Kat! Come within!" I whispered. In amongst the bedclothes curled my dear First Lady of the Bedchamber. We lay, our arms about each other, I with a great handkerchief about my nose, and much incommoded by the onset of my cold.

"No one can touch us now, Kat," I said with a gulp, half phlegm, half triumph.

"No, my pretty," she agreed, complacent and excited both. "We have achieved it now at last. Oh Lord, my pretty one, whoever would have thought it! This is a strange time for us." She hesitated. "Are you afraid?"

"No," I laughed. "I should be, I suppose, by rights, but I am too exhausted. I could sleep for longer than the Seven Sleepers did! But it is me the people want, Kat. I am the one they shout for. Only I can do what is required, be what is needed. I am in my right place, Kat, I know it. I was never meant to live and die at Bisley. And Kat, it is thanks to you – to your foresight, your cleverness..."

"Oh no," Kat answered, flustered, "no, I dare not take the blame for this... The burden would be too great."

"Then I take the blame myself," said I, "for I was eager enough and needed small persuasion. Kat? Whatever can have become of Xavier? Why has he not come to claim his reward?"

"He bides his time, chuck," Kat shrugged. "Who can say? Give him no thought tonight. Sleep now; there is much to do."

With rheumy eyes and aching head, the nation's hope, the realm's salvation drifted into slumber.

And now about me buzz a host of suitors. First is Philip himself, who lets me know through his ambassador de Feria that should I become papist and lead England back into the fold, he will have me; then thinking better of it, offers me his nephew Archduke Ferdinand of Austria. We Habsburgs, he says, will welcome you into our great fraternity. And now the court is full of men with names no one can pronounce – Augustin Gyntzev, Count von Helfenstein, Caspar von Breuner, Baron of Stubling, Fladnitz and Rabenstein. A full-length portrait of Archduke Ferdinand is carried in with some difficulty. Swedes we have also, singing the virtues of Prince Eric. Now the Archduke Charles is proposed. But how could I marry a man I have never seen, I simper? Would he be prepared to come in person? In disguise perhaps?

Ambassadors sneak up on me when I am at play, watching the

dancers at a ball, to probe my views when they believe my mind unguarded. They purse their lips and withdraw.

Marriage with the Earl of Arran becomes a possibility. We would unite England and Scotland. I meet the earl in secret, and find him unstable. The King of Denmark sends me a heart of crimson velvet pierced by an embroidered arrow. The Duke of Finland comes to plead the cause of Eric of Sweden.

And nobody believes my declaration: I shall never marry; I am determined to be governed by no one. This celibate life is so pleasant and I am grown so well accustomed to it that I would rather enter a nunnery than marry against my will. But on the other hand, I add – for I have no wish to send them away unhappy – should I ever wed, then your master...and your master...are both high in my regard; pray tell them so.

And where is Robert all this time? With me, ever with me. I have never been so well content in all my life.

You see, it is a very pleasant thing to be a queen! One rises late. One takes breakfast in one's chamber. Now, still private, one attends to one's toilet. That is, my ladies move about me, comfortable and competent. They wash my hair – my person is already bathed, Kat in attendance – and dress me in my finery. We paint my face with an egg-white mixture. I have a tailor and a hosier who advise me. Russet, tawny, orange, peach and crimson suit me well. I wear cloth-of-silver slippers, and I twine pearls into my hair.

Once I had discovered silk stockings I wore them constantly, and cloth stockings only in winter. I have at my disposal French gowns, robes, cloaks, loose gowns, kirtles and stomachers, and many dozens of petticoats; a new pair of shoes each week, and any number of feather fans.

The vision I am now become, I walk abroad. I dance; I pray; I read, and write letters; I consult with my ministers; I receive reports, and ambassadors. I read and I translate. I hunt and hawk; I dine; I banquet; I am entertained by masque or play or music. I am attended by my Gentlemen Pensioners who escort me where I go, all young and beautiful and muscular, and none of them an inch under six foot.

I have a score of palaces at my disposal. I begin the year at

Whitehall, Greenwich, Hampton Court or Windsor; then to Oatlands my hunting lodge with its tall trees full of rooks; or Nonsuch with its white marble fountain and its statues of the emperors of Rome; to Whitehall for the spring; and then in summer I make progresses and visit the fine houses of my more favoured subjects; and in autumn I return to Oatlands, Windsor, Nonsuch, and so again to Whitehall.

This is a way of life I think it will not be difficult to grow to like.

I remember when I first saw my bedroom at Nonsuch. Like the little country boy I once had been, I gaped wide-eyed.

"Kat! There's a bath room! A room especially created for myself to bathe! And lined from floor to ceiling with looking glass!"

We stared, the two of us, at this great marvel. There stood the bath tub, made of mottled porphyry, on a little dais, ornate in itself. And every wall was glass, with ourselves reflected, and our shining eyes and open mouths. Kat clapped a hand over her face.

"My lady! oh my lady! You must never stand upright in this room unless the door be locked. A person entering unforeseen would see you from all sides. You could not hide!"

Next day we had a fine firm lock put in place upon the door of that dangerous and voluptuous little room.

I discovered in myself a love of pageantry, a sensuous appreciation of the drapes of gold and silver brocade that hung in the Long Gallery at Whitehall when we welcomed visiting dignitaries, the crystal drinking cups, the flowers arranged in curious device with profusion of summer fragrances, the roses twined about the doors to make an arbour within a room, the contrast between milky pearl and purple velvet. I found that rich attire became me well, and, well protected by the width and spread of the farthingale, I never needed fear discovery of that strange secret I possessed; beneath such kindly panoply my hidden prick might lift and thicken to its heart's content, all unobserved.

"They say that Robert Dudley is your lover..."

Oh, foolish tongues to wag on such a wayward matter! Would that he were – that he could ever be!

Robert and I were like two children that had been all their lives shut up in some dark room with but the wherewithal to keep alive. Now the latch was lifted and the door ajar, and we had come forth, and found the world to be a castle of riches, with, beyond, a meadow of delight, and all for us to pick and sample. And, by appetite greedy and by nature sybaritic, we took with both hands.

We rode fast horses in the royal parks, racing each other, laughing, with no velvet-gloved gaolers waiting for us at our return. We danced long into the night at the gorgeous winter balls, the myriad candlelights a-glimmer and the scent of sweat and perfume mingling in the crowded chamber. We took a barge upon the Thames at dusk, supping at friends' houses, and returning with the lights dancing in the black water, and the sound of drums and flutes accompanying us where we went. We passed time in the stables discoursing upon the merits of Irish or Spanish horse; we never spoke of Amy. Of course there was gossip. I knew what they were saying:

"Why has not Lord Robert sent for his wife now?"

"It is because he has set her up in a house in Oxfordshire."

"Buried her in the country, eh?"

"Buried? Ah, not yet, not yet..."

"Other men's wives have come to court..."

"They say court life does not best please her..."

"I have heard she longs to come to court, but is forbid."

"They say Lord Robert has made other plans."

"They say she is unwell."

"Was it wise, dear lady," Kat began one day, "to give Lord Robert Dudley his own rooms in Whitehall?"

"That is his due, as Master of Horse."

"But so near to your own?"

"Where else should be the rooms of one's dearest friend but near at hand?"

In a loose gown, well padded beneath, a robe about my shoulders, I was accustomed to visit Robert's bedchamber. A maid-in-waiting would accompany me, and Robert's manservant Mark Tamworth let us in. The room was dark and warm from the hearth's glow, and we would drink wine and eat Corinth cakes and talk into the night.

Once I said: "Things have fallen out well for us, Robert, we who went so latterly in terror for our lives."

"It was my constant prayer that we should know such happiness. We trod a maze, with enemies at every corner. Good fortune, had we known it, watched over us the while, and brought us safely to this haven."

"By a hairsbreadth," I agreed.

He leaned towards me, smiling. "Will you never tell me the answer to that childhood question, even now?"

"What question, Robert?" I asked innocently.

"You know well enough. You said that you would tell me when you were ready. Don't play with me, Elizabeth; there is no need. The moment never can be more appropriate than now, with our fears and dreads behind us. And in some ways, the situation is curiously the same, and the question therefore relevant to the present time. And now the answer is become more pressing, since my future hangs on it."

"Your future? Is there any doubt of that? Your future lies with me, here at my side."

"But in what capacity? I tread a no-man's-land between the part of friend and servant; this makes me doubtful and unsure."

"Unsure?" I laughed. "There is not a doubtful bone in your body, Robert; you are certainty itself. You walk, ride, move, dance, all as if the earth were yours to command; and I love you for it."

A look leapt to his eyes, as quickly suppressed.

"You love me as a lapdog or a sunny day," he answered lightly, though I know he hoped for reassurance.

"It's odd, I know, that I should so freely have used that word," I admitted cautiously. "I have always felt that I cared more for you than you for me. Once when we were children I asked for a kiss from you, and I recall you gave it most ungraciously."

"I was a fool," he responded at once. "Ask again. Ask now..."

His eyes, those wonderful eyes, looked into mine. A coward impulse seized me. "Now I am in no asking humour," I replied. I sensed my maid-in-waiting stiffen; I had half forgot that she was there. I pulled myself together.

"I too tread a fine line," I said to Robert, "not always knowing whether to respond to you as friend or sovereign. At this juncture, with a mob of suitors baying for my hand, a kiss bestowed on you would carry more meaning than it should. And I would never know whether it was my power you reached for or my person."

"Then let me make that plain at once," said Robert with a flash of anger, stung no doubt because there was some truth in what I said. "You had no power at all at Woodstock, and little at Hatfield, and less in the Tower, but my devotion never faltered. We were good friends as children; you were like a boy to me. I had no thought of who you were but as a fellow archer, rider, chess player. Do all those years mean nothing, when we were friends because I was I and you were you?"

"I have never doubted your friendship," I said, much moved. Who could have told us in those distant days that Edward would die, and Mary also, and that I would steer clear of both assassin and foreign bridegroom, each equally to be avoided? No, his care for me was true enough. But must I, who now possessed that dark deceiver, power, because of it alone, be the first to speak of love? I let the moment pass, and after, soon withdrew.

On one of the occasions when I rode alone with Robert we drew rein where a little stream led into the river, forming a small creek thick with overhanging willows. The grass grew high, the heat haze hung, a tremulous misty green, dusty and peaceful. Clouds of butterflies rose from the meadow flowers. Beneath the trees the river was slow moving, with bushes of wild roses growing down towards its edge. We could see the pebbles on the river bed, and shoals of tiny speckled fish. Blue damsel flies darted.

We dismounted; our horses drank.

"Warm enough to bathe," said Robert.

I laughed scornfully. Did he suppose I would undress?

"Not you," he added, joining in my laughter. "Me."

"You?" I teased. "Would you provide an entertainment for me?"

"It would be my pleasure," he responded graciously. And yours too was his implication.

"Very well," said I, and sat down in the grass and spread my skirts.

"After all," said Robert, with an affectation of diffidence, as he unlaced his doublet, "you have seen me bathe before."

My mind flitted briefly back to childhoood days when Robert, Barnaby and Henry Sidney – and sometimes even Edward – had plunged romping into shallow waters, splashing, sparring, ducking one another. I recalled a pleasing melange of pert bums and jiggling pricks; and with a little surge of pleasure I remembered that even at eleven years old the youthful Robert had the best legs and the most attractive shape. I settled comfortably amongst the grasses and a warm sweat of anticipation suffused my body. I watched Robert undress. I caught my breath, startled at how beautiful he was.

I think that I have never seen a man more perfectly formed, clothed or unclothed. He was tall, his legs were long, with sumptuous thighs, lightly furred with fine dark hairs. His chest was bare, his belly smooth, his prick large even in repose, his balls of like vigour. His arse was firm and well shaped – years of superb horsemanship could work as much, I noted with appreciation. His arms were muscular from swordplay and archery. Naked he was well at ease. He stood now, legs apart, with no attempt to hide his parts, well aware that he was worth more than a passing glance. He smiled at me. His eyes glowed. There, they said, you wanted to peruse what I can offer you...you always like the best...if you have any doubts, resolve them now.

Then suddenly he turned, and leapt into the river. He made a monstrous splash. I leaned forward, panting. My cock lurched, and I put an ineffectual hand down to my skirts. I watched him swim, that bright Adonis. The sunlight glittered on the waterdrops that fell from his raised arm.

I longed to join him. I longed to throw off my cumbersome clothes and jump in beside him, to wrestle and to tease, to press against him in the water, belly to belly, prick to prick. A great despondency came over me. I understood it very well. I desired him with every breath in my body. The irony of it all was that a crook of the little finger would bring him to me. And then...what then?

Robert heaved himself out of the water, streaming droplets, confident of his reception. I forced a smile.

"Bravely done!" I said. "You put Leander to shame."

He crouched beside me, some young god of the stream, pagan, expectant. "And my reward?" he breathed.

"The knowledge that you pleased me," I hedged.

"Ah!" he groaned, plainly disappointed. "And did I swim the Hellespont for this?"

"What would you have more?" I asked, melting at his rampant maleness and the beauty of his nakedness.

"A kiss, and quickly, before I start to shiver," said he.

He leaned over me and his lips touched mine.

"Enough – you'll dampen my clothes," I protested.

Sulkily he withdrew, and jumped to his feet. He shook himself and ran about to dry, rolling then in the long grasses. All of this I watched, pretending I did not. He dressed.

"You are chary of your favours, madam," he observed severely, helping me to rise.

I smiled. "That is because I know they will be the more valued when at last I offer them."

"Well," he smiled in return. "I see I must be content with that."

That evening, late, I came to his room unaccompanied. I was dressed in a loose gown as before, well padded at the hips. They call the cushion-like accessory that gives such an effect a 'bum roll'. It was the fashion of the day. I wore my hair loose, having perfumed it with coriander.

Tamworth opened the door to me. Robert was not yet abed, but stood beside a table, goblet in hand.

"Elizabeth..?" his eyes flickered in surprise, in sudden hope.

I said nothing. I glided over to him and put my arms about him. He responded instantly. I kissed him, my mouth greedily seeking his, our tongues now interlocked. We held each other fast. I kissed his face then – eyebrows, eyelids, all about. I twined my tongue about his ears; I surprised myself by the vehemence of my passion. I bent my head and kissed his neck, his chest. He groaned ecstatically.

"Elizabeth..." he whispered, and his glance strayed to the bed.

I shook my head, forcing myself back to equilibrium.

He understood. He gave a wry smile.

"My reward?"

I nodded.

"Well," he said. "I see I need not fear the Earl of Arran or the Archduke Charles."

I smiled, and put a finger to his lips; and then I left him.

There had been a certain complacency in his tone, and in his assumption that I had come to him as queen.

Poor Robert. All that had occurred was that another man had for that moment lusted for his body.

II

They do not like Robert, these courtiers of mine.

The Earl of Arundel, Henry Fitzalan, my Lord Steward, had been a faithful servant to my grandsire; a man in his forties, dark and bearded, he was a good-humoured well-read fellow, and gave splendid entertainments. He it had been who had spoken up for me when Bishop Gardiner accused me in the Tower. Insular and proud, he looked backward rather than forward for his inspiration. He strongly resented Robert's rise to fame, and having been imprisoned without trial by Robert's father he would be unlikely to bear warm feelings towards the son; but he resented Cecil also – it was the lapse of the old order that disquieted him, as a result of which a few years later he resigned his post, and went across the seas to Padua, seemingly to take the waters for his gout.

Then there was the Earl of Sussex, Thomas Radcliffe. Chief Steward by hereditary right, a man of the old nobility. He it was most involved with the negotiations for the proposed marriage with the Archduke Charles, and certainly thus found Robert's presence an annoyance; for it was no secret that the rumours flew concerning Robert and myself. A man in his early thirties, Sussex was devoted to me; but he could barely bring himself to be civil in Robert's company, and plainly detested him. Sussex, however, was so much my honourable servant that he may simply have believed that Dudley, son of a traitor to the realm, was not a good enough reason for the queen's possible rejection of a better suitor. He was then soldiering in Ireland; his dislike of Robert was to manifest itself on his return.

Thomas Howard, Duke of Norfolk, was, however, too much with

us. He too, scion of an ancient family, a descendant of King Edward III, therefore cousin of mine and a Plantagenet, made no secret of his disdain for so-called upstarts such as my secretary Cecil and my Robert. Like Arundel, to whom he was related by marriage, he looked back to the past. He had a long oval face with a sensitive mouth and lugubrious dog-like eyes, an auburn beard, and an expression indecisive and melancholy. He had been much in evidence at my coronation, walking before me, bearing Saint Edward's crown, officiating at the banquet, dressed in silver lined with sables. Younger than Robert, he was a graceful dancer, a fine rider, skilled in many accomplishments. Had Robert not been at court, he, Norfolk, would have shone more brilliantly. When he and Robert were both created Knights of the Garter I had hoped their visible enmity would ease. It did not.

Robert did not give a fig for the finer feelings of the old nobility. His quarrel with Norfolk echoed down the galleries.

"I hold you a poor Englishman to give your support to the notion that Her Majesty should marry the Archduke," Robert said. "No loyal Englishman would wish Her Majesty subject to a foreigner."

"Oh? Perhaps you think I should give my support to the notion of a marriage with yourself?"

"Her Majesty might do worse."

"I warn you, Dudley, that unless you cease your presumption you may well not die in your bed!"

Was he masterminding a plot to murder Robert? We heard whispers of it.

We appointed him our Lieutenant-General in the North and sent him with our army to prevent French troops from setting foot in Scotland. At that time I trusted him. That he possessed a Hand of Fortune game that dealt in the rise and fall from power I thought merely a curiosity. That a portrait of the Plantagenet King Richard III hung in his house at Kenninghall did not seem at that juncture sinister.

Now as well as his amiable brother Ambrose here at court Robert had a sister Mary, a most lovely creature, one of my ladies-in-waiting.

Standing, holding the casket where I kept some of my rings, she looked at me uncertainly.

"Your Majesty...may I speak?"

"Of course, dear Mary – though I think I guess the source of your misgivings."

"My brother..." she began.

"I knew it."

"Your Majesty has been so gracious..."

"Not at all," I demurred.

"So many gifts...so many honours..."

It was true enough. Our Robert was a Privy Councillor, Knight of the Garter, constable of Windsor Castle. He now had house and land at Kew, and the monies due to him as Master of Horse; and other favours besides.

"He has deserved them all. Mary, he is the ornament of my court. He is the perfect courtier – handsome, gallant, witty, full of vigour, skilled at tournament and dance. I had no notion of the richness and diversity of his accomplishments when first we rode from Hatfield. There is no man so superb, so dazzling in perfection as he."

"A sister sometimes sees another side," said Mary drily. "His vanity? His singlemindedness? His selfishness?"

"We all have faults...but you would say more?"

"Pardon me for my boldness. It is only my great love for you both that causes me to trespass on your goodness. I fear..."

"You fear?" I prompted.

"By raising him so high, you cause men to grow jealous of him, and I fear their hatred. They say cruel things of him. They say – "

"These whisperings are the petty murmurings of spite."

"But some of them are true," she whispered.

"To what do you refer?" I asked her sternly.

"They say what does a man who flaunts his closeness to the queen when all the time he has a wife at home."

"Well, that is nothing," I scoffed. "Robert visits Amy...now and then."

"A little more of then than now," said Mary.

"But I need him here. He has his duties. I cannot spare him to make social visits to the country. I hope you do not find fault with me for this?"

"No indeed, Your Majesty," said Mary warmly. "No, the fault lies with Robert. If you could make him see as much... If you could ask him to be kind to Amy...it would do much good to his reputation. And she is not well."

"She has an illness of the breast; I know that."

"And more, a sadness of the heart. They say that such is caused by lack of love."

"I will speak of her to Robert," I said.

But I did not, and nor did he. When he and I were with each other, we only spoke of things that mattered to us.

Among the many prerogatives of a king or queen I trust that no one would deny the paramount importance of the right to seek and satisfy the pleasures of the flesh.

I assumed at that time that as a lover Robert was of necessity forbidden me. I would have greatly loved to take him to my bed; but Robert loved a woman, and it was plainly not in my best interests to disillusion him. I was, however, in full manhood, twenty-six years old, with power to do as I chose and with male needs to be fulfilled. I sent once more for Thomas Parry.

I looked at him with affection, this irascible companion in misfortune, now grown corpulent with good living. We sat each side of the table, as so many times before, our papers spread between us.

"Thomas," I murmured, leaning forward. "Do you recall how once you found a wench for me, and I in male attire, and we walked the night-time streets, two men together?"

Thomas chuckled then. "We have seen chequered times... But," he frowned, "mere pleasure in recollection is, I hope, the only reason for Your Majesty's reference to that escapade at this present moment."

"It is my wish, Tom, that you would find me a youth... an ingle. I know that such exist. I think it would be an easy enough matter for one of your discernment and knowledge in the world's ways."

"What are you about?" he growled. "You cannot prowl the streets as you are now become! The risks – the danger... No, it cannot be done – much as I am always glad to please Your Majesty in all things."

"You misunderstand me, old friend. You would send the boy by water to the Whitehall backstairs. You will tell him that a gentleman awaits. It will not be the first time that those old steps, that back way, have known the night-time arrival of a drab of one sex or another. There is a privy passage leading from the upper apartments, straight to that door."

"But what if you are recognised? What if the boy should guess the name of his unknown paramour?"

"How may he?" I replied. "Who of the common folk has seen the queen except in jewels and robes and gold? And since the queen is a woman, there can be no link between Her Grace and some lewd gentleman of the court who sends by night for a street boy. And you, Thomas, shall be waiting at the door, and lead our guest to where I shall be." I convinced him, talked him round; for I believed there was no danger in it. With Blanche to sit at the upper end of the privy stair on guard; with Kat to accompany me down and attend my divestiture, and Thomas to oversee my rendezvous, I was certain to be safe.

I must confess to a rising excitement as, emerging from a sea of petticoats, I regained my true self. Kat helped me to bind my luxuriant head of hair in a red jewelled velvet cap. My hair, pulled tightly back from my brow, was completely hidden – much as is seen in the portrait I had painted for Eric of Sweden, when all agreed I was the image of young Edward. That was my only vulnerability, and it was well dealt with. Therefore I made a personable male in my doublet and hose when I entered the small room where the lad was ready for me.

"My lord, this is the boy," said Thomas self-importantly; and withdrew.

A yellow-haired scrap of a lad he was, some fifteen years or so, a Bankside whore skilled at his trade. Unasked, he stripped for me, flaunting his lean young body to my gaze; then with the lightest of kisses on my mouth, he moved down till he knelt before me, and took out my prick, made much of it, then turned about and, bending to a chair, offered his buttocks to me. I took him. Sodomy, said Brother Xavier, so long ago, can be very pleasant. My physical need was well satisfied in that moment.

Was this my true self then, that elusive thing, now finally encapsulated here, a nobleman hunched over a street boy, a man that, like so many others, sought release in his own kind? I paid the boy well; he thanked me; but I said no word to him, my voice – that great betrayer – silent. For the duration of my gratification I was transported, who knows where, adrift in time. With passion spent, a mental void remained. The boy was gone; I was alone. What did Robert do, I wondered, for the easing of his needs? Not for a moment did I suppose that they were satisfied within the marriage bed; he was never from my side. Moreover, I had heard such tales of Amy – querulous, hysterical, unwell – no, she could never please a man of Robert's nature. What did he do? Had he ever been across the river to the stews? What did I know of him?

I tugged my hair clear of the velvet cap. Into the room came Kat, bustling, frowning, plainly apprehensive.

"Oh my lady – John – take off those clothes – it makes me ill to see you as a man. And with your hair long like a woman's – what are you now become? - not one sex nor the other! Here is your gown. For God's sake, dress, I beg you!"

Hurriedly we worked to lose that lewd courtier, and with Thomas's help all the final touches were then put to send that villain packing.

A little flushed, the queen in a loose robe came from the passage, reclaimed Blanche from her post, and crept back to her bedchamber. There Her Gracious Majesty lay in her great bed with its painted silk hangings, and wept into the pillows.

Her Majesty is not long down-hearted. It is summer time. She mollifies poor Cecil, driven to distraction by her prevarications; she oversees the reform of the currency; she fends off rumours that she intends to make Lord Robert her consort when his personal circumstances permit; she indulges in diurnal verbal fencing with poor Alvaro de la Quadra the Spanish ambassador. She dines at Robert Dudley's house at Kew; she returns to Richmond by torchlight, starry-eyed at the recollection of their conversation.

What did we say? It was nothing; it was merely the contented ramblings of two people that are glad to be together. We laughed; but at nothing in especial; and the hours sped by.

Yet I have no sooner quit his company than I long for him again.

He came to my bedchamber. Of course, we were not alone. Kat was with me, and Mary, Robert's sister. I sat in bed, the bedclothes well around me. My bed gown was of white silk. Kat brushed my hair.

"Sit beside us, Robin," I invited. Robert lodged himself upon the bed.

"Tell me your news," I breathed, and looked into his eyes.

"What, since I last saw you – a hundred years ago at supper?" he smiled.

"You are right – it was a hundred years, and in that time you must have had a million thoughts!"

"And all of them of you."

"Tell me some hundred of them; we have time."

"My lady is a radiant angel – "

"Wait – first let us establish to whom you refer, Rob. Your lady? Who is that? Some holy statue – or some wench I know not of?"

"Why, you clown," he grinned, "who else but you could so possess my heart, my soul, my very being?"

"Do I, Robin? Do I all that? Tell me."

"Your hair, my love, is soft as satin. Mistress Ashley, brush it not so rough. Give me the comb. I'll show you how it should be done."

"Do as he says, Kat."

"Now, where was I? Hair as soft as satin. Face like a radiant star."

"We have had 'radiant'. 'Radiant' was the angel."

"Forgive me. Face of that haunting beauty we associate with Diana, moving by moonlight in the misty forest, spangled with silver."

"The forest spangled, or the lady?"

"Everything; we are talking about moonlight."

"No, we are talking about my beauty."

"Forgive me again. My concentration lapses when I am so close beside you...so close that I can smell the perfume of your skin, and breathe into your ear...so."

"You have raised goose bumps all the length of my arm!"

"Let me see."

"What, must I show my flesh to any passer-by that asks it?"

"I have heard that when men look on treasure they grow mad. I fear to lose my reason. But I would lose it gladly for the sight of that for which men cross the seas at risk of life and limb. It would be a small price to pay."

"Nevertheless I shall not ask it of you, Robin dear. I prefer your reason to your artifice. What if you truly loved me, and ceased posing as a lover? How would you be with me if you truly were to speak of love?"

"My eyes speak it...constantly."

"They do?"

"Look at me...test me."

"No. When I look in your eyes my own reason is somewhat at risk."

"And I thought you so bold."

"I am bold!" I blazed; and our eyes met. As if an invisible beam shone from eye to eye, our gaze held, motionless.

"Now do you see true love?" Robert asked in a low voice.

"Love?" I breathed. "I would not know it if I saw it. What is it like?"

"It is like what you see before you, no more nor less."

"Oh Robin – if I could believe it..."

"As I understand it, we believe in what we see, and where we yet doubt, faith steps in to sway the balance."

"I have that faith," I answered.

"Then we are invincible," said he.

I shook myself clear of those bright orbs' enchantment, aware of Kat beside me, sensing her unease.

I gave a brittle and unconvincing laugh. "Leave me now, Lord Robert; and sweet dreams to you."

"They will be sweet, your gracious Majesty; for they will be of you," he answered easily.

Comfortable in the return of his courtly superficiality I smiled.

He kissed my hand, bowed, and was gone.

"I think it wrong you should encourage him," Kat said afterwards. "What good can it do? He is a married man, and you could never wed him even were he free as air."

"I know that," I replied. "It doesn't matter. But why do people frown so upon simple pleasure? It pleases me to talk of love with Robert; and it pleases Robert also. Where is the harm?"

"It is common tittle-tattle that you have borne his child!"

I giggled. "That is my favourite rumour. I love to hear it. I believe we have had two or three infants already. We are a fecund pair."

"Have a care of your reputation, madam," answered she severely. "Women and queens must learn to do so."

"Oh Kat," I laughed. "Such rumours are so easily disproved. Where are all these brats?"

"You know very well," Kat said. "After a midwife has been led blindfold at midnight to a secret place and delivered a healthy babe of a young woman with auburn hair, the babe has been conveyed – "

"By night," I grinned.

"Hidden in a basket, amongst the cheeses," Kat relented and began to smile. "And taken to a goodwife far from London – a buxom dame who'll ask no questions. Why, I believe there are no fewer than twenty such, scattered about the realm, all buxom, and good-hearted and discreet, mothering these little auburn-headed infants."

"I wonder I've had time for policy," I smirked. "I seem to have spent much time in childbed."

"We laugh," said Kat, sober again. "But the gullible believe it. Therefore, be circumspect with my lord Robert."

"What does it matter?" I shrugged. "As you say, we can never marry. It is but play. The world should guess as much. Why, anyone would do the same if they were me. Who could not love Robin? He is entirely perfect. Is he not, Kat? Is he not perfection?"

Kat smiled indulgently. "Aye, he is so. And why should you not be happy with him while you may?"

As usual, we outdistanced all the rest, Robert and I, and here among the trees, at Windsor, we dismounted, leading our horses slowly at a walk.

Robert turned his gaze to me, his face half in shade.

"Forgive me if this moment is inopportune," he said.

"For what purpose, inopportune?" I enquired.

"To speak of sober matters."

"Ah – then perhaps it is so."

"Elizabeth," he said. "It pleases us to play and jest; but answer me in all seriousness... You know I love you."

"Indeed I do not."

"You do – your heart knows it. I believe that I have always loved you; indeed, if one may judge love by the consistency of devotion, the inability to forget for an instant the image of the beloved, then I confess myself love's adept. I shall always love you."

"Rob, I think I would prefer our foolery."

"No, hear me out," he said. "I shall always love you. But tell me, have I any hope that this love may find satisfaction – albeit long hence – at some distant date? What I mean by this preamble is..." and now he dropped to one knee and looked up at me, "...would you, most wonderful of women, ever so demean yourself as to honour your poor servant with that marriage of which everybody speaks but us? Answer!" he begged. "Even though by a refusal you would pierce my heart!"

I breathed again. So he was not so serious as he implied.

"I have said that I will never marry," I repeated gently.

"Yes, but," and he gave a wry smile, "nobody believes you."

"They doubt the word of a queen!" I said in mock outrage.

"No... the heart of a woman," answered he.

"Oh, stand up, Robin," I laughed. "Rob, Rob, you are in no position to speak to me of marriage – you have a wife at home!"

He stood, slowly. "Amy has a malady which her physicians say will kill her within the year."

"Very well, then ask me at that time," I said pertly, with a toss of the head.

He looked so grim and downcast that I relented. I said: "I speak now with my heart, Rob. If ever I wed Englishman it shall be you."

"That is all I wished to hear," he answered.

"Oh my God!" groaned Robert, seated, hunched, his face buried in his hands. "How must it seem to you? I swear – I swear it is not so!"

I comforted him as best I could, stroking his hair, taking one of his hands between my own. He grasped my hand as a drowning man a straw. He turned those wondrous eyes upon me, looking up with tear-stained cheeks. "Tell me you believe me innocent. Nothing else matters."

"What do you think happened?" I whispered.

"I think she took her life, though I would deny it to anyone else but you. She sent her servants away, every one; she sent them to the fair. It would appear she wished to be alone, and – she was subject to strange fancies – this again I would deny to others. She said often enough that life held nothing for her – she prayed for deliverance – none came; therefore she reached for it herself. She was in pain. There is a certain reason in what she did. Or may have done."

"Perhaps she simply lost her footing on the stair."

"Yes, this could well be so. But tell me honestly, who will believe it?"

Robert retired to his house in Kew in great gloom and despair, while a jury at length brought in a verdict of death by misadventure on his wife Amy, found dead at the foot of her staircase, her neck broken by the fall.

God knows I did not wish her dead. All the difficulties rampant in her existence were a hundredfold increased by her demise. When the furore died down, when the muttered calumny concerning Robert and myself would finally dissipate with time's passing – for it was common knowledge that we two had plotted her death like two stage murderers, cackling the while, clamped in a lewd embrace – yes, when all was quiet again, Robert would surface a free man.

My dread was that he would persist in his love for me, love that I as fervently requited, and with eminent reason, one day would kneel to me once again and point out that we were both free to marry, and that if I loved him, as I said I did, then why should we not do so? He would give reasons, all political, why our marriage would be in every way acceptable. He would persuade Cecil to approve.

Then he would turn to me, adoring, ardent, confident of my reciprocal tenderness. And I, what could I answer? What reason, what excuse for my continued procrastination, my inexplicable coquetry? Must I then watch the diminution of his love through weariness, reproach and disappointment? Must my existence dwindle into a repetitive conundrum, of waking one more day to tease him and to tell him no?

TEN

I

"Marry me!" purred Robert, his lips close to my ear.

Behind him the crimson satin awning quivered in the wind; at his feet the deck was strewn with flowers.

"Marry you? Where have I heard that song before?" I teased, settling against his shoulder.

A year had passed. To see us, merry and laughing, at the Midsummer water party on the river, you would have thought that neither Robert nor myself had ever heard such words as wife, mysterious circumstances, jury, suspicion, murder... How easily these things could be forgotten! He had not loved her. He loved me...he loved Elizabeth. The magic lanterns danced along the water's edge; the water glimmered, green, gold, silver; but the waves, I remember, rocked the boat in which we stood.

"I believe that I ask it every day, and with equal predictability you refuse me," said Robert.

"Nothing is predictable; therefore ask and ask again."

"Be assured that I will do so. As the force of the river wears a passage through the most obdurate of rocks, so shall the force of my love wear down the impassivity of your resistance."

"I hope so, dearest eyes, and so never fail in your tenacity. And after all, I do not believe my resistance so very strong," I smiled.

"It is a wall," he groaned.

"It is a weak wall. One more push may do it."

"Marry me!" said Robert.

"Bishop de Quadra." I called out to him where he stood in conversation with Cecil. "Robert and I would be wed – what better moment could there be than here upon the choppy Thames, and by your own fair hand?"

"Elizabeth!" gasped Robert, stupid with disbelief.

"Come, bishop, here we stand. Or shall we kneel? This is my bridegroom – have you ever seen a more handsome fellow? Any woman would be proud to take him. I know that I would. Ah, Robert, look – the bishop is confused and knows not what to say. I fear his command of English is not sufficient for our purpose, and afterwards he might be inclined to deny what he has done, saying he had been confused. And that degree of uncertainty is not what we wish from our marriage, Robert; no, we must be sure, and all the world also must be sure. It is too important a matter for jest, do you not agree?"

"Lord forgive you, madam; you are insupportable," Robert agreed. "How you raise and dash my hopes! You know that I would marry you in a ditch if you so chose it."

"And soil my shoes? Unmannerly rude churl, to wish my pretty shoes spoiled!"

"God's teeth, you know I wish no such thing. No man alive would tolerate your careless teasing of one who idly dotes upon you."

"And do you, Robert? Do you dote upon me?"

"And you know it."

"And I upon you, Rob, with all my heart."

The baffled bystanders upon the deck gave us glances of despair, as arm in arm we moved away, laughing as the boat lurched.

Vile weather raged that summer, fearful storms. We lost the spire of St Paul's in a lightning flash, and intermittent thunderstorms brought sleet and hail that made folk think of those dark days when Edward died, and look askance at me for signs of incipient decay. A loss was suffered, a personal one for myself – Thomas Parry died, all sudden, of no particular cause, it seemed.

"I was fond of that man," I admitted to Mary. "I have known him almost all my life."

I do not believe that he was loved of many, Thomas. But how intricately his life had been bound with my own – what curious secrets we had shared! The nighttime prowl to the female whore's house, the surreptitious pots of blood that he secreted into my apartments to give the lie to rumours that I had no monthly terms, the letters he smuggled to me in the household accounts, that street boy he brought to the backstairs at Whitehall... A pang of sharp regret now pricked me. And where might I now go for my lewd male pleasures? How could I ever satisfy that devious itch now Thomas as pander was gone, other than with my own fair hand?

"Your Majesty is troubled." Mary murmured. "Let me soothe you."

Her hands upon my brow were soft and cool. Robert's sister. Robert's hands... I leaned back and she caressed my face. Her fingertips were firm and gentle. She put her cheek close to mine.

"Your touch...miraculous..." I praised her.

"Robert is not the only one who loves Your Majesty," she replied, and our eyes met.

Briefly I let my mind wander in contemplation of those thoughts her words provoked. It occurred to me that her husband Sir Harry had grown somewhat austere – was he a lover to her as well as a mere father to her children? At that time she was mother to Philip and Ambrosia, Mary and Robert as yet unborn. How little we know of those close to us! I believed she loved me. I believed that were I woman as she understood me to be, we might have grown to know another kind of love together. I would have liked to please her with that love.

Weary of those recurrent problems – the obnoxious Lady Catherine Grey who believed herself heir presumptive to the Crown and acted accordingly; and Mary Queen of Scots who had now quit France to take up abode in Scotland and believed herself already Queen of England – I settled down with Robert on that summer evening to lose myself in diversion. We sat on velvet cushions, my ladies nearby. We played the Truth Game, and ate sugared comfits. Musicians strummed in the window embrasure.

"What is your dearest wish?" I asked, casting for compliments.

"You know it well – to marry you!" he laughed. "And what is yours?"

"Never to marry," answered I.

"I doubt that is your dearest wish. Now come, deal not in half truths. Your dearest wish..."

"To live to old age," I replied, "with an unblemished reputation. And after, to be well spoken of."

"H'm," said he, as if he would take issue with me, but thought better of it. "My turn. Who is your ideal man?"

"A cheap trick to gain praise!" I accused.

"As yours was," he retorted.

"Very well. My ideal man..." I leaned back, nestling amongst the velvet. I paused: then I continued dreamily: "It is a sea captain."

"A sea captain?" frowned Robert. This plainly was not he.

"I have a half remembered image from my childhood," I replied. "I must have seen him on one of my father's ships. A big tall man, with hair as black as a raven's wing, but curly, with gypsy ringlets, and a gold ring in his ear; and a pointed black beard, and great broad shoulders. When he smiles, a dazzling flash of teeth. A tanned skin, bronzed by sun and wind, and those blue eyes grown pale from looking into distances. And thighs like tree trunks, and a swagger to his walk."

Zachary Mountshaft! Where was he now, that big dark man in whose strong arms I lay and slept, a boy.

"I am sure that no such man exists," said Robert, "so big, so dark. What, and a skin like leather? You who are so fastidious... And they never wash, these sailors. Once at sea, they stink to high Heaven. And they are well known for buggering one another."

I laughed a foolish high-pitched laugh. I let the moment pass. I might have then asked Robert what he thought of such. Was he affronted at the notion? Had he ever...in some weak moment...with a boyhood friend – ? What did I know of his most private thoughts? Dare I ever ask?

"One must seek comfort where one may," instead I answered drily.

"Habituated to the cabin boy's arse, your sea captain will not know what to do, faced with a woman of appetite."

"I think I may yet persuade him to look my way."

"I doubt it not, my dearest Majesty. I pray he stays aboard his ship and never comes ashore to disturb our equanimity."

"Equanimity? Is that what we share, you and I?"

"Tonight we do. Would it were ever thus!"

"Always agree with me and do as I say, and it shall be so," I laughed.

"Such is my desire and my intent. Ask me who is my ideal woman."

"No, for I see you have decided to flatter, and therefore I would not believe you."

"I never flatter. I speak from the heart. My answer will prove as much."

"Very well," I said comfortably. "Tell me your ideal."

"Small, dark, and somewhat plump," said Robert carelessly. "Not well read...easy to manipulate..."

"Who is this monster?" I scowled. "You live dangerously, Lord Robert."

"No more than you, who tantalise me with that vision of a sea captain, something I shall never be."

"I may have other ideals than you, I trust?" I said in dudgeon. "You are not the only species of well-formed male that strides this earth. Others exist beside."

"That being so, may I not also possess another ideal than yourself?"

"No, Robert," I said firmly, "and herein lies the difference. You may not."

How we did spar; and he was never afraid to cross me.

"I have come to a decision as regards my marriage," I announced. "It shall be the King of Sweden."

"The King of Sweden is an imbecile," said Robert contemptuously.

"Nevertheless, he is my choice. Do you imply I lack discernment?"

"In this instance, yes; though not habitually."

"And what business is it of yours, I wonder, Robert Dudley? Who are you to give opinion on the dealings between one monarch and another?"

"So it pleases you to be monarch on this occasion? Very well then – who am I? I am a loyal subject, and the matter of my sovereign's marriage is very much my business."

"So much so that you would be my bridegroom, I suppose?"

"You have given me to understand that such would not be entirely displeasing to yourself."

"You were mistaken. I would never dream of dishonouring myself by marrying you."

"Then I beg Your Majesty's permission to go away to sea."

"Go and welcome... Robert! Stay!"

There was none like him. The very arch of his dark brows made my heart pound, the very flare of his nostrils. His mouth so firm and sensuous, his aquiline nose, his well-trimmed beard and fine moustache, the fringe of hair that lay on his broad brow, his lovely limpid long-lashed eyes...this alchemy was my overthrow.

He dressed superbly. In crimson silk or amber, in a doublet of gold satin sewn with knots of pearls, a cap set with gold and rubies and a plume of apricot, he strutted with easy grace, sure of his beauty. His long, long legs – the eye ran admiringly from crotch to ankle, every inch perfection – his strong and graceful hands, his noble bearing, all contrived to present to the world an image of the greatest excellence.

We were inseparable, delighting in similar pursuits, and whether it be dance or hunt or conversation, liking well each other's company. And we had kissed as lovers; we had stood belly to belly, the thickness of raiment disguising intimations of our body's lusts, arms about each other, mouth on mouth, tongues intertwined. He pleaded for more; and I said: Later...one day hence...when the time is right...be patient; and the months went by, and all the sum of our most certain passion were those hot and ardent kisses.

Now came to me a man I would not have seen but that he sent me an odd message – "He brought word from Thomas Parry." And Thomas had been dead these eighteen months, and we had understood his kin provided for.

Blanche put down her book, and, ever wise and wary, counselled me.

"Let you and I, Your Grace, see him alone. It is long after Thomas's death, and sometimes folk presume upon the name to gain some favour. I have seen this man as he waited; if he is a kinsman he is of the poorer branch."

The man knelt at my feet. His clothes were shabby, weather-stained and old. Of his person there was little to recommend it. Although he had attempted to make himself presentable, nothing could disguise the shifty eyes, slack mouth and ingratiating manner calculated to arouse suspicion in the observer.

"State your business," Blanche said. "We have other suppliants that wait without; be brisk."

"My name is Francis Crale," said he, "drinking companion to Thomas Parry, now deceased."

I feared the worst, and guessed Blanche shared my deep misgivings. I remained immobile, gorgeous in my purple velvet spattered with the milky hues of pearls. My foot tapped irritably.

"We understood you to be Parry's kinsman," I began.

"I never said as much," he answered, avoiding my eyes. "I drank with him. And in their cups, men talk."

"What do they say?" I asked with a thudding heart.

"Such an odd tale...such a story which concerns Your Majesty. I would not believe it for a moment. Indeed, now I see Your Majesty my courage fails me and I fear that I was duped; for you are in truth the most glorious of...women."

"What was your purpose in achieving access to our presence?" I said coldly.

"Your Majesty may see by my appearance that the world has not been good to me." He shivered, picking at his hands. The month was October, but yet the room was warm. "I tried to earn an honest living. I have not been fortunate. This desperate measure was my last resort."

"You are here to ask for money?"

"Only that which keeps me clothed and fed." His face was sweating. He brushed his hand across his brow. "I would not be a burden. I am a loyal subject, good and true."

"Have you spoken to any other about the drunken matter you once shared with Thomas Parry?" I asked then.

"Not a one, I do assure you." His little eyes were bead-bright. "I thought if I should do so, he whom I told would come hotfoot upon the same errand as myself, achieving what I would achieve."

"How if I permitted you to remain here for a while at Hampton Court, in a chamber of your own, and gave you honest work? You would then be in my employ."

"Your Majesty!" he said. "It would be more than I deserve! I do accept your gracious bounty with a thousand thanks!" He took my hand and kissed it fervently. I shuddered in disgust; his mouth was moist and burning. "Blanche, oversee it." I described where was to be his lodging. "And Crale, your discretion must be absolute."

"I swear it, oh I swear it!" he assured me.

"What will you do?" Blanche asked me later, frowning.

"Set a watch upon him," I replied.

"He plainly must not live," said Blanche.

I hesitated. "He will not blab. He believes himself in green pastures now. I thought him ailing," I added. "Perhaps in the course of nature..."

"That man you sent as servant..." The word came to us before a day had passed. "He died...they say it was the smallpox."

God's death, what ailed me? I was hot and cold; it seemed I had some kind of fever. I called Kat to me, and I took a bath to freshen me. My heat seemed alleviated; I considered myself well recovered. I settled to my correspondence, but my head ached and I found the heat returned. Dr Burcot came to me, pronounced me feverish, and frowned.

"I like not this," he said in grave tones.

"No more do I, believe me, Dr Burcot," I said tartly.

"Your Grace, I fear that you have the smallpox," he declared.

"Impossible! I have no spots. It is a fever. It shall run its course and ease, as fevers will."

"My liege, I have seen the signs before," he answered firmly. "In the city it spreads as if borne upon the breeze."

"But we are not in the city. I will have no gloom mongerers about me. I refuse to have the smallpox. Be off with you, ignoramus. Get this knave out of my sight!"

I sat over my correspondence, hot as a summer noonday. I could see them glance at me, my ladies, then at each other. Their apprehension infuriated me. I returned to my letter. The words shimmered before my eyes. I was obliged to take to my bed.

They hung over me, anxious faces, whispering, muttering, pleading with me to name a successor to the throne. I had the wit to let them know that Robert Dudley was to be Protector of the Realm – beyond that I would not permit myself to think.

Mary bathed my brow. I retain no clear memory of that swift and dreadful illness. All merges to a dark and throbbing void, with Mary at my side, her arms about me, and her lips upon my eyelids. An itching skin, a paper-dry throat, pains of the head – these so possessed me that I barely knew now who I was nor where. Then he whom I had thought incompetent, that Burcot, was before me, fussing, ordering, with the result that I found myself wrapped in red flannel upon a mattress before a blazing fire, a curious concoction poured into my throat. I turned, reached out a hand, and screamed. The smallpox – the pustules of that vile disease – were clearly defined upon my hand.

"Now calm yourself, madam," said Dr Burcot gruffly. "This is good news. This is the sign for which we waited. If the spots had not broken through I could not have answered for your life. What would you rather – a few small spots or death itself?"

"I may be disfigured – " I gasped.

"This is no time for vanity," admonished he.

I snivelled into my pillow. He would never love me, scarred. He never truly thought me beautiful.

"Your Majesty!" said Dr Burcot urgently. "You will live!"

The candle burned low. I lay in bed, my fever gone, habitual clarity of mind returning to me. I had been fortunate, unbelievably so. I had survived, and, the mirror told me, now that the pustules had healed, unmarked upon the face. I turned my eyes toward Mary who sat sewing by the fire.

"You cannot see in this dim light," I remonstrated.

"I was not sewing; merely lost in thought."

"I believe I owe you my life, Mary."

"Not at all. It was Dr Burcot who did everything."

"No. In my delirium it was your face ever present, always close by, always there beside me."

"It was my pleasure. But Kat was nearby also."

"A little further off, I think," I smiled.

"Your Majesty," Mary turned her face to me. "We are alone, or I would not say this to you...but I cannot hide it from you, nor do I think that I should do so."

"Speak on."

"Your Majesty...I know your secret."

Silence, but for the shifting of the logs.

"It is true that I attended you most intimately while your fever raged," she whispered. "I did so out of love."

"And your knowledge – did you share it with anyone?" I lay there, icy cold who had been so febrile.

"No one," she replied in low tones. "Whom should I have entrusted with that kind of truth?"

"Not – Robert?" I pursued, barely able to speak out the words.

"Not Robert. I would not be the one to tell him. He would consider himself the laughing stock of Europe."

"Ah, you think so?" I gasped angrily.

"I know it," she replied.

"Robert loves me," I said. "All the world knows he loves me."

"No," she answered soberly. "He loves a woman and a queen. And he honestly believes that his devotion to you merits an honourable marriage. How might he regard this – shattering of his hopes? I pity him with all my heart. And...I pity you."

"There is no need," I answered carefully. "Or is it that now I am recovered you intend to share your discovery with others?"

"Don't speak to me like that, I pray you!" she cried. "So unfeeling and so hard. Do you know me so little? Did I not say I loved you? Do you not believe that?"

"I assume you loved whom you thought I once was."

"That essence which I loved exists yet," she replied. "But knowing what I know, I could not serve you in the same capacity as previously. Be assured of my devotion – but – I shall leave court, with your permission."

"To go where?"

"To Penshurst or to Ludlow Castle – it matters not. I intend to live in retirement with my children. You may trust me completely. I shall not speak of what I know."

"Mary, dear Mary – let me explain. I would not wish this burden on you without full knowledge of the way it came about."

"I do not wish to hear it," Mary answered. "I intend to put it from my mind. It is too terrible a secret. I wish that I had never found it out and myself a thousand miles from here. I would prefer to leave, and live my life elsewhere."

"I do not wish to lose you, Mary."

"But you will not prevent my going?"

"No."

"Then I shall go. But there is another reason..."

I knew it. Mary stood and came over to my bed. She placed her hand upon my pillow. Like mine it bore the scarring of the pox. But her case was other. The pox which she had caught from nursing me had spread; her face was pitted, pockmarked and disfigured. She lived, but her beauty was gone, and when she came again to court, she shunned all company.

Looking at my face in my small hand mirror I perused all that I saw. I was more fortunate than anyone had a right to be. Unblemished. My skin clear. Such beauty as was mine intact yet. And, past two alarms, my secret safe. To whom should I give thanks? Was this the work of God? I shuddered. Yet it must be so.

Upon the table stood the hourglass given to me for my New Year's Day gift by Sir Thomas Heneage. It was a lovely thing, encased in black velvet, garnished with gold. The sand came trickling through; and I was already twenty-nine. I remembered how old the Princess Mary had seemed when I first saw her; she was then about the age which I had now attained. The Dean of Westminster said that my unwed state and lack of issue was terrible as a plague. Resplendent and bejewelled I might hold age at bay for – how long? But time would not stay for me for ever.

Oh, time! I needed no hourglass to remind me of its passing. It wearied me to fend off constant pleas that I should marry. Things were well enough as now they were – the pleasing intrigues of the labyrinth of policy, the pleasures of dance, hunt, pageantry, the adulation of my people. The unquestionable love of Robert.

"Robert..." I took his face between my hands and kissed it. He held me, ardent, still aware of how nearly death had separated us. He loved me; but this deep sure love of his was born of our long-suffering, of all the years had brought us, good or bad. He loved my faults, my oddities. God's teeth, he would have loved me had the pox wrought devastation to my skin.

I longed of a sudden for the superficial love of those who would worship image alone, leaving my true self all undisturbed; I longed to turn from sobriety and enmesh myself in triviality. I needed reassurance of my persisting charms; too much could never be enough.

II

Thomas Heneage was a gentleman of the Privy Chamber and he was very pretty; and plainly he adored me. Christopher Hatton was a Gentleman Pensioner, a royal guard in red and yellow damask; he was yet more beautiful than Thomas and the best dancer at court, and passionately in love with me. God's death, it was no more than my due! Heneage was my own age; Hatton seven years younger, therefore a little more of a trophy. Robert hated both.

Hatton, coming from the Inner Temple, knew well how to entertain with masque and dance. They have their revels, these lawyers, with their Master of the Game and their Clerks of the Green Cloth and their Lord of Misrule. They wear green velvet and green satin and carry bows and hunting horns and in the Hall itself they hunt a fox and cat with hounds; and dance and feast and perform their plays for New Year's Eve and Twelfth Night.

"Come then, share your festivities," I said. "Let's have it at Whitehall."

The torches blazed as we settled in the winter evening to watch the young lawyers with their play of *Gorboduc*. This representation of the ills that followed civil strife was understood to be a protest at the claim of Mary Stuart to our throne; therefore comfortable in our shared agreement that so blatant a wrongdoing was to be despised, we gave all attention to the play. Long, long were the recitals therein, wearisomely long! Yet very splendid was my Hatton, crying:

"O cruel fates, O mindful wrath of gods,
Whose vengeance neither Simois' stained streams
Flowing with blood of Trojan princes slain.
Nor Phrygian fields made rank with corpses dead
Of Asian kings and lords can yet appease...
Yet O ye gods! If ever woeful king
Might move ye, king of kings, wreak it on me
And on my sons, not on this guiltless realm
Send down your wasting flames from wrathful skies..."

Big he was, Hatton. Why, he made Robert look dainty, and Robert was not small. My eyes ran with approval over Hatton's massive shoulders and thick neck, the muscles of his thighs. I surmised his buttocks big, and logically there would be a cock of like proportion. And handsome! Big brown eyes and very dark of brow. These great hulks of mutton are but too often maladroit, lacking all politesse; but Hatton was as graceful as a deer.

The play over, a masque followed, and I watched him dance. The torchbearers came forward, calling on us to join the dance, a galliard it was, with its cabrioles and capers. It might be said that I first felt the twinge of lust for Hatton when he was three feet in the air and surrounded by cupids. Those wicked little urchins know well how to pierce the heart.

"I cannot believe in my good fortune, oh most gracious Majesty," said Hatton to me as we danced. "I did not know it, but until this day I have been only half alive. Now with the most careless glance from Your Majesty's eyes I am reborn and come alive."

"Indeed my glance upon you is in no way careless," I replied, "but as carefully directed as any Cupid's dart."

"Too much..." he murmured, plainly overcome, "too much honour..." and he turned those great brown eyes upon me with a doting ruminating gaze that made me smile – and why? Because it reminded me suddenly of the robust contemplative stare of the big Cotswold sheep, a sight forgotten until now, and remembered with a surge of merriment. That Robert scowled but added to the moment's piquancy.

And then there was the Earl of Ormonde, Thomas Butler. Black Tom they called him. When he first came from Ireland I half thought my tall dark sea captain was come to me at last out of the fervour of my fancy – tall, brooding, swaggering, he strode our narrow court in thigh boots calculated to unbalance equanimity.

They lusted for me, all of them, I swear it – Heneage my pretty courtier, Hatton my adoring swain and Ormonde my strong adventurer. And Robert must learn he had not ultimate claim upon me.

And here was the truth of it: there was no reason now why I should not agree to wed him. He knew it and I knew it. We had come through the dangerous days of Amy's strange demise. The country cried out for a marriage. Or at least, its mouthpiece, my councillors, so cried out. They would have accepted Robert had I foist him upon them. He would not have been a popular choice, but such was my standing that I could have made them take him. They knew of no reason why we should not then have borne an heir, and thus silenced the claims of Mary Stuart and the Greys, great-granddaughters of King Henry VII, younger sisters of Lady Jane. My hesitation was now inexplicable. It was plain for all to see that I loved Robert; why, even Sussex who despised him had been heard to say that if he were my choice, so be it; he, Sussex, would serve him faithfully. It pained me deeply to hurt Robert by my continuing procrastination.

There was one night... He came to my room; naturally we were not alone. Kat was there, but sitting in the shadows; and there was dear Kate Carey with her, paying no particular attention. Robert and I played cards, companionably. We talked of perfumed gloves: "I am told," said Robert, "that they lose their perfume should you put them against apples and quinces" – and we talked of Cambridge, of choirboys, of whether we liked marchpane or Corinth comfits best. Neither could have foreseen the rush of passion engendered by this slow increase of plain simple pleasure in each other's company. It was a goodnight kiss, intended but to last a moment. Suddenly it was other. Our bodies clung. A mutual hunger held us. Dressed, as we were, there was no danger of my passion disclosing my true nature, and I blessed the padding that made possible my disguise; beneath it I was hard as a tree, and, it seemed to me, as big. It surely was the same for him. His voice was not his own. Hoarsely he spoke my name. We knew then that we desired each other to the depths of soul and being.

"Let me come to you – " he pleaded. There was no reason to refuse so obvious a conclusion to our patent need one of the other. Only that reason – only that one reason I could never give. What if I told him? No, I never could. What was it Mary had said, he would consider himself the laughing stock of Europe? He was so proud; how would he take it to learn I had been fooling him? Oh, not fooling him in contempt, of course; but yes, contempt indeed, by virtue of my long deception. How could he ever forgive so complete a betrayal? I could not ask it of him. And I would not. Would it not drive him from my arms for ever, and straight towards the bed of some vile female who could give him all that I could not – heirs of her body, and that kind of love which so many men required, which Robert now required of me?

If he were not here, if I sent him far away...? I cast about for an idea which I thought perhaps would not displease him.

"How would you like to wed the Queen of Scots?" I said, and tapped him on the nose, for I would show him that this matter was a light one between ourselves.

He laughed; he naturally assumed I jested.

"That way," I continued carefully, "we would have Scotland in our pocket. And I – "

And I would be free of his disturbing presence, free of the need to humiliate him by my refusals; lonely without him, yes, but still possessing his love without the pain of constant denial. He would be King of Scotland, I of England; we would rule our combined lands, two mighty monarchs, lovers though apart, like giants that faced one another from distant pinnacles.

"In order to become a suitor for her hand," said I, like one that holds a plum between thumb and forefinger, "it will be necessary to make you an earl."

His eyes flickered and lit up, control asserting itself immediately. Whether or not he took seriously my proposal for his northern marriage he would go through its initial preparation with glad heart.

Cecil read the words. Lord Hunsdon handed me the peer's mantle lined with ermine. I placed it around the shoulders of Robert, who knelt at my feet. Overcome with warm affection I could not resist tickling his neck. Dark hair curled behind his ears. I longed to kiss those curls. Robert remained eminently dignified, yes, even reproachful. For him it was a famous day. His brother Ambrose, Lord Warwick, handed me the sword and baldrick; I girt it about the neck of the new created earl and on his head placed cap and coronet. The trumpets sounded. Earl of Leicester, Baron Denbigh, Robert's status was now assured.

It meant much to him; but in truth he stood in high regard before, and higher, in my estimation, when he knelt to me at Hatfield, penniless.

What would he more? A queen to court, and Kenilworth to play with. How he loved that tumbledown old castle I bestowed upon him! It was his own, and he might do with it as he pleased. Now he would sit at a table spread with plans for forecourts, keeps, and towers; gardeners buzzed about him with their fine designs and herb samples and their talk of French style and Italian. Let him be happy. He would be less so in the icy northern wastes in company with Mary Stuart. He would think fondly of me, and in his fancy he would make love to me, and I by absence would grow more perfect in his mind. I had heard the Queen of Scots was querulous, demanding – bearing all the faults that Amy manifested. He would remember then the good times we had shared and how he once paid me that compliment: you were so much my friend you might have been a boy. And I meanwhile would think of him, would picture every line of his majestic form as I lay in my bed at night, my hand upon my cock. And thus our love would be preserved, untarnished by quarrel or reproach, and I would be spared the accusation in his eyes when I once again refused him.

"The Queen of Scots has wed Lord Darnley."

"Lord Darnley? But what for? Is it not the world's best kept secret that he loves his menservants, his grooms, his kitchen boys?"

"So well kept a secret that 'tis hid from the Queen of Scots herself!"

Although there was some sniggering at Whitehall I was nonetheless monstrous vexed. This did not well accord with my plans.

"But I offered her the Earl of Leicester," I frowned. "Is she mad?"

"Her refusal of the earl," said Cecil drily, "may have somewhat to do with the earl's refusal of her."

"What refusal? Robert agreed!"

"To your face, Your Majesty. How dare he not? Privily he wrote other to her Scottish Majesty."

"Robert!" I cried. "How dare he! Where is he? Where is that villain, that miscreant, that – traitor to the realm?"

Strong accusations, but I was very angry. And the wretch was unrepentant.

I encountered him in the Lower Gallery. I poured out my fury.

"I am not your pawn, Your Majesty," said Robert calmly, though his eyes were unnaturally bright. "A baron of the realm is not sent here and there like a stallion, to mate to order."

"Baron or no – and I who made you baron can unmake you – you go where I so send you, whether it be overseas, as seems most preferable to me now, or to the bed of Mary Stuart."

"Would you cut off your own right hand?"

"I would not; but I would send you to Scotland."

"I shall not go," he shrugged. "I know you better than you know yourself. You do not wish me gone."

"Yes, that is so, for it is very convenient to me to use you as an indication of my presence, for when folk see you like a little dog they know your master is close by."

"You speak senselessly. And it is my intent to remain close at hand until that day you come to your senses and agree to marry me."

"Never! I shall never marry you. I could not tolerate the nearness of one surpassing all in arrogance."

"No, not all. There is yet one more arrogant than I."

We paused in our recriminations. Beyond Robert's superb shoulder I saw Thomas Heneage amongst a group of others, all listening, all pretending they did not.

"Thomas, dear friend, escort me from this place," I said; and eagerly the pretty fellow hurried forward, all delight. We left Robert fuming in the shadows.

"Lettice Knollys, Kat? What do you mean?"

"You must have noticed, dearest," Kat replied. "You have not treated our Lord Robert well. That is a proud man. And – that is – a man must have an outlet for his passion."

"But Lettice Knollys? She is so unlike me! Is that the kind of woman Robert truly wants?"

"Dear my lady," Kat never slipped to call me John now. She had schooled herself over the years, and even when she privily attended me, even with the proof of my masculinity before her eyes, she never lapsed, but called me thus: dear lady. "It is you," she said, "whom Robert truly wants. Whether it be for your body or your power, who but Robert knows? And maybe not even he. But you have made it plain he cannot have you. There is none like you; to court one that resembled you would give him pain. Therefore he seeks an opposite."

Lettice Knollys was so. She was rampantly womanly, was Lettice. Countess of Hereford, she had two young children; she was twenty-four years old. She had a face like a cat that has dined off roast swan followed by a dish of cream. Her hair was a rich chestnut. Her eyes and mouth were knowing to the point of lasciviousness. Her expression promised pleasures of the bed. Disguised as we all were by shoulder pad and stomacher, there yet seemed every indication that in her case clothing hid large breasts, and small work of the fancy were it to suppose great buttocks and plump thighs, such as men are reckoned to enjoy. I was not blind; I saw that she had charms. I did not take it kindly that Robert saw it too.

How childish were we then...I gazing into Thomas Heneage's eyes, which were a poor substitute for Robert's; and Robert smouldering at fair Laetitia, with the blaze erupting if he caught me watching. Throughout that cold winter, when the Thames was frozen solid so that people walked upon it as if it were a thoroughfare, all my superficial favours were bestowed upon Heneage. I danced with him, I paid him compliments, and God's death but he was a very pretty fellow! Yet amongst all my coquetry I had time to murmur to that villain Dudley:

"An you bed Lettice Knollys you shall never come to mine."

"As yet I have not done so," Robert answered calmly. "But you try my patience sorely and I am perilously close to that which you fear."

"I fear nothing, least of all your amorous ruttings."

"Ha!" he snorted. "You long for them."

I knew that after such an insult I would never speak to him again.

"Have I Your Majesty's leave to retire to my own place?" he asked me, "for there are sights at court which are bad for my digestion."

"Go, by all means, and preferably the swiftest."

His town house then was Durham House, down on the Strand, well known for its high turret, whose light shone like a beacon all about. He would not be happy there. He would sit and brood and think of me at play with Heneage. Let him go. Or else to Kenilworth. Let him go build a tower, plant a garden, rusticate in Arden.

With shame I now recall how the vagaries of our philandering did so engross me that the slow beginnings of Kat's illness were quite lost upon me. With true nobility and for devotion's sake she kept it from me, laughing when we laughed, participating in all gossip and game, and all in silent suffering.

When she might no longer keep the truth from me and from herself, with grim prognosis offered by our best physicians, she retired from court, and, often as I might, I visited her and sat with her, and brought her of the fairest food and drink. Blanche took her place in my bedroom. Ah, I loved Blanche dearly, but she was not Kat – my dear companion with the merry heart and great propensity to laugh. How she had always giggled inappropriately to make me smile and raise my spirits; never fearing to upbraid me, but loyal, oh so loyal – a loyalty begun of necessity, continued of pure love.

"Do you remember – ?" she would say, her eyes alight; and at her bedside where I sat, I would wander with her down the tortuous byways of the past – the first time that she sneaked a pot of rabbit's blood into my chamber on a tray, and almost muddled it with the herbal cordial; the rowdy romps at Chelsea and the lovely nakedness of big Tom Seymour; and the fright we had when Blanche revealed she had not been deceived by my supplanting – and the old dark house at Bisley, and the day I first put on my female clothes – and Brother Xavier, who had worked it all, and had not come to claim his due. And then her eyes would fill with tears, and she would say:

"My lady – oh my lady – whatever will you do without me?"

And however merry we had been, I never left her chamber without weeping.

It was in the summer that she died – my dearest friend, so pale and sallow who had been so plump and rosy, a merry laughing woman for the quieting of whose fears a boy from Bisley sat upon the throne of England.

"Send for Robert Dudley."

"He is from court, Your Majesty."

"Send for him. Say that I command it."

"Robert..." – how I clung to him. "There is none like her, none. I am lost...no one will ever know how much I did have need of her... She has been with me all my life...now I am so alone, bereft – all is desolation."

"Peace," he said, holding me. "Peace...I am here... I am always here for you..."

Blanche told me grimly: "You must find another woman you may trust as you did Mistress Ashley. I am older than you. If I were to follow in Kat's footsteps, where would you be? Already I am suffering from shortness of sight... You must make another confidante."

"I dare not."

"Nevertheless, you must."

I cast my glance doubtfully at the group of ladies that giggled and sewed and diced nearby. With poor dear Kat gone, Mistress Eglionby was the Mistress of the Maids, and my maids and gentlewomen seemed so young to bear such a secret – Mary Howard, Catherine Knyvett, Anne Windsor, Dorothy Brooke... Then there were my cousins Kate and Philadelphia Carey, both lovely girls and devoted to me; and Ann Russell the Earl of Bedford's daughter. This latter was the one I leaned towards as confidante. A sweet girl, short, with a snub nose and slightly protruding teeth, she had a pleasant manner, and was liked by all. But was she of such mettle as to bear a confidence of such magnitude? I knew Blanche spoke truth. I must seek one or two that I could trust. But whom? And yet it must be done.

It was by a circuitous route that she who was to prove my most trustworthy friend came to my notice.

That September the princess Cecilia of Sweden came to our shores with a vast entourage in all senses of the word, for she was with child. The infant, my godson, Edward Fortunatus, was born; and christened with great ceremony at the Chapel Royal of Whitehall, Norfolk his godfather. It was a brilliant occasion, with a myriad candles glinting upon mother-of-pearl and coral, crystal and cloth-of-gold. Lord Northampton, fifty-three years old and a recent widower, participated in the ceremony and fell violently in love with

Helena von Snakenburg, a maiden of fourteen, one of Cecilia's train. Nothing would please him but that he should marry this fair maiden, and, curiously enough, the child returned his ardour. When Cecilia left England, Helena remained behind, this possible because I gave her the position of Gentlewoman of the Privy Chamber. She was entirely delightful, very pretty, with hair so fair it was almost silver. She wed Northampton five years later, and I understand it was a gentle and undemanding marriage; however, he died soon after and Helena remained with me. I had no idea then how dear to me she was to become.

It was all celebration in the Chapel Royal as the winter closed about us, for Robert's amiable brother Ambrose, halt and lame and walking with a stick since his return from warfare at Le Havre, married Lady Ann Russell, and my sweet Maid of Honour became Lady Warwick. She wore silver blue over purple velvet threaded with silver, Ambrose in purple velvet shot with gold. But by far the most beautiful wore purple satin; he was the bridegroom's brother, Baron Denbigh, Earl of Leicester, and he had sworn that he would come to me on New Year's Night and that he would take no refusal.

"You agree?" he gasped.

"If you abide by my conditions."

"Aha, I suspected as much," he grinned cynically. "Name them."

"I agree to sleep with you on New Year's Night; you agree to give up all pretension to an interest in my lady Lettice."

"Ha! So you were jealous!"

"Not at all," I answered loftily. "I am merely thinking of the reputation of one who would be consort to a queen."

I had him there. "I accept your condition," he replied. "I sleep with you; and I renounce Lettice. And yet," he added, looking at me narrowly, "I do suspect you of some deviousness..."

Dear Robert. How well he knew me!

"Who would credit this?" he marvelled. "And who but I would tolerate such treatment, uncomplaining?" And he laughed with pure good humour.

In my great bed at Whitehall Robert and I lay side by side, he naked, I heavily nightgowned, the curtains drawn about us. But I had ordered the sheets to be so laid that we were separate, each enclosed by linen and velvet, each warm and comfortable, each apart.

"And for this I have given up Lettice Knollys!" he snorted.

"I said that I would sleep with you; I always keep my word."

"You are a trickster, madam. Lord knows why I love you; I must be distract."

"And do you love me?"

"God's truth, if you don't know that by now..."

"I do know it."

He turned so that he lay against me. He began to kiss me. Encumbered by the sheets we lay in each other's arms. He moved to lie upon me; I withdrew from our embrace. He rolled on to his back, and lay there breathing hard. "So it is passion that you fear...?"

I said nothing. Was ever man in such a wretched case as I? Fear passion? I longed for it. I ached to lie with him as man to man, to feel his hand about my cock, to lie beside him naked and to let what might occur. Oh! the laughable irony of being desired for my person by a rampant male who thought me woman – why, it was a scene straight from a playhouse! If one had warned me that by putting on petticoats I would put myself into this painful and piquant predicament, I would never have quit boy's hose.

What if I were to tell him, now, here in this bed? Ah – my courage failed me; I dared not. He loved me as a woman and a queen; I dared not ask him to love me as a man.

In the darkness Robert's voice spoke, low and thoughtfully.

"I try to understand you. I understand that you fear marriage. You have seen only trouble come of it – your father, your mother, poor Catherine Howard whom you loved... You ever have maintained that you would never marry, yes, since you were eight years old. I understand that. But you have ultimate power now. You need not wed for policy; you might wed for love. You would then know that marriage need not be a threat, but a sustenance, a haven. You would lose your childhood fears. Yet if those fears are so ingrained that you fear to put on the shackle of the wedding ring, there yet remains to love. And you do love me. Not passionately, I suspect, but deeply enough. But you withdraw from consummation. You fear motherhood. I have spoken to Dr Huicke. He tells me that he has advised you never to conceive, because of the fine sensibility of your nature.

But you seem reluctant even that I should simply love your body. With my mouth and my tongue I could give you such pleasure, and all without danger. Why will you not permit this, I wonder? What is it? What is the secret fear, stronger than passion, stronger than pleasure?"

I said nothing. He was letting his thoughts ramble; I was not required to answer.

He leaned up on one elbow and gave me a light kiss on the temple.

"There is a mystery about you," he murmured. "And I have always been a seeker after truth. There is a hidden key, and I shall be the one to find it. I promise you, Elizabeth, the maze that you have created has an entrance and a centre, and one day I swear I shall discover both."

"I pray you do," I said, excited and afraid.

ELEVEN

I

Rycote, in Oxfordshire, that loveliest of shires, was our Arcadia. Here we found peace and contentment, pleasure and merriment, and, with few about us from the court, the illusion of the freedom of the common man. Whenever we required as much, my dear friend Marjorie and her husband Sir Henry Norreys were pleased to welcome us and make us glad.

"This place has always had a particular hold on my affections," I told Robert. "When they brought me to Woodstock a prisoner we stopped here on the way. Against the recommendation of Sir Henry Bedingfield, they treated me with love and kindness here. It was a little haven of delight – quiet rooms and clean, sheets perfumed with lavender – and this for one accustomed to sleeping in the confines of the Tower. And Marjorie is now become my own good friend."

"This does surprise me," Robert laughed, "since you call her your own crow, for her black hair. You are fortunate that she permits us to cross her threshold."

"Not at all. My rooks, my brave black birds, are held in high esteem by me, and all the world knows it. And here we can be at peace. No quarrels here, Rob, only harmony."

"Agreed, while we are here."

The previous months had not been easy. Mary Queen of Scots had brought forth a male heir, her claim to our throne thus heavily substantiated. Renewed hostility to Robert was given leadership by Norfolk. He warned me privily against Robert's overweening ambition; he told Robert it were best he quit the country. The court declared allegiance – Robert's friends wore blue, the Norfolk faction yellow. The dead Amy's brother was offered a bribe to bring forth evidence to show that Robert had the woman pushed.

A curious ceremony of reconciliation then occurred. The King of France poured oil on troubled waters by choosing Norfolk and Robert as worthy of receiving the Order of Saint Michael. For this they must make peace, each eager for the honour and each proud at heart, and, differences submerged, they wore the ritual robes – the white velvet and white silk, the cloth-of-silver trimmed with silver lace, the russet velvet furred with leopards, and the black velvet white-feathered caps.

"I wish to be your friend," said the sombre earl to Robert. "Therefore I will speak honestly to you. You are wasting your time in your pursuit of the queen. Her Majesty must wed the Archduke. If you hamper the negotiations by your importuning, all England will despise you. Throw in your lot with those of us who work for a profitable marriage. There is no other reasonable alternative for you if you wish to keep your dignity."

"I dare not leave off my suit to Her Majesty," said Robert innocently, "for she will fear I of a sudden find her personally distasteful."

Norfolk compressed his lips and turned away. No, they were not become friends, for all the silver and the velvet.

But Robert was no easy friend. Secure in my affections, he took public liberties at which men took offence. He should not have used my kerchief to mop his sweating brow at tennis; he should not have permitted his servants to throw their weight about. God's death, I had poor Bowyer my usher who guarded my door come to me demanding whether Robert were king or I queen, for Robert had been swearing at him and giving him orders; and if I chose to be agreeable to the wayward Irishman Ormonde, Robert had no business to sulk and quit the court, obliging me to send for him.

"I was a fool to return," scowled Robert. "Any new face pleases you, and today it seems you like them Irish."

"Robert, be sweet. What may I do to placate you?"

"Marry me," he laughed bitterly.

"Maybe I will."

"You think so little of me that you jest on such a subject?"

"I will marry you – in secret – unless I change my mind."

"What is your plan, if you have one?"

"Let us behave like children in the dark who go step by step, not knowing what lies ahead. Let us intend to marry. Let us make all arrangements as if we were to marry, but each with the freedom to withdraw if he so wishes."

"If *she* so wishes," Robert corrected.

"No," I said. "If *he* so wishes."

Like my playmate of so long ago, Robert was amused by the game, and teased by the glittering prospect that might be his at its conclusion. He agreed to wait for me at St Swithin's churchyard, and I came thither slowly, by boat, setting out from Greenwich with Kate Carey. We landed at the Three Cranes' Wharf, here entering my coach. We sat within, and waited.

I was consumed with a curious excitement, a nervous exhilaration. Robert was waiting for me at St Swithin's church – I knew it: I had sent a servant to verify as much. If I would, he would wed me. I chuckled then. The church would wed us – two men in holy matrimony. Oh Hymen, great god of marriage, what would you have to say to that? And oh Robert – what would you have to say upon our wedding night? But ah! to play with the notion – almost to wed – to wait here, in my coach, with starry eyes, and dwell upon the night's conclusion... Robert and I wed, lovers before all the world.

"How long shall we wait here, Your Majesty?" said Kate.

I laughed, all suddenly at ease, my reason returning.

"Until Lord Leicester has departed," I replied. "My messenger will inform me of that time, and then, when it is too late, we will go to the church." I smiled then at her face. "You think I am unkind. Believe me, it was all in foolery; and what I do is for the best."

Long after Robert and his men-at-arms had quit St Swithin's church, we drove there in our coach and found him gone. We turned back towards Greenwich. There by the roadside he was waiting, on horseback, with his attendants. I called for my coach to halt. My heart absurdly light I jumped down from the coach. Robert dismounted.

"You – " he groaned. No word was bad enough.

"I know it," I cried, running to him, flinging my arms about him. "You make me every kind of fool and I permit it."

"You knew I would not come."

"I knew it – but still I waited."

"Come back with me," I urged. "We'll lie on cushions in my barge."

He made arrangements for his horse and came into the coach with me.

"I go along with every silly scheme," he sighed. "I want so much what you might offer me... I am like the child in the tale that pursues the golden bubble in the woods, and loses his way, yet still pursues, because the bubble is so bright."

We had come to Rycote following our visit to Oxford, of whose university Robert was chancellor, and where we had been greatly entertained. *Palamon and Arcite* was the play which they performed for us. So many beautiful boys surrounded us there; one hardly knew where best to look. When Theseus' hunt showed in the quadrangle scores of boys believed it to be true and tried to take part – why, they would have leapt out of the windows in their eagerness. Boys en masse – how very pleasing is the concept! Pink and glowing, dewy as primroses – virginal – all untainted by the cynicism of age, glowing with health and spirit! Oh Rob, I thought despondently, the time that we have wasted...

Leaning from my upper window at Rycote Manor, in my nightgown, with my hair loose and the sun upon me, I looked lovingly down on Robert who sat on horseback below, enticing me to ride. He wore dark green, and looking at his laughing eyes and vivid smile, I thought he seemed some elf of the woods, nay, Oberon himself, come forth to lead me to some occult rite. Thus fancy; the reality was that I preferred to lean upon my window sill, sun-warmed and smiling, watching him. After he had gone I would return to bed and curl up in the warm sheets, reading Ovid's *Metamorphoses*, and nibbling cinnamon comfits, till I chose to rise. No doubt I would indulge in private pleasure, with a crumpled kerchief clasped about my prick; and later, washed and dressed and lazy still, walk in the gardens and the meadows amongst the grazing sheep, and half believe that I was in the Golden Age. I looked down at my Corydon contentedly.

"It is too early in the morning," I resisted.

"Past ten!"

"Precisely. Too early."

"The best part of the day."

"You know that I have never been at my best before noon."

"If this be not your best, when you are now so perfect, I fear for my reason when I shall see you better than you now are, tonight."

"The darkness will help hide my deficiencies."

"Madam, you have none!"

I reached down to him, leaning. He reached up, and though he stood upright in his stirrups our hands could not meet. The distance was a little too far. There seemed a pleasing poignancy in this, perhaps because the gap was symbolic only; in actuality I could reach Robert when I chose, and touch him when it pleased me.

It pleased me to do so that very night.

I entered Robert's room; Tamworth withdrew without a word. I lay upon the counterpane. Eagerly responsive, Robert put his arms about me, holding me against him.

"Come into bed and lie between the sheets," he said.

"No; be content with what I do."

"And what has prompted this nocturnal visitation, sweet?" he said, curbing his patent disappointment.

"We are in Arcadia here. Today I walked in meadowland, knee deep in summer grass. The birds sang all about me. From my opened window I could smell the roses that twine about the sill. Here, I brought you one. When I am gone back to my chamber, put the rose beneath your pillow."

"No; against my heart."

I began to kiss him. He responded eagerly. We clung together. He spoke my name in breathless tones. I pressed against him, well content.

Shortly afterwards I crept away. In my own room I leaned upon the window sill and looked out at the perfumed darkness, silver-shadowed by the moon. There was enchantment here. I had been foolish. I had come to Robert as myself, a man in love. A boy from Gloucestershire, one who remembered childhood meadows, Cotswold sheep. Vexed, I understood that it would not be so for Robert. He would assume that the queen of England came to him and lusted for him; he would suppose himself one step nearer to the throne.

To hear me talk, one would suppose it was all Robert, Robert, and no more besides; it was not so. I was obliged that autumn to deal angrily with the matter of the succession, pestered by members of my own Council in my Privy Chamber – Norfolk, Pembroke, Northampton, and Robert also (brought, I suspect, to help keep me calm in a situation dealing with a matter known to be repugnant to my sensibilities).

"Ah, Robert, you also! What a false friend, to lend your voice to these rampagers. I had thought that if all the world abandoned me, you would not!"

"I?" gasped Robert. "I would die at your feet!"

"And what has that to do with anything?" I said scathingly.

Before a delegation of both Houses I then spoke my mind. I wore robes of crimson velvet. I had spent hours in preparation of my speech, but when I came to utter words, my own vehemence guided me. I told them I would wed as soon as I conveniently could, and they must take a prince's word for it. I warned them that by naming a successor I would submit that person to such practices whereto I had been subject in my sister's reign. And let them not think that I would ever by violence be constrained to do anything. Though I be a woman – I always liked to stress this point – yet I had as good a courage answerable to my place as ever my father had. "I am your anointed queen. I will name my successor when I so choose; for it is monstrous that the feet direct the head."

Next we had wrangling over subsidies. Then there was Scotland.

That winter it was well known that the Queen of Scots was cognisant at last of what manner of man she had wed; but we were unprepared for the resolution of her matrimonial problem. Lord Darnley was murdered, and his boy lover with him; and after one week of mourning, the stricken queen had gone dancing with her paramour. Already compromised by rumour when her Italian lute player David Riccio had been stabbed to death before her eyes – and some had said he had been her son's father – she must tread carefully now; and I warned her so by letter. Prosecute the murderers, I urged, let your own innocence be seen before the people. But the Earl of

Bothwell was tried and acquitted at a most suspect trial, and within three months he was with Mary at Dunbar and she had wed him. Subsequently she surrendered her person to the nobles of her realm and was ignominiously taken to the fortress of Lochleven. Under pain of death she had been forced to sign a document of abdication, and her infant son was proclaimed king. They had no warrant nor authority by the law of God or man to be as judges over their prince and sovereign whatsoever they may have believed that she had done. Terrible as these matters were for that anointed queen it was much in our mind: *what would it mean for us?* What would it mean that courtiers could rise against a queen if aught should be discovered against her integrity?

I would have had my armies enter Scotland to restore that woman to her rightful place, solely because she was that country's queen. Invasion...Mary's death – the Scottish lords and I gave threat for threat. But finally the lady made her own solution. She escaped and crossed the Firth and landed on our shores, with a saucy demand for clothes of mine to wear and an urgent plea that I should send for her.

"To do so," Cecil said, "would be to acknowledge her as heir"; and I did not. She remained in the north, and trouble buzzed about her.

"Norfolk has sounded me out upon whether I would support him should he marry her," said Robert cautiously.

"Would you so?" I answered equally cautiously.

"Patently someone must marry her," Robert said. "It is the only way to negate the threat she represents."

"They hoped to treat me so, for the same reason, when my sister Mary ruled," said I. "Some quiet inoffensive little duke as far from these shores as possible. But Norfolk? Is that a good move? What does the noble earl himself think, as far as you may surmise?"

"I think he does not know his own mind."

"Encourage him discreetly...sound him out."

Robert grinned. "This is the man who once told me that he objected most strongly to my practice of kissing the Queen's Majesty without being invited thereto."

I laughed. "He is a very pompous fellow, our Norfolk. It would well suit his vanity to be considered for the hand of a queen. I think it proper that yourself and brother Warwick should join the commissioners at Westminster in their investigation of her conduct and complicity in the murder of her husband."

Letters of a most incriminating nature were found in a casket. I was obliged to urge the hapless queen to justify herself as best she might; but she was ever silent. To send her back to Scotland would have been tacitly to agree to her certain assassination, nor could she be permitted to seek aid in France; therefore in comfort and with all proper ceremony was she installed at Tutbury castle.

But meet with her – never! Though she might press for it for all that she was worth, I never would agree. That epitome of womanhood – mother, wife, mistress – renowned throughout the known world for her feminine beauty... I knew well enough that were we to stand face to face, I, tall and lean and spare, for all my willowy perfection, would beside her seem a male.

Norfolk, our premier duke, the sad-eyed scion of Plantagenet ancestry, had meanwhile bought the old monastery of Charterhouse and named it Howard House. Perhaps he transferred his portrait of King Richard III to hang in his Long Gallery. His wife had died in childbed, and they said that his despondency led him to strange fancies, a leaning towards popery, an obsession with the glories of the past. Sensing an admirer, Mary wrote to him. I learned this from Kate Carey's sister Philadelphia, Lady Scrope.

"He denies all interest in the Queen of Scots," Robert said.

"My lord of Norfolk," I began. We sat at Whitehall, lingering after supper, several others grouped about us. "I hear that you detest the Queen of Scots and suffer much from rumours which link her name and yours in harmonious conjunction?"

"Your Majesty, I have seen the Casket Letters," Norfolk replied. "I was appalled. I discovered therein her inordinate love for Bothwell, her loathing of her murdered husband; in short, such as every godly man could not but abhor."

"And you believe these letters true, and not the work of forgery?"

"I do, the matter contained in them being such as could hardly be invented or devised by any other than herself."

"And therefore, naturally, the idea of marrying the lady certainly disgusts you."

"Certainly! There is no doubt upon that score."

I smiled, and leaned a little forward. "But later perhaps? With the passing of time – time which heals all and fades all stains – perhaps it would become a different matter? If it were for the good of the realm?"

The sudden silence jarred like a faulty lute string.

Norfolk flushed. "No reason could move me to like her that had laid claim to the crown. Send me rather to the Tower. That is a lady who takes absolute measures." He laughed brittlely. "In such a marriage, no man could be sure of his own pillow!"

"But afterwards," said Robert, "he looked thoughtful."

"Rumour monger!" I accused him playfully – but thoughtful also.

Norfolk's comportment that summer was most questionable, sometimes present on our progress, sometimes absent without reason, and his manner shifty and constrained. Time and again I paved the way for him to confess that of which he was most surely guilty. He must ask my permission did he wish to wed the Queen of Scots. To take any course without that first step would be treason.

"You come from London, my lord?" I called gaily to him when he made obeisance to me in the gardens of Richmond. "So what news? Is there any news of...a marriage?"

"None," he answered, and, our brief exchange interrupted by one of my ladies, he bowed and withdrew, and no more said.

I invited him to dine with me, alone at my own table. It might be said we dined on pleasantries. I made myself agreeable. He would not be drawn. At length I laughed, reminding him of that which he once said: "I pray you, take good heed to your pillow!" – so broad a hint as should make me ashamed; but even then he would not speak; and yet he plainly plotted, even if at that stage it was no more than the secret letter and the sounding out of friends.

"There is much more!" said Robert. "Forgive me, but all this summer I have been in converse with him, and now I must reveal all that I know."

We were at Titchfield then, home of the Earl of Southampton, a petulant and pleasing boy of six and twenty, the despair of his young wife, whom he had wed three years ago all sudden and without parental consent and now discarded for the love of boys. One could not but admire – while pretending to despise – such flagrant disregard for appearance. Every servant at his table was a little gem, each boy, as it would seem, chosen for the pertness of his arse, the shapeliness of his thighs, the lasciviousness of his expression. Even while highly discomposed as a result of Norfolk's curious perfidy, I could not but be well entertained by such a shameless modus vivendi as now presented itself to my gaze. God's death, but bums were pinched and fondled, earlobes nibbled, with barely an attempt to conceal the same. A mean dark humour on my part envied that young earl, ill mannered though he plainly was, and not long for this world, it seemed, for having an incipient consumption.

To be powerful and concupiscent – such as I might never be – to care little for appearances, to indulge the whim of the moment, to see a pretty boy and send for him...this seemed a pleasing prospect indeed to one for whom such was forbidden fruit.

"What do you think, Robert?" I teased him lightly. "Could you be happy here? Do you admire the earl's wild ways?"

"I find the matter of the utmost repugnance," answered Robert stuffily.

With no change of expression I said: "Tell me all you have discovered concerning my lord of Norfolk."

"It is much worse than we supposed," Robert said. Dear Robert. His tone was self-important. Some of that he told me I knew already; some made me understand the full extent of the difficulties that lay ahead. There was a vast plot a-brewing. Mary had every intention of seizing the throne, and Norfolk of marrying her. Cecil was to be ousted. As for myself, my fate was plain. There would be civil war; the north was to rise in rebellion, and East Anglia also. Spanish troops were to land on the north-east coast. Mary had sent a ring to the duke in earnest of her good faith, and also a cushion with a meaningful device that showed a knife which cut down a living vine. A Florentine banker named Ridolfi was suspected of bearing coded messages, but nothing was yet proved. We placed the Duke of Norfolk in the Tower; we could do no other.

Led by Northumberland and Westmorland, there came rebellion in the north; another in Norfolk. Their ingratitude enraged me. Many rebels we executed, but many we pardoned and released. And now a Papal Bull was published, absolving all subjects of their allegiance to me. Was ever monarch so tried by pontiff? 'Pretended queen' he called me, inciting my own people to rise up against me! But our rebellions were put down. The loyal outweighed the malcontent. The Norfolk rebels confessed their aims to be: the queen's death, the imprisonment of Cecil and the infamous Dudley, and the releasing of the duke.

The Duke for his part continued to incriminate himself yet further. Messages to and from his cell were passed in leathern bottles or dropped into the privy and collected by such servants as knew nothing of fastidiousness. We permitted him to return to Howard House, an ill and penitent man, swearing his innocence. Here he could be watched more easily; and that same Ridolfi came and went.

The duke of Norfolk, forbidden to quit his house, set about to enlarge and improve it, and thus there came a constant stream of workmen with their hods and baskets, and some others to watch them for what they might bring in and out. Rumour was not enough. Rumour said that an invading army was expected to land at Harwich, that Norfolk had refused to aid the Duke of Alva in his plan, that Norfolk had sold plate and jewellery to finance the same. Ridolfi then, watched and with our permission, went beyond the seas, and here blabbed, while ciphered letters fell into our hands. A bag of gold and letters was then intercepted, sent from Howard House, and Norfolk's secretary made confession, and gave concise directions. The key to the cipher was hidden under the carpet, below a map of England just outside Norfolk's own chamber. Further papers were hidden among the roof tiles. Letters were discovered from Queen Mary, love letters, letters implicating Norfolk to the hilt.

Yet I was ever reluctant to send him to his death, this man of the blood royal. I held back from the playing of God's part, the sending of a soul upon its journey to eternity. He was a man who meant well, but foolish, melancholy and misguided, a man from a bygone age. By his plottings he brought others than himself to disgrace, and one of them was none other than that wayward young Southampton, whose dissolute household I had once found piquant.

Norfolk was executed for high treason. Southampton was taken by the Watch at night in Lambeth Marsh, with that vile intriguer Bishop Ross; and passed two years in the Tower for his treasonable activities. He made somewhat of a name for himself there by his childlike tantrums and his smashing of his food plates. After promises of future good conduct, faithful service to the crown, and spotless demeanour henceforth, he was released, and straightway begot a son, possibly the most beautiful youth ever to exist. Beloved of many men, adored in sonnet form, young Southampton was to live and thrive to plague us all.

But why dwell on the vagaries of boy lovers? What matter young Southampton's fascinating ways, when Robert Dudley finds the same 'a matter of the utmost repugnance'?

II

Having in mind for some time that which Blanche had well advised me concerning the sharing of my secret with another lady, I fixed upon Ann, Lady Warwick, wife of Robert's brother Ambrose, as my confidante. Of her kindness and devotion I had no doubt, nor of her sweetness of nature. These qualities, I believed, would combine to sustain her in the undoubted turbulence of spirit which my disclosure would certainly effect.

I broke the news in conversation upon cushions in the summer gardens of Richmond, as we sat in the shade eating strawberries and fanning ourselves against the heat. She made it easy for me to broach the subject when she confessed that Ambrose and she were not like to bear children because of Ambrose's tendency to shun the marriage bed, seemingly for a half-admitted attraction to his own sex. Ann bore him no grudge for this but loved him nonetheless, and such a sympathy, I judged, must predispose her mind towards my own case.

"You were a good friend to Kat Ashley..." I began.

"I loved her dearly."

"I also, more than anyone could ever know... Kat took a secret with her to the grave...it is my desire to make you privy to that secret, dearest Lady Ann, and when I do, my life and reputation will be in your hands."

"Your Majesty," she whispered awed. "I am yours to command."

"Long ago," said I, "Kat came to Gloucestershire with Thomas Parry and the young princess, her charge. They dwelt at our royal manor of Bisley. They resided there at Over Court House, and here made the acquaintance of a little boy, a boy of the same age as Elizabeth, who by a freak of fortune had been born in Bisley, though he was the son of the Duke of Richmond, and grandson of the old king. The princess caught a fever, and she died..."

Curiously, it came easily enough to me to tell the tale, almost as if it had happened to another. She heard it all in silence, asking nothing, her eyes ever on my face, as if she would take in more than mere words, as if she would see soul itself by some conjunction between her understanding and my own.

"It was for Kat's sake that the deed was done," I said, in that low urgent voice in which I made confession of the event. "It was all for Kat – her fears, nay, terrors, being such, that it then seemed the best course possible. And once the deed was done, we never could go back, but must brave it out or be condemned for ever. And though it may be said that we were wrong, yet I believe it was for the best, and do maintain it yet. I am the best there be for what I do. I am of King Henry's blood, and if I had not undertaken what I did, England would be the worse for it. And now I need your help and support, dear Ann. Will you of your great kindness grant it to me?"

"I will," she answered steadfastly.

"What, unconditionally and without further persuasion? Am I to be so fortunate?"

"I hear your story and am touched by it. If there be blame, it is not yours. And I have served you faithfully ever since it has been my good fortune to know Your Majesty, and am accustomed to the service, and I long ago chose to believe that anything Your Majesty did was right; this I believe still, and shall. When I am alone and my thoughts free to roam, I shall no doubt meditate much upon the strangeness of it all; but of my fidelity have no doubt."

A cynic might observe that Lady Ann could act in no other manner and yet retain her status; but I knew this had not occurred to her, her loyalty was absolute.

"Thank you," she said, "for sharing it with me and trusting me. I am honoured by Your Majesty's confidence and that I join the worthy fellowship of those considered faithful enough to bear a burden of such magnitude. And may I ask which others, beside Robert of course, are privy to this wondrous secret? If Ambrose knows he has not told me."

"No," I said carefully. "Ambrose does not know."

"But Robert, of course – ?"

"Oh yes; oh, Robert has known from the first."

"And Cecil?"

"But certainly. And the Duke of Norfolk; Sussex also." I lied easily once I had begun. "Mary Sidney, naturally," I added, glad to find veracity in my generous boasts at last. "Of course," I then continued, "none will ever admit as much to the other. It is never spoken of. My female gender is assumed. It makes it easier. If we all believe in our hearts that I am woman there never comes the slip of the tongue, the knowing aside."

"I understand. I also will never speak of it. But," she added then, wide-eyed, "what a marvel here amongst us! It strains credulity! However did...? I mean – forgive me, but – it is well known you have your female health...why, I myself have been approached by those would know if Your Majesty was capable of bearing children...and I know your laundresses have reported stains of blood..."

"Why, child, blood is easy to acquire," I answered, smiling at my ghoulish answer. "Failing the blood of slain pot-rabbits, there is always one's own – you know that I am sometimes bled by my physicians for my health, from arm or foot... This has proved useful to me as a source to silence tongues."

"It is all most marvellous," said Lady Ann. "But what I find most marvellous of all is Robert. How brilliantly he counterfeits! Why, you would swear that he believed you woman and yet hoped to marry you!"

"Yes," I said caustically. "You would swear so indeed."

"I have it on the best authority," said I to Robert archly, "that what so disgusted you at Titchfield is not unknown to your own brother

Ambrose. What do you say to that?"

"Where did you hear that?" snapped Robert.

"Enough that I have heard it."

"What nonsense!" Robert answered irritably. "Whoever said as much deserves a whipping. Ambrose? It's laughable. I know it is not so."

"How do you know?"

"Why, many a time when Ambrose and I were lads..." He paused.

"Yes, Robert Dudley? What did you and Ambrose?"

"Now tell me that you would not be surprised to hear that any full-blooded youth seeks to know womankind to try his manhood?"

"And you maintain that in your search Ambrose was with you?"

"I swear it. Believe me, you were misinformed. Why, Ambrose is no more boy-lover than myself, and," he laughed – a little too heartily, I thought – "you know very well I am not so."

The seaman knelt before me and kissed my hand. He was rough and gnarled as any ancient oak, a gargoyle hewn from the wood of his own ships. His hair was black and curly, and his beard thick and grizzled; in his ears he wore small golden rings. His mighty frame now bent before me seemed yet large as some men standing. His leather boots creaked as he rose. I rewarded him and he withdrew. I watched him fondly as he strode away.

"What is it about these men of the sea?" said Robert in mild exasperation. "You smile at that great oaf like any lovesick wife in a seaport. Thank God the man was so ill-favoured or I might well have seen in him another rival! Have you no shame? He was a pirate!"

"I love my pirates, every one," said I. "They risk their lives at sea for me, knowing I must disown them should they fall foul of Spain. They drive the Spaniard from his course so that he flies for safety into Plymouth laden down with gold to pay Alva's troops in the Netherlands – gold which we may borrow when it suits our purpose. How could I not love them?"

"I know your policies," said Robert irritably. "But there is more. What did you tell me once of a tall sea captain? That he was your ideal, a fantasy created from your youth? I swear you live in hope that one day such a man will crawl out from between the planks of some tall ship, along with the woodworm, his boots awash with seaweed, his shirt perfumed with fish oil and his language unintelligible to the discerning."

"I swear I do," I laughed. "And I pray that this same Hercules will carry me away to sea, there to discover unknown worlds away beyond the Western Isles."

"Without exception," Robert said placidly, "all sea captains are short, stocky, red-faced, leather-skinned, and ugly as toads."

"Then Robert, you have nothing to fear."

"Madam," said Robert, much on his dignity now, "there are at least half a dozen swains whose company at this time you patently prefer to mine."

It was true that I had chosen to distance myself a little from Robert to spare him the pain of my refusals; and one way of so doing was to surround myself with others. But more: if I am honest, which I sometimes am, I loved the presence of adoring gentlemen, and time was not on my side. I must feed on compliment and love letter and ardent glance while yet I might – and by the saints, for such I had a mighty appetite.

La Mothe Fénélon, ambassador from France, came courting me on behalf of the Duke of Anjou. We began by speaking of the marriage of King Charles, that feeble evil-minded brat, to Elizabeth of Austria. The ambassador responded: "I regret I may not congratulate Your Majesty upon your own marriage."

"Alas," I sighed. "Posterity has small cause to be grateful to me...but I have never been courted by a suitor worthy of me. The man I marry must be of royal blood, or rank comparable with my own. Handsome of course...fastidious..."

"But there is only one possible suitor then, Your Majesty, and that is the Duke of Anjou, brother to our king."

"I believe he is much younger than myself?"

"Your Majesty is ageless; and Anjou bears himself already like a man!"

I turned to Robert. "Robert! He bears himself already like a man... Yet," I sighed extravagantly, "he will always be younger than me..."

Robert chuckled. "So much the better for you!"

"Enquire about him, Robert...tell me what Monsieur is really like..."

"Thin and pale," reported Robert gleefully, "and his face is almost yellow, and his legs thin as two broomsticks. Notwithstanding, he is dominated by voluptuousness, drenched in perfumes; and of course, he is a papist."

"Jealousy makes poor account," I retorted. "I have heard that he is handsome. I have a plan. I shall go on a progress to Kent and he shall sail across to me and we shall watch the moon rise from the deck of his sailing vessel."

It was given out that the marriage negotiations failed because the French demanded Anjou should be king with equal power to myself and should pursue his religion as if he were at home. The truth was I wanted no more to do with him as a suitor since he said I was an old creature with a sore leg. It was true I had an ulcer a little above my ankle. But no one is old at thirty-eight, least of all a queen such as myself.

"Your Majesty, there is always his younger brother; he longs to worship at your shrine."

This sounded promising. But —pockmarked? How pockmarked?

The Earl of Oxford rode to my notice upon a snow-white steed, lance in hand, at the tiltyard at Westminster.

Edward de Vere. His ancestors fought at Bosworth Field with the victorious Henry. He was named after my half-brother. Why, I remembered him when as a boy of eleven he had handed me a posy at his father's home in Essex, with a Latin oration and the wickedest eyes ever seen on a boy so young. It had been a brilliant occasion of hawking and hunting and masques by torchlight. Later, discarded by his mother, he had become one of Cecil's wards. Now he was twenty-one; and here he was, an ardent and accomplished youth, eager to rise, eager to adore me.

And this I knew as I invited him to dance with me.

He was not tall. He had a small face, a smirking mouth, with sensuous lips and a neat moustache. His eyes were hazel and disarming. He had brown curly hair and slender eyebrows. He wore black satin. He was a scholar, a poet, a Cambridge man. He had already killed a man – a boy cook, who, it was said, ran on to his sword. What had really happened? There was some gossip...there was always gossip about Oxford. How well he danced!

Later that evening he played upon the virginals. 'Dolent Depart' it was, a sweet and melancholy air. Dancer, horseman, poet, scholar, musician – and but one and twenty! And the prettiest legs! My eyes ran along the curve of his thigh: the light caught it in a shimmer of satin stocking. Blessed fashions, that delight the eye with such enjoyable revelation...

"My young lord, you possess all the graces," said I in compliment.

"The only Grace worth possessing is your Grace," said he, "as far beyond my sphere as is the cold and lovely moon."

"You are mistaken in your surmise, my lord. Sweet Cynthia is not cold; her heart, to those that love her, is warm."

"Then it shall be my delight to discover the same," answered he, "for her bright gaze has enchanted me and I am henceforth her bondslave."

"You will find her not an unkind mistress."

That December I attended his wedding. He married Cecil's daughter Ann in Westminster Abbey, and we banqueted at Cecil House in Covent Garden. Though I wished her well, the little innocent, for Cecil's sake, I doubted that her marriage would be a path of primroses.

When we went into Warwickshire that summer, it was Oxford who was the hero of the festivities at Warwick castle. There was a mock battle, with forts set up, and fighting men, and Oxford leading the assault, sword in hand, a knight against a dragon – yes, there was a dragon; and fireworks that lit up the night and showered their cascades of gold into the River Avon.

"My house will seem but poor by comparison," said Robert. He was a little sullen because Kenilworth was not yet as he wished it to be – a poor unfinished barn fit only for owls, he scowled.

"As long as neither of us is required to do that which at present pleases neither of us," I laughed, " – to wit, to woo!"

I was in merry humour. I had kissed the Earl of Oxford in the brilliant illuminated night, the heavens glittering with fire above the dancing crimson river.

"Have I your leave to go beyond the seas?" said Oxford.

I hung two cherries in his pretty ear. "You have not. Why should you wish to leave these shores? Have you not all you long for here? A pretty wife...?" I teased.

He pouted. "All the world knows what I think of marriage."

"A holy state, young Oxford."

"Even Joseph was a cuckold."

"How you do love to shock, my friend," reproved I gently.

"Say you so? I speak but as I find. I think the Trinity a fable and the whole sorry tale a fabrication."

"Your notions are too dangerous for you to travel overseas. For your own safety you must stay at home."

Nonetheless he sneaked away. He ran off with Lord Edward Seymour and they flit about the Low Countries and played at soldiers. I ordered him home. Reluctantly but swiftly he obeyed.

Now he frequented the company of players. Sir William Cecil, now Lord Burleigh, despaired of him. "He haunts low taverns and he lives with lewd companions."

"Is this so, my naughty boy?" said I to Oxford.

"I envy them," he answered.

"Whom do you envy?"

"Those same players. Theirs is a freedom we at court may never know. I am well at my ease amongst them. The inn yards and the mean streets, these have charms the great house never can possess. A vibrancy, a stronger pulsation of the spirit. The men themselves – the joy of counterfeit, the abandonment of self-imposed restraint, the pleasing loss of dignity... Why, I have joined them in their revels. I have put on woman's garb!"

"You have, my dear?" I smiled. "And how was it, this metamorphosis?"

He grinned bewitchingly. "I found it pleasing. And I was a very pretty wench."

"I well credit it. What did you wear?"

"Blue taffeta. Tight-waisted. Lord, but the laces pulled! And a hairpiece of golden curls."

"You should dress so for me some time."

"Your Majesty, I will!" he cried delightedly. "I love the intricacies of deception," he confessed. "I love to think that a man may pass for a woman, or a woman for a man. Amongst the players, who are male, we sometimes let a woman play, and none watching guesses it. You cannot tell from the careless glance which sex is which; and therein lies a curious pleasure."

The Earl of Oxford in a French farthingale, a small pearl cap, a tiny ruff, slashed puff sleeves, a bodice drawn tight, edged with lace... How he did mince and strut with dainty steps, and, being short, did, as he promised, pass at a distance for a wench.

I laughed. "My dear! I think it is your small moustache that gives away your secret!"

"Damn me, " cried Oxford. "I should have known I could not fool your Grace! They warned me you were devilish astute!"

"They told you true. Take it from one who knows, sweet friend, you have a little way to go before the world believes you female."

"And what is so special about a man who likes the company of players?" Robert said contemptuously. "My own players, which bear my own name, are the best in the land. You know it. You have seen them. Therefore I myself frequent the company of players. I saw James Burbage's worth from the start. And when he has acquired a building to be used specifically for plays, he will be famous the length and breadth of the land. So, wherein lies Lord Oxford's own particular brilliance?"

"How peevish you are, Robert. No one denies your patronage of Burbage's players. But Oxford has a mischievous streak; he puts himself among the players in the very inn yard, eating and drinking with them for the pleasure of it. He takes part in their plays and dresses as a woman. He has tales to tell of pert and pouting boys that take the lady's part - pretty queens and lisping angels, of street brawls and bad-tempered inn keepers, of the cheers of the crowd, and the tears also; I love to hear of such..."

"Oxford is a brat, and a lying brat at that. These colourful tales come from his own head. He is also something of a drunkard, and a man in his cups sees the world a merrier place. Your interest in him is misplaced, and, if I may say so, occasionally insulting."

"In what way?"

"In that when we were at Warwick and they brought us news of the slaughter in Paris on St Bartholomew's Day and I feared for my nephew Philip Sidney living then in Paris, you cared more for

Oxford's company than mine."

"Indeed I did not."

"You cared nothing for poor Philip, whether he lived or died, nor for myself that fretted for him."

"By all the saints, the welfare of young Philip Sidney is most dear to me."

"It was not then. You fondled Oxford's ear when I had not yet heard whether Philip lived or died."

"Oxford has perfect ears, and we know Philip to be safe."

"We did not in that month of August, and I say you cared more for Oxford."

"Truly, Robert, you must curb your jealousy; it makes you an object of ridicule."

"Ah – if that is how I seem to you..."

"Robert! Come back! How dare you stalk out of the royal presence!"

"And now, my dear Your Majesty," purred Oxford, "have I your leave to go beyond the seas? The love of travel is unquenched in me; I grow stale and decayed in London, and only Italy can purge me of these morbid humours."

"Italy no less?" I teased. "Have you not heard that which is said about Italy? All the vices of the known world, every man a sodomite, the twin skills of poison and perfume at his fingertips! And you would venture your young and tender person in this wild and wicked wonderland!"

"Exactly so," he sighed. "I am such a fool, would you not say? I know not what I do."

"I say you know exactly what you do," I answered fondly. "Go then, with my blessing – but be sure to bring your stories home with you, for I shall demand a close account."

He kissed my hand, and looked up at me with expressive eyes. "What, Your Majesty, all my stories?"

"All."

"I go much in the nature of a quest," said Oxford, sober, owlish, as youths become when thinking that they have discovered the secret of how the world wags, none other knowing the same. "I go to learn to know myself, and, through myself, the whole of creation."

"I would expect no less," I agreed, amused.
"No, truly," he maintained. "I have been to Dr Dee and spoken at great length. He sees a strange and marvellous future for me. He says I must pursue my search for knowledge of my fellow man, and write all I discover. He tells me I will be famed far and wide – " he frowned " – and yet unknown."
I clouted him about his pretty ears, but gently. "Leave off your riddles, my buffoon. Go find yourself in Italy, and bring it safely home."
Dear Oxford. I called him my Boar, for his emblem of the blue boar. Robert said it was an apt name.

"The court is well quit of him," said Christopher Hatton. "Your Majesty, my love for you is so great that it eclipses all other. You will not even know him gone, for by passion's alchemy my own love shall expand beyond the narrow confines of my heart to fill each room in which you find yourself, and you shall breathe it as the very air."
He was ever thus, was Hatton. In conversation florid, and, away from me, the writer of such letters as would make one think we had been lovers for all time. "Bear with me, my most dear sweet lady. Passion overcometh me. I can write no more. Love me, for I love you." His devotion was entire. If ever I felt melancholy or unloved, an afternoon in Hatton's company put all to rights. I wish for every man or woman one such.

And what did Robert the while? God's death, I believed him choosing carpets; I was wrong.
Robert had by then quit Durham House and occupied his own house in the Strand: Leicester House. He had a passion for Oriental carpets. His floors were a paradise of colours – peacock blue and crimson, tawny and jade, with leaves and flowers and curious curves in mathematical design; a man need never lack diversion for the eye on Robert's floors.
Some time in late autumn he invited me to sup with him at Leicester House, and all unsuspecting I arrived. I was wearing my black taffeta all starred with pearls, and matching pearls in my hair; at my throat a small ruff, and from my head dress a long diaphanous

veil. I carried a plumed fan, apricot-coloured. All this became me well.

We entered through the gatehouse and so into the forecourt. Torches lit our way. The great gables and the battlemented tower were mere dark shapes in the greater darkness. The wind blew chill and dank from the river. We climbed the staircase to the upper chambers. When, seated, I admired Robert's carpets, thinking thereby to please him, he gave little indication of proud ownership. Indeed, he seemed most ill-at-ease, even shifty. We dined. Then sent he all his servants from the room. Two of my ladies yet remained. The room was warm and close from the fire. Its glow caught wainscot and gilt picture-frame and Robert's troubled face. He fell to one knee.

"It has ever been my way to throw myself upon your mercy," he then said, "to speak truth and to pray for your forgiveness."

"Lord, Lord! what have you done?" I marvelled.

"There is no gentle way to tell you," he said gloomily.

"Nonetheless – ?" I encouraged patiently.

"Forgive me," he said once again. "Driven desperate by your coolness towards me – unhappy and bereft – I have courted Lady Sheffield, and now she is with child."

I compressed my lips. Nothing of my feelings showed. "While it is true that I am unfamiliar with the ways of childbearing," I said with dignity, "I understand nonetheless that babes are not conceived by courtship alone."

Robert squirmed. While it was gratifying to behold him there upon his knees it was also so ridiculous that I said irritably: "Oh, cease this false humility and sit down on a chair."

He obeyed. "I have offended you," he said.

I shrugged. I had no intention of showing him as much. "You are a man," I said in pious tones, "and men are prone to lapses of the flesh. Let me congratulate you upon your fecundity."

"It was the weakness of a moment," he said miserably.

"What? Not an all-consuming passion?" I said curling my lip.

"Indeed not, as you well know."

"You mean you do not love the lady?"

"God's eyes, I most certainly do not. I love you and always have and shall, but you have made your indifference plain; and in despair

I turned to another. I was foolish; I was weak; and I regret it bitterly."

"Lady Sheffield..."

"It was either to be she or her sister," Robert answered dismissively. "Both were eager for me; but Lady Sheffield was the more demanding."

"God's death, you have not wed her?" I cried suddenly alarmed.

"What do you take me for? I never was a fool," snapped Robert. He sighed. "Or was I? Poor lady, she seemed mad for my love; and I could not refuse."

"Wretched Robert, to be so persecuted," I cooed in the tones of one who would sympathise.

He winced. He was uncomfortable; and rightly so.

"So, you will be a father." I said in ironic congratulation.

"It would seem so. In the summer, as they say."

"A bastard infant," I mused. "Are there others, perhaps, of which you have not told me?"

"God forbid! No!"

"Because, Robert, though I may be tolerant once, I may not always be so."

He was silent.

"And was it the once, or many times?" I probed. "How many couplings does it take to make an infant of the Dudley stock?"

"It was," Robert coughed, "more than once."

"Oh, greedy Robert! The weakness not of one moment, as you suggested, but of many!"

"Had you deigned to marry me the matter might have been other," Robert murmured in a tone a little tinged with accusation.

"I think not," I replied, with a cynical laugh which he naturally misinterpreted.

"I wish that you would reassure me," he said humbly, "of your continuing goodwill towards me."

"You have it," I said shortly. "But keep the lady from me."

Angry, hurt as I might be at his unwelcome news, I could tolerate it, nay, even treat it with a certain sardonic humour. Lady Sheffield, even with child, was no threat to my position in Robert's heart, I knew it. I guessed him vexed at his misfortune, a secret foolish encounter now made a public show. I could almost find it in my heart to sympathise. But other rumours gave me more cause for concern.

"Robert!" I screamed. "You are after Lettice Knollys once again! Is there to be no end to your rutting?"

"You wrong me – I swear it," Robert said unhappily.

"Her very husband does accuse you."

"He is deranged."

"And yet it is well known you press for his return to Ireland, saying he is most fit for the position of authority. Which is he – mad or competent?"

"Whichever he is, it is a matter of no interest to me."

"As long as he leaves his wife behind in London!"

"Oh? Is she in London?"

"Get from my sight! Go father a dozen more brats upon these drabs so eager for your manly charms; for I swear those same charms mean nothing to me now."

"Elizabeth! You are unjust."

"I am your queen. Address me by my proper title."

"Give me leave to go from court."

"Aye – to the arms of that adultress!"

"No, to some cave or mountainside where I may live as hermits do."

"A hermit, in amber satin? You will be one of the wonders of the world!"

And so we raged at one another. But when I was ill, it was Robert who sat up with me all night, who soothed my brow and held me close and comforted me with loving words. I clung to him, my hair moist with fever.

"Oh Robert, Robert – how have we grown so distant?"

We were at Dr Dee's house in the spring. I smiled to see him as he came to his door to greet us; with his long hair and his long grey beard, his bright darting eyes and stooping build, he was becoming more and more like the image of the magus feared by the untutored. His house was old and rambling, sprawling along the riverside, all corners, nooks and crannies, all passageways and sudden darkness; and everywhere his books – in his library a vast array, but also on his tables, chests and window seats, as one who reads and is inspired and leaves one book to peruse another elsewhere.

I remember he spoke to us of demons – demons that controlled each celestial body, and, within ourselves, that which he called the star demon, whom each must discover for himself, through the tapping of celestial powers.

"Angels tell us only of God," he said, "but demons tell us of ourselves – that darkness within, which each one of us knows, when the voice of God is silent. When we perceive our own demons then we become as gods. The world is as a lyre, thrilling with the music of invisible strings. When we attune ourselves to them we are at one with the hidden energies of all Nature. Our senses are a part of this great harmony, and subject to the influence of astral bodies, from which power flows directly into the spirit, permitting us to see the wonders within ourselves."

Then he asked to speak to Robert and myself alone, each privately.

I sat opposite him. He had spread my natal chart upon the table, a wondrous chart, all stars and moons and arrows, dotted with tiny calculations in his small neat hand.

"This coming summer is a time of great importance to you," he said. "I see risk and danger, and Venus herself. Strange aspects; but an auspicious time which must be looked directly in the eye. Could it apply to anything in especial?"

"This summer I am invited to Robert's castle of Kenilworth," I laughed. "Robert has plans... I believe it is to be an unforgettable experience!"

"It may well prove to be so," said Dr Dee.

I frowned. "But this is not my chart. I am a subject of the sign of Virgo, as you know. This is a natal chart for one born under Leo."

My eyes accused. John Dee returned my gaze.

"A stranger to you, Your Majesty," he agreed. "But one whose voice has been too long suppressed and silent. Pay heed to him, this Leo child, this stranger. Feed his needs – he is a trusty friend to you."

"But Robert was born at midsummer; this is not Robert's chart..." I faltered.

"No; it is not the Earl of Leicester's chart. It is the chart of one more close to you than even he. This coming summer, at Kenilworth, is an auspicious time for a Leo subject, one who has been too long denied. No Leo subject likes to be ignored, and you have not been kind to this one. Draw the clouds from off this hidden sun. Accept him at last; permit him to exist."

"I dare not," I shuddered.

"You who pride yourself upon your courage...and speak of fear?"

"I have too much to lose."

"Or the greatest prize of all to gain?"

"What did he say to you?" I asked Robert as we came away.

"That is my secret," he replied, and smiled. "And what to you?"

"The same," said I.

TWELVE

I

A warm trickle of sweat moistened my inner thigh; to one already overheated in petticoats, these side saddles were the very devil. It was as hot a July as I had ever known. Our cavalcade made its way along roadways thick with fine white dust, between hedgerows of roses, wreathed in honeysuckle, lacy with meadowsweet. We passed fields of wheat and hay meadows, where folk laid down their tools to cry 'God bless Your Majesty!' and to wish us well. Warwickshire burned gently beneath the radiant sun.

Now we spied Robert's party riding towards us, Robert in amber and gold like a very ray from that sun, and perspiring freely in the same.

"Welcome, welcome!" cried he expansively to one and all. "Follow me – a shady pavilion awaits you, and great good cheer therein."

He had had erected at Long Itchington an enormous purple tent, with tables laid and places set, and music the while, and jugglers and tumblers who, notwithstanding the sun's blaze, leapt and cavorted, their lean bodies glistening. Thereafter we were brought towards Kenilworth in the summer dusk.

"And now," said Robert, "shall you bid a brief farewell to the bulk of your household, which is to lodge at Warwick. You, my dearest Majesty, shall come with me, and I ask nothing more than that you put yourself, your very precious person, entirely in my hands. A welter of wonders, a miracle of marvels awaits you at Kenilworth. For the next eighteen days time is at a standstill and you and I are wanderers in an enchanted land... trust me; I am your guide, the fortunate he that leads you into this maze, at whose heart lies love and self-discovery, and wonders a thousand times more fair and strange than may be sought beyond the western seas..."

I smiled in great affection. Hyperbole came easily to one who as my Master of Horse had created pageant and tournament and procession for as many years as I had reigned. And yet I knew that love itself inspired my friend's determination that this visit should surpass all other.

"Tell me, Robert," I said, reaching for his hand. "What was it that John Dee promised you when he looked in his scrying glass at Mortlake?"

"He told me that I should achieve my heart's desire," said Robert simply.

"But that, I think, depends partly upon myself?" said I.

"Partly? Oh no, entirely," Robert assured me.

"Then have no fear," I answered quietly, "for I have decided that if it be in my power, this selfsame heart's desire, being of like substance to my own, shall be granted ere we quit your castle."

Robert bowed, perhaps after so many disappointments and delays, unwilling to believe as much; but I had seen the longing in his eyes.

Kenilworth floated insubstantial as a dream, a phantasm of dazzling lights, above its dusky grey lake. At its gates a pretty youth representing a sibyl, dressed in a diaphanous gown, came forth to greet me, calling me the Prince of Peace. He had no sooner finished his verses than one Hercules the porter staggered out, lanthorn in hand, as one awoken from sleep.

"Who knocks? What noise is this? What rowdy train of travelling folk that wake honest folk from their beds?" Then as we laughed and gained admittance we drew level with the lake and here the first of the marvels now came to our attention – a floating island veiled in smoky mist and lit with torches. Hereupon sat a most beautiful youth with long flowing hair and all dressed in white silk, the parts of his body clearly defined as he stood up and spoke.

"I am the Lady of the Lake... The lake, the lodge, the lord are yours for to command."

We drew rein to listen. No lady he, and such was plain enough, and in delighted tolerance we accepted his pretty lie and heard his poesy. On the bridge as we went further, we passed pillars decorated with the symbols of earth's abundance – apple trees, cherries, wheat, grapes; birds cunningly contained in cages amongst foliage, fish and fowl on platters; bay trees bringing forth flutes and lutes; and at last the ragged staves of Robert's emblem, hung with armour to show that he would lay down his life for me. Cannons roared salute; we entered.

And now Robert pointed upward to show me that the blue and gilt clock upon the tower was to be made to stop here and now. Time was indeed to stand still.

Excitement, apprehension, dread, anticipation, all now stirred within me, warring elements that left me in a strange and sweet confusion. When Time was once more set in motion, what of myself and Robert? What would have become of us?

I was startled at the perfection of his planning. I could fault nothing. I had given him Kenilworth, a partly tumbledown castle, it being his pleasure to own the same; and we had teased him for his tower building and his garden plans and his Italian gardeners; but he had made a palace of that pig's ear.

Now there were glittering windows, gilt hangings, ornate chambers and stairways, carved oak panelling, great beds with curtains of blue and silver, edged with lace and fringed with gold. And everywhere glass – blue glass candlesticks, glass goblets and bowls, great looking-glasses, glass tables and statuettes, all with a myriad lively sparkles caught in the dancing flicker of the glow from flame and sunlight. And naturally upon the floors the oriental carpets so beloved of the castle's lord, a sea of crimson, emerald, blue.

From my chamber a small room led, containing a little marble bath, with fishes' heads and tails fashioned for its ornamentation; and a lock upon the door – "For that I know you value your privacy," said Robert.

He had thought of everything. As Blanche prepared me for sleep and I settled into the bed with its bear and ragged staves at each corner and its hangings of white tinsel silver, purple velvet and copper-gold, my heart felt heavy with misgiving, and I half believed I would not dare make my confession after all.

I wished that Kat were here. She would have known what was best.

We might have laughed about it; for it was droll enough, my situation. She laughed so easily, did Kat. If ever I missed her it was now.

"Blanche, Blanche, what shall I do?" I whispered. "Shall I not tell him? Shall I keep my secret to the grave, Robert believing me a woman? See, the very sheets bear his insignia, as if he would possess me as I slept, as if he would enforce his will upon me even absent. I am full of fears. I dare not risk the loss of his love. I shall say nothing, but then risk his anger and his hurt. His love for me speaks in every thread of silver, every twist of gold. What must I do? Advise me, Blanche."

Blanche tucked my bedclothes about me with a firm and final flourish. "Elizabeth," she said severely, as if I were six years old, "no man is worthy of the endless cogitation that foolish females indulge in for his sake. My advice is to leave them all alone, every one. I have known but one only that I could tolerate at close quarters, and he only for that his circumstances obliged him to seem female. In this particular instance I say you are old enough to make up your own mind concerning Robert Dudley."

Old! Yes! That was it – I was old. Panic seized me. I was too old for him to love me. A youth of nineteen would consider me an ancient crone. No, that was not so; Oxford loved me, worshipped me – but I was no longer young...

"Blanche! Bring me a looking-glass."

"It is too dark to see," Blanche grumbled.

"Light candles," I commanded.

I sat up in bed, my hair a-tumble. The candles, held by a plainly disgruntled and disapproving Blanche, showed me a pale face, ghostly in the glow, framed by the darkness. I flung the mirror from me.

"It's true – I am old and ugly. An ancient, and I dared to think of seduction and allure...so old, so old..."

"As old as Robert Dudley," Blanche agreed, "no more nor less."

A little chastened I repented of my wailing. "My neck is good," I conceded. "And my face has no wrinkles."

"And believe me," Blanche continued drily, "as for seduction and allure, Robert Dudley thinks on these things, age or no."

And now we stood in the pleasure garden, watching the dancers. Above us, the great Norman keep made shade. The garden lay before us like one of Robert's oriental carpets, patterned with foliage, with white marble statues, ornate obelisks and pale stone bears that twined about their ragged staves. A fountain surged up at the centre of this profusion, a marble structure thick with elaborate sea monsters, shells and naked nymphs; rich in fish, lush with cascading water. All along the castle walls coloured birds flew amongst columns and arches studded with bright jewels, screeching their alien song, flashing their startling plumage. Sweet music played for the dance; and I remarked those guests that watched, as I did, fanning themselves, murmuring to their companions: Henry and Mary Sidney, Ann and Ambrose Warwick, Lettice Knollys, Philip Sidney and his friend Fulke Greville. Safely back from his tour of foreign parts – and I use the phrase in its fullest sense – young Philip had blossomed into vibrant manhood. Robert's glance softened every time it fell upon his pretty nephew. Fair-haired, slender and graceful, he was the darling of his parents' eye and also, I surmised, of Fulke Greville's. If I were not mistaken, there was a growing love there.

"Elizabeth..." said Robert in low tones. "I have witnessed you upon countless occasions and in many places, but I swear I never saw you lovelier than you are now and here at Kenilworth."

"I wish you would not speak to me so," I replied, fanning myself excessively.

"Why not?"

"I prefer you when you are merry and amused and clear-headed. This lovesick foolery is more fitting for callow youths and gullible maids. It does not become those of riper years."

Robert chortled. "Come now, so sedate so suddenly? I assure you, I despise all talk of the advancing years. I am more youthful now, by all the saints, than ever was I as a young man. And the same is true of you."

"Oh, Rob," I sighed, "I am afraid we make ourselves ridiculous by talking of love... We should seek to be attaining wisdom, as befits our years."

"Madam, I forbid this kind of talk in this enchanted place," said Robert gaily. "Did I not tell you that time stands still since you are entered here?"

"It stands still, yes, but at the point at which I entered, as you say. And how old were we then?"

"I am forty-two," said Robert, "and you are ageless. And I love you and you love me; there is no more to say. Now, may I come to you tonight?"

"You may," I said; and gloom such as I had never known descended upon me, and the dancers danced, and the music played on beneath the unstinting heat.

Naked I stood at the window of my room, illumined by the sudden flash of firework, now gold, now green, now crimson, now silver. The noise was unbelievable, so close were these fiery explosions fixed; and with every further cannonade the sky grew bright and fizzed and sparkled, darkening briefly, to return to its blaze of brilliance. I shrank back from the window. I moved slowly across the floor towards the bed, and curled my body into the perfumed sheets. Here I sat, arms clasping knees, head bowed, awaiting Robert's presence as if he were a messenger of doom and not the man I loved.

Here he came, Robert, the handsomest man at court, whose years of devotion I was now about to reward with a revelation so devastating that I doubted our friendship would survive the shock.

"Wait – " I said quickly. "Not yet. Sit by the bed, or stand, or what you will; but not into bed – not yet – if ever."

Robert flung himself into a chair.

"Doubts, hesitations, even now?" he said, yet patient the while. "You surely do not fear I shall be maladroit? Let me assure you of my competence. For God's sake, Elizabeth, give me the chance to prove to you once and for all – "

"I do not doubt it," I interrupted. "It isn't that. Rob, there is no kind way to – it would be amusing if it were not so terrible – indeed, I fear that a certain hysteria rises – I pray it does not overcome me – "

"Whatever are you trying to say and failing so lamentably?"

"Do you remember how you often asked me to answer a question – something you once asked Princess Elizabeth when she was a little girl? And I have never answered it, all these years?"

"Yes, but it doesn't matter; it isn't important now."

"It is," I answered glumly. "I never could answer that question, because the maid to whom you asked it – was not myself. There! I have said it now. I am not that little girl of eight years old; I never was. I am someone else, an impostor. Therefore I never could give you the answer you required, although I longed to do so. I am not the princess, daughter of Anne Boleyn, though I am of royal blood and of as good a stock as she; otherwise I never would have consented to play her part. I have deceived you as to my true identity; but I have never deceived you as to my love. I have always loved you, and I urge you to remember that, when you at last absorb the truth of what I tell you now."

"I have never considered myself a stupid man," said Robert carefully, "but I must confess I do not know what you are talking about."

"I know; I sound distract; it is not so. I longed to give you all you once desired; but I dared not share my fearsome secret. I believed you would not love me if you knew – "

"If I knew – what? – that you are not Elizabeth, preposterous as that appears? But this is nonsense! I see you are Elizabeth, I see it with my own eyes. I see you are the woman whom I have loved for so long, she who so infuriates and delights me – she, moreover, whom I have seen crowned with holy oil and courted by all the princes of Europe. You choose to play some game now and I see that I must play it too. And so, in God's name, madam, if you are not Elizabeth, then perhaps you would be good enough to tell me who you are?"

In a small voice, shaking with that mild hysteria which I feared would rise into my throat and choke me, I replied: "I am a boy from Bisley."

There by rights ought to have been a stupefied silence; but instead a vehement thunderbolt of a firework rocked the night outside my window, and we both jumped. Robert at once regained composure.

"A boy from Bisley?" Robert said in the controlled and patient tones of one dealing with a halfwit. "And where and what in God's name is Bisley?"

"It is a village. In Gloucestershire," I answered, pleased to be able to answer a question so straightforward. "If you recall, it is a royal manor, owned by the crown. It is," I added, "famous for its fulling and dyeing. Cloth merchants come from far and wide... The Cotswold sheep, you see, is unusually large."

"I doubt it not," said Robert weakly. Then he said: "Did I hear you aright? You said a boy...?"

"I did."

"Do you mean to tell me that you – one of us is mad, I know, and I begin to fear it is myself – that you are a man?"

"The males in my family on my mother's side are always beardless and of good complexion. I doubt I could have passed as female all these years had it not been so. Though natural skill abetted me," I added with a certain modest pride. "As for the rest, it has been easy, for I have been dressed in petticoats since I was ten years old and ridden side saddle as long, and learned how to walk in small strides. Kat Ashley and Blanche Parry taught me all I know."

"Spare me the details of your obscene masquerade, please," said Robert coldly. "No, this is too much. I need to know I am not dreaming."

He stood up. He gripped the sheet. He tore it from me. He reached down and put a hand between my legs.

"By God, it's true," he said unnecessarily. He turned away and began to pace about. The fireworks crackled and hissed, their brilliance showing him now as a shadow, now as a hunched and striding figure. He spun round. I saw the blazing of his eyes.

"Who knows?" he hissed. "Who else knows?"

"Only Blanche. But then I had to tell another woman, when Kat died, for safety's sake. So I chose Lady Ann, your brother's wife. And your sister Mary found out for herself when I was ill. There are no others more, though I believe that John Dee guesses it through magic art... Thomas Parry knew; and Lord Thomas Seymour, and Queen Katherine Parr – but they are dead. And there is a priest in Bisley, but he may be dead also; I have not heard from him."

"Mary and Ann!" screeched Robert. "Before me?"

"Yes, but they are sworn to secrecy, as you see. After all, they said nothing to you."

"But not Ambrose?" he checked.

"No; no one else knows; only those two women, good friends both."

"Not Burleigh? Sussex? Arundel? And Hatton? Oxford?"

"No! None of those! What do you take me for?"

"Indeed I know not what. You swear it? You swear no one knows but Ann and Mary, and your lady, Blanche?"

"I do swear it, by all I hold most dear."

"So," he said thoughtfully. "There is no loss of face for me."

I remembered what Mary had said: he would consider himself the laughing stock of Europe.

"No," I said drily. "Your reputation is intact. You are yet the Queen of England's supposed lover and known by all to be beloved of the most powerful woman in the land."

He was silent. He sat down. A firework filled the chamber with a flood of emerald. Robert's face showed, green, preoccupied.

"Rob," I said, entreaty in my voice. "Nothing has changed. We two have loved each other now for more than twenty years – kissed, comforted, teased and vexed each other – surely there is some foundation here – ?"

"You must be crazed," he answered, a stranger speaking. "Nothing has changed? Everything has changed."

"Because it is a man who loves you? Is that so difficult to take? What about your nephew of whom you think so highly? What about the lovely Philip?"

"Philip? What has he to do with this?"

"Men fall in love with him wherever he goes. He has just left, across the length and breadth of France and Italy, a trail of broken hearts to show his passing."

"Philip inspires admiration," Robert protested. "Admiration only."

"Hubert Languet is in love with him, and pursued him to Vienna to tend him when he was ill; he writes to him every week – and he's a handsome fellow and renowned for his learning; I daresay his affection is returned. And since Philip has come back to England he is very close indeed with Greville. I speak of it to show you that it is no shame for one man to love another."

"But between you and me," said Robert, "it is not so simple; and you well know as much."

"Why so?"

"Why so? Why?" he spluttered. "Because you deceived me, you set out to deceive me – year after year – all counterfeit – all lies – how you must have laughed behind your hand!"

"No!" I protested angrily.

"And how you must have chuckled, you and that gossip Ashley: 'Today he kissed me', 'Today he said he loved me', 'What a romp', 'If only he knew!'"

"Robin! It was not so!"

"You shall have no further occasion to smile about it with the dour Mistress Blanche. I shall make sure of that."

I grew cold. "You – you surely do not mean to make the truth known. I would not have believed – "

"Madam, I would sooner die than let the world know I had been so fooled!" cried Robert. "Rest assured of that. *Madam!*" He heard what he had said, and laughed ironically. "What must I call you now," he said contemptuously, "some half and half thing, neither man nor woman? Indeed I know not what to say or think nor how to act."

"Much as before?" I suggested tartly.

He shook his head. "Impossible," he answered brusquely. He added, looking about him, as if justifying his position to a circle of spectators – a court of justice perhaps. "It is too much to ask of me. No man would be expected to – no man of pride and self-esteem – and certainly not myself! It is preposterous, beyond the bounds of reason. Elizabeth!" he stared at me, distraught. "How could you? How could you abuse me so? And I so loyal, faithful, for so long!"

"But – what have I done?" I cried stung. "Am I to grovel for your forgiveness? I refuse. How am I at fault? I never have ill-treated you. Your wellbeing has always been most dear to me. It has been entirely to spare you these pains you now endure that I have kept my secret from you. I would not have deceived you for the world, but chance had forced my hand before we even met. The irony of my situation has been an ever present torment to me. I loved you from the first and would have proved it long ago as any lover would; but respect for your manly sensibilities," I continued savagely, "restrained my carnal impulse. I guessed that you would strut and rage, much as you are now doing. You were in love, yes, but you must love a woman – such was plain enough – and therefore woman you were offered."

"Offered?" he spat. "I was never offered you in any form I could accept. It was always tease and then retire."

"I was obliged to hold back when I would have offered more."

"What did you think that you could offer me?" said he contemptuously. "Boy that you were, man that you now show yourself to be?"

And now I was enraged. I flung back the sheets and stood up facing him, all erstwhile doubts and fears concerning my power to please him quite forgot.

"There is no fault or imperfection in what I offered you and offer still. I am as finely formed as any and have been desired and praised for my male beauty by men with better judgement than yourself. I am not ashamed to stand here as I am. What you now see before you is as fair a sight as any in the land and you would be a fool to tell me otherwise."

Robert sat there fixed, immobile, staring. Finally he whispered: "And by God, it's true."

He stood up shakily. "But what would that then mean?" he murmured. "What would it mean for us? For me?" He put up a hand to his brow. "I must think...I need to think..."

He turned to go. Suddenly he paused, as if a long forgotten fact had occurred to him. I was the queen.

"Your Majesty," he said weakly but with dignity, "have I your leave to depart?"

"You have not," I answered.

"Nevertheless..." said he, and without looking back he quit the chamber.

"Robert! Come back!"

But he did not. The room grew crimson, golden, green; the sharp explosions cracked and burst; and I stood shivering, in the brilliant confusion.

"He will never accept it," I said to Blanche with gloomy resignation.

I found that with dawn's light came a certain clarity of thought, a calm that overlaid the turmoil of the night's grim solitude. I saw that I would have to learn to live bereft of Robert's goodwill, that staff upon which I had leaned for so long so carelessly. However, I (who more so?) was long grown used to loneliness. I would once more override it.

"But we shall quit this place," I said to Blanche.

"I think you should not," Blanche replied, assisting me into a loose white gown. "It will be talked about, and speculation rife. We are expected to be here for eighteen days, and Robert's enemies will take advantage of the affront put upon him, should you leave."

"Well, I care nothing about that," I answered airily. "Robert should have considered as much when he strode from the room."

"If Robert had considered it," said Blanche, "he would have been a sly conniving courtier; whereas I believe him to be an honest one who speaks from the heart."

"To my detriment," I winced. I heard again the contempt that rang in his voice. *And what did you think that you could offer me, boy that you were, man that you be?* "Enough of Robert. I have no wish to see him or speak with him and shall spend the day here in my chambers. Besides, the heat here is oppressive; it is too hot to walk abroad."

"Your Majesty will disappoint the goddesses and nymphs that wait about the lake to sing your praises."

"Let 'em be disappointed. They are in good company."

But with the food that was brought in to me came notes from Robert. Pushed under the door came notes from Robert; servants brought the same.

"Your gracious Majesty, hear me..."

"Your Majesty, let me but speak to you..."

"Elizabeth, I was wrong – the night has left me wiser..."

"Your Majesty, I beg you, do not deprive this poor realm of your light. Here, where you are not, no sun shines and we shiver in perpetual night..."

I could not, dared not believe, after the harsh words of his anger and reproach, these gentler messages that seemed to atone for them. It was true he had murmured something that seemed favourable to me when he gazed upon me naked. But now I began to doubt it, wondering if I had dreamt it, conjured it out of longing. Surely he hated me now? These messages were merely the courtier speaking, words born of a wish that none should see that we had quarrelled under his roof.

Sitting in the window embrasure, one knee drawn up to my chin, munching apricots and reading Ovid, warm in the sun's heat, I smiled and sighed. Ah, to be a private person – to be that time-honoured object of the courtier's envy, the silly shepherd! Then would all such mollification be substantial. To be sure, now Robert repented of his harsh words; but no monarch ever would know whether such came from the heart, as Blanche suggested, or from the rational mind that knew his future bound up with his sovereign's.

"I will not see him," I replied.

All day I kept to my chamber, deaf to pleas that I should come forth. But as the day cooled and because the hunting of the hart was promised, I was eager to be out and on the chase; and with those guests that loved to hunt I rode and put the business from me that was troubling my mind. When we returned to the castle, a Wild Man, all shaggy and unkempt, carrying a green bough, ran with us alongside, chanting paeans of praise the which we paused to hear. But these words went deeper, did they not? A plea for all misunderstandings, weepings and lamentings and quarrellings to cease, friendship to be renewed, lovers reunited? This had the ring of something writ to fit the occasion! I found I knew the man; it was George Gascoigne, the poet, in this disguise of Sylvanus; he who was to write:

> But in my glass, which is of trusty steel,
> I can perceive how kingdoms breed but care,
> How lordship lives with lots of less delight
> Than common people find ...

He led us on towards an arbour; I perceived he had contrived to bring me there for a purpose, the which was now revealed, for from the arbour came forth one masked and in a long green robe. Some wood god, no doubt, but plainly, in spite of mask, the lord of Kenilworth, perspiring warmly.

"Whom do you represent?" I enquired, leaning a little to him.

"My name is Deep Desire," he answered.

"Of whom for whom?" said I.

"Of wretched Robert Dudley for that same prince first greeted by the Nymph of the Lake."

My heart jumped. I understood that he had chosen to address me thus with meaning. It was commonplace of course to name a female monarch so, but in this instance I believed it signified more.

"This prince accepts your greeting," I replied.

"Then grant me this," cried Robert, "that I may be restored to my former happiness, and set free from the vile dungeon of your displeasure! Your Majesty has been to hunt the hart – it is here, at your feet!"

Sylvanus then flung down his bough. This act of homage so alarmed my horse it reared and plunged, and caused a crowd to run about us; but I calmed the beast and called: "No hurt, no hurt; all's well." I spoke to reassure the throng; but I looked towards Robert.

II

Night time. Robert came to my door; Blanche let him in and left us. He hurried to my bedside and reached for my hand and kissed it.

"Sweet Your Majesty," he said, and stood and looked at me. Looked at me honestly, knowing who I was. And I saw love in his eyes, as it had ever been.

"It was gracious of you to receive me," he said contritely. "Dare I hope that I am forgiven? I was churlish, but – in my defence – I was taken aback."

I laughed a little at his understatement. "I do forgive you for your outburst – but do you forgive me for deceiving you? Believe me, it was not my wish."

"I was all night awake," he said. "My thoughts came tumbling; I was all confusion. I thought back – remembered – I began to understand things which had seemed inexplicable. Again and again I asked myself and now ask you: why could you not tell me? Why could you not trust me?"

"You made it plain it was a woman that you loved, a queen. I feared to lose that love."

"But Ann and Mary learned the truth and loved you still. Why should you have believed me less constant than they?"

"Oh, Rob! You wanted marriage – sons – and failing that, you wanted us to be lovers. And every time I spoke to you of men loving men, you became so pompous and censorious!"

"I deny it most strongly."

"Robert!" I accused. "You said Southampton and his boys disgusted you."

"And so they did, for that they flaunted themselves and were not discreet. But – "

"And you mislike Lord Oxford with an inordinate distaste."

"I do, for that he is a mincing fool. But – "

"And you denied that Ambrose liked his own kind."

"To protect his reputation!" Robert spluttered. "I believed you female, did I not? And women are reputed to find sodomy repugnant. I was afraid for Ambrose."

"So now you agree that he is thus? And all those tales of you in your young manhood – ?"

"Lies; all lies."

"And Philip? How you sprang to his defence when I said Hubert Languet loved him!"

"Philip seems to draw towards him, lodestone like, all older men that have a fondness for a pretty youth. Poor Peter Ramus, lately slain, led him in Paris to all his boy-loving friends, of which Languet was one. I have no doubt that Languet is besotted. If I am honest I own to some jealousy. I have always found Philip very beautiful; but I am his uncle and I may only look."

I smiled. I patted the bed beside me. "Sit down, Robin, sit with me."

He sat, in a chair close to the bed. He reached for my hand; I gave it.

"So, Robin," I said, a great content upon me at this restoration of our intimacy. "You are something of a hypocrite, by your own admission?"

"Not at all," said Robert. "It is yourself must bear the blame. Deception breeds deception. Passing as female, you obliged me to speak as I would to a woman. If you had come to me as your true self and asked me man to man..." He paused, still marvelling at the novelty of the concept. "...man to man, if you had asked me for my thoughts upon the nature of that kind of love, I would have answered in another kind."

"What would you have said?" I whispered, leaning towards him.

"I would have said that most men at some time or another have admired one of their own sex, often for prowess, sometimes for beauty; and that in many instances this admiration has grown into love; and in some further instances this love has manifested itself in physical form."

"And in your case, Robin?"

He hesitated. Then he said: "I have never known love with a man, but I have, as many men have, performed certain acts of pleasure...often...first, when I was a boy..."

"With whom?" I asked in blatant curiosity.

"With Barnaby Fitzpatrick. But we always kept it secret from Prince Edward."

"With Barnaby!" I cried delightedly.

"Yes – when we went swimming and outdistanced Ned – and often in the winter when we shared a bed. Then when I was a soldier in the Low Countries, in an army camp such things are commonplace."

"Robert Dudley!" I breathed awed. "It seems you are more cunning in these matters than I!"

"In most matters, I suspect," said Robert comfortably. "Horsemanship, archery, swordplay..."

"Arrogance, vanity..."

"There we are equal, I believe. But have you a name, my new-discovered friend, if you are not the woman I believed you? One I may whisper to you when we are alone?"

"All that is best forgotten," I demurred.

"I think you owe me an account of how you came to be that which you now are," Robert said, "and more, with your permission, I will hear it closer to you than I now am." He slipped off his robe and climbed into bed beside me.

"I do not recall that I granted that permission," I gasped, delighted at his boldness and our close proximity.

"No," he agreed. "But formality is irrelevant between lovers; and I have been patient far too long." He gave me a swift companionable kiss. "My first amazement over, I require to know your history, more strange, it seems to me, than any I have heard before..."

So I told him all that he would know. It was not easy, sitting side by side, and naked as we were, the first time we had ever been so; but except for a friendly arm about my shoulders he did not move close, but sat enrapt as those upon a stage who hear such tales of disguises and enchantment as must be told before the play proceed.

"So, you are Harry of Richmond's son," he mused at length. "A curious convolution of fate and chance, which I think would have pleased the old king. He loved that lad, and would have had him crowned, if he had lived."

"Though I am not Elizabeth," I said, "I am as well born as she. I would never have participated in the plan's inception had I not believed myself worthy to take her place. We were alike as two peas. I was able to convince everyone save Blanche of my veracity... I thought that you yourself would grow suspicious, for that I never could answer that question to which you would have a response."

"What question?"

"Oh, have you forgotten so readily, after causing me so much anguish because that I could not reply! I had to stave you off, and tell you I would answer when the time was right."

"Ah yes – oh, but that was nothing – it was a silly childish thing!" He laughed. "When she was eight years old or so, I asked her which of us boys she liked the best. That's all. She never would reply, much like yourself."

I laughed with him. "It happens that I know the answer. She told me. Rest easy, Rob: it was you. And, for what it's worth, I am in agreement."

Robert coughed, with unconvincing modesty.

"It is not easy for me now," he said. "I always thought of myself as bold enough, as competent a lover as any man. But in all honesty I find myself now green as any virgin. I have always dreamed of loving you, and you are right – we are the same as we have ever been...nothing has changed. At least," he laughed, "an earthquake has shaken the earth and rearranged it entirely; but the earth is that same earth." He paused. "John," said he, and, savouring the word upon the tongue, repeated it. "John...tell me something."

"Yes?"

"You said a number of men had desired you for your male beauty."

"I did, yes, I remember."

"This troubled me somewhat last night as I paced up and down. I will be honest – a raging jealousy consumed me! Who were these men? And when did this occur? It surely could not have been since I have known you? Since I declared my love?"

"Of course not," I assured him with a hug. "And did I say numbers? I am sure I did not. I was boasting, was I not, and angry when I said it? But it pleases me immensely that it made you jealous!"

"Then put me from my misery and my perplexity, minx."

"It is true that someone wanted me, knowing me male. It was one man only – Tom Seymour. He was my lover, briefly. He taught me love's ways. But oh...that was long ago. In all these years you have been my only love. I teased you with pretence – Heneage, Hatton... But it was always you who had my heart."

Robert was silent.

"Rob – it was long ago," I said anxiously.

"No, no," he said. "I don't begrudge it you. He was an honourable man, and handsome," he conceded, "though a fool."

"I would rather speak of you."

"I – ", Robert hesitated. "When you stood before me naked, John, I thought you beautiful. Eerily so, elfin. A creature called up by magic, now green, now crimson. Because of the fireworks," he added unnecessarily. "I understood how any man would want to take you in his arms. I wanted that. I would have liked to take you there and then – and partly out of anger. I was afraid. I had pictured it so often, how it would be when I first saw you naked. That is, it was Elizabeth I pictured. That image was still in my mind's eye as I looked at you. And you were still she but you were you. And now the two images have merged into one." He kissed me tentatively, carefully; and then passion rose, and he held me to him fiercely and possessively. We tumbled into a close embrace, our limbs entwined, our bodies pressed together.

I recall those eighteen days and nights in Robert's kingdom – a time when time itself stood still, subject to his command – as a mythical perfection, beautiful and vibrant; the Forest of Arden without the winter wind, the wood of Athens without its trickery, yet retaining the moonlight and the fleeting all-pervasive notes of music. As background to our new-discovered love, music played – the air rich with the sound of lute and flute and singing; and fireworks lighting up the night sky and the shimmering waters of the lake. As if to emphasise that we had strayed into Arcadia, the lake, the woodland and the castle itself were peopled with the folk of fantasy. The Lady of the Lake (that lovely boy), a welter of nymphs and nereids, a mermaid, and a monstrous dolphin – Arion himself – were ever present, called up by magic, as it seemed, at the sleight of hand of Kenilworth's magus lord.

We hunted in the woods, we feasted, we ate amongst the trees, seated on banks of flowers as lush as ever did Titania know; we laughed when Arion forgot his lines and pulled his mask off, crying he was none of Arion, not he, but honest Harry Goldingham. And then at night...

Two people who had all their lives longed to be lovers were now freed at last from previous deception and misunderstanding. All counterfeiting gone, all prevarication and confusion, we were become as that same Harry Goldingham, the masks flung down, our own true selves remaining.

And what were these? I was a man with auburn hair (the which a little aided by the use of herbal colouring), smooth-skinned and willow-slender, well proportioned, and more sensuous than I had yet supposed. Robert was the handsomest man in England, dark-haired (here also I suspected a small help from herbal remedy) with wondrous eyes; and tall and muscular, and passionate of nature. Almost I suspected that, freed from the need to placate and please the woman, he gave himself up gladly to the rougher more companionable pleasing of the man; certainly our kisses here were more ardent than ever we had shared when he had been more courteous. Our naked bodies moved against each other, sometimes moist and slippery with lust, sometimes warm and quiet with tenderness. Night after night we sought to know each other in as deep and intimate a fashion as was possible between two lovers who already knew and loved each other's minds. The world without forgotten, nay, extinguished, we gave ourselves up to flesh's gratification.

"Either the magic of the place has touched my senses," Robert laughed, " – though it should not be the case, since it was I procured the magic and know its cause – or else it seems to me entirely reasonable that you should by night be my companion in male lust, by day a woman of great majesty and beauty. I half suppose that this is now the way of things – that beneath their petticoats and farthingales, all these fair creatures are pretty boys who for mischief or strategy have decided to put on a disguise. And why not? We see it at Whitehall whenever there is masque or play. In my own company of players, comely lads dress in long gowns and paint their faces and hide their short locks with gorgeous hairpieces; and who would know the difference? They ask us to believe it; we believe it. Which is real, and which is insubstantial – who knows?"

"And yet I think your magic is in part to blame," I answered. "We meet as male lovers only by night, silvered with moonlight, hidden by shadow, speaking in whispers. There is a certain deceit about the midnight hour; things are less real than when the sunlight seeks them out and shows their faults in all their actuality."

"Oh, you and I are real, doubt it not," said Robert. "Tangible flesh on unspiritual buttocks; honest love juice from corporeal cocks; true salivation from true striving tongues – we are no mere spirits, believe me."

The theme of love, like a brook, trickled through the entertainments we were offered – a country wedding, with dancing on the green, and Morris men, and rustic songs of love. Though the bride was ill-favoured it was a merry spectacle, and to all in love, a happy reminder of their own good fortune.

I sat comfortably in a bower of rose petals, with Robert's hand on mine; the sun shone and the sky was blue. I looked about at the circle of courtiers, sitting like myself much at ease, watching the bridal party as it looped and threaded in the movements of the dance. Tonight once more I would lie in Robert's arms. I thought the world had no more wonderful gift to offer. My fears had been groundless. He loved me as I was. Could one be as happy as I and live? A sudden laugh drew my attention to the presence of the Countess of Essex, Lettice Knollys. I found it in my heart to pity her. I had so much, and she...poor thing, what had she? Whatever cause had she to seem so well content?

The sky was full of stars that last evening, when in a long low boat Robert and I lay, rowed amongst the pageant on the lake. By flaming torchlight we saw half-naked tritons blowing trumpets, their bare chests gleaming bronze and crimson. The Lady of the Lake came gliding by upon a barge almost as glorious as our own. Gilded fish glimmered in the silky water. Painted dolphins, lit from within, were drawn along beside us; and upon the banks musicians played. When it was our pleasure to retire, four cannon gave a loud salute.

At night Robert and I lay entwined. I voiced my fears.

"Our last night here. Nothing will be as perfect ever again."

"You are wrong, my dear, I promise you," said Robert. "There will be trust between us now, and truth, and greater love for that it is without deception."

And, like a fool, I let him persuade me this was so.

In the morning, time was set in motion once again; the blue and gilt clock face on Caesar's Tower showed that the dials moved in their diurnal course; and we quit Kenilworth.

The next stage of our royal progress was to be Chartley, Lettice Knollys's house in Staffordshire. Here she would be hostess to us, and, her husband Essex serving in Ireland, she would be responsible for our wellbeing and entertainment.

Anywhere, after Kenilworth, would have been dull, but Chartley surpassed itself. Here we met Lettice's pretty and insufferable children – two girls, Penelope and Dorothy, and the boy, young Robert Devereux, aged eight years.

"What a delightful child!" I praised him – for never let it be said I was not a model guest. All mothers love to hear their sons commended; it is well known. "Come, kiss me, boy." But the wretched brat turned from me in a huff, and hid behind a chair.

"Naughty! Naughty Robert!" Lettice chided; but I knew she was amused, the bitch, and of a sudden it occurred to me for whom the child was named. Another thought then struck me on that theme, but I put it from me as base and unworthy. Robert's little foolish fancy for that woman was well over, was it not, when that child was conceived? But several times during that dreary visit I caught myself eyeing young Robert Devereux for signs of wondrous eyes, fleeting facial expressions and the like. Ah no, he was a little monster, sullen and withdrawn, with a Welsh lilt to his voice from the constant company of his tutor Broughton, who would have him raised more Celt than Englishman. Besides, no son of Lettice could hold charms for me.

A dull uncomfortable visit, during which I of necessity slept alone, wondering sourly whether Lettice had given orders for my sheets to be unaired and my food laced with purgatives. Lettice was a vile unpleasant wily wanton, with all the allure of a crab-apple. All my ladies were in agreement. I say this should it be thought that when I speak of her I show unreasonable prejudice.

Robert laughed ruefully. "I was wrong; I'm getting old."

"Enough of that kind of talk," I reprimanded him, slapping him smartly with my fan. "You are but one year older than when you told me you were in your prime."

"Nonetheless..."

"What are your symptoms? I will prove them all imaginary."

He was despondent. Lettice's husband, Lord Essex, had died in Ireland, dysentery the cause. Rumour, ever spiteful and vindictive, accused Robert of a crime. Men were ever swift to malign Rob; jealousy, no doubt.

"How dare they!" I said, vexed for him. "As if you would so trouble yourself to rid yourself of Essex, when you have long since lost interest in the lady!"

But it recalled the days of Amy; and I understood my friend's depression.

In the summer Robert had gone north to take the Buxton waters. I could not take seriously his debilitation. I knew his humour to be dread of old age, not old age itself, and proceeding from that seat of melancholia the hypochondrium. Accordingly I permitted him his indulgence, his taking of the water, sniggering the while at what he must by choice endure at Buxton. No food – and Robert liked his food – but two spoonfuls of raisins rinsed with wine, and bread flavoured with currant juice; no lustful thoughts; no riding at speed; and, I teased, on festival days the shoulder of a wren for supper.

I missed him as I lay alone in summer palaces. I felt affection for him and great tenderness. To think he cared for me so much that he would willingly endure the rigours of the baths, still to retain that straight muscular build, the trim frame that I loved to watch and handle. Let him immerse himself in purity if it would please him so to please me. When he returned I would be the one to benefit from his restored vitality; and confident in this assumption, I awaited his return.

And it always was so. When he came back from his self-imposed tortures, purified within and glowing without, and joined me on my summer progress, it was almost as if he needed to prove to me the efficacy of his cure. He would murmur a plea that we should be alone that night. I would contrive to lose my ladies, who retired discreetly under Blanche's competent ministration; and he would come to me.

Then I would discover once again that all my fears were groundless, that magic did exist outside Kenilworth's enchanted timelessness. At Long Melford, at Kirtling House, at Audley End, we contrived to consummate our love. At Rycote often. And now at Wanstead...

Robert's new toy, this long low house barely seven miles from London...a peaceful place, surrounded by forest. It was all golden gables, doves, gardens. When it came first to Robert's hands it was ragged, bleak and careworn. Robert transformed it, made gardens grow, filled all the rooms with beautiful things, strewed oriental carpets upon the floors. Proudly he took me from room to room.

"This is your own chamber. No one shall sleep in this bed but yourself – and one other close to yourself at this moment. This is my chamber, the colours yellow and gold, curtains of damask... This is the Red Chamber, this the Green Chamber – "

"Whatever can this one be, Rob? We have already seen the Red Chamber."

"This is the Second Red Chamber!"

"So many – all with names!"

"And when this window is opened," Robert demonstrated, "what do you see? Leaves, only leaves. The tree grows right against the house wall. Here, birds shall sing for you so near you shall reach out your hand and they alight upon it; and the walls, you see, are painted with more leaves and more birds, for this is the very forest of Arden come to Essex!"

I winced at the name of the shire; it called to mind unpleasant things best forgot. I smiled. I kissed him.

"It is a perfect place," I said.

And it was so – a lovers' retreat, embraced by trees, and every night through the opened window that gave on the rustling summer leaves, came the nightingales' song. A special place, our own.

Here we pored over charts, guessing where Francis Drake might now be. We giggled, conspirators, at how we had given out that the brave fellow was bound for Alexandria for a cargo of raisins, when, all being well, he was by now veering towards the New World, towards King Philip's treasure fleet, bearing my goodwill embroidered on a green silk scarf – 'the Lord guide and preserve thee until the end'.

Drake was the kind of sea captain Robert permitted me, for he was ruddy, gruff and strident; no dark sea prince to carry me off to the Western Isles and steal my heart away. Drake had buzzed bee-like about the Spanish Main, seeking that nectar which bloomed about Nombre de Dios, and bringing ivory and spices, hides and precious stones, bringing Brazilian wood, and silver, silks and velvets, into Plymouth. His pale far-sighted eyes had gazed upon the southern seas, an Indian guide to show the way, a world of unimaginable splendours yet awaiting. Now with Hatton's *Pelican* and the *Elizabeth*, the *Marigold*, the *Swan*, the *Christopher* – those brave oaken barks that bore our hopes and dreams of greatness – he was gone to sail those southern seas. He sailed for those of us that could not.

Now in the Queen's Bedroom at Wanstead, Robert and I said prayers for him, that salty hero of the ocean, and part of our prayer was that he should return weighed down with gold. Gold! Spanish bullion! We hugged each other, merry-eyed, and romped that night in the lavender-scented sheets of the Queen's Chamber, excited further in our lovemaking by images of surging waves and palm-fringed islands, of casks of rubies, Peruvian emeralds, sapphires and silver, chalices and Spanish ducats.

"Grow old?" I teased him in the morning, ruffling his hair. "You would not know how."

The year began badly. Lettice, Countess of Essex, gave me as a New Year gift two hairpieces. Now they were beautiful hairpieces, and such had latterly become fashionable. But I knew well enough how much dear Lettice loved me. Had observation showed her what was all too plain to me?

Those of my ladies that combed my tresses now tried to hide the comb from me; its teeth chewed away my hair in greedy mouthfuls. The broad dome of my forehead grew daily more prominent. I smiled bitterly at my habitual delight in the Neville features – the smooth and beardless skin, the slender shapely build, the pleasing pallor. I had only seen my uncle Ambrose as a man of five and twenty. He had not thought to inform me – and perhaps he no more knew the fact himself – that in their fortieth years the Neville males were prone to baldness.

I tried on one of Lettice's hairpieces, the black one. It made me look like Lady Norreys, nay, even more crow-like than she, for that my nose was hookier. I could not wear it. I tried on the other, which was yellow. Now anyone possessed of a pale skin with a tendency to freckles, knows that yellow next the skin gives one the look of a sufferer from serious disorder of the liver. I could not wear it. Not yet, however, was it the moment for despair. A red hairpiece was another matter. Now keeping the stark beauty of my noble brow, the same was garnished by tendrils of auburn curls, upon which my ladies placed a cap of pearls. My eyes showed large and dark in my pale oval face, my lips full and coral-rose. The high lace ruff emphasised my lean jaw. My gown was silver and gold, my bodice overlaid with amber and gold, two rows of pearls cascading thereupon. A red hairpiece became me well.

One afternoon in the month of April, Helena, Lady Northampton, that lovely girl who came from Sweden with Princess Cecilia and became one of my ladies, brought a letter to me, frowning.

"It was not delivered; there was no messenger," she said.

"Not delivered? What can you mean?"

"Your Majesty, it was thrown. Thrown through a doorway. No one saw who put it there."

Well may the wretch have fled who brought such tidings. I read thus:

"Robert Dudley has played you false. He wed Lady Sheffield and then cast her aside. Now he has got Lady Essex with child and he has set her up at Wanstead; 'tis certain he will marry her."

So few lines so to unsettle me. I crumpled up that paper in my fist.

"Come, Helena," I said. "To Leicester House."

Robert's face, habitually of ruddy hue, grew pallid as my own. "But who could write such things?" he spluttered. "I am surrounded by those that hate me."

There be those that deceive by outright falsehood; and those that do so by default. Robert was of the latter. He was an honest man by nature and the direct lie did not come easily to him. Absence, silence, these were his methods. Face to face and I could wring the truth from him within a moment.

"Lord Henry Howard," he continued. "It must be he that writ this note. He was Lord Oxford's paramour and they quarrelled. Now he has grown devious and bitter. Why, Lord Oxford says he is the worst villain that lives in this earth, a very rat. It is the falling out of sodomites. It is well known that when this happens, they grow bitchy and vindictive."

I looked him in the eyes. "And do we, Robert? Do we?"

He capitulated. "I never married Lady Sheffield; this I swear."

"And cast her aside?"

"She will not leave me be. I offered her money. She accepted it. I wish I never had set eyes upon her."

"She is the mother of your son."

"Yes, God be praised, I have a son of her. But she means nothing to me now."

"Unlike that other," I said, dangerously quiet.

"You are more angry than I have ever seen you. I know it because you do not rage at me."

"Yet!"

"It is true I have made love to Lettice," he conceded then. "What can I say? The world will know it soon enough."

"Yes. Women have that unkind capacity to make visible that which at first was secret. And when, may I ask, did you resume that liaison which I believed was over?"

He coughed. "At Chartley."

"When we quit Kenilworth," I breathed, unable yet to take in the full extent of his treachery. "At Kenilworth also, perhaps?"

"No, not at Kenilworth. That magic world is yet intact."

"But once beyond its confines..."

"I am entirely guilty. I shall not deny it."

"And then you purchased Wanstead. For her, perhaps?"

"No – no – for you! For us!"

"Then why is she now there?"

"She has to go somewhere," he shrugged foolishly.

"She sleeps perhaps in the Queen's Chamber? She was always puffed up with conceit."

"No, no, she has her own room..."

"The one with the tree and the nightingales, maybe?" I sneered. "Well, and have you wed her?"

"No, and never shall!"

"And am I to believe so competent a deceiver?"

"Yes – yes, accuse me; I may not defend myself. In your eyes it must seem the ultimate betrayal. It was not so. Try to understand. I wanted sons; I wanted a solid dynasty."

"You wanted cunt," I spat.

"Well, I am a man like any other," he cried stung.

"No you are not," I countered savagely. "You are the man beloved of the ruler of England."

"And that is a dubious blessing," Robert muttered, "and brings penances along with joys."

"Does it so? Then quit the realm and see how well you are without me."

"Misery makes me stupid," Robert said. "I love you and adore you and would hazard life for you. I would have given anything to spare you this hurt."

I turned away. "I have no wish to hear your empty words."

"Hear my defence then, " Robert cried. "It was because of how we were at Kenilworth, not a rejection of the love we found there. It was then I learnt that I would never marry you – with all that that entailed – no sons and daughters of my name and yours. And I am no longer young; time will not wait for me!"

"Oh, that again!" I snapped. "Your vile preoccupation with the approach of the grim reaper! You are forty-four, the same as I. This is not old age! I'll hear no more of this! Your faculties are active, and you may very like prove fertile and breed sons for thirty years or more; for carnally you are plainly not in decline!" I looked at him. I felt hot fury surge in me. "God's death, I can verify for myself that you know how to fuck as skilfully as any – sometimes four or five times a night. Don't talk to me of age and time – these are irrelevances."

"You are more angry now than when you learnt of Lady Sheffield," he said then. "Why? It is the same. And we rode that one and grew close again. Why is this matter more outrageous to you?"

"Why? Because – "

I could not see it then. But soon enough it came to me. Before, he had gone with another woman, choosing her above me. Now, now that he loved me for my true male self, he had not chosen another woman – he had chosen womankind. There was a difference. I never could forgive him this.

"I once said that you showed no signs of growing old," I said. "But I was wrong." My voice rose and I screamed out like a fishwife. "Your hair is grizzled at the temples and your belly juts when you forget to draw it in. It is time you went to Buxton once again and stayed there! I myself am due to visit Wanstead next month – "

"I know it. Philip has prepared a masque for you."

"I want that woman far away. I want no sign of her about the place."

"She will be gone, I promise you!" Robert looked frightful, haggard.

"And you also!" I bellowed. "Go from my sight. Go to Buxton. You need every help that miraculous waters can give you to stave off age's ravages!" Breathless I paused. Coldly and with dignity I then concluded:

"And come not south again until I give you leave."

It was in a very different frame of mind from when I had last visited the place that I arrived at Wanstead for my Maytime visit. I knew that Philip Sidney had arranged a masque: I had no wish to disappoint him.

The trees were white with blossom; birds sang on every branch; the air was sweet with a fine perfume. My heart was leaden. On arrival at the house I prowled from room to room, opening drawers, turning down bedspreads, peering into cupboards. Had I found any trace of Lettice Knollys – the smallest kerchief, the torn scrap of a letter, a feather from her fan – I half believe I would have had the house burned down. I found nothing; Robert had kept his word.

Yet though Lettice was not present, Robert was. His spirit was in the air, his breath at my ear, his touch prickling my skin. Our laughter hung in every room – fools' laughter, as it had proved, wrought of illusion and deceit. As to the window with the tree beyond, I did not open it; I had no wish to hear nightingales.

What were we but a ridiculous pair? Middle-aged, foolish. Robert was right; he was growing old. His hair was becoming grey. He would soon have a paunch. His joints ached. He was one must take the waters to preserve his youthfulness. And what of me? My body was yet trim enough and the ulcer on my leg had healed; but I was growing bald about the pate. I suffered from tooth pangs. Some of my teeth were bad. Would I become as Philip of Spain, who once had kissed me underneath a tree in the rain, and now had had all his teeth pulled out and lived on slops? What right had I to talk of love or expect it from another? Best go forward passively to old age; what other choice was open to me?

"Your Majesty, they stay for you in the wood...the masquers are prepared, and only await your presence to begin..."

Dressed in white and gold I moved outside, my ladies with me. Amongst the trees in a green glade the Lady of the May awaited me. Philip Sidney gave me his arm, leading me to the revellers. I looked at him, startled anew by his astonishing beauty. So fair he was, so slender, each feature exquisitely formed. Desired by men and women both. By Robert also... He smiled at me.

"Your Majesty, I know I cannot hope to attain my uncle's perfection; but my heart is yours, and I pray my poor poesy may please you."

"Philip," I said tenderly, "your uncle is not perfect. He is a man, with a man's faults; and virtues also. I am well content that you should be here in his place. Tell me the story of the masque."

"The Lady of the May asks that you help her choose a suitor..."

A boy, a lovely boy, came forward, radiant in a gown diaphanous as gossamer, garlanded with flowers.

"I am the Lady of the May," this vision told me. "And I submit to you. Not because you are richly dressed – for May's flowers are as fair as any gold and silver – but because you are the most beautiful lady that these woods have ever received."

"Am I, Philip?" I smiled doubtingly. "Does this fair nymph speak the truth?" (And could an auburn hairpiece really do so much, I wondered cynically?)

"I swear it," Philip answered ardently; and God's death, I believed him. Philip Sidney, manhood's perfection, the ideal of our age – he would never lie to me; nor this bright vision, this shimmering boy who called me beautiful. In a dream I watched the masque unfold in the springtime woods, and twilight fell at last. Then the boy, leaving, called out: "Farewell; I wish you goodnight, praying to God that henceforth the flowering of May may long remain in you and with you." In the green and gold sunset he faded into the forest; and I turned to Philip, marvelling at my transformation.

"There was some magic here, I think," I said, almost, I believe, reproving him.

"If there was," answered he, "Your Majesty brought it with you. Magic attends you by divine right. You are enchantment itself, and all who see you fall under your spell."

I pondered this, half laughing, half triumphant.

"I shall not grow old," I said, almost to myself. "With or without Robert, I shall not grow old. I choose never to grow old."

THIRTEEN

I

He is handsome yet; but when I saw him first – he was then twenty-four – he was more handsome than had any man a right to be and live. When he came through the door, in company with Humphrey Gilbert his half-brother, it was all I could do not to gasp like a fish, forgetful of my royal dignity.

He came for letters granting him authority to sail westward in search of heathen lands. He was after fame and fortune. He was six foot tall; he had raven-black hair and a black beard, and eyes of startling blue. His skin was dark; he wore a pearl in his earlobe. All in all, he had those gypsy-dark good looks that Robert had when young, that selfsame strutting swagger that bespoke arrogance and wildness. His thighs were rippling muscle, and his shoulders broad. He called to mind that Lucifer I once saw in a mystery play in Mynchen Hampton market square when I was six years old:

> The Devil am I, come for Mankind's soul
> Look to me, man, for I shall seize thee whole
> My kingdom waits for thee at close of day
> And I have come to carry thee away.

"My mother was a Champernowne, Your Majesty," said he, "therefore I am a kinsman to Mistress Katherine Ashley. I hope to prove as loyal as she."

"I loved her dearly," I replied. "And all her kin for her sake."

"When you know me better, you shall love me for my own."

I saw poor Gilbert flinch; he feared his brother had been too bold.

But I loved boldness. He was Zachary Mountshaft come to me anew out of the mists of time, recalling nights spent in his manly arms, recalling the creak of timber and the smell of tar on the Bristol quaysides. He was the stuff of dreams incorporated into flesh. He was my sea captain come to me at last.

He was a close friend of the Earl of Oxford – and no one, it seemed, knew how to pronounce his name.

The Earl of Oxford had come back from Italy a mincing painted butterfly, so perfumed that the scent of him was like the approach of summer. Of Oxford's more well-known enemies, Oxford himself came a close third. His fluttering extravagant manner needled the undiscerning, and disguised what many knew – that beneath it lay a gifted intellect. It was almost as if he must play down – indeed deny – his talent. To see him fluttering about the court and hear his bantering, you could be forgiven for supposing him a fool and not possessing the fine mind and great depths which he took such pains to hide.

"I love the intricacies of deception," he had once confessed; and his own life displayed as much.

He brought me sweet-smelling gloves embroidered with roses and trimmed with whorls of yellow silk. He had given up all pretence of loving his wife and now they lived apart. When he learned that the wretched lady was with child he said that it was none of his, and supported his proud boast by a string of little scandals concerning pretty serving-boys.

On his sea journey he had been captured by pirates and dined off the story for a month.

"Stripped to my shirt – surrounded by a circle of the vilest ruffians imaginable – not a one of them under six foot in height – all raven-haired and swarthy, ears a-glitter with gold rings, bare-chested. Glistening with the sweat of lust they closed in upon me. Seventeen if there were a dozen, all plainly desperate for the need of me. It was only my high rank that saved me from being buggered there and then upon the deck..."

"Now tell me, naughty boy," I said, "somewhat concerning your new friend from Devon... I would know more of him. What can you tell me of him?"

"Item," said Oxford, ever the courtier, "he will surely fall in love with you; for he is damnable proud and only the most excellent is to his taste. He says he comes of Plantagenet stock; but he is a great braggart, so we will let that one pass. Item, his beard curls naturally and he has no need of curling tongs. Item, he says he has caused women's hearts to break; but I myself know him for a shameless liar."

"And now," I laughed, "most searching of questions, therefore think well before you reply. How do you pronounce his name?"

Oxford gave the matter his most serious consideration. "Myself I speak the name as if it were to rhyme with valley."

"Do you mean that others are in some disagreement?"

"I have heard Lord Surrey speak it as if it were to rhyme with poorly. And now I come to think of it, I have heard Charles Arundel rhyme it with barley."

"What does the man himself say on the subject?"

"Your Majesty, it would imply that one was monstrous ignorant if one should ask so direct a question. And besides, we should not understand his answer, for it would be cloaked in such broad Devonshire it would be unintelligible. I would suggest that, to spare us all embarrassment, Your Majesty make him a knight, and then we shall all say Sir Walter and be done with it."

As does so often happen with people who are to mean something to one another, there was at first no more to tell. The two brothers set about to furnish their expedition, causing some distress to the Privy Council by appropriating a boatload of oranges and lemons from Seville, and then, having left the fruit to rot and paying no compensation, setting sail. Fierce gales drove them back to Plymouth; the fainthearted fled; the brave set forth afresh, only to be driven into Dartmouth. All but one. My sea captain, in the *Falcon*, weathered the storm, ploughed on, and single-handed fought the Spaniard in the Bay of Biscay.

Then he set off to fight in Ireland.

The Earl of Oxford's talents lay in more peaceful quarters. Poesy and prose, it seemed, were to be his raison d'être henceforth. It was to be his purpose to refine and enrich our language; and this being Philip

Sidney's ambition also, the two grew to be rivals. Their rivalry led to an undignified brawl on the tennis court during which Oxford was heard to call Sidney a puppy; and there would have been a duel had I not forbade it.

Sidney quit London and went off to Wilton to write poems, for the which therefore we have Oxford's truculence to thank. Oxford threw himself into the company of players and, as Burleigh termed them, 'lewd companions'. When he had been in Siena, Oxford said, he had heard of two feuding families, sworn enemies, that were newly in accord and grieving, following the deaths by their own hand of two lovers, a boy and a girl from each of the warring factions, who had secretly fallen in love all unknown to their parents, and had chosen death rather than be parted through their parents' hate. He thought there might be a story here if only he might write it.

"What hinders you?" I enquired.

"I am a little short of money," he confessed.

I gave him land worth two hundred and fifty a year; and told him to go write a play.

I was surrounded by those that would love me. How welcome, after Robert's treachery, the sheep-like devotion of Hatton, the compliments of Heneage, and now, most piquant of all, the courtship of Alençon, prince of France. His dear friend and confidant came to plead his cause, Jean de Simier. A dangerous man, this – we had heard that he had had his own brother murdered for making love to Simier's wife; the wife had taken poison. Oxford noted all this down; he thought that he might use it in his play.

Whatever had been true, the man himself was captivating. He had that very dark hair that so pleased me, and a flashing smile, and a manner half suave, half merry. His purpose was to love me by proxy, and for all that there was talk of possession of the Netherlands and income of some threescore thousand a year to Alençon and peace with France and the thwarting of Spain, the matter in question was one of love. I must be loved.

There were some that muttered against the proposed marriage. Robert was one. Oh yes, Robert was back, albeit somewhat subdued. I could not leave him to stew in his own juice at Buxton. That infant born of Lettice had not survived, and it occurred to me that Lettice was not so young – well over thirty – and perhaps no longer healthy childbearing stock. But now I had no doubt that Robert would try again.

"What are you about?" he said to me between his teeth. "You play with these negotiations as a child with fire. You go too far; you will be married ere you know it – and what then? This headstrong haste – it's almost as if you have forgot..."

'Forgot your true sex...' I knew what he would say.

Robert had grown monstrous sober. Whether it were due to the disappointment of his hopes regarding a new dynasty, or to a late and growing sense of shock at the discovery of my true identity, I cannot say, but he had taken to religion with a damnable fervour and was all but become a Puritan. Lettice's father was one so, and I partly suspected a wish to please Sir Francis in Robert's taking up the cause. I knew Robert to be no more nor less devout than the next man, and did he wish to please me, he would do well to steer clear of this sanctimonious breed. They had with small originality called me 'a Jezebel who maketh herself a prophetess to deceive the servants of the Lord and make them commit fornication and eat meat sacrificed unto idols'. They spoke thus, Puritans, in gibberish; I had no patience with them.

Simier, therefore, was a most acceptable alternative. We gave him his own apartments at Greenwich, beyond the garden, and I visited him there, with Kate and Helena, to hear him talk of love. For amorous conversation and gallantry and teasing dalliance he was more skilled than Hatton ever was, and a thousand times more so than Robert.

Nor should it be thought that Simier's admiration was political. Since I had vowed I never would grow old, I swear time had indeed stood still for me, as Robert's clock had promised. My face, framed in its glowing auburn curls, retained a youthful smoothness, free from wrinkles, and of good complexion. My eyes, though a little near-sighted now, were orbs as brilliant as ever. My body was yet slender and upright; I moved gracefully, and rode as fast and far as anyone might care to name. There was no shame for any man that thought to court me; I was yet a prize.

I had been fortunate in health. No weakness brought me low. I had rheums and colds as any other, and the headache if I grew over-troubled; but that suppurating leg ulcer was healed, and I had never needed physician in any serious capacity other than when I had the smallpox. Blanche and Kat had both known simple herbal remedies for common ills and I would use the same without the need to ask for potions from my court physicians. I might discuss my ailments with them, but no doctor had ever seen me at close quarters save to bleed me. I would often ask their opinion; though I rarely took it. Dr Robert Jacob said, when I discussed the matter with him, that given my history and my bodily proportions – that I was not gross in weight, but youthful still – he foresaw no reason why I might not expect to bear children to the prince of France; for after all, the good doctor had had discourse with my ladies, and both Blanche ap Harry and Lady Warwick had assured him that I was a healthy woman. I thanked him gravely for his opinion.

"You must pull back from this outrageous venture before Alençon himself is allowed to come to England," Robert told me in the Red Chamber at Wanstead. "Were you all that the realm believes you to be, I would still so counsel it. England will never take kindly to the French yoke. When the people hear that Alençon demands the crown in his own right, and equal power with yourself, and the right to pursue his damnable popery while living here at our expense, they will revolt, and all that previous goodwill upon which you so pride yourself will be tarnished and soured. Let him not come. You know you cannot marry him. You know it! This foolery with Simier is all to appease your monstrous vanity."

I laughed. He was so plainly jealous – as were Heneage and Ormonde and Hatton. "No one may ever have too much love and adoration," I said. "And if one is an object of beauty it is almost one's right. I feel no guilt at Simier's attentions."

"You are besotted," Robert scowled. "I don't understand it. Does he put something in your drinks when you flit over to his lodgings? There can be no other explanation."

"There you are wrong," I answered with great dignity. "Do you recall the concept of the courtly lover? I think you do, for you were one such, and are no more. Look into your heart, Robert Dudley, and ask yourself why it is that your queen must go elsewhere for deep and undemanding love."

"Undemanding?" Robert scoffed. "On behalf of his master, that French monkey of yours demands your very kingdom."

Robert and I were plainly not on good terms.

I sat that evening in Simier's pavilion, sipping wine and thinking about Robert's accusation. It was a warm June evening, full of the scents of honeysuckle.

"The Earl of Leicester thinks you feed me love potions," I said, sipping. "And if so be that he is right, I must commend you on their efficacy."

"With you and me," said Simier smouldering, "no love potions are necessary. They are for the imbeciles and maladroit who know not how to love. A jealous heart spreads rumours of the great."

"You think the Earl of Leicester jealous?"

"The world knows it. He takes you privily aside to warn you against my master, a man who is all heart, all compassion, all adoration. You have been good to Leicester, showered him with benefits – and how does he repay you?"

"How? With advice, the advice of a friend and counsellor."

"The Earl of Leicester is no friend to you, madame," said Simier, dark-browed.

"How so?"

"He would prevent your marriage, and, thereby, your happiness."

"This is because such an action on my part will put me out of his reach for ever."

"No, Your Majesty, Lord Leicester himself has done that."

"In what way? Would you talk in riddles, my sweet monkey?"

"I would talk plainly. I tell you that Lord Leicester is neither a faithful counsellor nor a loyal friend. He would deny you that happiness which he himself possesses. How has he put Your Grace out of his reach? He did so when he married the Countess of Essex, secretly last year at Wanstead."

"He married – ?" I stuttered.

"Yes. I wondered if you knew. Sir Francis Knollys obliged him to do so, for that the infant which died should be born in wedlock. As I understand it," Simier continued, "it took place early in the morning. Lord Leicester left your side, went on ahead to Wanstead, married the lady, hurried her away, cleared up the wine and wedding cakes; and waited to receive you. I believe he entertained you splendidly. They do say that those who feel the greatest guilt are those that bring the greatest gifts..."

I felt the rage that rose within me burn me as a slow and steadily rising flame. I stood up.

"He shall to the Tower for this."

Or anywhere out of my sight – or anywhere that I need never look upon him more. Since we were then at Greenwich, it was deemed most convenient to place him in the Mireflore Tower, and there I ordered him taken under arrest. Oh! vain and empty gesture! Nothing I might do in punishment could ease the pain and torment I endured to know him married. And secretly, and in such wise, like a thief in the night! And I had thought him noble. This was not the act of one who loved me. Robin, Robin! He knew well enough that I would never marry. A true lover would have kept himself unwed likewise. God's death – I tolerated his fucking the wench and what – would he try my tolerance to this degree? It was insupportable! It was the action of a glutton, one possessed of the sensibility of a clod of earth. And this the man I once believed I loved and who loved me! How mistaken were we in that!

The rocks do not so cruelly
Repulse the waves continually
As he my suit and my affection
So that I am past remedy...

Ah! this betrayal, and from him of all folk! Droit et loyal. Is this loyalty? A dog shows more, a thousandfold.

They pacified me on all sides.

"Madam, all he has done is marry whom he lay with..."

"Lawful wedlock is no crime..."

"His loyalty is not in question. No one doubts the Earl of Leicester's loyalty – and love – for Your Grace."

"Show generosity. Show that nobility which of your true self you possess. Forgive him, of your kindness."

But Lettice was with child. The child might live. Robert would have lawful heirs. Bound by their familial affection, he and Lettice would grow close and caring. And he was mine, and mine alone! But why should I want him? He was growing paunchy, his face wine-rosy, and his hair no longer dark. And he was veering toward the strident and forbidding God of the Puritans, that preacher of Do Not. What drew me to him yet? Nothing. No, he was nothing to me; I had so much else besides. I could dispense with old lovers, and I would so.

"Let Lord Leicester be set free. But I shall not see him. Let him go to Wanstead. He should be happy there; it is the place where he was married. As for the woman he has wed, let her stay well clear of me. And now...let my French husband come to woo me."

Why had they told me he was ugly, dear Alençon? He was delightful. He had a sweet face, sober in repose, with very pretty eyes and well-formed brows. Lips like the bow of Cupid; and most shell-like ears. It is true that his complexion was marked from the pox and that his nose was over-large; but such was his gaiety of manner, his wit and his charm, that it was easy to overlook his faults; I found him very pleasing. And there was no doubt of his adoration of me.

Yet our love was founded upon a strange bond of which no one was cognisant but ourselves. We danced and dallied in full view of all the court; we gave gifts; we wrote letters – his particularly were of great passion and devotion. But in the privacy of his lodgings, in the August of his first visit, he confided that to me which I received as his most precious gift – the secrets of his heart. The truth was that he loved Bussy d'Ambois. Bussy, it seemed, was male perfection, all that a courtier and lover should be. Alençon missed him to distraction. It would be a great comfort to him if sometimes he might be allowed to talk of him to me. It was a measure of our great affection that he felt able to trust me with his true sentiments; and I encouraged him. I said that I was rare among women; I understood the love of man for man; it seemed most reasonable to me that one man should love another.

"Who more than I should deem it natural that you should love a man?" I told him. "All my life I have been attracted to the breed – a big arse and a muscular thigh have always caught my eye. The bodyguard you see about me are all handpicked for their strength and beauty. All are six feet tall and perfectly formed. When we are married," I added, "you shall bring Bussy to England, and we all three together shall be friends."

Alençon kissed my hand, nay, every finger and my wrist; and said I was an angel, he the most fortunate of men.

It was observed that Lord Leicester was in great grief. Jealousy of my forthcoming marriage was supposed, shame at his betrayal of me, fear for England's welfare; these were not the reasons.

I was still on speaking terms with that vile lizard, that married man. And on one such occasion I contrived for us to be alone. I had some information to impart to that complacent husband who believed that I should never dare to marry.

"I shall marry in despite of you," I told him, "for Alençon is one that loves his fellow man. We have spoken of it, he and I. It is common knowledge that his brother Henri is so; well, like one, like another. Therefore, when my Francis and I are wed, I shall reveal my secret; and we shall be lovers, he and I; but none shall know save you. And while you sleep with Lettice Devereux and grope in her fat thighs, you shall know that the Prince of France and I are about a like task. And you shall not sleep so easily, I think."

"You are mad," gasped Robert. But he believed me. He knew that I was monstrous angry with him yet.

"It is a very happy solution," I said smoothly. "Things have fallen very well for me."

"Is it out of spite? To hurt me? I see no other reason why you should behave so."

"You flatter yourself, Leicester. It is for love of Alençon; and the pleasure we shall know together in our bed."

Poor Francis. News came to him that Bussy d'Ambois had been slain in a duel. Alençon left at once for France, heartbroken. I placed a ship at his disposal. He wrote me love letters on his journey home. He promised me he would be back, to devote the remainder of his life to loving me.

Robert's infant lived, a boy. That same year, in the summer, I was very ill; it was a whooping cough and fever. My symptoms were physical; but I believe my bruised and tangled emotions the true cause. In my weakness, my vulnerability, I knew well enough what I would never face when I was upright and in control – I loved Robert still, with all my heart; and I ached with jealousy and grief. My tortuous liaison with Alençon was no substitute for true and honest love; I was all deceit, pretence, all outward show.

Blanche, aged as she was, nursed me, with a worried look upon her brow. I understood it. I recalled something that Katherine Parr had said to me in anger, when she knew that I was male – "There lurks the spectre of a slow consumption in the men of the house of Tudor. A matter, boy, which you would do well to heed."

As I lay there, tossing and turning in my sweat-drenched sheets, racked by an intermittent cough, my troubled mind recalled Prince Arthur, whose frequent fevers finally laid him low, the sweating sickness raging in the streets. Wretched Edward nearly died from quartan fever, long before his final illness took him to his tomb. My grandfather suffered from benign tertian malaria throughout his life, and, closer to me, my own father died of a rapid consumption. These thoughts tormented me more than the fever. It burned itself out; and I recovered.

"But madam," laughed Kate Carey – Lady Nottingham, as she became – with a curious brittle tone. "Why should Your Grace have been tormented so? Those vile diseases only happened to the Tudor males."

"Your Grace," said her sister Philadelphia, Lady Scrope, "was perfectly safe. Your womanhood has saved you."

"Being female," added Lady Cobham comfortably, "has so many hidden advantages."

But it was Helena, Lady Northampton, who had the courage to speak out to my face.

The four of them sat sewing, making a semi-circle about me. Their busy needles flew, and they bent their heads as Helena began.

"The others said I should not speak of it; but it is making me ill to keep up the pretence. I cannot bear it. And I believe it to be in Your Majesty's best interest if we are all honest with each other. Therefore

I brave your wrath to let you know, Your Majesty, that you have been discovered; but by those loyal to you – that is, we four only. There; it is said. We know not if we merit punishment for speaking out. We think not, for we love you, and we believe you hold us in regard. We do not even seek to understand the mystery, but we believe that you should honour us with your confidence; for our devotion has been apparent these many years."

"What is it that you think you have discovered?" I said carefully.

"The reason why you feared the diseases of the Tudor males," said Lady Cobham, "for that is what we suppose Your Majesty to be."

"The notion is monstrous," I replied, but faintly.

"Yes, and so it is," said Lady Scrope, "and Helena became ill when she first guessed it; and in her distress she confided her belief to us."

"It was your profile on the wall by candlelight," gasped Helena. "Without the hairpiece and with so little hair. I saw the truth. It was the night I fainted and had to be carried from the room. The image stayed with me. It was like a picture I had seen of the old king's father, King Henry the Seventh. It was the same. I told Kate. We pieced it all together."

"Only Blanche and Ann are permitted to attend Your Majesty when you bathe," said Kate. "And there are other things," she blushed. "In a word – we ourselves are women and we are close to you, closer than any in the kingdom, and we know it in our hearts. We once asked Lady Warwick outright – we dared not ask Blanche! And she was not able to convince us."

"I see," I said.

"We think that you should trust us," Lady Cobham said; and looked me in the eyes.

"We have already lied for you," said Kate. "They come to us, those gentlemen that would know all your secrets – those doctors that would send report to France or Spain on matters intimate. We tell them lies. We have already saved your reputation countless times!"

"And will continue so to do?" I asked them soberly.

"An it be with mutual trust," said Philadelphia. "We have agreed it."

"We supposed you thought us stupid," Helena said. "We are not so. We would prefer that you should value us for ourselves."

"Indeed I do so, and have ever done!" I cried.

"Then – may we question you upon the subject – may we so presume?"

"Come closer," I said. "Once it is told, we shall be bound together in a matter of some magnitude, ending only in death itself."

They all looked grave, their needles still, their manner showing proper solemnity. I smiled, curiously moved. "Rascals one and all, you put me to shame, prepared to serve me, guessing what you do, and knowing not the reason and the history. In your friendship I am most blessed of women."

None of them flinched from the word, but sat, silent, accepting, as I began my story.

The rain pattered dismally down upon the sodden streets. I looked forward to attaining the comparative comfort of my coach, where at least I would be dry. The Earl of Oxford hovered at my elbow, patently vexed with the rain, yet making small effort to seek shelter.

The crowds that pressed against the house walls cheered and cried "God bless Your Majesty!" I smiled and waved and thanked them.

"Your Grace," Sussex murmured, "we should go indoors. Your coach awaits..."

"I see it," I said. "Oxford, however, seeks to detain me. I believe he loves the rain. Perhaps because the raindrops hang in his moustache like pearls which match those in his ears."

"Indeed such pearls please me not at all," said Oxford irritably. He seemed to be looking about him, to right and left, frowning the while. Ahead of us, the road lay pitted with puddled hollows.

"We must move on," Sussex said. "I fear Your Majesty will catch a chill."

"Well, Lord Oxford?" I said. "And have we leave to go?"

"No – yes – wait!" said Oxford; now he was a-tiptoe. "Ah!" Now he showed satisfaction. "But Your Grace," he said, "the road is full of puddles. Your Grace's lovely shoes will be muddied..."

"No matter – it is no hardship to walk a yard or so," I answered briskly.

"I would not have you soil your shoes," said Oxford, beaming. From the crowd emerged a tall dark man, who bowed, unloosed his cloak and laid it on the ground in front of me, a carpet of peacock blue.

"Your Majesty," he said. "My humble cloak is at your service; also my humble self."

I smiled and thanked him graciously. Back from Ireland, he was eager now to seek advancement close to me. As I stepped across the velvet and entered my coach I heard Oxford clearly enough:

"God's teeth, Raleigh! Whatever kept you?"

II

"My intention is to sail towards the west," said Walter Raleigh. "My plan is to provision my own ships and make a settlement upon the western coast, myself as captain. We learn to trade with the Indians, exploiting such resources as we find. The glory to Your Majesty would be beyond expression. All I require is your permission to embark."

"God's death," I laughed. "And would you quit the court no sooner than you have arrived? No, I have other plans for you."

I made him Captain of my Guard.

How jealous they all were!

What though I gave him the use of Durham House with its turret study that looked out over the Thames? – he had nowhere to put his clothes and books. What though I dubbed him knight? – he was of royal blood; it was his due. But it was all that I could do to keep him by my side.

His head was full of dreams. He saw seas as high as mountains, lands where high cedars grew, and forests of strange fruits, where Indians offered up their secrets – that tree bark which cured the pox – that Nicotian weed which burned in the bowl of a clay pipe, panacea for all ills. His turret room was spread with charts of vellum ornamented with stars and moons, tritons and dolphins, closely intersected by the lines of the compass, highly spattered with those magic words Terra Incognita; his ambition directed towards the possession of ships – and in particular that vessel named the Governorship of the Lands of the West. His companions were chartmakers, Portuguese pilots, men who would map the stars. Their talk was of the North-West Passage to Cathay, of islands in the western seas, of the nature of God and the mysteries of the world.

Poor Hatton was quite out of his depth, weeping visibly – such was the extent of his ruffled sensibilities. He gave me three gifts: a jewelled dagger, an embossed book, a silver pail. The book contained a letter from him, conveying to me his love and his distress that I seemed to have forgotten him; the dagger was for him to plunge into his heart for grief; the pail contained Water, the reason for Hatton's reproach. I laughed, but kindly. I told him that I would place my sheep in verdant meadows so high they never should be flooded; I sent him a dove, reminding him that Noah sent a dove and it flew safely over water.

When we came from Greenwich to Westminster our boat would pass Durham House, and by dusk we could see the light that burned in that turret window. Raleigh would be there; and Heriot the mathematician, and Harry Percy whom they called a wizard, and Robert Hues, and Henry Howard, Oxford's disreputable crony. We knew they sat till late into the night. Whether it be in atheistic speculation or plans to sail to the isles of the west, or those adventures of the mind that are the soaring of the daring thought, I knew their converse would be worth the sharing. I longed to be amongst them. God's teeth, it was myself that was the jealous one!

With curious clarity I saw once again the cabin on that ship in Bristol harbour; Zachary Mountshaft, tall as a tree, and beautiful in all his manhood; and myself, small and adoring – 'Let me be your cabin boy! When I grow up we shall sail the seas together...'

God's death, I would not permit Raleigh to sail to those islands of the west if I could not go with him!

Sometimes our council meetings took place at Leicester House. It amused me to think of Lettice obliged to quit her home to make way for the business of the realm. I remember that on one occasion, with that business done, I prowled about the place in morbid restlessness. Here she sits, I thought, here weaves her tapestry. Here they talk...about me, no doubt. If only the air might be obliged to yield up its secrets! Here she sleeps – they fuck. I stared at that bed of walnut, with its crimson curtains trimmed with gold and silver lace, and a little footstool in the same colours. Robert was ever neat and precise in his colour matching.

The bed obsessed me. I pictured it with its sheets crumpled and moist with summer lust. How was it with them? Was their lovemaking wild and heated? Or always disappointing, Lettice turning away unsatisfied, Robert apologetic, sighing, thinking of me? I stood there at the door, entranced, oblivious to the world.

A sound disturbed me. Someone in the passage. I bolted from the room – that is, as much as one may do so in a farthingale. Hand on my heart I paused, as guilty as a thief discovered, two pinpoints of crimson in my pale cheeks as, despising myself for my prurience, I recollected what I was about.

I was face to face with a boy, a monstrous handsome boy some fourteen years old. He was tall and lean. He had dark auburn hair and a long face with a broad forehead. Stupidly, my fancy still so raging, I half expected him to challenge me, to ask me to explain myself, so clearly was he master here. But he dropped to his knees and bowed his head. I raised him, and he kissed my hand. Lettice's son, young Robert Devereux. At Chartley he had fled from my embrace and I had thought him a most poisonous brat; clearly he was not so.

I asked him about his studies. He murmured something in reply. He had left Burghley's household, where he had been ward, and was now at Cambridge. He told me that behind Trinity College lay an open sewer, and the boys threw rotting entrails at each other on their way back from their lodgings.

I smiled tolerantly. He was improved, yes, but he had a little way to go yet before he would become a courtier.

Into Plymouth sailed the *Golden Hind*, and thence to Deptford. What a tale they had to tell, Drake's mariners – and we had believed them lost! The *Marigold* had been lost, and all hands with her, in a fearful storm; but those ships remaining had sailed on, taking Spanish vessels, Spanish stores, loading the holds with silver bars, gold coins, more gold and silver by the ton. Jingling with music, resplendent with courage, they had sailed towards the great southern sea. For more than two months they had had no sight of land. They reached the Spice Islands; then on again, to the Cape of Good Hope, and along the coast of Africa, and northwards. They had circumnavigated the globe. Sir Walter Raleigh ached with envy.

We dined aboard the *Golden Hind*. Sir Francis Drake now showed us all the wealth he had acquired for us. Beneath those low creaking beams in the Great Cabin, upon a table, were spread the more splendid of the spoils. Upon a crimson cushion, emeralds, gold and diamonds. In a chest, more of the same; in careless abandon, as it seemed, emeralds and pearl; in sweet confusion pendants composed of little stars that winked and glittered in the light; necklaces, great rubies, gold rings. I placed my fingers amongst those gems, feeling the sensuous touch of jewels against the skin.

"Robert!" I turned to him, shining-eyed. "Touch this richness!"

Facing me across the table, Robert put his hands into the jewel chest. Our fingers touched, amongst the emeralds, diamonds, rubies. I could not but recall that wondrous night at Wanstead, when we romped, and prayed for merry red-cheeked Francis Drake, and grew ecstatic thinking upon Spanish gold. Our eyes met. Robert plainly shared my recollection. His eyes pleaded with me suddenly. *Forgive me – you were not always so cold.*

My lips parted, with the lust for gold, the lovely half-forgotten lust we once knew... Then I saw again the walnut and crimson bed at Leicester House; and turned away.

"So...talk to me of sailing westward..."

The meal was done, the silver gilt bowl borne away, the towel brought, my rings held while I washed my hands. Now I was free to sit on cushions and discourse with those that truly held my interest.

God's death, but he was beautiful, was Raleigh. He leaned upon his elbow, his warm eyes holding my own in a mellow gaze. His thigh closely embraced by white silk shimmered in the torchlight. When he spoke, the pendant pearl that hung from his earlobe quivered.

" – of sailing westward," I invited, leaning my chin on my hand.

Walter Raleigh knew better now than to speak in terms of ready money, actual ships, the economy of providing for the same.

"I stand upon the deck," he said, "my eyes straining into the sunset. The sea ahead is streaked with amber – russet – gold. As the sun sets, a fine line, green as emerald, shows for a moment – only for a moment; then is gone as it had never been. The strange mysterious rays of the dying sun flood the sky with silver light. But still no sign of land. We know so much now. We know that the earth is not pear-shaped, that the sea does not rise as we sail westward, that ships do not in sailing climb a hill towards Heaven. But so much is yet hidden from us – will ours be the voyage that makes all things clear? The sailors are asleep now. I am their shepherd; they look to me for protection. I watch them sleeping, sea dogs as strong and gnarled as English oak. I feel the burden of my responsibility. Who will ease the captain's care? My crew sleep; but I know that one is yet awake..."

"Your cabin boy," I breathed.

"My cabin boy," he smiled. "How shall I call you this time?"

"John."

"Always John," he teased.

"It is a sturdy name."

"Very well. John, my cabin boy. Shall you come to me on deck?"

"No. I will be in the cabin. Come to me there."

"I enter. I sit down."

"I see that you are weary. I smooth your furrowed brow."

"How cool your hand upon my skin. An angel's touch."

I placed my hand upon his brow. Indeed my hand was cool, his forehead warm. I stroked it. He frowned, returning to his thoughts. "We know that Toscanelli's planisphere was incorrect. We know that the Orinoco is not one of the Four Rivers of Paradise. But Heriot believes the Indians friendly, believes it possible for us to live in harmony with them. What we could learn from them!"

"I don't wish to hear about the friendly Indians, nor Toscanelli. The cabin boy needs to know that the captain is at ease."

"He is at ease, very much at ease. The cabin boy's hand is smooth as silk – uncommon in a lad."

"This lad has always looked after his hands. And were the captain to touch any other part of his body, he would find the youth as smooth, as yielding as he could wish for."

"Would you have the captain do so? How would young John take it should the captain touch him in more intimate part?"

"John wishes it; it is his most passionate desire."

"So be it then. The captain reaches for him, sits him on his knee; he

kisses him. He finds the cabin boy's lips very sweet."
"And then?"
"And then? What, would he more? Greedy boy!"
"He would. After all, there is no sight of land; the night is long; and what else is there to do?"
"Persuasive boy. Go to my bed and wait for me there."
"And shall I undress?"
"Certainly! Would you have me fumble with trunk hose?"
"Very well. I wait for you there."
"Naked?"
"Naked, as you required."
Our eyes, daring each other to venture more and more, began to sparkle.
"So, captain...now, what will you?"
"Any cabin boy that leads me on so must answer for the consequences."
"I am ready for them."
We began to laugh, comfortably, affectionately, and, I think, sharing a certain arousal. Behind us, disapproving courtiers shook their heads.

Splashing in that Water was a pleasure I enjoyed against a background of gathering threat and tension. Outrage amongst both high and low against my proposed French marriage showed itself in broadsheet, letter and gunshot. But there was other more sinister opposition, and when the French marriage plans had died a natural death, these other forces festered, horribly alive.

John Somerville was a plain and simple madman who set out to kill the queen and telling all and sundry what he was about. On being taken, he killed himself. Thomas Morgan was a man that came, as it would seem, to warn me of a plot upon my life; he was a servant of the Queen of Scots, and worked for my downfall. Henry Percy was the Earl of Northumberland and plotted treason; he was betrayed. Francis Throckmorton when arrested told of the intended invasion of our realm from France. Such things hung upon the whispered words of small fry, or the idiocy of chance – a letter torn to shreds at sea and cast to the winds, the fragments then blown back upon the deck and pieced together. Then came William Parry.

This was a man employed by Burghley to give news of English Catholics, but suborned by Thomas Morgan to work for the death of England's queen. This man, like Morgan, came into my presence on express purpose to give warning of a plot upon my life; and maybe I was close to death at that moment, for he bore a dagger hidden in his sleeve. He was betrayed by his associates, and tried and executed. I might have intervened and saved his life. I did not, for the words he spoke in his defence:

"I did intend to stab the queen. But when I saw her face to face I was overwhelmed by her likeness to King Harry, and I stayed my hand."

A man who brayed abroad my resemblance to my grandsire was a dangerous man. What if in his terror and his ecstasy he had convinced himself of the truth?

It was Hatton's task to interrogate the accused before they came to trial. I was protected by a web of steel – the intelligencers of Sir Francis Walsingham, that vast array of men that worked in secret, agents provocateurs, risking life and limb in alley, tavern, thieves' den, marsh and wharfside, mingling with the disreputable, becoming as they, doyens of a dark and secret world. It was such as these who worked in secret to make clear the guilt of Queen Mary Stuart, to reveal her true intentions. And amongst them all, the presence of Captain Jacques, the subtle Italian.

"He is a vile and dangerous villain, and no stranger to the swift knife in the alley when occasion demands it. Slippery as an eel, and cold of heart," said Hatton. "He is indispensable."

Jacomo di Francisci was his name. He had fought in Ireland; he was a reckless adventurer; and it was he that spied upon that Ballard who was given leave by Rome to murder me, that Jesuit conspirator, Mary's creature. Captain Jacques prowled the underworld, a lord of his own kind. "Loyal to me," Hatton said, and added: "at the present time."

In Walsingham's hands, then, and in Hatton's, I might place my trust; the law would work for me, and justice take its course and bring Queen Mary to trial and execution in the wake of her vile crew; but with the arrival of Martin Sawley I was on my own.

The man who would see me gave his name as Brother Xavier.

It was the moment I had dreaded. That spectre from my childhood sprung up now to harm me when I was most vulnerable. Assassins all about me, threat, secrecy, confession, distrust, like humming flies in the rancid air. Now, of all times... Where had he been, all these years? Why had he not appeared before? He must be old now, yet I saw him in my mind as he was then: his skull head and his smoothly-combed fair hair, his glittering eyes, his lewd smile, his proprietorship of me, his domination. I would not see him. And yet I must.

A man was led in, seemingly a monk. I bade my attendants withdraw, yet they were well within call. Alone now with this stranger I regarded him.

"You are not Brother Xavier!"

My mistake. Whatever I said now, I had betrayed myself.

"My name is Martin Sawley," said the stranger. "I am not Brother Xavier; I am not a monk. But I thought that I might gain your presence by this subterfuge."

How had he ever passed for monk? I saw now that his face was lean and sallow, pock-marked, haggard, and his eyes as hard as stone. He was no longer young. The forefinger of his right hand was gone; he wore a golden ring on the stump, careless of this deformity.

"I am a thief of the road," said he, "and I encountered Brother Xavier in the Black Sow on the Mynchen Hampton road. Your Majesty perhaps recalls it."

Oh, I recalled it well enough! The highwaymen and footpads, the tosspots and ruffians, purveyors of stolen goods; the gusty laughter and the weighted dice. "You should fear them," Xavier had said. "There's not a man here who would not do murder for a groat."

"You are a madman," I replied. "Why do you come here in another man's name? What of the man you impersonate? Why is he not here himself, whoever he may be?"

"Why? For that he was left for dead," the man laughed. "Dead in a ditch, with his head broken. But he told me a tale once, and I never did believe him. Now I'm here to try my luck."

"Have you been long in London?"

"Not so long."

"This man of whom you speak..." said I.

"The monk? Or so he said."

"And he is dead, you say?"

"As I understand it."

"But how may you be so uncertain?" I pressed urgently, with my fingernails digging into my palms. "Either he is dead or he is not. When did you speak to him?"

"More years ago than I care to remember."

"If your meeting took place so many years ago, why is it only now that you have come to me?"

"I thought it a crazy tale. I never believed it."

"Why would he entrust a secret of such magnitude to one such as yourself?"

He shrugged. "We were good friends. I was to come to London with him when he claimed his pickings. Maybe he guessed someone might do for him. How do I know? He was to meet me at the Black Sow. I waited but he never came. It happens. I took to thieving; I had other fish to fry. But now I'm down on my luck and I remembered Xavier and that old tale."

"Who told you he was dead?"

"A man who heard it from another."

"So it is not proven." I could not restrain a sigh.

"He must be dead," said Martin Sawley. "Otherwise he would have come himself. He would have been here years ago."

There was some logic here. "And you – have you spoken of this strange matter to others?"

"I might have."

"They would not believe it. As you say, it is a crazy tale."

"But one that could take root and grow, if fostered."

"You purpose to remain in London then?"

"I lodge within the Wall, in Cheapside. But low dens beside the Fleet ditch are not to be my dwellings for ever."

I marvelled at our odd exchange. It had been conducted in low whispers and on equal terms. We might have been two reprobates in some low tavern.

"Take up an honest trade," I told him, reverting to a semblance of proper dignity. "Leave off your life of roguery."

"I have other plans," he said. "I have brought my message and I leave you to consider what is best to be done. I shall come to you again. If I am hindered as I leave, I shall blab. But look to see me again. We have more to say to one another."

I permitted him to leave. I gave him money. I might well be so generous; I intended his death.

I sent for Hatton.

"I would see your Captain Jacques," I said.

Hatton arranged a meeting for me with the wily Italian by night. He escorted me in my coach to a certain roadside. A clump of dark trees gave landmark. Hatton withdrew; the rider who had been waiting for us dismounted and entered my coach.

Captain Jacques looked so much the dark intriguer that I wondered he were not suspected of all crimes imaginable. Tall and lean he was, with a black pointed beard and a scar upon his cheek, all eerie in the lanthorn glow. He was dressed all in black, with a long black cloak which he drew well about him, as it were to hide an arsenal of weaponry. I spoke to him of what I had heard concerning his reputation; I assessed him; and I daresay he me.

"There is a man must die..." I murmured.

I described who came to me. I had no doubt but that the slippery Italian could prise him out of his bolthole in the environs of Cheapside and the Fleet.

I was proved right. The deed was done, the business thus concluded. I had survived assassin's knife, stray shot, the machinations of the Stuart queen, and all the villains that Guise and the pope had sent at me. I would not go down to a low brute from the wilds of Gloucestershire.

It is always at the dark hours of the night that demons come. Murder...how easily it fitted into the devious toils of policy, expedient to the matter in hand, a nothing, a nudge to rid the path of obstacles.

How little did we guess, dear Kat and I, that questions of this nature would be bound up with what we began so long ago at Over Court, our great deception.

The taking of a life...

And more than one life? Was then Xavier himself murdered? By one I knew? Or by a stranger? By chance or by intent? Unbidden came into my mind something that Blanche had said at Hatfield, many years ago: "This monk then is become a danger to us..." What if, unbeknown to me, some well-wisher had made sure that Xavier never came to court? Could it be, as now seemed likely, that he had been dead these forty years and no threat to me at all? I would never dare enquire.

But what was I saying? Whether he were dead or no I never could be free of the spectre of him. Dead he might be, but he had spawned by careless talk a creature such as Martin Sawley – and were there others yet to come? While I yet lived I never could know peace of mind, the mental ease of a simple blameless life, whose course was not first set in motion by deception's hand.

And horror upon horror, now I found myself recalling Xavier himself, his eyes narrowed and bright, his voice as gentle as the cooing dove, his arms about me. "Peace, John, they will do nothing...you did not kill her...trust me..." His words, seeming at the time a reassurance, now took on a sinister significance. He had attended the princess in her illness. Had he ensured that the hapless maiden never recovered? Was the edifice of my supremacy built upon so vile a crime? Oh, God forgive us all, I must surely be mistaken. Fear and guilt were rendering me stupid.

What responsibility in this was mine? I might not avoid a degree of blame, I knew it. Circumstance and fate had so decreed that for the good of the realm a boy from Bisley had ascended the throne of England. That boy from Bisley had thus possessed the power to end the lives of England's noblest duke, and of God's anointed monarch the Queen of Scotland, and so many others of lesser stature – furtive plotters, conspirator priests from Rome. For these the blame was squarely mine.

It was for the good of the realm. I repeated it aloud. It was necessary.

And now, these foes of mine were dead. But at what cost, I sometimes asked myself? And in the darkness of the night I heard again that scream of William Parry at his trial —

"I here summon Queen Elizabeth to answer for my blood before God..."

"Madam," Robert said to me, "may I present my stepson Robert Devereux, Earl of Essex? Henceforth he is your most devoted servant, and that loyalty which it has been my greatest delight to offer to your person lives on in him, a vibrant living flame."

This lovely boy was here at court at last. What would he have been – seventeen? Sleek as a cat, with eyes like mist and a voice half-Welsh in its intonation. I noticed his long, long fingers. His gaze was warm, smouldering. Those born under Scorpio are thus; they draw the unwary to them with the attraction of a lodestone, and only afterwards, enmeshed in their silken toils, does one see the deviousness, the black despairs, the heedless rush towards destruction; and they are very beautiful the while.

But I looked over young Devereux's bowed head to where Robert stood. It had not gone well for my old love latterly. That son of his, that darling of his heart, child of his secret marriage, the Noble Imp, had of a sudden died, but four years old; and Robert in his grief and passion had, I thought, a little lost his reason, for he had spoken of God's requiring a sacrifice in order for him to regain the love he now believed was lost to him, that is, my love for him. I hoped that he had not said as much to Lettice.

His loyalty to me was plainly undiminished. I knew well enough he longed to be once more close to me. In all the fears we shared throughout the discovery of plots against us, he was steadfast and superb. When William of Orange had been slain and our own vulnerability exposed, Robert was the force behind the Bond of Association, where, as knights, they vowed to pursue and put to death all would-be murderers and whomsoever had directed them. He was the same that knelt before me beneath the oak at Hatfield, and as much as he, did I now long for the restoration of our old accord.

"I know that I have lost your favour," he confided to me, after Devereux had quit our presence. "I have committed that offence which is unforgivable in your eyes: I have grown old. You must have those about you who are young and handsome. Treat Essex as my gift to you. He is all that I once was and long to be again; and never can be more. I cannot be what you desire – perhaps the boy may take my place, and remind you of what once was, with us."

I put my finger on his lips. "Cease this gibberish, Rob. There is no one like you and never can be. Essex is beautiful and I shall treasure him. But you have always been my one true love."

"Not for a long while," he said ruefully. "Since Raleigh came to court, we lesser swains are quite overlooked."

"I have been less than kind," I said. "And I repent me of it. I understand your intention regarding Essex, but it is not necessary. I think we need some time at Rycote, you and I."

Robert's head upon the pillow, half turned to me, in my eyes retained all the beauty he had possessed when young. It is certain that his hair was silver grey and that his cheeks had acquired a ruddy glow; but all his features were yet strong and well-defined and handsome. I ran my finger along his profile and touched his lips. What devil in me had made me cruel to him? Old? He never would grow old. My love would sustain him. Whoever said that fifty-one was not a goodly age to be? Why were there songs of 'sweet and twenty' when the world knew that ripeness was all? I held him in my arms.

"Thank you for coming to my bed," I murmured. "Your lovemaking is more perfect than ever."

"We are well matched," he agreed modestly.

"I had half feared that your inexplicable devotion to your Maker would have kept you from me, fearful of His wrath."

"God forgive me," Robert answered, "but I love you more."

"You say you love me," I stormed, "yet you would go from me!"

I had thought Richmond my favourite palace, but I doubted it on this occasion. Perhaps it was the approach of winter, so dark, so unforgiveably dark, and the wild winds gusting at the window latches; and all this talk of parting.

He would go to the Netherlands and I had promised him the same, but now I would not have him go. No worthy cause was worth the separation from him. The Dutch had asked for our help; I had agreed. The knights and troopers were assembled, and Robert was to lead them as my Lieutenant-General. For Antwerp only Robert would do, only Robert represented what they needed; and Robert was in agreement. Ah, I understood so well! It was his last chance of glory. He, the greatest horseman of our age, longed to be in the field at the head of his troops; he hungered for the shouts, the praise, the freedom; he wanted to be all that he might be before the gout, the aches and weaknesses took too final a grip – he wanted to be glorious. Could I deny him this, who loved him? I could.

"Rob – stay..." I pleaded huskily, searching his face for signs of doubt and hesitation. "What if I die, and you so far from home? I think I am not well – stay, Rob – think how it would be, the seas between us, and I dying?"

There we stood, our arms about each other, weeping freely, fancies straining to imagine this grim prospect.

"Of course I must stay," said Robert chastened. "I see it now."

"Go!" I shrieked. "I'll have no sacrifices for my sake."

"And I'll not go, leaving you distract."

"I am glad for you to go. Indeed I do desire it!"

"You do?" He waited, hoping to be persuaded.

"No one but you can do what is required," I told him, proud and full of love. "You will be as you were when you rode to Hatfield on a milk-white steed, a saviour and a hero, the handsomest man in England!"

Robert gave a little self-effacing smile; it seemed that he agreed.

They welcomed him as the Messiah, the Dutch. Perhaps they did not strew palms in his path, but they strewed pageantry and prose, salutes of gunfire, bonfires, fireworks, and within the month had offered him the absolute government of all the provinces, and the buffoon accepted. All at once, it seemed, Lettice was preparing to set off to join him with a train of ladies and gentlewomen and coaches, with the intention to set up a court there which would rival mine – such was her boast.

Rage and recrimination followed, all by letter. I had forgot his natural arrogance. He had forgotten who was master. He wrote his apologies, he sulked, he begged me to send him to some faraway place such as the Indies, or to employ him in my stables, to rub my horses' heels – anything where he might abase himself and devote his life to praying for my happy preservation.

Serenity returned between us. "It is always thought a hard bargain when both parties are losers," I wrote, "as it is between us two...now will I end, that do imagine I talk still with you and therefore loth to say farewell...as you know, ever the same..."

He got small glory from that venture. He came home with debts and disillusion. The one affray where he had fought with a knight's bravery, decked out in fine array, had been the occasion when he lost that which he held most dear, the lovely Philip Sidney his most cherished nephew, mortally wounded. It left him broken-hearted.

"Come home, dear Rob," I wrote. "All shall be well."

"I am come home," he said with bitterness, "your poor old servant."

I would not have him speak so. And when it seemed the Spaniard was like to come against us, against our very shores, it was in Robert's hands I placed the kingdom. Lieutenant and Captain-General of my armies, with absolute power under my command.

"There is no one else so capable, so brave, so dear to me," I said. "It shall be you or no one that saves England from the foe."

"By all the saints," he told me, not without some admiration, "your capacity for self-deception is almost equal to your capacity to deceive the world. Strangest of all, after so long, you persuade me to believe that which I know well enough to be a falsehood – that I am young, and that you are the most excellent of women!"

I walked through the lines at Tilbury with a soldier's stride. The fifes and drums played. I had no ladies with me. I mounted; my horse was white. I was of necessity in my sleeves and skirts, but I wore a man's steel corselet from neck to waist. Ormonde bore my sword of state, and Robert led my horse by the bridle. Ever at my side, Rob, at my triumphs...

On a little hill we placed ourselves, where all could see. The soldiers cheered when I spoke. The body of a weak and feeble woman...the heárt and stomach of a king... Man and woman both? Whoever was I, sitting there, that summer day in the middle of the camp, declaiming? An icon – an image – a figurehead – a queen – a king. I was whatever they believed me to be.

I suddenly recalled those tales of a lord who fled from the lost battle and returned to his family home a fugitive, taking up abode in a secret room, his whereabouts known only to a faithful servant. The servant brings him food and all in secret, locking the door when he leaves. Then one day the servant dies; and the lord, locked in the secret room, dies for lack of food and air. Years pass. The door is opened, and with the sudden onslaught of the light and air, the old bones quite disintegrate.

Was I on that August day, with a woman's painted face, a man's war gear, my own true self at last, or was I like that lord? Without the trappings of identity, without the painted face, the auburn hair-piece, the spangled ruff, the glittering jewels, had I existence? Or had I become no more than a skeleton beneath the gilt, that once exposed, would cease to be, and crumble into dust?

We were never called upon to fight the Spaniard in the streets of London. The booms of spars and chains and ropes that Robert ordered slung across the Thames were never needed. It was victory at sea, God's victory, and our seamen's, and the great Armada sunk, destroyed, dispersed.

It seemed that we were celebrating that victory for ever. Cannon and firework, dancing, feasting, prayer – on and on the joy and gaiety.

But the image which most stays with me is that of Essex and myself at a window, our fingers intertwined, shadows dark against one more firework celebration, tears streaming down our faces; and Robert's last letter writ from Rycote, lying on a little chair beside us.

FOURTEEN

I

I died when Robert died. Oh, after the vital spark was quite extinguished my body jerked and twitched and went through the motions of a life, and those about me believed that I was living yet and maybe saw no difference in me; but the heart was gone.

He had not been well. Stomach pains. Low spirits. Summer's ending. Late August.

"I think that I shall take the Buxton waters."

Why not indeed? They had done the trick before. I had no premonition. I gave him some of my own herbal remedies to take with him.

"Safe journey," I said kissing him.

He wrote to me from Rycote where he was staying overnight. He wished me good health and long life. He said my medicine had done him good. He asked me how I was. Comfortable nothings. He was about to set out on his journey.

I could see him in my mind's eye, there in that place where we were always merry. A moment to spare, before the rigours of the day, while the horses were saddled below. A seat at the table by the window, where the trees were yet in summer leaf, and the placid sheep grazed. He would remember all our pleasant times. He sat and wrote to me. Merely one of many letters written over the years – but his last. Within the week he was dead. The fourth of September. He was fifty-five years old, no age at all.

Burghley brought the news to me. No one else dared.

"Oh no," I assured him. "There must be some mistake. He is at Rycote. See, I have his letter."

I would see no one. I kept to my chamber. I lay on my bed and wept. Two days must have passed. At last my ladies came to me and spoke me fair, telling me that my presence was required. I must come forth and celebrate my birthday.

Even now I think he is at Rycote. I believe that if I go there unannounced I shall surprise him. I shall upbraid him – gently – for the trick he played in sending that false rumour. It will be summer time, and I shall find him standing, with our two horses saddled, underneath the trees.

"Sweet Your Majesty," said Essex with a winsome smile, "don't grieve. I am here. You still have me. And when you call me by his name you will believe him to be here with you."

Essex ever had the diplomacy of a crumhorn; but he meant well, and as he pointed out so pertinently, he was here. Moreover he adored me and made no secret of the same.

Essex knew well enough that he had been offered to me by Robert as a gift, and I knew that he knew it; this at first bound us together, Essex being a willing gift and I a glad recipient. Sorrow must have made me senile – I believed him gentle and restrained, the which belief he encouraged with his tales of early life in Pembrokeshire, his lonely house amongst the sand dunes with the wind whistling through the holes in the roof, and no protection from the gales off the raging seas, and his wish to become a hermit there. He had proved his worth in the ill-fated Netherlands campaign and, dying, Philip Sidney had bequeathed to him his sword.

"I am your Robert come again," he told me. "We shall be once again as you were in the old days, when Lord Leicester rode upon a snow-white steed to offer his life to your service. We shall recreate those days! How wonderful they must have been... Inspiration! Glory! I wish I had been there. You must have guessed that you were about to forge a new Golden Age, where chivalry and loyalty were all! You must have looked into the future with such hope and expectation!"

Did we so? I had not the heart to disillusion him. As I recalled, we were simply grateful to have survived; and to take each day as it came was all we undertook to achieve.

But it is very gratifying for one that must paint his face with egg-white and alum to hide the wrinkles of age to be courted ardently by a good-looking youth; and no one disputed Robert Devereux's good looks. Almost no one...

"Two a penny, such as he," shrugged Walter Raleigh; and putting his finger to the side of his nose he made as if to know something I did not. He was Captain of my Guard, which meant that I had entrusted the protection of my body to him; and as such he had the appointing of the young Adonises that surrounded me and kept me safe. That evening he sent in to me one after another big broad fellow carrying the dishes, each one more handsome than the last. As that proud procession of rippling thighs, massive shoulders and bulging well-padded arses passed before me I smiled; and I was grateful to anyone that had the power to do that for me.

Raleigh and Essex never took to one another. There was the incident at North Hall, Warwick's home, on the summer progress; but the fault was all with Essex. A small matter – I had forbid Essex's sister our presence for that her marriage had been an elopement; but since her husband and Walter bore one another an old grudge, Essex believed Raleigh the cause of my hostility to Dorothy. Before all, Essex raged.

"This is Raleigh's doing; you stand in awe of him."

"You are mistaken," I said lightly. "It is you, my sweet, that master me. Have no fear of Raleigh."

"Fear? Of that villain?" Essex screeched – and yes, it was a screech, no less. "My sister is disgraced to please that Raleigh for whose sake Your Majesty sees fit so to humiliate me." Glowering at Raleigh who stood close by, continued Essex: "What is he? A reprobate, a landless man raised only by your favour, a man who knows the insides of the Fleet prison and the Marshalsea! A man who mercilessly slew the poor and wretched when he fought in Ireland! And I ask myself now whether it is right for me to give myself over to the service of a mistress that lives under the thumb of such a man."

This was too much. "Would you insult my friends, brat?" I cried. "You who are so free with your vile accusations. Look closer to home, look at the beam in your own eye: I mean your mother, that she-wolf who would be queen in the Netherlands and knows not how to raise a child to be respectful to its sovereign!" Hands on hips, I screeched as well as he.

"Then since no member of my family pleases Your Grace, my sister and myself will quit this place and burden you no more."

"Remove one inch from North Hall under my extreme displeasure," I warned him, startled at how much it pleased me to berate him: I was in fine danger of arousal. I would have liked to clout his ear, yes, and have him to respond in kind – what was I about?

Essex withdrew, tight-lipped. I lay in bed that night content and curiously alive. How very satisfying it had been to bawl at him! How he had scowled, how his dark eyes had glittered! I wriggled comfortably in the sheets; I had seen my lord of Essex's rage revealed; I knew him now to be one soon aroused to anger; I suspected we would spar again. Then Kate came in to bring me news that Essex and his sister had been seen to leave and take the road to London. I sent Carey after them to bring him back.

"Be careful, stripling," I said, wagging my finger at him. "I am master here and those would serve me had best remember it."

He bowed; but he was monstrous angry.

I made him Master of Horse and gave him Rob's old lodgings at St James's Palace.

"Let me go in search of gold," he pleaded. "Let me die for you!"

Rob had once said that to me. Where lay the pleasure in such a sacrifice? God's death, it was all I could do to keep Essex at court for this same love of glory. He rode the length and breadth of England by night to get aboard a ship at Plymouth to go save the throne of Portugal. If he is to be believed, he plunged through surf as high as his own head to be the first ashore and almost single-handed took the fort. He hurled his pike into the gates of Lisbon and challenged the Spaniard to come forth and fight him for the honour of his queen. I ordered him home, and he obeyed.

"My knight," I purred. "You please me well."

When he went to the playhouse he was cheered more than the players were. The whole world loved him.

He and I dined intimately; that is, we played at cards and dice. We played the game of chance. We were both great gamblers, but my dice were loaded – the very same which I picked up at the Black Sow on the Mynchen Hampton road. And if, the better to aid my prowess, I should grip him by the knee, or stroke the inner reaches of his thigh, there is no one may give me blame. It pleased him well, and he in response would lean and nibble my earlobe, and kiss my neck. We played the better for it.

Joining us at the table came young Wriothesley, Earl of Southampton, who had, like Essex, been a ward at Burghley's house.

He was then seventeen.

It will be understood that when Henry Wriothesley's name is mentioned there must be a pause for one to go and lie down in a darkened room. For sheer perfection he outweighed them all. How was it that Kit Marlowe described his charms? – his body straight as Circe's wand, his neck delicious to the touch, his breast smooth and his belly white; and along his back a heavenly path, curiously dinted. And how, I ask you, did Kit Marlowe know about the curious dints along that heavenly path? Envy answers me that everybody knew about Southampton's back and from intimate observation of the same. They said Thomas Dymoke was the first, and Edmund Pretty, and the Earl of Oxford, and Sir Henry Danvers and the young Earl of Rutland, and Piers Edmonds when he was in Ireland; and the besotted poet up from Warwickshire, who wrote him sonnet after sonnet; and Essex, of course – the whole world, it seemed, knew the curious dints down the heavenly path of Southampton's back. I froth at the mouth to think of it...

He was the son of that Southampton who lived shamelessly with men and left instructions that his lover Dymoke should bring up the boy. ("He makes his servant his wife!" screamed the wretched countess.) Young Henry was educated at Cambridge and Gray's Inn, but no lawyer he, no, more an altarpiece, a Ganymede, justifying his existence merely by his beauty. Long chestnut tresses had he, curled in ringlets, carefully placed over one exquisite shoulder. He liked to be seen in company with his cat. Yes, he had a cat, one Sebastian; black it was, with a white cravat and chin and nose, also white feet. It was borne in a basket by a pliant page. We thought it affectation to possess a cat when lapdogs would suffice; and he would sit and stroke it, and with the playing of his fingers call sensuous delights to mind.

> Fair Cynthia wished his arms might be her sphere,
> Grief makes her pale because she moves not there.

Southampton must have boasted to that subtle Marlowe how the queen herself, like all the others, had fallen captive to his charms.

There was one evening...

There were several present, one being Oxford, and, the torches dimmed, the gaming continued late into the night. Southampton who at that stage, it was generally agreed, had not yet lain with Essex, had been ogling Essex shamelessly, the worse as the night wore on; indeed, so much so that we others felt almost like panders to his blatant lust, as if we should fling down a bed for them to put an end to the business and be done with it. Essex, who in my presence was far too astute to do more than respond in the mildest of terms, preserved a pleasant equable demeanour, though plainly flattered nonetheless by the gorgeous youth's admiration.

When I as usual had won the game and counted up my winnings, those two chanced upon the notion of a wrestling match to settle their own score. Cumbered by clothes, the hour being late enough for follies such as these, and no French ambassador nearby to pass the news on to posterity, they chose to wrestle naked – a proven way to touch whom you may not at present fuck, much as dancing is. Those two lads then stripped off their clothes and stepped a little apart from us, and crouched facing each other, circling about, ready to pounce. Essex was the taller, lean and rangy and long-legged, with fine muscles and broad shoulders and a neat arse and a good big cock; Southampton was the prettiest loveliest creature, more smooth and shapely, with a plump round bum and a dainty prick; and that fine mane of hair that hung about his face like the leaves of a willow in midsummer. The torchlight lit their naked flesh to amber gold. Their limbs entwined, their bodies pressed against each other, their breathing came in low grunts and gasps, now belly to belly, face to face, and now twisted about, contorted, bent to postures lovely to behold. We watched in throbbing silence; then from time to time must call 'Bravo!' or such inanity, to dissipate the curious enchantment.

It was Essex had the mastery at last, and seizing the boy by the luxuriant tresses he forced him to his knees and made him look at him; the boy did not resist. His position brought his face against Essex's prick, the which was quiveringly erect. Southampton kissed it, so plainly offering himself no words were necessary.

A stab of envy cut through my guts so sharp I put my hand against my abdomen. In that instant I would have given gladly sceptre, orb and throne, to be so young, so beautiful, so honest in my sex.

Somehow the moment passed; the couple gathered up their tumbled clothes, and dressed; but from that time Southampton was Essex's man and so remained.

I circled a silver pendant about Essex's neck. It hung upon his glistening chest. "But I think you have already won your prize," I said.

Oxford, either through maturity or exhaustion, had grown more sober with the years. Some ten years ago, when he had been my naughty boy, it had been all brawls, all backstairs intrigue, duels on Lambeth marshes, a foolish passion for a woman of poor repute, and much distress to the long-suffering Burghley. But Oxford's troubled countess was now dead of a fever, and Oxford had married Mistress Trentham, a plump staid lady, maid-of-honour – they all must marry, for posterity – and she promised him stability. They settled in Stoke Newington, north of Shoreditch, and Oxford confided to me that it was his intention to quit court life, and devote himself entirely to the writing of plays. He had his own company of players, and also a company of singing boys. Moreover, he was on good terms with the innyard players and tavern poets, in particular that Warwickshire poet who was so passionate for Southampton. This Shakespeare wrote a good clear hand and was adept at transcribing Oxford's scrawling and illegible script.

My friend was hesitant to talk about his writing, partly because it was his true passion and partly because when he had published poems he had received but small acclaim.

"Nay, hostility!" expostulated he. "And why? Because I put my own name to the deed, and those who hate me – and surprisingly there be some such – vilified my poems for that they knew them to be from my pen. I was personally attacked – my style of dress, my manner, my repute. Well, I have learned from that. I never shall publish under my own name again!"

"Then how shall those of us that love you enjoy the fruits of your labours?"

But Oxford then became mysterious and said: "I have a mind to write a play set in a forest, and with something uppermost in my mind, it shall contain a wrestling match, and an amorous lady who gives a chain from her own neck to the victor, whom she loves."

"So gloomy, Walter? I would have you sit with me and talk of love aboard a vessel sailing westward."

"I am happy to oblige," he lied, and sat beside me on the cushions.

"Begin," I ordered comfortably, my skirts a-rustle as I settled.

"Daybreak," he said merrily enough. "I awake, my arms about that lissom cabin boy who never fails to please me when I am grown melancholy..."

And so he had been. His cherished colony, his settlers and his hopes for trading with the Indians, had vanished in mysterious circumstances, leaving only broken coffers and rotted books, deserted huts, and an indecipherable word carved on a tree. His kinsman Richard Grenville who had gone to the Azores on our behalf had engaged a fleet of Spanish war vessels near Flores and died in Spanish hands. Raleigh would have gone on that ill-fated venture had I permitted it; and now he was all taken up with plans of vengeance; but I had no intention he should go. And then there was his dream of El Dorado.

A Spaniard, Don Pedro Sarmiento de Gamboa, had been captured by two privateers and brought to Raleigh. This lying fool had filled my sea captain's head with yarns. Between the Orinoco and the Amazon there lies a city of gold, more gold than we have ever seen – streets, houses, palaces, all gold; the natives undefended, friendly, knowing not the worth of what they own. Why, they would trade it all for hides and horses!

This I could not believe; but Raleigh was enraptured by the notion. Behind his banter now, always that plea that he dared not utter: give me ships, give me your blessing, let me go!

"I cannot let you go," I told him, there and then upon the cushions. "Who would be left to me if you should go?"

"You are surrounded by those that love you," he said reasonably, as he had before.

"Boys," I said scathingly. "Brawling boys."

He kindly forebore to point out that it was well known that I had a weak spot for the same.

"I cannot believe I offer anything of value to Your Majesty by my inaction. I would be of so much more use aboard a vessel in your service. Name any venture – the getting of Spanish gold, the attacking of towns, the discovery of unknown lands – I am your man!"

"You are my sea captain," I said, and touched his cheek, "the man I have dreamed about ever since I was a little...girl. Handsome, brave, wayward – an adventurer of the mind. You forget, my dear, I am forbidden danger, exploration, all that goes with sailing westward; I am needed here at home. But you also are needed. You are the embodiment of my dream."

"I understand it, and am gratified by it," he answered tetchily. "But dreams are nothing if they may not be translated to reality. For both our sakes, permit me to bring home your dreams to you in substance. You would be sailing with me in my heart."

"It's not enough!" I cried. "I want to be with you in actuality. I want the hardships of the voyage, and its pleasures. I want to see the approach of land, to go ashore, to feel the sand of an alien beach beneath my feet, to see the tall cedars and the dark-skinned natives, to go further, further inland than any man has been before." I paused. "If I cannot..."

"...then you forbid it me," he finished angrily. "Envy alone – your envy – holds me back from my desire."

"Your desire is to be here with me!" I said enraged. "Have I not given you enough? Sherborne, castles, manors, jewels, cloaks?"

"Your Majesty has always been most generous," he replied unhappily.

"Then please me! Please me by remaining here," I urged, "my own sea captain, I your cabin boy..."

He gave a brittle smile.

"Raleigh," I said, dangerously quiet, "say I am your cabin boy and talk to me of our adventures overseas."

He chewed his lip. My blood boiled. Dare I send him to the Tower for insubordination such as this?

"Raleigh!" I growled, pounding one fist against another. "Say I am your cabin boy!"

He fetched a weary sigh. "You are my cabin boy. Our ship is sailing westward...we lie in close proximity...there is a cry from on deck – land sighted! We prepare to go ashore. I carry you, you being little." He caught my eye, and of a sudden smiled, and hugged me, relenting of his sulks. "We go ashore...I build a hut for us. Come night, I take you in my arms, and all night long the strange birds sing, and the soft wind plays in the tall cedars..."

Well, he soon provided reason enough to send him to the Tower. He secretly wed Bessie Throckmorton and gave her a son. As I say, they all must do it an they want continuance of their line. But Bessie? She was not even pretty.

"Because my first and only love is your sweet Majesty," said Essex, "I shall never betray you as others have done, by taking a wife in secret and leaving you to find out by chance. I do intend to marry Frances Sidney, it is true, but I do so to give protection to the grieving widow of my friend. Love does not enter into it; how could it, when my only love is you?"

"Is it true, Robin?" I said tenderly. "Am I your only love?"

"I swear it," he replied with glowing ardour. "Test me, set me an ordeal – I long to prove myself in your service."

"Overseas?" I said warily.

"It must be overseas," he answered reasonably, "since Your Grace has brought us peace at home."

"I need you here," I said.

He flung himself on his knees. "Let me to France; let me lead your armies that now support King Henry. I am the one can do it best; I am the only one fit to command."

"Oh, rise, Essex," I laughed. "There is no need..."

"How may I make Your Grace see the sincerity of my intentions? I must have the command in France. I shall remain upon my knees till you relent. Hard-hearted mistress, pity me!"

He would not rise; nor would I quit the chamber, for I was as determined to call his bluff as he to kneel there. My ladies tittered, seeing him; this made him the more stubborn. There he knelt, sore kneed, protesting his devotion. It pleased me to see him thus, I must admit – what is it about a good-looking youth in a position of subservience? It has a certain piquancy; the more so as his face becomes more flushed and scowling in his annoyance and discomfort, and his knees are plainly paining him, his pride keeping him there where he had sworn to remain. And which of us gave in? It was myself. After two hours had passed I lightly clouted him, and let him go to France.

Presenting a fine figure in his amber velvet trimmed with gold he proved a poor commander, and disobedient to my wishes, and when recalled, sunk into black melancholy, swearing that life was a prison he would soon be quit of, for it pleased the queen to ruin him; and unkindness and sorrow had broken both his heart and wits. Honourable, brave, he sought in warfare the personal combat between knight and knight, challenging the governor of Rouen to fight over the matter of my beauty, as if he were Sir Lancelot; the governor, a man of our own time, refused. And all the while Essex wrote to me of love in fulsome terms, as if indeed he were my verray faithful knight and I his lady.

I do not doubt that he loved me, but I knew it for a fiery and unstable passion, conceived of our shared belief in unreality. It was not unlike a hectic fever, swinging from gentle heat to fearsome leaping flame.

It was not like Robert's love.

Southampton became embroiled in an affair as fierce and bloody as was ever seen upon the stage. It concerned Harry Danvers, a youth of exceptional physical beauty who was then his lover, and henceforth, as was supposed. Harry, with his brother Charles, as a result of a longstanding feud, killed one Henry Long and fled to Southampton's house for refuge, which was granted. Much to-ing and froing then, the horses hidden here, the brothers there, and the crime discovered by a hapless serving-girl who washed the bloodstained shirt, and by a groom who handled the bloodstained saddle. Much riding by night and fleeing to the coast. Pursuit by the sheriff, the taking of a small boat, the threat to throw the sheriff into the sea, the flight to France.

Wicked? Aye, but those gorgeous wayward boys lived thus – with danger, fellowship, the flouting of laws; it was part of the febrile gaiety, the devil-may-care of it; and damn me, but I wished them well.

"So it comes down to this," I said to Raleigh in a tone of withering contempt. "I answered your pleas; I allowed you to go seek your El Dorado. You did not find it. And you came home because – I scarcely like to frame the words...because – ah, let not Essex get to hear of this! – you came home because you were tired!"

"I would not put it quite so baldly," Raleigh answered with some dignity; and plainly ill at ease.

"No? You would dress it in a hairpiece perhaps?" I jibed scathingly. "You have been given a chance not given to the common man. And you have failed. You went for gold; you came back with what they call fools' gold. An apt name in this instance, would not you say?"

"Your Majesty, men on the other side of the world have seen your picture and bowed down to it, thanks to me."

This, I concede, appeased me.

"But you went so far for *me* – for *us* – to do what I could not, and you could not achieve your heart's desire!"

"My heart's desire is peace from striving; I shall never attain it, for while I live I am a seeker."

He told me of the swampy forests, of the shellfish that grew on trees, the lake that bubbled with black pitch; the scaly reptiles in the yellow rivers; the poisoned arrows of the natives, and the men whose heads grew in their chests, with eyes where the nipples are. He had tales to tell of hacking a way through the undergrowth with naked swords, of hostile tribes and friendly, of waterfalls as high as churches, of the warm rains that drenched a man's shirt and the heat that dried it as swiftly. And of rumour – always ahead of them – rumour of gold mines, rumour of villages further down the river where lived sages who could answer all they wished to know, of eggs with wondrous properties of healing, and vile diseases that caused men's bodies to explode. Of fields where gold and silver stones lay for the picking – and El Dorado, always El Dorado, always out of sight, beyond the mountains, inaccessible.

"But you brought no gold," I said. "And you came home...because you were tired."

There was no place for weariness at my court. You must dance long into the night, you must ride fast, outdistancing the crowd, you must be beautiful always, and merry and light of heart and reckless – and ageless.

"Raleigh? He's old before his time," shrugged Essex.

"I doubt he ever went near Guiana," Southampton scoffed. "He anchored in a cove in Cornwall, and there sat and waited for some time to pass; now here he is, the greatest bluffer of the age."

And, as it were, drunk with the lateness of the hour, the company, the intensity of self-deception, I turned from nuzzling Essex's neck, and guffawed with the rest of them.

II

When was it that I first had inkling of Essex's hunger for the crown? When did the comparisons with Henry Bolingbroke begin, he that took his cousin's throne? And Essex was my cousin.

"He was not an easy man," said the long-suffering Raleigh. "He must always be first."

There was a bevy of fine sea commanders at Cadiz under the leadership of Lord Howard of Effingham – Sir Walter Raleigh, Sir John Wingfield, Sir Francis Vere and Lord Thomas Howard – but it was Essex who grew restless and began the fray, who quibbled at the admiral's orders and knew best, Essex who must be first through the shattered walls, destroying all before him. Against my express orders he then scattered knighthoods like largesse amongst his followers.

"It was I who said we should remain in Spanish waters and await the treasure fleet," Essex cried, "but I was shouted down."

"We shall not continue petty shipboard squabbling at Westminster,"

I replied. "The crux of the matter is that you came back without gold, and the Spanish treasure fleet sailed by you unobserved."

"Gold, always gold!" snarled Essex. "The true gold – a noble heart, a man loyal to you, leading his troops, sword in hand – this you value not at all."

"This voyage cost me dear; and I expect a profit on my capital."

"Your Majesty talks like a merchant," he spat.

"You overreach yourself, sirrah," I said angrily; but as I turned away I saw Master Dutton in my mind's eye, bent over his accounts.

If I would not praise Essex as he wished, there were those who would. He had but to ride down Cheapside and the multitudes would follow, cheering, bellowing adulation; and the great beard he grew was emulated by the masses and was called the Cadiz fashion.

"I have heard that you intend to give more honours to Sir Walter Raleigh," Essex came to me in dudgeon. "I am always overlooked when favours are bestowed, and first in line when you hand out displeasure."

"You are never overlooked; it is not possible to do so."

"Your lack of faith in me will make me ill."

Always so. If he considered himself slighted he took to his bed. From thence he wrote of his despair, his detestation of existence, his devotion to myself in spite of my cruelty. I was not cruel; but he believed himself much wronged. He calmed himself, it seemed, by visits to the playhouse, where his favourite play was *Richard II*, which he saw so often that he must have known the words by heart, and Henry Bolingbroke who caused the king to be deposed he understood to be a portrait of himself. Neither was the implication lost on me.

"He lived by his own laws," said Raleigh. "We could never work together; he attributed the vilest motives to my actions."

Their expedition to the Azores left Raleigh understandably bitter. Essex, as commander, had been lacking in diplomacy, and proved mysterious and unreliable and pugnacious. Raleigh kept his dignity, and limping from the wound he received at Cadiz was become the very model of the noble seaman grown grizzled in the service of the realm, the trusty sword dented by brave use. Essex raved and ranted and began to seem an angry child. When the Lord Admiral became Earl of Nottingham, Essex locked himself in his room and, it was said, buried himself beneath a heap of blankets. Raleigh interceded for him. True, Raleigh was not without his faults – anger was one, and taking no regard to the future was another – but events that followed coloured my view of those two sparring partners; when the day came, Raleigh was loyal to me.

It was to Wanstead that Essex retired when he would sulk. It was an odd business, I reflected, visiting him there, place of so many fair and foul memories for me.

I sat beside the bed, that great bed where Robert and I in balmier days had romped together, grown ecstatic over the prospect of Drake's gold. Now Drake was dead, of the flux, off Nombre de Dios Bay. The present was personified by Essex, Essex who sat hunched in his nightshirt, hair and beard in disarray, taking sops at my hand from a spoon, persisting in his claim that my careless treatment of him had made him ill.

"Come now, be sweet again," I cajoled. "Be Robin to your Bess, as we have been before. Return to court, where you are sorely missed."

"If I return, you will seek fresh occasion to humiliate me."

"No indeed. I only reprove you when I believe the occasion merits reproof. Nothing would please me more than to have you back with me, the darling of the court."

"And *your* darling?" he probed pettishly.

"You were ever thus," I said warmly. "Do you recall how your dear stepfather so proudly handed you to me – this most precious gift, he called you – knowing that you and I were to be close?"

A reluctant smile touched Essex's lips. "Yes, I remember."

We looked about us, as if Robert were still here, and might have entered the chamber. But instead, from another room, came a great guffaw and a crash of furniture, a coarse oath, the sound of boots running up and down the staircase.

"My good fellows," Essex laughed affectionately."They will roister, however I reprove them."

("He loves the company of his soldiers – a breed of low ruffian that knows only drinking and fighting, and they are eager for reward," warned lawyer Francis Bacon. "Nor has the earl wherewithal to reward them. A dangerous combination.")

"There was once a tree here at the window," I observed, "and when the casement was opened, you looked into the heart of the tree."

"We cut it down," said Essex. "It grew too near the house." Then he clutched at my hand and kissed it. "Loveliest of women," he said, muffled by the beard and bedclothes, "sacred Gloriana...merry Bess..."

Hugh O'Neill, Earl of Tyrone, routed our army in Ireland at Blackwater, and the chieftains rallied to him and ran amok in Ulster. Essex came back to court. "I am the only man to lead our army of retribution. Let me bring this rebel to his knees."

And he went, with Southampton and Harry Danvers and his swashbucklers.

Maybe an army such as this was what was required for this situation, I thought in perplexity. Maybe Essex's own peculiar brand of bravado and chivalry, at the head of his die-hards, was the solution; for no one yet had achieved a happy compromise in that troubled land.

It was not to be so. Amongst those wet and swampy bogs, surrounded by his acolytes and lovers, power went to his head. He disregarded my commands, he acted on his own account and dubbed nigh on one hundred knights expressly against our wishes; and he wrote arrogantly of what he had done, and begged to be allowed to return to England and justify his action.

I refused him that permission. There were few prospects less attractive than that of Essex truculent and aggrieved and burning with fancied wrongs against himself, storming back from Ireland in the company of a gang of rake-hells ready to die for him.

It was exactly this that now occurred.

Autumn, and a stormy downpouring, with the sodden leaves thick on the mud-stained tracks, the soughing trees swaying and the great clouds scudding wraith-like in the turbulent skies.

The court was then at Nonsuch, my pretty hunting lodge set amongst its downs and woodlands. The time of day was early morning.

Dozy, never a morning person, I entered my bath-room, that

luxurious little room where the walls were all of mirrored glass. Philadelphia, Lady Scrope, and Kate, Lady Nottingham attended me and then withdrew, preparing my clothes, my face paint and my choice of hairpieces. I settled into my bath. My thoughts were far away. I barely heard the distant squeals, the protests, then the dark gruff voice. I stood up, frowning, looking down for my discarded robe, my towel. When I looked up, I was looking into the eyes of the Earl of Essex.

He was behind me, standing in the doorway. The looking-glass on the opposite wall showed us both – myself stark naked, Essex travel-stained, filthy and unkempt, in mud-soiled boots, with spur and sword; and on his sweat-streaked face an expression of such incredulity, disgust and loathing as I will never in my life forget.

What did he see? A man, with scrawny shanks and hairless chest, a limp cock beneath a few sparse hairs – this first he would have seen. And then? A wrinkled visage, hooky nosed, with sharp bright eyes, a forehead bare of hair, but some grey tangled locks that hung about the shoulders. As Essex saw me, now I saw myself. Not Cynthia the Goddess of the Moon, nor Diana, Virgin Queen of Huntresses, not Gloriana, timeless beauty for whom men were proud to die, nor Bess the merry companion of young lads that longed to be her lover – but an arch-deceiver...an old man.

"Hand me my robe," I said.

Dumbly he did so.

"Madam – we could not stop him!"

"He burst past us and threw us aside!"

Kate and Philadelphia were distraught. I calmed them.

"Go with my servant," I told Essex. "Wash yourself and come to me within the hour; and we shall talk."

"You were always a man?" blanched Essex. "You were a man even for Leicester?"

Resplendent in my finery, immaculate, the image which the world acknowledged, I received him. Chastened he sat by my side.

I almost had it in my heart to pity him. He was like a man beaten down by a blow, dazed and thunderstruck, almost inarticulate in the numbness of his shock.

"I was completely fooled," he murmured.

"You saw what you wished to see," I said. "You set yourself to be a knight in the service of a lady. You were the courtly lover. But I was as much at fault as you. I lived through your eyes. I believed myself what you believed me to be. We were both deceived."

"But you were always male," he whispered. "How could it be? How was it done?"

"It doesn't matter, Robin. It was all many years ago."

"Although I do not understand, I shall still serve you. But – this awesome secret – am I the only one who knows?"

It was clearly apparent that Essex must for his conduct in the Irish war give account of himself before the Privy Council. "This secret is known to the Privy Council," I replied. "But naturally, it is never spoken of. Merely understood."

"Does Raleigh know?" gasped Essex.

"Oh no!" I answered. There would certainly be no containing Essex if he believed himself the dupe while Raleigh sniggered at his ignorance. He was visibly relieved. Yet I believed him more unstable now than previously. He seemed glazed, stupid, all in disarray. Upon his volatile character this alarm had fallen as one blow too many. I could no longer trust him. Not that I doubted his chivalry, his protestation of devotion; what I feared for was his sanity. And what he might declare in his confusion.

With Essex's revelation came my own. In that appalling moment when our eyes met I began to see all things anew. A hideous clarity exploded upon my previous self-deception. I had believed myself protected from the ravages of time, a gorgeous flower about which the eager bees buzzed; now I suspected that those lovely lads so kind to me before my face were other when they were away from me. I imagined them laughing together down there at Essex House, all so beautiful, all so young, and as they had derided Raleigh's expedition and sneered at him for that he was more than forty years of age, I fancied they derided me. What? What did they call me? Old old woman? Painted crone? *Silly old queen?*

And if they did so, it would be no lie. I was a living falsehood. I was the auburn hairpiece, the starched ruff, the pearls, the spangled farthingale, a walking relic from another time.

They all were gone now – Robert first of all; Sussex my great support; Heneage my old admirer, the same age as myself; dear Hatton, who remained unwed, because, he said, no woman could rival myself. Burghley was gone now; and Alencon whom I might have wed; Arundel; and my cunning Walsingham; and my old foe and wooer Philip of Spain – all dead now, all gone. And then came the snapping of the last thread that led back into the past – Blanche ap Harry, so old now that her skin was crumpled like an ancient parchment, and her sight gone; and she, paper thin, and yet retaining to the end her faculties.

"I did not think that you could do it," she confided to me, her voice a whisper. "And look at you – you have outlived them all."

What consolation that? When Essex saw me as I was, I lost belief in my eternity. I was sixty-six years old. I was an old man dressed in woman's clothes, no more nor less.

"He is to see no one," I gave orders to Lord Keeper Egerton. "No one is to visit him, neither wife nor friend nor kinsman."

Imprisoned in York House for his rash and irresponsible deportment in Ireland and his unlooked-for return, it suited Essex's own state of mind to concur with my prohibitions. He sank into despair. He had no wish to see his friends. He turned to God, not with serenity but in religious frenzy. He was upon his knees for hours on end, composing sermons, sending letters to Southampton urging him to turn his back upon fleshly delights and worldly pleasures – a thing that Southampton had done all too literally for years. He was tormented by ill health, that 'Irish flux' of which his father died, but, as Egerton reported, amazed, he took this torment as proof of God's good hand upon him.

Southampton the while ignored his friend's pious advice, and was to be seen every day at the playhouse, while those reprobates whom Essex brought from Ireland roamed the streets in bawdy brawling, loudly demanding his release.

God's death, whatever might I do with him! If only he were to be discovered at some plot; if only he would rise against me publicly, in some way that his guilt might be seen by all, his ultimate punishment justifiable. But Essex only prayed.

"I would tear my heart from my body with my bare hands rather than betray the trust of Her Majesty," he declared. I knew what he referred to. But such a protestation in no way reassured me. It was crazed, extravagant.

At last I ordered him released, but not to come to court, nor into London. He wrote mournful letters to me.

"Forgive him, ma'am," said Philadelphia. "He won't betray you. For all his wildness he is honourable. Let him come to court."

But in my heart I knew there was but one end for the man who had seen me as I was. I prayed that he would rise up in revolt.

"The queen's mind is as crooked as her carcase." Essex had said that publicly. Plain enough his meaning. What else had he said?

"Essex has said many wild things about Her Majesty," the rumours ran. "You would suppose him mad for what he says."

"Walter..." I pressed close to him. "He must die...what may we do? How may it all be done?"

"With so many bad counsellors about him," Raleigh promised me, "he will do it for himself."

Essex House was filled with discontented soldiers – younger sons, the disaffected, thieves and cut-throats, those who bore a grudge. Buckhurst whom we sent as messenger reported that it was like an army camp there, Essex the captain, and his men everywhere about, some sleeping in the courtyard, and horses ever at the ready, and constant coming and going, a surging simmering excitement like a great cauldron about to boil. What was their intention?

We remained at Whitehall, Raleigh and I. We sent messengers to Essex House, demanding that Essex make clear his purpose. He imprisoned our messengers. He took to the streets. His little army rampaged, calling on the citizens of London to rise up in his support. They did not. In curious confusion Essex's followers roamed Cheapside and Ludgate. At last they trickled back to Essex House. Our forces surrounded it. Essex and Southampton climbed on to the roof with swords in hands, roaring their intention to die fighting. They were dissuaded. They were taken to the Tower. Southampton took his cat with him.

Essex and Southampton and the others were tried at Westminster, the two earls both found guilty of high treason. What other verdict could there be? Essex had set himself up as Bolingbroke. I truly believe that his intention was to be king, a wish that may have grown in fervency when he discovered an impostor on the throne, the which discovery had made him mad. If I, who patently was not Elizabeth, could rule the land, then why not he?

He was executed privately; that is, within the Tower. He had to die; there was no other course. He was doomed from the moment that he saw me naked; and I believe he knew as much. He was thirty-three years old. He died nobly. He said nothing to my detriment. They said his death speech was an honourable one, but most of it, they said, was lost upon the wind.

But I was merciful towards his noble friends. Southampton? Who could destroy an ornament such as he?

Sir Giles Brydges, warden of Sudeley Castle, Lord Lieutenant of Gloucestershire, welcomed me to his home. He was a sturdy round-cheeked man with a neat beard and moustache. He led me proudly about his domain, showing me the improvements he had made – his yew hedge, in especial, with its alcoves formed to be like a Long Gallery.

His wife, the elegant Lady Frances, explained to us that the entertainments would last for several days, and during the revels I would meet folk from thereabouts who came expressly to declare their loyalty.

Cotswold shepherds! Here they came, men from the wolds, square-faced fellows, ruddy-skinned and hearty, for all the world as if my childhood was now come to life again, the past unrolling its memories in living shape before my eyes.

"These hills afford nothing but cottages," they said, "and nothing can we present to Your Majesty but shepherds. We carry our hearts at our tongues' ends, being as far from dissembling as our sheep from fierceness. This lock of wool, Cotswold's best fruit and our poor gift, we offer to Your Highness..."

"Their speech is rustic," murmured Lady Frances. "Does Your Grace well understand? I can translate the humble hillside way of talking, if you wish."

"By no means," answered I. "I understand it well enough."

I thanked the shepherds, who, with much forelock-tugging, bowed and moved away. Amazed, appalled, I stood and looked down at the lock of Cotswold wool which I held between my jewelled fingers. Beyond those woods, and somewhat south from here, lay Bisley. Here I stood at Sudeley, the castle in which Katherine Seymour died, the castle owned by Thomas Seymour, who had pursued me in his lust. And in my hands a scrap of Cotswold fleece, gift from poor shepherds with a living to make in bitter weather on these uneven hills. I had fled that life, where sheep ruled all, knowing my destiny lay elsewhere. The Cotswold sheep...hardier than the Hereford, for all the Hereford has a longer coat.

I twined the lock of wool about my finger, with the pearls. A wheel, it seemed to me, had come full circle in that moment.

"From your old lodging at Rycote, this Thursday morning ready to take my journey..." Robert's last letter, which I had kept these fourteen long years. I put it against my cheek. Ah, Rob, I said, your journey took you further than you thought... There was none who loved me with the depth of love you gave me over all the years, in all our troubles and our joys. Forgive me, Rob, I had to give the order for his death. I know you loved him dearly, and the same did I. I do believe that no less than the throne would have contented him. And this I will pass on to no one but the true successor, and peacefully. You understand this. You understand I had to have him killed...but ah, God's death, the light and life have gone out of the kingdom with him.

"Raleigh!" I shrieked, looking wildly about me. "I want Raleigh! Send for Sir Walter Raleigh!"

"The hour is late," began my lady Ann.

"Send for him; he will come."

"Your Majesty...my dear," said Raleigh kneeling.

"Rise!" I wept; and pulled him to his feet and clung to him. "Raleigh, Raleigh – swear you will not die!"

"I will not die, I promise you," he said against my ear.

"And when I send for you, you will be with me instantly."

"You may depend upon it."

"Ah, Walter, things are not as they once were. They look no more for El Dorados. They look only northward, where King James stands twitching, waiting for his summons."

"He will have a long wait," Raleigh said, "and for myself I do not choose to think of him. Here, we live in the Golden Age, and after, is a void."

"You and I perhaps live in that Golden Age," I smiled. "I think we sail the seas yet, sea captain and cabin boy, our faces to the west. But as for others... Spanish gold and terra incognita – these words no longer quicken the blood as they were wont to do."

"Give me a ship and I will prove you wrong!"

"Essex would have gone with you," I said.

"I would not have had him in my company," Raleigh answered.

"Nonetheless he would have offered himself," I said. "He was a seeker, like yourself. But the time was wrong for him."

When Kate died, it was one death too many. Kate Carey as she was, my Lady Nottingham, and younger than myself, should not have died. She was to have been my safeguard, after, to protect my body from the embalmers. But she had been my friend. Why, she had been with me in the coach, when I had teased poor Robert into waiting for me at the church, when we were young, when he believed me woman. Was nothing to be left to me?

I sat with Ann and Helena and Philadelphia, those ladies unto whom I had entrusted this responsibility.

"I have given orders that no embalmer shall come near my corpse," I said. "You three will do all that is required; and no other."

"You will not die; you have many long years left to you," they wept.

Many long years...I did not want them.

It was a dismal winter. The wind howled about our palace of Richmond. I began to suffer from a head cold. I was troubled with strange dreams at night, dreams that pursued me into the light. I began to see again that devious priest that set me on this twisted path. He came to me night after night, in a white robe, that may have been a winding-sheet. I saw him on the stairway once, and at a window, beckoning. Sometimes he was behind me; I felt his cold breath on my skin; and when I turned, he was not there.

"Chance has played into our hands, John. This falls beyond my wildest hopes. Who would have thought it possible – and yet it is so!"

Night after night came Brother Xavier, like a white owl, who, they say, presages doom. At first he seemed to stand in that far doorway, hesitant, as if awaiting a summons, but then he grew bolder and stepped forward, coming towards the bed whereon I lay. If he should ever touch me...if he should ever reach out his cold hand and touch me...

And now I saw his head was bloody and his face, always skeletal, a cloven skull, with gaping eye sockets, and his jaw hanging askew. "He was left for dead in a ditch, his head broken...died in a ditch..."

Then I would wake up, sweating, icy cold and fearful. I dreaded night. I would not go to bed.

"Come, leave these cushions, dear Your Majesty," says Philadelphia. "You have been sitting here so long. You will be more comfortable in your bed."

"I am well enough here," I answer, and I stare into the fire, hugging the cushion to my chest and scarcely hearing her.

Other things are more loud now and more clear to me – Robert most of all. Robert, pestering me to answer his question, speaking to me from behind the locked door of the Tower: "It would mean so much to me at this time..." Robert's face, green in the fireworks' glow: "Who knows? Who else knows?" Kat Ashley, laughing, cuddling me: "You could wed Tom Seymour, a big man and a cock to match!" The feathers flying from the pillow in the chamber at Hatfield when we romped and thought our secret safe – and suddenly they become a shower of Spanish gold coins and when I reach for them they slip through my fingers. "I offer you a true and loyal heart." And then Essex, standing there dumbfounded, in his mud-stained clothes.

There should be no embalmers at my corpse. If so be they disobey my orders and my ladies cannot fend them off, I have instructed Captain Jacques to deal with the embalmers and make sure they tell no tale. All is provided for.

I have left my throne to Scottish Jamie. It is no secret that James loves pretty boys. He had his eye on Essex; he was in constant touch with him, and Essex wore a momento of James about his neck. I believe the idea was for James to rule with Essex at his side. Well, there remains Southampton. I chuckle to think of poor James, with that exquisite darling awaiting him, a mixed blessing, no doubt, to the unwary Scotsman. But what a coup – to leave my inheritance to one who loves boys and who dares to show that love, a king honest as I could never be. I find the notion pleasing.

But I am afraid. I clutch the cushion to me till my nails dig into the velvet. *Send for Sir Walter Raleigh. I want him now!*

"How dare we tell her?" they whisper, from a long distance away. "Sir Walter Raleigh is in the west country."

"Send for Sir Walter Raleigh!"

In front of me is a curtained door. My eyes fix upon it. There will come through that door one who beckons me. Sometimes I think it will be Brother Xavier, ghastly and grey, a death's head with a gaping leering grin. And then I know that I am wrong, and it will be my handsome sea captain, broad of shoulder, with wicked eyes, to carry me away towards the islands of the west.

But I shall have the last laugh. Whoever comes for me and lays his hands upon me will find nothing here. He will find the auburn hairpiece, the pearls, the ruff, the jewelled farthingale. But I shall not be there.

I shall be a hundred miles away, an old man sitting by the hearth in Bisley village, toothless, cackling, smoking the Nicotian weed, waiting for news of the old queen's death, while the sheep bleat on the greensward at my window, and the wind comes whistling across from Mynchen Hampton.